Cat Got Your Diamonds

Cat Got Your Diamonds

A Kitty Couture Mystery

Julie Chase

CROOKED
LANE

NEW YORK

Published in the United States by Crooked Lane Books, an imprint of The Quick Brown Fox & Company LLC.

Crooked Lane Books and its logo are trademarks of The Quick Brown Fox & Company LLC.

Library of Congress Catalog-in-Publication data available upon request.

ISBN (paperback): 978-1-68331-197-3
ISBN (hardcover): 978-1-62953-842-6
ISBN (ePub): 978-1-62953-843-3
ISBN (Kindle): 978-1-62953-844-0
ISBN (ePDF): 978-1-62953-845-7

Cover design by Louis Malcangi.
Cover illustration by Anne Wertheim.
Book design by Jennifer Canzone.

Printed in the United States.

www.crookedlanebooks.com

Crooked Lane Books
34 West 27th St., 10th Floor
New York, NY 10001

Hardcover Edition: November 2016
Paperback Edition: March 2017

10 9 8 7 6 5 4 3 2 1

Chapter One

*Furry Godmother's secret to
stunning Shih Tzu tutus: More glitter.*

I squinted through my freshly cleaned shop window at a lively group of women snapping selfies with the Magazine Street sign in front of a New Orleans police car and broken-in storefront. Humidity had twisted their hair to Albert Einstein proportions. An officer, standing several feet away, looked as confused as the jewelry shop owner sweeping broken glass. Crime wasn't usually a problem in the Garden District, but this was the second jewelry heist in a week. The whole conundrum made me extra glad I owned a pet boutique. There wasn't much of a black market for animal couture, and my baked goods had an expiration date.

Thieves aside, it was a beautiful New Orleans day. Ninety-seven, with a real feel of one hundred thirteen. Home sweet home. Hard to believe I'd ever left. Even harder to believe that somewhere beyond the sprawling mansions and Mighty Mississippi was my cheating ex-fiancé and our tabby, Penelope.

Pearl Neidermeyer was in front of me yammering away. "Lacy? Hello? Lacy Crocker, are you listening to me?"

"Yes, ma'am." I smiled at the woman who'd taught me ballet for three months as a child. "Every word." My mother had put me in every form of dance and pageantry for years before she accepted the painful truth. I was my father's daughter, made more for observation than participation.

I also shared Dad's love of animals and art, which had led me to opening Furry Godmother, a custom pet boutique and organic, animal-friendly bakery. My degree in fashion design was finally paying off. My favorite ensembles were captured on film and hung around the room in collages of antique, gilded frames. Animals had been my life's passion for as long as I could remember. Who knew that one day I'd be making custom creations for a literal catwalk?

Below the photographs, white oak shelves lined three walls, heavy laden with products, mixes, and baking supplies. The turtles and aquarium took residence on the fourth, a nice touch for atmosphere and entertaining children. Wide shop windows welcomed ample light from Magazine Street and invited shoppers inside for a peek or sample. A row of white minichandeliers hung from the ceiling, classing up the joint. My pink-and-green color scheme was adorable with punches of yellow for zip.

Mrs. Neidermeyer's bangle bracelets jangled as she paced. "Those Fat Cats are making a big entrance at the gala. They're building custom carriages. I can't compete with custom carriages, so our costumes need to pack a punch."

I rubbed my palms together and pulled myself away from the window. "Your dancers need something spectacular."

"Exactly."

Images exploded in my mind like movie theatre popcorn. Shiny, dazzling popcorn. I lifted a finger. "I have an idea." I opened the drawer behind the counter where I kept notepads, cardstock, and a rainbow of sticky notes. I snagged my favorite pink sketchpad and smiled. "The costumes I create for your Shih Tzus will be so stunning, every dance coach on the East Coast will want your name." I grabbed a pencil and scribbled notes. "I'll start with silver sequin jackets."

Mrs. Neidermeyer shook her head and pressed her lips tight. "No jackets. The darlings can't perform properly with their legs all wrapped in sequins. Remember practicality. It's not a photo shoot, darling. This is the Jazz Festival we're talking about. We need to make a real impression at the Animal Elegance gala. The judges must be awed."

I snickered, dancing my pencil over the paper, sketching lines and curves where crinoline and glitter would meet in sheer pageant perfection. "People do think I'm a little odd."

She moved closer and set her stupendously bedazzled flip phone on the counter. "I said awed. Not odd." Her frown said she didn't necessarily disagree with my being odd.

Sometimes I forgot I was the only one who thought word-play was hilarious.

I inhaled deeply and leaned my elbows onto the counter. My long, pale-blonde ringlets swung around my arms. "What do you think of something like this?"

She scrutinized my work. Her lips twitched, but she shut the smile down quick and tight. "I need seven. Make them spectacular. No jackets. Don't forget this is your time to shine, too, dear. A few media mentions from an event of this caliber and you can put your name on the map as a designer."

The upcoming French Quarter Jazz Festival had Garden District residents in a tizzy, planning the finest fundraisers and galas for their favorite organizations and charities, including Animal Elegance, the swankest gig of them all. I'd already secured a contract for Furry Godmother to provide refreshments for the pets. Still, dressing Mrs. Neidermeyer's Shih Tzus was the biggest opportunity of my career so far.

"Okay. I'll get to work on these and give you a call when they're ready." I turned the paper in her direction. "Seven sparkly Shih Tzu tutus. No jackets. Must dazzle. No problem."

She nodded, attention riveted to the pad where I'd doodled the quick mock-up. "Excellent. Can we get four dozen peanut butter pupcakes delivered to the gala as well? Make a sign so they'll know they're from me."

"Sure." I scratched a note on the paper. "Good choice. The venue contracted me for bottled waters, dish rentals, and a mix of tuna tarts and turkey tots. Pupcakes will make the perfect dessert."

"Bag the pupcakes individually and tie them with purple and green ribbons. Satin, not that cheap curling nonsense."

"Got it." I suppressed an eye roll. As if she needed to clarify. *Only the best* was practically this district's motto. Plus, I took accessorizing seriously.

Returning home to New Orleans four months ago hadn't been easy, but an ugly breakup with my ex-fiancé, Pete, had helped the process along. It probably wasn't even a coincidence his name rhymed with *cheat*. Though *two-timing creep* was more accurate. *Cheat* implied a certain level of "Whoopsie. Did I do that?" Pete had maintained two full-time relationships, using his complicated schedule at the busy DC hospital to keep us both in the dark. One more reason I preferred pets to people. Pets never lied.

Mrs. Neidermeyer perused the bakery display while I drew up her work order. The oversized rings on her hands glittered under florescent studio lighting, casting rainbows over the display case and floor. "Everything is riding on this gala. We need costumes that will make the audience gasp, check their programs, and remember our names. We must enchant them."

"No problem." A win for her would be an enormous victory for Furry Godmother. "I will do my best to impress."

She cast a suspicious look my way. "When can I expect the finished costumes?"

I checked my emaciated calendar. Three little notes dotted an expanse of blank white paper. The Himalayan Rescue Foundation needed six dozen tuna tarts. Happy Tails Day Spa needed twelve dozen canine carrot cakes. A local equestrian event had requested custom sashes for all participating thoroughbreds. I had time to make fifty tutus and still brainstorm the new line of Paris-inspired designs I hoped to launch next spring. "When do you need them?"

"The dancers need time for a proper dress rehearsal and the gala is in a month. Sooner is better. We're planning group photos before the gala."

I twirled a length of hair around my finger. "Two weeks?"

She nodded stiffly. "That will do."

Making tutus would be fun, but I couldn't wait to get to those poodle skirts. I'd dreamed about them all through the spring. I sighed. There was nothing like Paris in the spring. I scratched the date onto the work order and handed Mrs. Neidermeyer a copy.

Her eyes glazed over, gaze lost somewhere else in the room. "Mrs. Neidermeyer?"

"Hmmm?" She patted the counter between us, unseeing. "Your order slip."

She'd honed her pale-green eyes on Mr. Tater, my store's investor. I hadn't heard him come in. Remembering to replace the bell inside my door after cleaning the windows had proven impossible. Half the time, I only remembered the bell was missing when I made plans to clean the windows again. She wetted her lips, and I dropped the slip on the counter where she'd eventually find it with her roving hand.

Mr. Tater made his usual circuit around my store's interior, touching random items on shelves and exploring the pet treats inside my displays. His thinning gel-spiked hair went well with the gold rope necklace and pinstriped dress shirt tucked neatly into jeans worn around his navel. Unfortunate wardrobe aside, Mr. Tater was catnip for the over forty and single crowd. He'd amassed a fortune with his savvy business investments and liked to flaunt his money more than most, a trait this town appreciated. He was also a shrewd and generous businessman. He'd signed on as my investor when I couldn't secure a proper loan and had refused my parents' help.

Mrs. Neidermeyer's hand landed on the slip. She stuffed it into her oversized designer bag and strode toward Mr. Tater with purpose in her eyes.

Then an olive-skinned man with the profile of a prize-fighter sauntered through the door, drawing my attention away from Mrs. Neidermeyer and Mr. Tater. The man cast his glance around before heading my way. His stride was as predatory as his gaze.

I skittered back a step. "Can I help you?"

He lifted his eyebrows and appraised me thoroughly. He brushed long, calloused fingers over a stack of brightly colored head wraps beside my register. "Interesting shop you work in."

"It's my shop, actually. I make all the organic pet treats, custom clothing, and accessories."

He chuckled, toying with the stack of accessories. "What are these supposed to be?"

I bit the insides of my cheeks. He was antagonizing me. "Those are headscarves for small dogs or cats, possibly a large guinea pig or teacup pig."

His gaze moved from the material between his fingers to Mr. Tater, and he stepped back among the racks, feigning rapt interest in the turtle tank and neighboring aquarium along the far wall.

"Lacy." Mr. Tater peeled my attention from the rude man and greeted me with a handshake. "How's business?"

"Great." I hoped it sounded believable. I couldn't afford for him to give up on me yet.

Mr. Tater rocked back on his heels. "Excellent. May I have four pawlines for Priscilla?"

"Certainly."

He moseyed back to the bakery display case. "She can't get enough of the new recipe. What did you change?"

I slid a pair of plastic gloves over clean hands and opened the case. "Trade secret, Mr. Tater, but I'll throw in an extra pawline to make up for not telling you. How's that?" I smiled at him and the store I loved.

"Five pawlines? She's going to love me today."

My pawlines were a pet-friendly version of famous New Orleans pralines. The pawlines were made with bacon fat and wheat flour instead of pecans and brown sugar, but dogs couldn't get enough, especially Priscilla, Mr. Tater's Pug-Beagle mix. Breeders called the combination a Puggle. I called her downright adorable.

I stacked his pawlines in a logoed bakery box lined with pink paper.

Mr. Tater turned his attention to me and lowered his voice. "I've contacted a security firm about installing a system here. A sales representative will be in contact."

I sealed the little box with a golden fleur-de-lis sticker and handed it to Mr. Tater. "Is everything okay?"

His forehead creased. "Don't you want an alarm?"

"Oh, I do." Assuming I could run it once it was installed. "Is this because of the jewelry store break-ins?"

Mr. Tater leaned against the counter, his brows raised in surprise. "Have you heard anything?"

"No. Only what I've seen or read in the news." I tipped my chin toward the front window. "Maybe you could talk to the officer across the street before he leaves. Get the inside scoop."

He shook his head. "There were a few petty thefts at the restaurant. Last night there was an issue at the Gallery."

Goose bumps ran down my arms. He had good reason to worry. His restaurant, the Barrel Room, was the busiest in the city. A bad reputation could ruin business. And the Gallery was Mr. Tater's jewelry store, positioned at the district's edge. "Wow. Did you make a report?"

"Of course. It took all morning to sort it out." He watched the scene outside. "I can't believe there were two hits in one night."

"Scary," I said.

Mrs. Neidermeyer pressed a palm to her heart. "Is there anything I can do?"

"Oh, no. Forgive me." He placed a set of air kisses on each side of Mrs. Neidermeyer's face and smiled. "There's no need to concern yourself. I'll get a security system installed here right away and nip this thing in the bud."

Mrs. Neidermeyer nodded solemnly.

Tater excused himself and disappeared onto the crowded sidewalk beyond the windows.

I followed him as far as the door and flipped the "Closed" sign before tugging my gloves off.

The dark-eyed man lingered near a rack of tiny top hats.

I made a show of looking at my watch. "Can I help you choose a treat for your pet?"

He licked his lips and smiled. "How about something for my big dog?"

I wrapped frustrated arms around my middle. I'd survived the DC area long enough to know a hooligan when I saw one. Several colorful suggestions came to mind for his "big dog," but Mrs. Neidermeyer's presence restrained me. I couldn't afford to lose her business by behaving less than ladylike. I formed my most threatening smile. "I think it's time for you to go."

Mrs. Neidermeyer cleared her throat and joined me at the door.

The man laughed. "Look at that. Time to go." He winked at Mrs. Neidermeyer and slunk into the sunshine.

She dabbed a handkerchief against her forehead. "Well, I never." She fussed with her clothes and hair, looking utterly disgusted.

I pulled the shades on my windows for good measure. "Are you okay?" I had half a mind to report the jerk for upsetting Mrs. Neidermeyer, but unfortunately that wasn't a crime. Not even in this neighborhood.

"I'm fine. You don't get to be my age without meeting your share of perverts and derelicts." She dropped her hands to her sides and straightened her spine. "I'll be expecting a detailed mock-up of those tutus for my approval."

"Of course."

She left with her chin high and a pageant-worthy wave over one shoulder.

I flipped the dead bolt and straightened the welcome mat with my shoe, admiring the deep-cherry stain I'd used on the knotted oak floor. The planks were easily a century old and worn smooth from decades of foot traffic.

Every shop on Magazine Street seemed the perfect mix of history and art. Both quirky and timeless. I'd hit the jackpot finding an available rental space and an investor the same month I came home. The crew at All-American Construction had turned the empty space into a cozy studio with built-in shelves and a bakery display in a matter of days. They even hung my chandeliers. Everything was perfect, and it was great to be home.

Speaking of home, I had dinner plans across town.

* * *

My little black Volkswagen bounced up the rear driveway at my parents' house. I pressed the accelerator with feather-light pressure and prayed I wouldn't need a whiplash collar. The windows in my first car, a white convertible, had stayed down year-round thanks to this driveway. Too many fast trips up the lane had rattled something loose inside the door panels. As a veterinarian in a pet-centric community, my father never had time to fix the windows. Plus, it was his policy that I attempt everything myself first. If I failed or got stuck, I could call for help, but not until I'd tried. I never did get the windows fixed, but I could do an unfathomable amount of other things thanks to his infuriating policy. Ingenuity was a Crocker family virtue.

I parked beside Mom's new Mercedes and pulled in a deep breath of thick Louisiana air. Telltale scents of earth and ozone lingered around me, enticing me to sit in the swing and watch clouds flutter past. Leaves on the old oak tree overhead turned their veins skyward in anticipation of the brewing storm. Their mossy beards floated on the breeze.

Mom met me on the back porch of our family's century-old Victorian. She thought cars parked out front looked tacky. Her honey-blonde hair was pinned up on one side, showing a shock of gray. A lifetime of smiling had left marks at the corners of her mouth and eyes, as if her face anticipated the next round and waited in position. "Well, you look ready for a trip to the library. All that outfit needs is glasses and a bun with a pencil shoved through it."

"Pencil skirts are classic, Mother."

"I agree. They're quite popular with my girlfriends."

I sighed. This was a story I'd heard before. "They're all grandmothers."

"Well, it's true." She tugged the door open and held it as I passed.

Our cozy family home was a five-thousand-square-foot Victorian dollhouse, complete with scrolling gingerbread woodwork and muted mauve-and-olive color scheme. Mom's great-grandfather commissioned it in the late nineteenth century after selling his plantation. At that time, wealthy Americans found it distasteful to live in the French Quarter. Personally, I loved the Quarter. What I didn't like were the debutante balls and cotillions.

Mom passed me on the way to the kitchen. "Dinner's nearly done." Her vibrant floral wrap dress and matching red pumps were stunning together. I'd gotten my passion for fashion— and unfortunately my ski-slope nose—from her, but little else. Even our opinions on design trends were night and day. Where I saw geeky chic, for example, Mom saw a schoolmarm.

I followed her on a whiff of something wonderful. She stopped to examine an array of steaming pots on the stovetop. "I don't know what's happening here." She turned in a circle, flummoxed. "Imogene," she called, "where are you and what can I do to help?"

Imogene was my nanny until high school when she switched to tending house. She'd been in the family since my grandmother hired her as a home health aide late in life. She and Mom had become fast friends. She kept the estate going while Mom grieved the loss of her mother. After that, she never really left. Imogene became like an aunt or surrogate mother to me, filling in as caretaker, chef, and tutor whenever Mom's community engagements had taken her away.

"Oh, no you don't!" Imogene's voice thundered through the first floor, accompanied by the rhythm of highly motivated size-six sneakers. "I've got an eye on everything." She rolled into view, arms open, and pulled me against her. "Miss Lacy." She stepped back for a better look at me. "You're too skinny."

She always said that. "You know that's a compliment, right?"

"Not where I come from."

I hugged her again. "You come from Marigny, not Mars. I think *you* look perfect."

Marigny was once a plantation seated down river from the French Quarter. Today it was shabby chic and considered a local secret. Great clubs and food. A short walk from the Quarter, funky and eclectic. It suited Imogene perfectly, much like her beliefs in local lore and mysticism.

"I'm old." She poked her puffy salt-and-pepper hair. "I'm starting to look like the Bride of Frankenstein."

"You look like home to me." She'd advised me on everything from boys to outfits. She understood how out of place I felt at Mom's parties, at my school, in my skin. The only things that helped me sleep as a child were her stories and a sprinkling of invisible dust from her fingertips to ward off the weary dreams. Imogene came from a long line of shamans and had a whole bunch of beliefs and practices I didn't understand. All that had mattered to me was that I loved her and she loved me and we were family.

"What's for dinner? It smells amazing."

"Oh." Mom returned from ferrying pitchers of ice water and sweet tea to the dining room. "We're supposed to be trying a new recipe, but Imogene won't let me help. I made beans and rice for dinner. There's a big salad in the fridge. I visited the French Market this morning and picked everything myself. Purely organic. The only additive used on those beautiful veggies was love." Her obsession with whole foods was contagious, eventually leading to my first experiment in healthy pet treats.

I pulled the salad from the fridge and unwrapped the plastic covering: bright-green lettuce leaves, tossed with sliced carrots, onions, and every shade of bell pepper known to man. "This is beautiful." I carried it to the dining room and laid it on the table built for twelve. Then I grabbed a stack of plates from the cupboard and set places for my parents, Imogene, and me.

Voodoo, the family cat, sauntered into the dining room and rolled in a shaft of sunlight. She was an ageless, sheer-black rescue, the third in my lifetime, and one of many Voodoos before her. Adopting adult black cats was a kooky tradition started by Dad's grandpa, the first veterinarian in our family, when he replaced their aged cat with a new one of a similar size. The intent was to avoid the discussion of death with his very young son, but the unanticipated result came years later, when neighborhood whispers of voodoo and witchcraft began. How else could Dr. Crocker keep the family pet going for decade upon decade? One day, the cat had a graying muzzle, and the next day it was inky black again. Proof of voodoo had never seemed so sound to the profoundly superstitious citizens of the most haunted city in America. Great-Grandpa enjoyed the misunderstanding so much, he started calling the new cat Voodoo, and the tradition kept going strong for seventy-five years.

I straightened the final plate and smiled.

Dad arrived a moment later and lathered up at the sink like he was prepping for surgery. "Good evening, ladies."

"Hey, Daddy." I ran my hand over Voodoo's soft coat before taking my place at the table.

Dad had kept local pets healthy for as long as I could remember. We'd celebrated his fifty-fifth birthday shortly after my return in March. Dad was contagious, always animated with purpose and buzzing with energy. He sat at the head of the table, white shirt sleeves rolled to his elbows, surprising me with a nudge on the knee.

"I heard you're making the tutus for Mrs. Neidermeyer's Shih Tzus this year. Mable Feller must be mad as a cat in a mailbox."

I smiled. Mable had made all the gala costumes for decades. Designing the tutus for Mrs. Neidermeyer was an honor and a bit of validation in local circles. "I hope she likes what I make. There's a lot riding on this job."

Dad dug into his red beans and rice with gusto. "You'll have business coming in from every pet lover in America soon. If New Orleans is chosen for the next National Pet Pageant, the line outside your store will reach all the way to the river."

"Only you would make the leap from designer of seven tutus to national kingpin." I poured a glass of ice water. "I think Furry Godmother might finally be taking off. I have some baked goods on order, and I think the sashes for Pegasus Farms will put my work on the equestrian lovers' radar."

Mom sighed, bored with our conversation and continually unimpressed by my life goals. "Come sit with us, Imogene," she called into the kitchen. "You make me nervous bustling around in there."

Imogene pressed the door open with one hand and peeked out. "I can't. This is serious business. You talk. I'll listen."

Dad dotted his mouth with a crisp linen napkin. "She makes me tired just watching her. I don't think she ever stops."

"I'll stop when I'm dead." Her voice carried over the clanging of lids and pans. "Plenty of time for rest up ahead."

Dad stuffed his smiling face with rice and chuckled.

I forked a wedge of lettuce. "The jewelry store across the street from my shop was broken into last night and so was Mr. Tater's jewelry store. He's having a security system installed at Furry Godmother."

Dad chewed slowly. "I'm sure it's nothing to worry about." The confidence in his tone didn't reach his eyes.

The strange, dark-eyed man who visited the store earlier came to mind. His presence had made the hairs on my arms stand at attention. Men like him didn't make appearances at Furry Godmother. Too bad I couldn't keep it that way.

I paddled the ice in my glass with a spoon and turned my eyes on Dad. "Do you think my shop could be of interest to thieves?"

"I don't see why. You empty the register every night." He raised his brows, questioning.

"Yes." I shook off the creeping feeling. A sensible jewel thief wouldn't look twice at my store. I was jaded from my time in Arlington. I shuddered and pushed the thought away.

Mom sensed the lull in conversation and got busy catching us up on local gossip and hearsay. She rattled off a list of events on her agenda and lamented over invitations she'd yet to receive. Overall, the meal was fraught with personal questions and poorly concealed suggestions that I find a husband. In other words, the usual.

I left an hour later with two lidded containers of whatever Imogene had concocted on the stove and a gut full of indignation. Mom's dinner references to "proper career paths" and the "quick passage of a woman's childbearing years" propelled my Volkswagen toward Furry Godmother. In keeping with my life's pattern, I'd lay awake all night rehashing and dissecting her every word and tallying the ways I disappointed her until dawn. If I were destined for insomnia, better to use the time productively.

I unlocked the front door at Furry Godmother and made a beeline for the storeroom. Ideas bubbled through my mind as I loaded my arms with everything I needed to mock up a knock-'em-dead tutu for Mrs. Neidermeyer. Airbrush gun, glitter spray, tulle, ribbon. Check, check, check, and check. I wedged my tackle box of craft supplies between my elbow and ribs and caught the store keys in my fingertips. I'd show Mrs. Neidermeyer a tutu she'd never forget and give my mother a reason to appreciate my career.

The familiar sound of my front door sucking open startled me. I'd locked the door—hadn't I? Heavy footfalls moved across the sales floor on the other side of the supply room wall. I tiptoed closer to the doorway, listening for a clue as to who'd followed me inside. Jewel thieves crashed into mind. I pressed my back to the wall and hid in the shadows, holding my breath and formulating a plan. Was I being robbed? Would a thief harm me if he found me?

Images of an earlier mugging flashed in my memory. I'd been young and naïve then. Fresh from the bubble of my family's upscale lifestyle and a few years on quiet college campuses, I'd chosen to walk home alone from work at night in Arlington.

Stupid.

I pinched my eyes shut and gave myself a pep talk. *You want to live, Lacy?*

Yes, I did.

I'd make a run for the back door. I opened my eyes and scooted to the rear shop entrance. I'd have a better chance if my hands were free, but the odds of unloading my arms without alerting the intruder to my presence were zero. I carefully pushed the key into the lock, balancing a tackle box of craft supplies and pressing thirty yards of tulle between my cheek and shoulder. The tumbler rolled, and I silently counted to three.

I jerked the door wide, dropping most of my burden with a crash, and dove into the rear lot armed with monstrous fear and an airbrush gun. A cat dashed through the shadows, and I dropped my keys onto the pavement near my feet. Panic seized my limbs. I needed those for my escape vehicle! I crouched to scoop the keys up.

My shop's back door burst open, and the dark-eyed man from earlier rushed across the threshold with a grimace.

I screamed, jumped to my feet, and froze.

He took long, quick strides in my direction.

My fight instinct fought with my flight instinct. The shriek that left my lips was worth a dozen horror movie deaths. Faced with an attacker and no one to hear my cry, I used the only weapon at my disposal. Gold glitter paint sprayed from the airbrush nozzle in my hands, covering his eyes and thick black hair in fairy dust.

"Gah!" he growled and swiped his face, letting loose a slew of ugly swears. He stumbled, and I bolted, dialing 9-1-1 as I moved. I'd come back with the police to get my keys and car.

Forget diamonds. Glitter was a girl's best friend.

Chapter Two

Furry Godmother's accessories quick tip:
Without rhinestones, they're just handcuffs.

Ten minutes later, I sat on a bench outside my store again while a carousel of red-and-blue lights lit the evening sky. I'd waved down a squad car on Magazine Street. The cops inside had insisted I return with them. The door was ajar when we got there. I followed the officers inside, rehashing the terrifying details as quickly as I could. "You know what? I'll write it down."

The officers exchanged a pointed look while moving methodically across my spotless floorboards.

I rifled through my desk drawer for a proper writing pad and pen. "It's best to list every detail as soon as possible after a crime. I went through something similar once. Well, not really. The last time was much worse." I bit my lip to staunch the flood of words. Emotion stung my eyes.

The officers headed for the stock room.

"Check the rear lot," I called. I settled my pen on the paper, but details didn't come as clearly as I'd hoped, not in the form of words for a list. Instead, I sketched the crazed look on the man's face as he chased me into the lot. I'd thought he was angry when I saw him, but there was something more in his expression.

"Ms. Crocker." An officer returned to my side. He looked at my sketch. "I'm going to need to ask you to wait outside."

"Oh." I handed him the sketch. "This is the burglar. I don't usually draw faces, but that's close. Maybe I can work with a sketch artist at the station."

He ushered me forward, nudging me out the front door. "Don't go anywhere." He stood a few feet away, watching until another cruiser, a crime scene van, and an ambulance pulled onto the curb.

A shiny black pickup barreled into the mix with a short bark of a siren, as if announcing itself was an afterthought. The truck now partially obstructed my view of the fire truck that had also arrived in response to my emergency call. Why were they still here? Obviously, there was no fire. The paramedics had gone inside and stayed. I glared at the truck. How many more people did it take to cover a break-in?

The man who climbed out of the truck looked more like trouble than a cop. Charcoal T-shirt and dark jeans. Brown cowboy boots and a frown. He gave me a once over and strode inside.

Indignant and out of patience, I followed him.

The uniformed cop followed me.

Furry Godmother was tidy. Nothing damaged or out of place, though my skin prickled just standing where a robber had lurked.

I slowed my steps when the stock room came into view. The officers and the man in cowboy boots were spread out, mumbling and nodding at the open rear door. A pile of tulle and assorted items I'd dropped littered the ground at their feet.

I rubbed the chill off my arms. Unease pooled in my tummy. There were too many officials here. None was leaving. Something else was at play.

As if he sensed my presence, the cowboy turned and lifted his gaze to mine. "Mrs. Crocker?"

"Miss Crocker."

He made strides down the hall and into my personal space. He flashed a badge I couldn't read through my scrambled thoughts and searched me with hard, emotionless eyes. "I'm Detective Jack Oliver." He extended his hand.

I pulled back instinctively. A bad vibe weighed the air around me.

Detective Oliver sucked his teeth. He had a scar through his left eyebrow and a number of similar white hash marks beneath a dusting of facial hair. The same marks dashed his neck and disappeared under the line of his collar. "I'm going to need you to accompany me to the police station."

The cops dropped my discarded supplies into evidence baggies.

"What's wrong? What's happening?"

He cocked his head and scrutinized my face. "Why don't you tell me?"

"I came back for supplies. I heard an intruder, so I escaped through the rear door. A man followed me, but I got away. I called nine-one-one, and I told the officers everything on our ride back here. Would you like a description of the intruder? I've made a sketch."

Detective Oliver stepped aside, giving me a clear view of the space outside the open door. Paramedics squatted near something large and eerily familiar. Under their careful watch, the brown-eyed man lay facedown in a mess of tulle and glitter-speckled blood. An officer dropped my airbrush gun into an evidence baggie.

The detective shifted his weight and braced his broad hands on his narrow hips. "Did he look anything like that?"

Well, yes. Yes, he did.

* * *

The police station smelled like stale coffee and body odor. Too many men in a confined space. My visit to their sanctuary had interrupted mealtime, by the looks of things. An array of po' boy wrappers and throwaway containers cluttered the table in the small interrogation room where Detective Oliver had asked me to wait. As it turned out, the stink wasn't body odor. It was their dinner.

A colorful collection of costumed tourists and citizens filled the lobby, sprinkled with a few prostitutes cuffed to benches and a loudly snoring drunk sleeping it off.

I pulled a bleach wipe from the stash in my purse and wiped down the seat and tabletop. Gross as the little interrogation room was, it looked like the Hyatt next to the Petri dish in the lobby. I doused my palms in antibacterial lotion and opted to keep my purse on my lap.

"So, Mrs. Crocker." Detective Oliver reappeared with a pad of paper, manila folder, and pen. He took the seat across from me. "You called nine-one-one to report the intruder."

"*Miss* Crocker," I corrected. "Yes." Memories of the man's lifeless, sparkly face sent heat through my cheeks and chest. I refocused on breathing to avoid fainting. After the night I'd had, rolling onto the police station floor was something I wouldn't come back from emotionally.

"Did you make the call before or after you hit Miguel Sanchez over the head with your paint gun?"

I exhaled. "I didn't hit anyone. I sprayed the intruder with the glitter paint and ran." He should have looked fabulous, not bloody. Or dead.

Detective Oliver trained cool blue eyes on me. "You don't seem shaken. In fact, you're extremely calm after what you've been through tonight. Any particular reason a dead body outside your shop doesn't bother you?"

I nodded, recalling the strange, bodiless sensation from the hours following my mugging in Arlington. The horrific events rushed back with a jolt. The scents of street garbage and images of sleeping homeless people were instantly as real and vivid as they were that night. I'd never seen my attacker coming. He was big, wielding a gun, and clearly agitated, probably on drugs. The cold metal of his gun had seared an invisible line into my chin. I touched it, to remind myself it wasn't real. "I may be experiencing shock."

He stretched long legs beneath the table, bumping his feet into mine and readjusting for the error. "Shock, huh? Most people would be outright distraught after the night you've had."

"I am." I folded my hands. "If someone hit him, then there was a second intruder. Are you certain the fatal wound was a blow to the head?"

Detective Oliver narrowed his eyes. "Yes."

"Were there any other injuries? Defensive wounds, maybe? Has the medical examiner determined the time of death by body temperature compared to the time frame between my emergency call and when the squad car picked me up?"

He poised a pen over the notepad. His careful expression wavered. For the briefest moment, he looked like I'd sprouted a second head instead of proposed a line of insightful questions. "I don't know what you're up to, Mrs. Crocker, but I'll ask the questions."

"My name is *Miss Crocker*." I inhaled deeply to settle my nerves but was assaulted with the collective stench of deep-fried sandwiches. "I'm exploring the possibility of a struggle. A struggle would have left evidence on the victim, like DNA or microfibers, which could prove my innocence." I'd helped Pete study for his medical examiner's national certificate. These questions mattered. A detective should know that.

Maybe I had gained something from our train-wreck relationship besides feelings of general mistrust and anxiety.

"Why don't you stick to sewing mittens for kittens and stop playing cop. Sanchez died from blunt force trauma. The handle of your paint gun cracked his head from behind like a coconut. Remember?"

I hugged my purse, unsure if he simply meant to remind me of the cause of death or prompted me to recall my doing the murdering. "It's an airbrush gun."

Detective Oliver lifted a finger. "I have the murder weapon in evidence with your prints—and only your prints—all over it." He raised a second finger like bunny ears. "I can place you at the scene moments before time of death." Third finger. "We have an emergency call from you reporting an intruder whom you admit to attacking. Is there anything else you want to share with me now, rather than later?" He removed a paper from his notebook and slid it toward me.

"My sketch."

"He looks wild. Surprised. Maybe frightened. Any idea why?"

My shoulders tensed. "No." Humiliation burned my cheeks and panic tightened my chest. "I don't like what you're insinuating. If you knew anything about me . . ." I squeezed my purse tighter. I didn't want him to know anything about me. I wanted to go home and take a shower hot enough to wash away the heebie-jeebies.

Detective Oliver slid his notebook off the manila file folder and flipped the folder open. "Lacy Marie Crocker. Thirty years old. Five foot three. Blonde hair. Blue eyes. One hundred twenty pounds." He lifted his eyes to mine. "Born and raised in New Orleans. Daughter to Dr. and Mrs. Crocker. Undergraduate degree in molecular, cell, and developmental biology. Graduate degree in fashion. That's quite a jump in career paths."

"It happens." By the time I'd finished my first degree, I realized premed was Mom's plan, not mine. I'd always dreamed of outfitting women who walked red carpets, not pulling all-nighters where the sick and injured bled, urinated, and vomited on me.

"You left Arlington four months ago, then came back and opened a pet store. How am I doing?"

"Furry Godmother is a pet boutique and organic bakery." Emotion cracked the words as well as my tough-girl façade. Sitting across an interrogation table from an obnoxious, kind-of-mean detective was the lowest moment of my life. Worse than being mugged. My character hadn't been called into question then.

Somewhere outside the interrogation room, a woman screamed for her go cup and a bathroom. It was legal to take alcoholic drinks with you when you left a restaurant or bar in New Orleans. Establishments offered disposable cups for the road. I doubted the policemen planned to return hers.

I inhaled long and slow, recalling my endless childhood hours of debutante training. I sat taller and breathed deeper. "Mr. Oliver, I am now, and have always been, an upstanding member of our society. Would you like my written statement, or can I go?" I itched to cross my legs and kick him under the table.

"It's Detective Oliver, and I know who you are, Mrs. Crocker. But being a Crocker doesn't exempt you from the tough questions. There's been a murder. You had the means and opportunity."

"I'm not married and you know it. Doesn't it have my marital status in that file of yours?"

He hitched his lips into a crooked grin. He dropped the file open against the table. Empty. He turned his cell phone to face me, previously masked behind the file.

"That's your big insight into who I am? My résumé and a copy of my driver's license?"

"Online résumés are quick references these days. Social media profiles are better, but you seem to avoid those. So why'd you leave Arlington, Crocker?"

I inhaled deeply. "That's irrelevant to your investigation and also none of your business."

"I'll decide what's relevant." He lifted his pen.

"I don't think you can hold me here, so I suggest you change your line of questioning or I'll leave." My voice quivered on every word, though he didn't seem to notice.

"Fine. Describe the night's events again, slowly."

I twisted the straps of my purse around my hands. The stench of police sandwiches had dissipated to a dull afterthought. The spicy scent of cinnamon and cologne drifted across the table. "Mr. Sanchez came into my studio earlier today. He looked around for a few minutes and left at closing. He didn't buy anything, and he wasn't very nice. When he burst through the door tonight, I sprayed him with the glitter sprayer and ran."

The detective's eyebrows knitted together. "Did Miguel Sanchez threaten you?"

"Not verbally." My fingertips whitened. I unraveled the straps and massaged my fingers, reviving circulation.

Detective Oliver shut the file and swiveled a pad of blank paper in my direction. He wedged his elbows on the table and steepled his fingers. His sharp blue eyes were cold and clear as glass. Almost surreal. A girl could get lost in those eyes if they weren't accusing her of murder. I drew the spicy cinnamon scent in through my nose. It took a moment for me to realize his lips were moving.

"Sorry that you felt threatened today. Was there anyone in the store who can corroborate your statement?"

"Mrs. Neidermeyer."

He nodded. "I'll check into it. Write your account of the events here, and you're free to go."

I fought back tears of relief and frustration. "I have to call for a ride. My car's at work." I liberated my phone from the jumbled contents of my purse. My instinct was to call Scarlet, my lifelong best friend, but she had enough going on. Better to call Dad now and Scarlet later when I had time for a proper breakdown.

Dad answered on the first ring.

"Hey." I twisted away from Detective Oliver, wishing he'd had the decency to give me a little privacy. "Are you busy?"

"What's wrong?" Dad went on alert. "Lacy? I hear it in your voice. Let me help."

I chewed my bottom lip, struggling to maintain my composure in front of the detective. "There was a break-in at my shop, and I'm at the police station filing a report."

"Are you okay?"

Mom whispered frantically in the background. Probably demanding the details to a story he didn't yet know.

"I'm fine. Can you give me a ride home? My car's still on Magazine Street."

Detective Oliver pretended to write in his notebook. His eye movement suggested he was eavesdropping.

I wrapped up the call quickly. "My parents are coming."

"I assumed."

I glared. "Nosy much?"

"Very much. Comes with the job."

I rolled my eyes and dug for a breath mint to busy my tongue before I said something I'd regret. "I didn't kill Miguel Sanchez."

"You keep saying that. You want to know what I think?"

"Not particularly."

"There's no sign of a break-in. I think you knew Miguel, and you let him in, but something went wrong. What was it?"

I twisted the mint in my mouth to keep from screaming. "First of all, no. Second, if you thought I killed him, you'd arrest me. You need to get back to the crime scene while it's fresh. Miguel Sanchez was a creep, but he didn't deserve to die, and I didn't kill him."

Detective Oliver shook his arrogant head. "You want to know what I think?" he asked again.

I held my breath to keep from saying that he obviously *didn't* think.

"Occam's razor." He shoved a stick of gum in his mouth and left the room.

My jaw dropped.

Occam's razor was a theory that said the simplest answer was usually the right one. In other words, my prints were on the weapon and I admitted to attacking the victim with it, so I must be the killer.

I curled my hands into tight fists on my lap, unsure if I could leave the room before my parents signed me out. "That theory is stupid."

* * *

Mom and Dad took their sweet time coming for me, probably deciding how to manage the gossip. As if dropping out of medical school wasn't enough. Now I was associated, however loosely, with a murder. Mom shuffled into the room where I waited while Dad signed some paperwork at the front desk.

She rubbed her forehead. "I can't believe I'm picking up my only child at the police station."

I forced back a wave of nausea. "They think I killed someone."

"Nonsense. Jack's an excellent detective. He'll figure this out." Her gaze danced over my face and along my torso, either scouting for injuries or checking for suitable attire.

I still had on the old librarian ensemble from dinner. What was suitable attire for a trip to the police department?

Mom was in all black. "I called our attorney before we left home. He'll get ahead of this."

I nodded. I was in jail, and she had made time to change clothes and talk with legal representation. "Can we go home?"

She marched into the lobby, and I followed.

Detective Oliver lounged against the big wooden desk, smiling at Dad. They shook hands. *Unbelievable.* Detective Oliver lifted his chin to me as I passed. A little white business card stuck between two long fingers. "If you think of anything else you want to tell me."

"My statement's on the table."

He tapped the card against the desk and nodded, dismissing us. "Have a nice evening, Dr. Crocker, Mrs. Conti-Crocker."

My head snapped around as my parents hauled me away from the station. How had he known Mom's last name was hyphenated? I turned my eyes to her. She'd called him Jack. Not Detective Oliver. *Jack.* "Do you two know him?"

Mom patted my arm. "Of course."

My jaw dropped. "What do you mean, 'Of course'? Why do you know a homicide detective?"

Dad opened the passenger doors for Mom and me. I dropped into the back seat and leaned forward between their headrests.

Mom adjusted the mirror until her eyes came into view. "Your father treats Jezebel, his cat."

Detective Oliver was a cat person. I considered that for a moment. "Is he always such a pain in the ass?"

Mom clucked her tongue. "Language, Lacy, really." She checked her lipstick in the lighted visor mirror as Dad pulled onto the road. "Jack's one of the good ones. He's from the area and he's a veteran. He moved home to take the detective position a few years ago. He's a bit of a recluse, but I suppose in his line of work, it's hard to get close to someone you might have to arrest later."

"I've never heard of any Olivers in this area. Isn't he a little young to be ex-military and a detective?" I pulled up a mental snapshot. "He can't be older than me."

Dad turned onto my street. "He joined the army after high school. Did a few tours overseas. Lots of our military men and women get degrees while they're enlisted. He is young, though. I'd guess him at about thirty-five."

A few tours overseas. That explained his people skills. "He doesn't look thirty-five."

Dad's eyes caught mine in the rearview mirror. He slid the Mercedes into the driveway of my fixer-upper shotgun home near the river.

"What about my car?"

Dad twisted in his seat to face me. "I'll swing by and drive you to work tomorrow."

I swung the door open. "'Kay."

He waited until I went inside and flipped on my porch light before pulling away.

Tears welled and rolled freely over both cheeks as I watched their car disappear around the corner. Panic sprouted anew in their absence, lining beads of sweat across my brow. Someone had been killed outside my shop. Why?

I collapsed onto the couch and pulled a pillow onto my lap. I'd abandoned my tutu supplies in the getaway. That left me twelve empty hours to imagine scenarios of how Miguel was murdered in the ten minutes I was gone. I wasn't sure if that was better or worse than dwelling on the list of ways I disappointed my mom or what I'd like to say to that obnoxious detective.

It was going to be a long night.

Chapter Three

Furry Godmother's Safety Tip: Don't cross your mama.

Dad drove me to work after breakfast. He shifted the car into park. "Do you want me to walk you inside? Take a look around?"

"No." I sighed. From where we sat on the empty street, there was no indication a murder had taken place beyond the hand-painted boutique windows. Summer sunlight glistened across the beautiful gold script spelling "Furry Godmother," erasing the touch of dew left behind by the night. Tiny animals with silver wings and wands flew around the curly golden words. The success of my store depended on me. Whatever had happened the night before was over, and I had to get back in the saddle before people got the wrong idea. I had nothing to hide, and I needed the district to see that.

I shoved the passenger door open and stepped into the day. Fresh-cut grass peppered the air, and I crinkled my nose against a sneeze. My arms and legs warmed instantly. The white eyelet of my sundress grazed my thighs when I turned to look back at Dad.

He leaned across the seat toward my door. "I could bring you lunch later."

"No. Paige works today. I planned to buy her lunch and catch up." Paige was once a regular on my babysitting circuit. These days she was a Brown University co-ed on summer vacation.

"Tell her I said hello. I'll wait here until you get inside and turn the lights on."

"Fine."

The dead bolt's tumbler rolled smoothly. No sign anyone had tampered with the lock, but Miguel had gotten inside somehow, and there weren't any indications of forced entry. I flipped all the switches on the wall plate beside the door and waved at Dad. His car didn't move. I walked through the store and held my breath when the back door came into view. A dagger of emotion stabbed my chest and stole my breath. I slapped the line of switches on the back wall, illuminating every inch of the storeroom. I nudged the bathroom door open with my boot.

Empty.

My heart hammered as I opened the front door and waved to Dad again. This time he waved back and edged onto the road.

I turned on shaky legs and marched into the storeroom to clean up my mess.

At nine, I put my chin up and unlocked the front door.

Everything in my southern upbringing said that opening the store was inconsiderate and that I should locate the victim's next of kin and bring them a casserole, but I didn't know Miguel or his family. I did, however, own a fledgling business in need of constant attention.

That was the hardest thing about death, in my opinion. Life went on. People who stopped moving forward started fixating and that never ended well.

I flipped the sign on the window from "Closed" to "Open." A handful of strangers climbed from waiting cars and headed my way. I peeked down the sidewalk. Nothing going on down there. The little cluster of shoppers stopped before me.

A pair of brunettes smiled. The taller one raised her eyebrows. "You're open?"

The half-dozen people on the sidewalk were waiting in their cars at nine in the morning for my store to open. It took a moment to process. They didn't have pets with them, and I didn't have any orders scheduled for pickup. My store was lucky to see a dozen customers before ten most days.

A man with wire rim glasses cleared his throat. "You said you're open?"

"Oh. Oh!" I stepped aside, bracing the door with my hip. "Pardon me. I'm . . ." The words drifted, incomplete. *I'm what?* I was shaken from the intrusion last night, from being accused of murder, from cleaning a crime scene five minutes ago. None of those thoughts were ones I cared to share.

No one waited for me to finish.

I followed them inside and gave my spiel. "Furry Godmother is a pet boutique and catering company. I think everyone should feel like Cinderella at the ball, so I try to make that happen here. I make custom clothing designs and bake fresh, organic, pet-friendly treats every morning with ingredients that are safe and healthy. The chalkboard has a full menu and pricing on treats. Design prices vary." I pointed to the adorable white framed chalkboard beside the display case. "I take custom orders if your pet has a special event coming up, and I make house calls for fittings and delivery. Royal Packages include both catering and an ensemble of your decree."

A portly man squinted at the bakery sign. "Pet catering? What kind of party needs a pet caterer?"

I smiled. "All kinds, really. Birthdays, weddings, holidays, Bar Mitzvahs. Any event where your pet is the star or where your loved ones will have their pets with them."

He shook his head. "That's crazy." Clearly, he wasn't from around here.

I smiled as sweetly as I could manage on three hours' sleep. "You're welcome to sample anything you'd like. My products are made from ingredients found in most kitchens. Some are pretty tasty. The peanut butter and banana pupcakes, for example, are made with all-natural peanut butter, bananas, water, oats, and eggs. No additives or preservatives, just real foods."

The little crowd hung on every word, oddly. Probably to see if I'd kill him.

No one opted to try the pupcakes. I unloaded a fresh box of cookies and muffins into the display case, changing out the shelf signs and wax paper liners and then arranging the pretty pieces aesthetically in neat rows. Thank heavens for mindless paranoia-blocking activities.

Sunlight moved across the front window as I wiped the shelves and boxed products one by one. Rubberneckers and lookie-loos came and went in unprecedented numbers. Very few people made purchases. Most wanted a recount of the night's events. Some were brazen enough to ask but left unsatisfied when I changed the topic.

I cleaned the shelves and replenished stock until the shop was immaculate.

The door sprung open, and Mom's silhouette burst inside. She glanced at the startled shoppers loitering along the walls, then rolled her eyes. "Busy morning?"

I puffed air into my cheeks. "I've had plenty of traffic."

"I figured as much. There was a report on the news after breakfast."

I'd intentionally avoided the morning news and mentally prepared for the worst. "Well, there's nothing to see here. I'm not sure what they're waiting on."

Mom clucked her tongue. Her silk Versace dress dashed her calves as she walked. "You shouldn't be here today. You should be at home resting."

"It's my store. My responsibility."

"Have you called Scarlet? She'll be beside herself, if she isn't already. I assume she gets the paper."

"I don't want to upset her."

"Good plan. Why would a childhood friend be upset that you were nearly killed and couldn't be bothered to call?" She heaved a sigh, unwilling to argue in public. "I don't know why you insist on the hard path through life. You're still a Conti-Crocker. The sooner you embrace it, the easier life will be again."

Easy for her. Not easy for me.

Mom was a Conti. Contis were old money and near-royalty in society's upper crust. Dad was a Crocker. Crockers were new money. Dad's family thought old money was a joke. How could people appreciate something they didn't earn? Mom's family called families like Dad's *faux riche*. They thought real money came from a lineage of power and influence, not from generations of hard work and a few good investment choices in the twentieth century. I'd been caught in the middle of the Conti-Crocker cold war for years, and I hated it.

I softened my smile. "I don't see two paths, Mom. I see this one." I'd never fit in to her world, and I'd beaten myself up about it for twenty years. Finally, the proverbial lightbulb flickered on during my junior year at an overpriced Ivy League college, and I quit. Temporarily. I pulled up roots and applied to Louisiana State. No one at LSU knew or cared about my grandparents' money. I was free to choose what I wanted to study and who I wanted to be without the burden of Conti-Crocker expectations. I'd proudly signed a long line of student loan papers and moved into a dingy little dorm room that smelled like stale beer, burnt popcorn, and sometimes sweat and dirty clothes. I wanted to see what I could do on my own. What kind of life could I craft? Mom had declared the whole thing a phase and expected me to move home after graduation, but I went to Arlington instead. I studied fashion at the Art Institute of Washington, met Pete, and shacked up after our engagement. We had more bills and aspirations than income, but I didn't care. Whatever happened was in my control, and the power was intoxicating. Until Pete ruined it.

As it turned out, Mom was right. I couldn't run from my legacy. Pete had somehow known all about the Contis and the Crockers before he'd ever asked me out. The truth about his scheming for my family's money came out during our explosive break up.

Mom gave the store a cursory glance, then refocused on me. "I saw Paige getting a frozen coffee. She'll be here soon so you can get some lunch."

"I'm fine."

She tapped her nails against my counter. "I'd ask you to talk about it, but I suppose this isn't the time."

Every ear in the store turned our way. I tugged the neckline of my dress. The "shoppers" had stealthily made their ways to displays within feet of the register. The room was smaller. The air was thinner. My eyes crossed.

"Lacy."

My gaze snapped up.

Mom smiled patiently. "Have you heard from the Llama Mamas?" She pressed her lips together and widened her eyes. "You can tell me the truth." She whispered the last sentence, careful of prying ears.

That explained her impromptu visit.

The Llama Mamas were a group of local plantation owners raising llamas and alpacas for charity. They carted their animals all around the county, educating, entertaining, and selling llama wool and weanlings. All the proceeds went to a children's research hospital in Baton Rouge. The Llama Mamas were Mom's biggest competitors for the "good gigs." She was incited to fund the Jazzy Chicks several years ago after attending an event at a plantation and receiving her share of dirty looks. The Llama Mamas called her a city dweller and accused her, politely, of not being true to her heritage because our family had sold the plantation and moved to the Garden District. That was in 1890, but as far as Llama Mamas were concerned, the Contis were sellouts.

Now the Llama Mamas and Jazzy Chicks basically tried to out-kind one another by volunteering everywhere they could to raise money for the hospital.

Dad said this was why he'd never retire. Staying busy kept him at a safe distance from the deranged competitions of socialites.

I shook my head. "Nope, I haven't heard anything."

She blew out a frustrated breath. "Well, if you do, call me. They're up to something, and I need to know what it is. I wouldn't put it past them to knock on your door for costumes." She leveled me with a parental stare.

"Got it. Hey, Mom?"

She tilted her head.

"Have you heard from your lawyer? I need to find Miguel Sanchez's killer before my reputation's ruined. If I'm not cleared soon, people will assume the worst." Even if the police solved the crime later, the damage would be done. "If people think I'm dangerous, my store will fail, and it won't stop there. Dad's business will suffer by association. No one wants a murderer's dad caring for their pet." I couldn't let my problems ruin a business he'd spent my whole life establishing. "Not to mention, the Crocker name will be sullied."

"Sweetie, you're fixating."

"I'm not. I'm . . ." *Jumping to huge assumptions*. Very different.

"Listen to me. Keep your chin up and let Jack do his job. He didn't survive the military by being a dummy." She tapped a finger to her temple. "Meanwhile, you need a fresh window display. That one's two weeks old, boring as one of those sad two-hour walking tours and faded by the sun." She frowned at my *Alice in Wonderland* display. "That Hatter looks like hell."

"Did you talk with the lawyer?"

She scoffed. "Don't worry, darling. You'll get wrinkles. Jack will figure this out."

"That guy practically declared me guilty. He's the enemy right now. Maybe you should stop calling him Jack. It makes him seem like a friend. It's like when you named the vacuum."

She rolled her eyes. "You were terrified. I had to give Vinnie a name so you'd let Imogene do her work. The name made him less intimidating. Names humanize us. You know that."

I shook a finger at her. "That's my point. Vinnie isn't a 'him,' he's a vacuum. We don't want to humanize Jack either. Names confuse things. Jack's out to get me, and Vinnie ate my blanket." I swung a palm into the air. No need to rehash this. I took a breath. "Detective Oliver isn't a friend. He doesn't get a name. One day you're calling him Jack, and the next thing you know, he'll have you on the witness stand saying you saw me kill Miguel Sanchez."

Mom set her handbag on the counter and pulled out a drawing. "Well, that escalated quickly. Let's just say calling him Detective Oliver, after I've called him Jack for two years' worth of Jezebel's checkups with your father, seems unfriendly to me. It's the opposite of southern hospitality, and you know I'm from the school of catching bees with honey."

I counted silently to ten. "Who names a cat Jezebel?"

She made a sour face and fanned the wrinkled paper from her purse. "Jezebel's a lovely Snowshoe Siamese. Here."

"What's that?"

She smoothed the paper on my countertop, carefully uncurling the corners. "I made a sketch of what the Chicks need for their costumes."

A large yellow-and-orange chicken wearing a black top hat was centered on the page. Beside him sat a rectangle with black lines.

I pointed at the rectangle. "What's that?"

Mom slumped. "It's a piano. We're teaching the hens to play. We've ordered four pianos, but I'll need you to take over after assembly. The pianos need to dazzle."

"Mmm-kay. Paint, glitter. Got it." I squinted at the little drawing. "Are those chickens in tuxedos? How do you want to keep the top hats on?"

She shrugged. "Bobby pins?"

"No." Tiny elastic chin straps came to mind, but I'd have to research that. Designing top hats for piano-playing hens was new to me.

"You'll figure out the top hats." Mom's eyes sparkled as the door opened. "Look who's here." She met Paige with a hug. "Paige, I'm tickled to death to see you. Your grandmother's been talking the Chicks' ears off all month about your homecoming. How's college?"

"Good, Mrs. Crocker. It's nice to be home."

"Well, you come by anytime for a visit, okay? Tell your mother and grandmother to do the same. Anytime at all," Mom cooed.

I giggled. I could almost see Mom's mind scrambling through a list of things to do in case one of those ladies took her up on the offer to drop by unannounced. Good old-fashioned hospitality came at a price. Mom would have to keep the house spotless at all times. Just in case. There'd be a standby pie on the counter and fresh pitcher of sweet tea on hand until Labor Day.

Mom waved good-bye to me and gave the lingering shoppers a scowl.

Paige tossed a mile of thick brunette curls over her shoulder and looked down at me from her model-sized frame. "Can you be cool or do I need a bodyguard?"

I narrowed my eyes. "Ha ha."

She dropped her bag on a shelf behind the register and leaned her elbows on the counter. "You want to talk about it?"

I shook my head. I'd babysat Paige when she wore diapers but hadn't seen her outside of Christmas and Fourth of July in years. I didn't make it home often when I was away. "Thanks for agreeing to work here part time this summer. Exactly how long are you my slave?"

She smiled. "I'm home for eight weeks." Her pretty coral blouse emphasized her youthful tan.

I kneaded my hands in mock mischief. "Excellent."

Paige laughed. "What can I do first?"

I scrunched my face. "Do you know anything about Miguel Sanchez? Any guess who'd want to kill him?"

"You mean besides you?"

I frowned. "I didn't want to kill him."

"Is that why you airbrushed his face with gold glitter and hit him over the head?"

I bit my lip. There was nothing wrong with the grapevine around here. "I wasn't the one who hit him, but Detective Oliver claims my prints were the only ones on the sprayer." Evidence wasn't on my side. Though it was circumstantial.

"Whoever killed him must've worn gloves." My prints were on everything because I was the only one who worked here until now. I opened a search engine on my phone.

Paige squeezed against my side, craning her neck for a better view of my phone's screen. "Since it's about a hundred degrees out there, I suppose the gloves were *just* to cover his prints."

"Yep." I typed Miguel's name in and got about a million hits. Apparently, *Miguel Sanchez* was a popular name. "If the killer wore gloves, he must've come here expecting to commit a crime."

A little gasp rose from Paige's lips. "Do you think someone came here to hurt you and had a run-in with Miguel? Maybe the intruder killed Miguel because Miguel could identify him later."

My blood chilled and my voice squeaked. "You think someone came to hurt *me*?" I hadn't considered that option. For good reason: I didn't like it.

She turned her back to the register and looked me over. "What happened?"

Tears pricked my eyes. "I don't know. He found me escaping out back, and I airbrushed him. I'm not sure what he did before that, but it looked like he trampled my Vive la France designs. He might've tripped over the box. I'd planned to launch the new line early next year, but I'll never look at Eiffel Tower appliqués the same again. Spring in Paris is cancelled."

"Doubt it." Paige's pink lips pulled down at the corners. Her structured silk blouse and polka dot swing skirt made her look exactly like the debutante she was. "I also doubt anyone could want to hurt you. I can't believe anyone wanted to hurt Miguel either. Mack says everyone loved him."

I set my phone on the counter. "Mack who?"

"I don't know. She works at the Barrel Room. I stopped by her place last night for a drink. She filled me in."

My tummy flipped with possibilities. This information could save my store, my name, and my future. I checked for obvious eavesdroppers and pulled Paige with me to the far corner of the checkout counter. "Tell me what you know."

"Mack said Miguel hung out with her crowd. She said he was well liked, quiet, and smart. She seemed really into him."

A more cynical woman might've translated those characteristics to womanizing, conniving, and shrewd. "Who's her crowd?"

"Locals our age. Restaurant workers. Bartenders. Everyone's home for the summer."

"Go on."

"Some people called him Tony."

I frowned and turned my phone over in my palm. "Is Tony a nickname for Miguel?"

Paige shrugged. She lifted a finger to the front door where a familiar silhouette appeared. "Here comes your boss. We'd better look busy."

Mr. Tater welcomed shoppers on his way to meet us at the counter. Purple crescents lined the pale skin beneath each eye.

I bit back the explanation that he was not my boss.

"How are you doing, Lacy? I came to check on you as soon as I could get away from the office. It's terrible. I didn't know if you'd be open today. Are you sure you should be here?"

"I'm okay. I think opening the store was best. I don't want to look any guiltier than I already do, and I have nothing to hide, so here I am."

He looked over his shoulders. "Business seems good."

"I think they all came for a look at the crime scene." And the local villainess. "There wasn't much to see and it happened out back, not in the shop." I couldn't blame people for their curiosity. Murder's scary, and in a neighborhood this size, what happened to one person felt like it happened to everyone. Heck, local tour guides still pointed out the former homes of celebrities and a restaurant once frequented by Mark Twain. "Sorry I didn't call you." Should I have called him?

"You're probably overwhelmed. I heard all about it on the morning news."

Paige groaned. "I swear they run that clip every five minutes on Channel Six."

Mr. Tater ducked his head. "Listen, that's the other thing I came to talk with you about." He slunk behind the counter to join us. "I'm negotiating the deal of a lifetime with management at Harrah's Casino. If I get this contract, Harrah's will serve Barrel Room wine at every bar in the house."

"Wow." I lifted my hands in celebration. "Congratulations."

"Thank you. Although I'm afraid I need to pull funding for your store for a little while."

"What?"

He raised pleading eyes to mine. "Your lease is paid through the end of the month, but I can't send the next check until this investigation is finished. I've got too much riding on this casino deal to have my name associated with a murder. The finance and legal departments at Harrah's are looking for a way to gouge me. If they claim I bring any sort of risk to the table, I'll be out more money than I care to think about. Please understand. This isn't personal." He forced a tight smile. "I'm sorry, Lacy. I'm sure you'll be fine until the case is closed and my Harrah's contract is signed. We'll revisit this in a few months."

Months? I set my phone on the counter. Stunned, I opened my lips but no sound came out.

Mr. Tater averted his gaze.

I tipped my chin to the ceiling, praying he was a terrible jokester who'd take back his words immediately.

Paige broke the silence. "What if the investigation is wrapped up by the end of the month? Then will you make the next lease payment?"

I blinked. Hope inflated my flattened lungs. I needed his backing. Mr. Tater had secured the space for Furry Godmother. He paid the monthly lease and the utilities in exchange for a portion of my profit. Sure, the contract between us said he'd forfeit his percentage of my profits if he stopped paying his part, but what was he losing? I wasn't exactly raking in the profits yet. Furry Godmother was a new business. What could I do now? My credit had maxed out with my new home loan and start-up costs for the business. At the rate I was going, I'd still have outstanding student loans when I became an octogenarian. I couldn't keep the business open without Mr. Tater's help, and I couldn't close up either. I'd invested in stock and small accessories, not to mention baking and studio equipment.

What would I do with all those turtle tiaras?

Paige elbowed me. "Did you hear that?"

"What?"

"If." He lifted a warning finger. "*If* you're cleared of the charges before the next payment comes due, I'll make the payments, but please understand, Lacy. It's not personal. It's business."

I nodded. "I'll figure it out. I promise."

Paige released a whistle. "Hello, handsome." She grew impossibly taller.

I followed her gaze across my studio.

Detective Oliver headed our way. A shiny silver detective badge hung around his neck on a beaded chain. "Mrs. Crocker."

I gritted my teeth. I hadn't seen him come inside. "Detective Oliver. Once again, it's *Miss* Crocker."

Mr. Tater nodded at the detective and saw himself out. No doubt distancing himself from the woman accused of murder.

"I'm Paige." She shot a long, thin arm toward him. Energy zipped in the air around her.

He dipped his chin. "Nice to meet you." His unusual blue eyes captivated and frightened me. The barely existent color of his irises fluctuated in the sunlight through my shop windows.

He rested a hip against the counter. "Anything you want to tell me today, Miss Crocker? Something you, perhaps, weren't ready to share last night at the station?"

I glanced at my phone on the counter. "Yes."

"Yes?"

I squared my shoulders and tried to look bigger. An impossible goal when standing beside Paige. "I don't think Miguel Sanchez was the victim's real name."

Paige dragged her gaze from Detective Handsome to me. "What?"

I peeked at the screen on my phone. "Some people addressed him as Tony. Tony isn't an acceptable nickname for Miguel. In fact, Tony is only used to shorten the name Anthony. So Miguel wasn't his real name." Or Tony was the fake name. Either way, why would anyone need a fake name?

Detective Oliver crossed thick arms over a broad chest. "I know Miguel Sanchez was an alias. His real name was Anthony Caprioni. He's from Jersey. What I don't know yet is why he used a fake name or how you know this."

"I asked around." I should've expected the detective to know at least as much as I knew after three minutes online and one conversation with someone Miguel's age.

"You know, I've been wondering, Miss Crocker. You moved home after nearly a decade away. Why was that?"

I dragged nerve-slicked palms down the fabric of my dress. "It's like I told you last night: personal and none of your business. Besides, this isn't about me."

"Maybe it is. Humor me. Why'd you rush back to the place you'd left at your earliest opportunity? Your family's not sick. No one died. You look healthy." His eyes slid over my face and torso. "Why the sudden life change? You're too young for a midlife crisis."

Ha. He'd be surprised.

"Looks to me like an escape on your part. So what were you running from?"

Stress. Heartbreak. Disappointment. Betrayal. "I wasn't running. I came back because New Orleans is my home. And I didn't leave at my first opportunity. I went to college like everyone else."

"Why'd Mr. Tater invest in you?"

"How do you . . . ?" I filled my chest with air and curbed my temper. Of course he'd researched me. His only suspect. "You should probably ask Mr. Tater. Unless you already know and are only here to provoke me again."

"I know everything." He tapped his temple. "Anything I don't know, I will find out. Soon."

"Since you're here, can we focus on the actual investigation, please?"

Detective Oliver smiled. "Absolutely." He widened his stance and circled a wrist, indicating I should enlighten him.

"If my prints were the only ones on the sprayer and the sprayer was the murder weapon, then the killer wore gloves to hide his prints. He must've come here to commit a crime. Could the killer have come for me? I don't keep enough cash on hand to justify a break-in, and my inventory is mostly made of supplies waiting to become something fabulous. Beads and rickrack aren't exactly in demand."

The detective looked like I'd sucker punched him. "You think you were the intended target? Who would want to hurt you?" He pulled a pen from his pocket, flipped a business card face down, and shoved the pair across the counter to me. "Make a list."

I guffawed and locked my hands behind my back. "I don't have a list of people who want to hurt me."

"Then give me one name."

It was as if time had frozen, immobilizing all the fake shoppers. The store seemed to hold their collective breath and stare.

My cheeks burned. "No one wants to hurt me. This is the Garden District. We don't have crime. We have fundraisers and parades. Whatever is going on here has nothing to do with me."

"Yet you brought up the possibility."

I pinched my lips together and shot Paige a look. She'd put the thought into my mind. Better to change the subject. "I'm trying to understand why there aren't any other prints on the murder weapon. If the killer wore gloves, which he must have"—I eyeballed the detective—"then why? Why come here with gloves on? What was the plan?"

"You tell me."

I dug my heels into the floorboards and locked my knees. "I don't know. That's why I'm asking. Are you always so impossible, or is this special for me?"

A glint of humor flashed in his eyes. The corner of his mouth twitched. "I have a few stops to make. I'll decide whether or not I can make a case against you after I run the rest of my leads. Until then, stay out of my investigation. No more nosing around." He set the business card on my register. "Remember who the detective is."

My jaw dropped. "I'm not nosing." I'd talked to my employee for five minutes about Miguel. Hardly the makings of an all-out investigation.

"I mean it, Crocker. I asked around about you. Folks say you're obstinate to a fault, but obstruction is against the law. Do us both a favor and keep that in mind. Curiosity never did the cat any favors."

My hands fell limply to my sides. I forced my jaw and eyebrows to relax. "I'm not obstinate or a cat, thank you very much."

"I notice you didn't deny the curiosity."

"That part's true, and it normally works to my advantage." But if someone didn't unearth the killer by the end of the month, I wouldn't just lose Tater's backing. I could be in an orange county jumpsuit. And Detective Oliver definitely wasn't going to get the job done by badgering me.

He smirked. "Do yourself a favor, kitten, and let this one alone." He breezed out the door looking arrogant and bossy.

Paige collapsed onto the counter with a theatrical sigh of collegiate proportions. "How do you keep it together around him? He talks and I want to circle him like a shark, but I have no idea where to begin with such a man-beast."

"Good lord. Get up." I pulled her arm. "He's not nice. That's how I keep it together. I think he wants to put me in jail. And he called me kitten. How misogynistic is that?"

Paige pressed a fingertip to her bottom lip. "I think it's hot."

A few shoppers nodded in agreement.

I groaned. "That's it. No more of that. He's the enemy. You can work on removing the window display while I get to the bottom of this mess. This is business. No hormones allowed." Luckily, mine had dried up with my last relationship and barren bank account. Even those extraordinary blue eyes weren't enough to sidetrack me from clearing my name.

Kitten my foot.

I was small and mighty. Like a fire ant, a bee, or something else I'd think of as soon as my temperature returned to normal. I plucked the neckline of my dress away from my piping-hot chest, then marched into the storeroom to turn down the thermostat.

Chapter Four

Furry Godmother's secret to a happy life:
Keep your friends close. Sometimes they have wine.

Everything about Miguel Sanchez puzzled me. Why move so far from home? It wasn't a grand business opportunity. Surely, restaurant work in New Orleans was no better than what could be found in New Jersey. Why did some of his local friends call him by his real name? What use was an alias if he didn't fully embrace it?

I adjusted a stack of bunny bonnets on my *Alice in Wonderland* display as I pondered the same questions. The white rabbit looked smart, as always, in his little vest and monocle. He'd know the answers. I patted his soft head and traced his little golden chain with my fingers. I'd admired his pocket watch since preschool, when I discovered the book on Mom's overcrowded shelves. We'd read fairy tales together until the gilded edging rubbed off the pages.

I had tried to emulate the anything-is-possible feeling at Furry Godmother with every addition to my collection. Each Royal Package featured a different fairy tale theme. All concepts were spun with love, sprinkled with glitter, and executed with the fervent attention to detail with which the good Lord had saddled me. Alice was my favorite, but the display was admittedly faded, and according to my mother, it was time for a change.

I hefted the book from the display and wiped it with a soft cloth. The best place to read *Alice's Adventures in Wonderland* was under the sprawling bearded oak tree in our backyard. The pages of my childhood copy were colored with evidence of my love—mainly water spots from sudden thunderstorms and a rainbow of fingerprints in shades from fruit popsicle to chocolate. Scarlet had her own copy, and we'd chased our share of rabbits under that tree.

I bit into the thick of my lip and rubbed a thumb across the screen of my phone. Scarlet was excellent at snooping and shenanigans, but I really should leave her out of my mess.

I dialed and pressed the phone against my ear.

"Hello?" The sound of her voice formed an immediate smile on my lips.

"Hi. It's me. How are you?"

Silence.

I pulled the phone from my cheek and peeked at the screen. I hadn't lost the call. "Scarlet?"

"Okay." The soft click of a closing door sounded through the phone. "I shut myself in the bathroom. That gives you about two minutes before they come for me. Skip the small talk."

Ah. The joy of motherhood. I laughed.

She didn't. "Ticktock."

"How would you like to go out to dinner?"

"Are you kidding me? If I can leave Carter and the kids at home, I'll go anywhere you want."

"Excellent." Mischief was always more fun with an accomplice. "How about the Barrel Room?"

"A winery. Is that a taunt? Do you need a designated driver or something?"

Ideas rolled over schemes and plots in my head. "Something."

"Fine. I'm in. I hear amazing things about their chicken. Can I meet you there at six?"

"Six is perfect."

A choir of small voices lodged complaints at her door ten seconds later, and we disconnected.

I locked up at five with a head full of questions and no more patience for faux shoppers. I flipped the "Closed" sign in the window and wiped my brow. The scorching southern sun burned through the studio's interior, illuminating dust motes suspended in the air and fingerprints pressed on my freshly polished glass. I puffed into overgrown bangs. Time to clean up.

I went to the back for my spray bottle and cloth.

Something niggled in my mind. *Fingerprints.* Everyone left fingerprints unless that person planned ahead. What crime would a person plan ahead for in my store? Could someone want to heist my inventory of beads and swatches? Did they long to illegally acquire miniature stage props and custom pet designs? I had everything from guinea pig wedding gowns to wigs for rabbits in the stock room. Maybe I'd been too quick to discount the possibility. Competition in the world of pet shows was stiff, but was it deadly? Even if robbery was the intent, breaking in to steal or sabotage my critter couture was a long throw from murder. The other possibility wiggled back to the foreground. What if someone'd come to hurt me and Miguel got in the way? Did I have a mortal enemy? A nemesis? A stalker? And if that were the case, why had Miguel been there? Did his visit yesterday afternoon have anything to do with his return last night?

I collected my supply bucket and scrubbed the shop furiously, removing fingerprints from the windows, door, and bakery display. I wiped the shelves, counters, and doorknob. Dust carried in from the streets clung to my floors. I drove my Swiffer around the room on a mental grid, careful to reach every nook and cranny, then set my Roomba, Spot, to work for the night.

I made one last trip around the stockroom, skimming my gaze along box tops and fabric bolts, begging the inventory for clues. Frustration coiled in my chest. What had happened to Miguel after I left last night? My phone buzzed, and I turned it over in my hand. A text message from Scarlet.

Carter's home. The kids are fed. I'm on my way.

Thank goodness. I hit the light switches and jumped over Roomba-Spot on my way to the front.

I stopped short at the sight of unusual pink light filtering through my front window. "What on earth?" I crept closer, confused by what had happened during the few moments I'd been in the back room. There was something on my window. Had someone vandalized my store in broad daylight? Surely not.

I stepped outside for a better look and confirmed the disgusting truth. Sticky chunks of strawberry smoothie clung to my freshly cleaned window, sliding over the glass like a plague. I could practically hear the ants lining up for a party. An empty go cup rolled on the ground where I'd accidentally whacked it with the door.

Shoppers and pedestrians stared but didn't stop.

A fly landed in the muck, and I gagged.

I texted a picture to Scarlet, then hustled inside for a bucket of soapy water and a squeegee. I was going to be late for dinner.

Twenty minutes later, I left for the Barrel Room with renewed vigor and the scent of sunbaked smoothie in my nose. Scarlet's time would be limited by little ones in need of baths and bedtime stories. I slid behind the wheel of my VW and cranked the air conditioning.

Traffic poked down Magazine Street, blissfully unaware of the dark turn my week had taken. It'd been twenty-four hours of craziness, and I was ready to go back to my previous life's troubles. Gossiping neighbors and a disappointed mother beat the daylights out of wondering if someone nearby wanted to destroy me or my boutique.

At the pace of a lumbering hound, I made my way to St. Charles Avenue, where I motored alongside the proud and stately streetcar in companionable silence for several blocks. The Barrel Room bordered Uptown, and it was already packed. I slid into the last available space in the lot and scanned the area for my best friend's Escalade.

Scarlet waved from the sidewalk. Her opposite hand pressed against the small of her back, amplifying her distended silhouette. Wild, red hair mounted into a sloppy bun on top of her head. Flyaway strands stuck to freckled cheeks. She looked runway ready in a perfect orange wrap dress and matching Pucci headscarf. I tugged my humidity-wrinkled sundress and made a mental note to up my game.

I met her with an awkward hug. "Wow. You're not easy to get close to these days."

She raised a perfect eyebrow above oversized sunglasses. "Keep it up and you're buying."

"I'm already buying." I tugged the glass door open and icy air poured over my shoulders. "What kind of person invites a pregnant woman to dinner and expects her to pay?"

"Pretty much everyone I know, unfortunately."

A young woman in a pressed white shirt and black skirt interrupted with a smile. "Two?"

Scarlet shuffled forward, tipped slightly back at the hips. "Yes, please."

The hostess gave her a sidelong glance. "I guess you don't want to sit at the bar."

She sighed. "Oh, no. I want to. Trust me."

The hostess led us to a table dressed in maroon linens and set for two. "Your waitress will be with you shortly."

Scarlet wiggled into her seat and leaned across the table on both elbows. "What happened to your window? That picture looked like my kids had been there."

My mouth dried with the memory of hot strawberry goop on my rubber gloves and giant southern bugs running into the rancid mess. "Someone threw a smoothie, but the window's fine now." I waved a dismissive hand.

Scarlet made a disgusted face. "This district is losing its mind." She steepled her fingers on the tabletop. "What are we up to tonight?"

I mocked offense at her question. "Can't a girl buy her best friend dinner without an agenda?"

"Where's the fun in that?"

A fish-faced man in black slacks ferried two glasses of ice water to our table before winding his way through the dining room in the opposite direction.

Scarlet lifted a finger, effectively stopping my answer, and chugged her water like a woman lost in the desert.

I shoved my glass across the table in case hers wasn't enough.

"Thanks." She blew out a long breath and curled her fingers around the offering. "Better. Now tell me why we're here."

"You've heard what happened to me last night?"

"No thanks to you, but yes."

I ducked my head and lowered my voice to a whisper. "The detective assigned to the case thinks I did it. Can you believe that?"

She matched my posture, leaning her belly into the table's edge. "He died outside your boutique. You were there. Your prints were on the murder weapon. Honestly, I can't believe you didn't call sooner."

Never underestimate the efficiency of a sturdy grapevine. "I didn't want to stress you out, but it turns out I can't process something like this on my own. My brain keeps rejecting it as reality."

"Understandable." She lifted my glass of ice water to her lips. "So, did you do it?"

"Hey!"

She smiled wildly, crushing a piece of ice between her teeth.

"That isn't helpful. Paige says Miguel hung out with local kids home from college, specifically one who works here, Mack."

"Those *kids* aren't that much younger than us. Don't make me feel old."

"They are kids. If I could be twenty-one again, I'd make some serious alterations."

"You regret your youth. Is that why you killed him?"

I shot her a droll expression. "Keep it up, beach ball, and I'm going to take your water away."

"Mean. So we're here chasing hunches and interrogating co-eds."

"Exactly." I set my forearms on the table and it wiggled. "Also, Detective Oliver confirmed Miguel wasn't his real name, so I thought we could ask the staff some questions and see if anyone has any information that might tell me why he went by an alias or what he was doing at my shop last night." I readjusted my arms and the table wobbled again.

"Fun." Her wide, conspiratorial smile warmed me. "Do you have a plan of attack or is this a free-for-all?"

"Planned attack." I flipped the table cloth up and located the issue. Two bolts holding the nearest table leg were barely hanging on. "The best way to solve a problem is by working out from the center. In this case, Miguel's the center, so I need to know everything I can about him and follow leads from there." I pulled a compact multipurpose tool from my purse and cocked it open to the screwdriver attachment.

"Are you fixing the table?"

"It's unstable." I cranked the tool until it didn't budge, then gave the table a shake. "There." I dropped the cloth and tossed the world's handiest gadget back in my purse.

"You should leave a bill for that."

I dusted my palms. "I think we can figure this thing out before the detective. Tater's pulling my funding until my name's cleared."

The waitress arrived with menus. Scarlet chose grilled chicken. I ordered a strawberry and pecan salad, light vinaigrette, and a pitcher of water.

The waitress smiled. "Of course. Can I get you anything else?"

Scarlet smoothed the tablecloth. "Yes. I have a question. Have you worked here long?"

The waitress beamed. "Almost a year."

Scarlet's smile grew. "Did you know Miguel Sanchez?"

"Yes." Her smile collapsed, and her gaze darted to me.

Silly of me to think the rumors of a local murderess hadn't made it this far.

"Miguel came to a lot of after parties. He's a really nice guy." She clamped her eyes shut. "*Was*. He was a really nice guy." When she reopened her lids, both eyes were heavy with crocodile tears.

I held back an eye roll. "Were you two close?"

Her head bobbed. "Oh, of course."

Doubtful. "What's an after party? Like after a concert?"

She screwed her face into a knot. "No. Like, after closing. We stay late to clean up and hang out."

I inventoried the room. Most of the waitstaff looked her age. Early twenties. It made sense that they'd hang out after hours, probably to eat any unsold food and make up for lost tips with free drinks from the bar.

Scarlet tapped a fingernail against her glass. "I heard there were some thefts here recently. Is that true?"

The waitress rocked back on her heels. "A few."

I gawked. Scarlet had heard that too? Sometimes I loved the Garden District grapevine. She was on a roll. I got comfortable and let her work.

"Would you say the thefts began after Miguel came to town?" Scarlet was in takedown mode. No one got away with anything when she was like this.

The waitress blanched. "Most of those missing things were probably just lost. Dropped in the lot or somewhere else. This is a winery in New Orleans. Plenty of people leave here half crocked."

The over-fifty crowd cluttering the tables didn't strike me as the sort to go anywhere half crocked. The Barrel Room in Uptown wasn't exactly a nightclub on Bourbon Street. The ambience was pure swank, and the location was premiere. Uptown was high rent, located upriver from the Garden District, and speckled with plenty of chic shops and residents.

Scarlet dismissed her with a smile. "I'm sure you're right. Thanks for your time."

"'Kay."

I folded my hands on the table as the waitress turned and ghosted away. "Nice work. How'd you know there were thefts here?"

Scarlet dipped her head magnanimously. "I didn't. I just figured if that guy was a thief and he hung out here, probably he took something. What'd you think of her answers?"

"I think she likes the attention Miguel's murder brings her, but she's lying about him. He was rude and demeaning. How could everyone like him? If he was Mr. Congeniality, why would he have been obnoxious to me for no reason?"

"What do you mean?"

"He came in yesterday, skulked around, taunted me, bought nothing, and left. Who does that?"

"Scary."

I shook my head. "He was weird. Mrs. Neidermeyer called him a derelict."

Scarlet smiled. "I would've loved to have seen Mrs. Neidermeyer's face."

"She was shockingly poised."

"Well, color me impressed. New subject."

"Agreed."

"Carter's brother's back in town."

"Chase?"

She nodded. A coy grin smeared over her face.

"Don't." Yes, I'd admitted to thinking he was gorgeous ten years ago, but we weren't in high school anymore, and I had bigger issues to deal with.

"Fine, but he asked about you."

"What happened with him and Courtney? I heard they were engaged." Before he met Courtney, I was a sophisticated senior and he was a lowly sophomore. It would never have worked between us. He and Courtney were a much better match.

Scarlet's expression softened. "You're not the only one who can escape a snare. Her dad's firm went belly up, and they planned to save the family fortune by marrying her into another one."

"Ew." Maybe we had one thing in common—we fell for jerks.

"Yep."

The waitress returned with our meals and the check.

I dug in. "Whoever made this salad is an angel. I think it came directly from heaven."

"I'm not eating salad in heaven. Calories had better not count there." She sipped her water and scanned the room.

"Ooh la la. I swear that man looks better every time I see him."

I followed her gaze to a stool at the bar. "Ugh."

Detective Oliver raised a glass in our direction and winked. He actually winked.

"Don't look at him." I clucked my tongue and impaled a lettuce leaf. "He's following me. I should've known." *Get your own leads, buddy.* I turned my attention back to Scarlet. "How often do you see him?"

"He turns up from time to time at local functions, fundraisers, luncheons." She circled her fork in the air as she spoke. "I wouldn't mind it if he followed me a while."

I frowned. "Stop it."

"Well, I'm married, not dead. Have you looked at him?"

Yes. "No."

"Liar." She sliced her chicken with more dutiful care than necessary. "Well, you wouldn't regret the effort. He has the prettiest green eyes."

"They're blue." I froze. Busted. "Fine. I've looked, but it's not like I had a choice. He's trying to pin me for murder. You know what else? He asked some really nosy questions and called me 'kitten.'"

Scarlet gloated with an open-mouthed smile. "What sort of questions?"

I deepened my voice to mimic Detective Oliver. "'Why did you leave Arlington to open a pet store?' He makes it sound like I sell stray cats to questionable restaurants."

"Everyone loves your work."

I chomped on my salad. "See? What does he know? Maybe I left Virginia because I had an awful, terrible, very bad

64

experience there. Maybe Pete's cheating was my way out, and I wanted a fresh start. Am I not allowed a fresh start?"

"Did you tell him about Pete?"

I stuffed my mouth with strawberry slices and said nothing.

"I didn't think so. He's single, you know."

"Shocker."

Her satisfied expression irritated me.

"So what do you want me to tell Chase?" she asked. "He could help take your mind off the drama."

A shadow fell over our table. "Evening, ladies."

I choked. Water trickled from the sides of my mouth. Detective Oliver stood at the end of the table looking tall and inexcusably smug. "Everything okay over here?"

I dabbed the tablecloth with my napkin and wiped my mouth. "Are you trying to kill me?"

"I'm just checking in. Sounds like you're getting set up for a date. Anyone I know?" The intensity in his stare made me squirm.

How did he do that?

Scarlet batted her eyes. "My husband's brother. Would you care to join us?"

Detective Oliver turned to me. "I can't tonight, but thank you."

She lifted her hand to him. "Nice to see you, Jack. I'll bet you didn't know Lacy's my best friend."

He shook her hand, then offered me his.

I snapped my attention to his scrutinizing eyes. "You accused me of murder last night."

He braced giant hands over narrow hips. The move created a gap between his jacket and shirt, revealing the shiny detective badge on his belt and sidearm at the ready. "I believe I *asked* you if you killed him. Politely, too, if memory serves me."

"It does not."

"Are you sure you can't join us?" Scarlet repeated. I glared at her.

"Not tonight."

I didn't like his tone, as if another night was an option. "What were you hoping to accomplish by following me here?"

"I'm here to ask a few questions and pick up dinner. Seems odd for an innocent person to think I followed her."

I squared my shoulders and lifted my chin. "You're doing it again."

He feigned innocence.

I looked to Scarlet for help. "Did you hear him? He thinks I'm a killer."

Detective Oliver rubbed his jawline. "Any particular reason you chose this restaurant for dinner tonight?"

"Yes."

"You want to expound on that for me?"

"Not really."

The waitress sauntered up to Detective Oliver and wetted her lips. "Anything I can do for you, Detective?"

"Nah. I'm just saying hello."

She dragged her gaze from him to me. "I thought you'd want to know a few of Miguel's friends are staying late tonight. If you want to hang back and talk with them, they'll be here after we close."

Detective Oliver's jaw clenched and popped. He slid a sarcastic look my way.

Scarlet smiled. "I can't seem to stay awake past nine. I'm out, but maybe the two of you . . ." She motioned at the detective and me.

The waitress perked up. "You're welcome anytime, Jack." She walked away with a swing in her hips.

I chuckled. "Jack? You and that very young, half-your-age waitress are on a first-name basis?"

He scowled. "Yes. It's normal. Do you ask people to call you *Doctor* Crocker?"

I returned his sarcastic look. "No. I'm not a doctor."

"But if you were, you'd expect that? Figures."

"Hey." My fingers curled on my lap. "I didn't say that."

He tipped an invisible hat in Scarlet's direction. "Nice to see you again." He shook his head at me. "Do us both a favor and go home tonight, kitten. Poking around in my investigation will only get you into trouble."

I swiveled in my seat and glared directly at him. "You'd have to be doing an investigation for me to poke it. So far, you're just harassing the victim. Me."

He lumbered to the cashier station and shoved a toothpick between his lips.

From my vantage point, he seemed to be smiling.

Scarlet sighed.

I gawked at the swooning woman across from me. "Stop it. None of that. He's the enemy."

"If you're right, the enemy just bought our dinner."

I searched the table, my lap, and the floor. The bill had disappeared. "Dang it." Now I owed him a thank-you. "I wish he'd stop stalking me and solve this murder before I'm out of business."

Scarlet levered her body from the chair with a grunt. "You should tell him that. Then call me with the details." She waddled off in the direction of the ladies' room.

I headed toward the cashier to complain, but Detective Oliver was long gone.

Chapter Five

Furry Godmother's secret to longevity:
Avoid heat stroke, matchmaking, and retired socialites.

After dinner, I paid my dad an impromptu visit at his office. The big, white barn behind my parents' house had been there nearly a century. I was twenty years younger in its presence. I'd grown up behind those walls, playing hide-and-seek with Scarlet, mending local pets with Dad, and later rolling in the hayloft with tourists, bad boys, and anyone else my mom was sure to hate.

Soft, yellow light illuminated the window above Dad's office sign. Dr. Crocker, VMD. I crossed the lawn barefoot, enjoying the sensation of warm grass against the soles of tired feet.

I let myself in with a flourish, sandals dangling from my fingertips. "Working late again, Dr. Crocker? You're making the rest of us look bad, you know."

He leaned over a small tan-and-black pug puppy, stethoscope pressed to the little guy's chest. "What can I say? It's nice to be needed."

"You're always needed."

"Well, thank you for saying so, sweetie. I'd like you to meet Dudley. Dudley, this is my baby girl, Lacy Marie."

I crossed the room to kiss Dad's cheek and get my hands on the chubby puppy. "Hi, Dad. Hi, Dudley." I set my sandals aside and rubbed Dudley's head. My voice slipped straight to baby talk. "What's the matter with you, little cutie patootie?" I lowered my face to Dudley's and rubbed his neck and ears. "What could be wrong with a little guy as sweet as you? Huh?"

Dad pulled a treat from the pocket of his white lab coat and palmed it for Dudley's inspection. "Mr. Fisher says Dudley isn't keeping anything down and he's lethargic."

Dudley sniffed, uninterested in the offering.

Dad now worked his appraising eyes over me. "How about you? How are you feeling?"

Like I was born under a black cloud. "Great." I scooped Dudley into my arms and cradled him against my chest. "Did you check for worms?" I fingered through his short fur. No signs of fleas or ticks. "Is he an indoor baby or an outdoor baby?"

"Indoor." Dad flashed a light into Dudley's eyes. "Lives in Uptown with Mr. and Mrs. Fisher. No kids. No other pets."

"House plants? Maybe mild poisoning?"

A man in plaid pants and a Mr. Rogers sweater appeared in the doorway. "No plants indoors, though we keep a garden out back and spend plenty of time in it."

Dad cleared his throat and waved the man in. "Mr. Fisher, this is my daughter, Lacy."

"Hello." I cuddled Dudley. "What do you grow in your garden? Do you use pesticides?"

Mr. Fisher looked puzzled. "We grow peppers, tomatoes, that sort of thing. No pesticides. Are you a veterinarian also?"

"Oh. No. Um." I glanced at Dad. "I'm so sorry." I set Dudley back on the table. "I stopped to see my dad and this little sweetie was here, so I helped myself to him for a minute. I should go wait in the house."

Dad squeezed my hand. "No, no. Lacy's quick as a whip. She grew up at my ankles, watching every move I made in here, and she's a natural with animals. I've never seen one who didn't take to her immediately or vice versa."

"Oh." Mr. Fisher's face brightened. "You're two of a kind, then. You must be proud."

"I am."

I needled Dad with an elbow. "It's in the blood."

Mr. Fisher nodded approvingly. "Do you work with animals also?"

Heat crept over my cheeks. This was the part where half the people in town thought I was crazy and the rest assumed narcotics. "I own Furry Godmother, the pet boutique and organic treat bakery on Magazine Street."

His gaze ran briefly to my dad before returning to me. "Are you happy?"

"Absolutely." A strange sense of pride curled though me, and the truth of that word settled into my spine. "I am."

Dad peeked at me over the wire frame of his glasses. "Mr. Fisher and his wife are psychologists. They opened a practice in Uptown."

"Oh." The word dragged into multiple syllables on my tongue. Psychologists. I cringed. He probably thought I sounded nuts, but I *was* happy. Happy counted. Why did I care what Mr. Fisher thought?

The men stared at me. I needed to say something. What was the question? "A private practice? That must be so interesting."

"Not as much as you'd think. People spend entirely too much time worried about nonsense, things that may never happen and others they have no control over. It's exhausting."

I knew the feeling.

Mr. Fisher scooped Dudley off the table and cooed into his ear. "Maybe we should stop by Furry Godmother tomorrow and get you a sweater like Daddy's so we can be matchers."

I lifted my gaze to Dad's. "I'd be happy to have you come by, but he should skip the sweater. A pug in Louisiana needs lots of water and a fan. It's ninety-five degrees today. Are you hot in that cardigan?"

"Heavens no. Poor circulation. You'll understand when you get older."

"You get chilled easily? Do you keep the house warm? Ever use the air conditioning?"

"Never. My wife and I enjoy the heat. The temperatures are part of what drew us here. We spend as much time outside as possible. Our old bones don't hold the warmth in for long."

Dad realized what I was thinking and clapped my shoulder. "I think we cracked this case. The heat's getting Dudley down. His flat nose and smaller air passages make the heat extra hard on him. It's good that Dudley's an indoor baby, but this breed needs somewhere to cool off regularly. Maybe there's a place in your home where you can keep a fan running for him. When you go outside to garden, be sensitive. These guys are prone to heat stroke. If he seems down, let him inside. Some little changes will make a big difference. Do this and Dudley should be back to himself in no time."

Mr. Fisher nuzzled his puppy. "So he's not sick? He's going to be fine?"

"I didn't see anything to worry about, and the heat would explain his lethargy and loss of appetite," Dad said. "You can feed him boiled chicken for a day or two if you'd like. Give me a call if he doesn't turn around, but I expect all good things."

"Thank you." Mr. Fisher gave Dad a one-armed hug, smooshing Dudley between them.

We followed him to the driveway and waved at his retreating taillights. My sandals dangled on fingertips behind my back.

Dad gave me a once-over and scratched his head. "That was a solid deduction. I'm not sure if it's age or fatigue, but I miss the obvious more and more, always seeking some deep-rooted malignancy." He turned both palms skyward and laughed. "Heat."

"Occam's razor." I mentally mocked Detective Oliver's obnoxious voice.

He nodded. "It's not too late to join the family practice."

"I'm barefoot." If there were a place in the world record book for most consecutive bad first impressions, I'd easily hold it.

"I'm sure he didn't notice. You delivered fantastic news. That's what he'll remember."

I gave him a disbelieving smile. "No more school for me. Besides, I like what I do, and I owe my left kidney to the student loan people already."

"Wow. Fannie Mae's gotten tough on repayment terms. Very specific, too."

"Ha ha."

Dad laughed.

I collapsed into a rocker beside his office door and slid my shoes on. "Mr. Tater dropped by to see me today. He wants to distance his name from the murder. If the police haven't found the real killer before the lease comes due, he won't make the next payment, and I'm up a proverbial creek."

Dad lowered into the rocker beside mine. "Well, that's unfortunate. What will you do?"

"I'll take on as many side jobs as I can for extra cash this month." Assuming anyone would let me work for them. "Maybe I can make the payments until things blow over. I still have two weeks this month."

"Let me help you. I'll make the lease payment."

"No."

"Then let me make your student loan payments so you can concentrate on the lease."

"No."

"Lacy, really." He frowned. "Your education was my responsibility. No one asked you to take out those loans. At least let me help until you get this straightened out."

"Nope. I'd agreed to go to Mom's alma mater and study medicine. Once I changed schools and majors, I took over the debt."

"That's nonsense. Now you're just being stubborn. You're only punishing yourself."

"I'm not punishing anyone. I'm being my own woman. Standing on my own two feet."

"How's that working for you?"

I huffed and let my head drop against the back of the chair. "Awesome."

Lilies and cone flowers swayed in the mulch along the walkway. Flowers were a feast for the eye this time of year in the Garden District, but it was hard to enjoy them with the collapse of my business looming.

Dad's warm hand fell on my arm. "Let us help you."

"I'm not taking any more money from you. You're preparing for retirement. You should be saving your money. I have a thousand years of work ahead of me. I'll handle it one way or another."

Dad leaned forward in his chair, bracing forearms on knees. "I hate to break it to you, sweetie, but you're an only child. The kingdom is all yours eventually."

"Don't talk like that. You're going to live forever. Mom, too."

"Well then, I'm definitely not retiring anytime soon. I've got to stay busy or your mother will put me to work at her parties."

A large delivery van pulled into the driveway beside my car. A man in white coveralls jumped down from the driver's seat and turned the pages on his clipboard. "Mrs. Crocker?" He approached me with a skip in his step.

I pointed to Dad.

"See what I mean?" He scribbled on the line and returned the clipboard.

The man tipped his hat, and men in matching white ensembles unloaded stacks of chairs and folding tables from the truck.

Dad pointed to the house. "Take them in through the back." He pushed onto his feet. "Speaking of parties, we're having a completely casual gathering tonight. A midnight chocolates-and-wine fiasco. One where I have to wear a tie and entertain all the other husbands who don't want to be here."

"Sounds fun."

"You should come. It'd mean a lot to your mother."

Guilt flooded through me. I loved Mom but hated her parties. "I would, but I can't. I've got a ton of work to do."

Dad watched with furrowed brows as men hauled linens and glassware into his house. When the back door snapped shut, he drifted his gaze back to mine. "You might meet a nice young man from a good family."

I covered my eyes with my fingers. "*Et tu, Brute?*"

"I'm just saying, don't mark all men as the devil because of one moron's actions. Pete was the exception, not the rule."

"Got it." I dropped my hands into my lap.

"Your mother and I just want you to find someone who makes you happy. We don't want you to be alone one day when we aren't here anymore."

"Well, thank you for your love and concern, but I'm already happy." I wrenched myself upright. "Tell Mom I wanted to stay for dinner, but I need to work on Mrs. Neidermeyer's tutus, make a plan for paying next month's lease, and solve a murder. Busy, busy, busy."

Dad rubbed his forehead. "Don't step on Jack's toes. Our relationship will only go so far to get you out of an obstruction charge."

"Everyone keeps throwing that threat around. *Obstruction. Interference.* Aren't you supposed to tell me I shouldn't look into this? I should stay safe. Batten down the hatches. Yada yada yada."

"Probably." His apologetic grin said it all. I got my insatiable curiosity honestly. From him.

I kissed Dad good-bye and cut through the flow of delivery men to my car. It was nice that my folks didn't want me to be alone, but I had enough problems already without adding another.

* * *

The scenery changed quickly on my way home. Majestic nineteenth-century mansions morphed into the squat strips of housing that made Uptown the unique and lively place I loved.

I slid my car against the curb and zipped inside, locking the door behind me. My place was a classic shotgun home built to house workers in the early 1900s. Like all the others, it was designed to be dull, drab, and utilitarian. Honestly, the architects should have known better. This city didn't believe in any of those things. Nowadays, the shotguns on my street were brightly painted, renovated, updated, and generally bedazzled into unique blends of art and history. One day I'd have enough money to do more than paint and hang art. Until then, I considered the aging light fixtures and stained floorboards part of the cultural experience.

My phone sprang to life with the unmistakable sounds of *Psycho*'s shower scene. Pete-the-Cheat was calling. I fumbled for my phone and rejected the call. My heart hammered stupidly. Pete had left bundles of messages in March and April, but I never returned them. By May, he'd called fewer than once a week. Even fewer in June. This was his first call in July, and the month was halfway gone. I'd heard it all. He was sorry. He wanted to make amends, return some of my forgotten things, and apologize in person. I didn't want to see him. I couldn't picture his face without recalling his secret double life, his other girlfriend, and the fact he'd only asked me out as part of a long con for my family's money. Whether he'd eventually cared for me or not was irrelevant, and keeping a second girlfriend was a solid indication he hadn't. I dropped my phone onto the coffee table and groaned. Unless one of the things he wanted to return was Penelope, I had no interest in him or his hearty line of BS.

I poured a tall glass of ice water over lemon slices and stewed. The Barrel Room waitress had served up Miguel's friends, and all I needed to do was go back at closing and talk to them.

I stacked tutu materials on the couch and curled onto the cushion beside them. I folded and cut sections of tulle while trying not to acknowledge my laptop on the end table. No time for the computer. I had work to do. First, I needed to create one perfect sample tutu. Then I could do research until dawn if I wanted.

I unrolled seven lengths of hot-pink ribbon and elastic.

Mrs. Neidermeyer was in the studio when Miguel came in. She'd called him a derelict. His friends called him Tony. Detective Oliver called him Anthony Caprioni from New Jersey.

I grabbed my laptop. "I'll do one quick search, but that's it." I typed Anthony Caprioni into the search engine. Dozens of articles came up.

He was a thief.

I scrolled through page after page, then checked the criminal justice site in his old county. Anthony Caprioni had a record twenty counts long. It started when he was eighteen, and I was willing to bet there was a sealed juvenile record before that. Probably a lifestyle he'd developed young. Statistically speaking, if he'd been arrested so many times, there was likely an iceberg of things he'd gotten away with hiding beneath the surface. That, or he was the world's worst criminal.

Miguel had cased my store. He'd asked about the products. He must've known I didn't have anything with significant resale value. Surely, a life of crime had given him a more discerning eye. His latest arrest was in relation to a diamond heist. Alarm bells screamed in my head. A jewel thief! A few searches of the local paper around the time of his arrest revealed Miguel had had a partner in the crime but rolled on him for a reduced sentence. The phrase "no honor among thieves" came to mind.

I rubbed my temples and shoved the laptop away. Miguel stole diamonds. It was highly likely he'd been involved in the local jewel heists.

Even so, I ran a pet studio. So why'd he break in that night? What did he want? Not jewels. Could he have also been a thug for hire?

A shiver raised gooseflesh on my arms. What if that smoothie on my window wasn't a random act of vandalism? What if this was about me after all?

Chapter Six

Furry Godmother's quick tip: Sunshine is
an excellent source of vitamin D and inside information.

I squinted into bright midday sun, soaking vitamin D into my skin and sucking the caffeine from a jumbo iced latte into my slumping system. I'd slipped out for coffee after Paige arrived. Another restless night had left me shuffling squint-eyed around the shop by noon. Nothing a little caffeine couldn't cure, I hoped. Magazine Street was my favorite part of the Garden District. Miles of hip and artsy shops stretched in either direction, lively and chic, inviting and invigorating. If anything could get my blood pumping, it was a few minutes on the brightly painted bench outside my studio. That and the frozen coffee melting in my cup. Wind whipped through my hair, tussling the strands and throwing away the sleepless night. The rich scents of freshly fried foods at a restaurant three doors down mingled with the sweet aroma of flowers in storefront window boxes.

I took another pull on the big green straw as I admired my window display. I'd been up until dawn reading every article

I could find on Miguel, poring over his social media accounts and trying fruitlessly to deduce the reason he'd come to Furry Godmother. The most I had to offer him was a connection to my family's money, but he was a thief, not a kidnapper. I might've had more information to work with if I hadn't let Detective Oliver get under my skin. I'd considered returning to the Barrel Room a dozen times before midnight, but each time, the detective's smug face came to mind, warning me to stay away from his investigation. That man was looking for a reason to cuff me.

I shook the cup and exhaled defeat. What I had were too many questions and a looming lease payment I couldn't afford. I'd noodled myself cockeyed hoping for an epiphany and still had nothing.

Paige bounced into view, and I jumped.

"Sorry. I didn't mean to scare you."

I managed a limp smile. "I was concentrating."

She settled on the bench at my side. "How are you?"

"Befuddled."

"Oh, well, you look pretty."

"Thanks."

She crossed long, thin legs and locked her fingers over one knee. "I miss it here when I'm away at school. Did you?"

"Every day."

"I can never explain it right to my friends. They don't have places like this in their lives. They aren't attached to their hometowns in weird, dysfunctional, codependent ways like me."

"Like us," I corrected. "You have to grow up here to understand, I think."

"Yeah. Did you know this street has always been my favorite? To me, Magazine Street is like if the French Quarter and Grandma's fancy social circle had a really cool baby."

I shook my coffee and pumped the straw. "Agreed." My tummy gurgled. "How's it going in there?" It felt like lunchtime and frozen coffee wasn't making the cut.

"Good. The gawkers thinned out. Still no sales. I came to see if you want to set up a new window display while it's quiet. Do you have a design consultation?"

I checked my watch. "Not until three." I shot to my feet on a caffeine and New Orleans high. My petal-pink maxi dress billowed around my ankles, a striking contrast to Paige's white pleated miniskirt and navy cap sleeve blouse. "Let's change the display."

"Excellent." She hopped up beside me. "I finished taking the old one down."

Cool studio air shocked my skin into goose bumps and added spring to my step. I inhaled the yeasty aromas of fresh-baked pawlines and gave silent thanks for an evening of insomnia. I'd lost a second night's sleep wondering what really happened to Miguel, but I'd gotten ahead on the daily baking. My display was full, and there were enough treats in the freezer to last a week.

Paige hefted a box of discarded items from the *Alice in Wonderland* display. "What will it be this time?"

"Let me check the stockroom for inspiration." I grabbed the box and headed to the back.

The empty window was a canvas awaiting a masterpiece. The new display should stop pedestrians in their tracks and beckon them inside, hopefully to spend some money.

"Something divine," I whispered to the shelves and piles of beautiful materials. "Ah ha." I gathered bags of white fiberfill, bolts of blue chiffon, and a caddy of glitter with my spare sprayer.

I floated back to the front, dropped my caddy on the counter, and faced off with the empty window.

Paige uploaded digital photos of the gowns I'd created for a Weimaraner wedding at Jackson Square on Monday and saved them to my computer.

I lined the window in chiffon and doused it in tufts of fiberfill for a heavenly backdrop, stretching and puffing the latter into soft, cloudlike forms.

"How'd you get all these puppies to endure formal wear?" Paige asked.

"Magic." I gathered the line of undressed animal mannequins from the previous display and arranged them in the faux clouds.

"Yeah, right."

"I sprayed the pieces with perfume so they weren't interested in chewing them off." Also, I kept a generous pocket full of treats. I'd learned that secret from Dad. All tricks aside, my patience was long, and that was the key to everything. "Can you toss me the glitter and sprayer?"

"What color?"

"Silver for clouds and angel wings. Gold for the harps and halos." I strapped small white wings on the naked pet forms.

Paige moseyed over with the glitter caddy and leaned against the wall. "I don't like it."

My hands froze on a cat statue. "Why not? It's pretty."

"They're angels."

I snorted. "You don't like angels?"

"Not these. It looks like all those pets died and went to heaven."

"They're supposed to be guardian angels." I eyed the blooming display. She was right. I stripped the wings and shook my head. "I'm off my game."

"Head in the clouds?"

"Ha."

She left the glitter on the windowsill and went back to the computer. "You're the artist. I might be wrong."

"You're not. It's me and this day." I pulled handfuls of clouds away from the soft-blue backdrop. "I could do a fairy theme." The wheels of creativity spun reluctantly into motion again. "No. Scratch that. Let's do a garden theme. I can put red gnome hats on the bunnies, bring in some wooden flowers and make a faux pond with iridescent gift wrap, add some pretty stones and turtles in tiaras. Paige, you're a genius."

"That's what they tell me."

"Humble too." I gathered the excess fiberfill into my arms and fisted a group of unnecessary wings. "I'm going to restock this and make a few gnome hats for those bunny statues. Shout if you need me. I might have to dig for some decent toadstool materials."

She gave me a salute and went back to scanning my digital pictures.

A dizzying carousel of ideas spun through my mind as I unloaded my arms and searched for perfect accessories.

The phone rang, and I fell into my chair's waiting embrace. "Hello?"

"Mrs. Crocker?" a strange voice chirped across the line. "This is Maddie Graves from National Bank. You left a message about a business loan?"

I pinched the bridge of my nose. I'd forgotten about the desperate late-night calls I'd made to loan officers. "Yes. Hi. It's Miss Crocker." I gave Maddie the run down on my debt, income, and immediate need. She gave me the boot, unless I could find a cosigner.

"Thank you for your time." I disconnected with as much dignity as I could muster and dropped my forehead against the desktop.

"Lacy?" Paige called from the hallway.

"Yeah?" I rolled my head for a look at the doorway.

She tiptoe ran into the stock room, a look of horror on her pretty face. "Margaret Hams is here."

The message in her raspy whisper and red face was clear. I should know this name.

"Margaret Hams?" Didn't ring a bell.

Paige planted her palms on my desk and dropped her face to mine. "From the Llama Mamas."

"Oh dear." I stood. I couldn't be seen talking with a Llama Mama. Not unless I wanted my mama to have a coronary. If Mom showed up and found a member of her competition here, she'd die on the spot and come back to haunt me. "Did she say what she wanted? Did she look mad? Is she alone?" Was this a trick? A ploy for information on Mom's Jazzy Chicks?

"She didn't say, I don't think so, and yes. Should I call your mother?"

"No!" I waved my hands in big arcs. "Never ever tell her about this. Let me get rid of Mrs. Hams."

I scurried into the shop.

A woman with a stroller peered into the bakery display. Paige rushed to her aid. "Can I help you?"

I scanned the room for a woman who looked like a llama lover. There was a boy with his hand in my turtle tank and a portly man with glasses on a necklace examining portraits on the wall. Where was Margaret Hams?

A woman in turquoise culottes and coral blouse caught my eye. She fingered the mess I'd left in my half-decorated window. The patch on her quilted handbag might as well have been a big *X* on the treasure map: *Love a Llama*.

I treaded softly, scanning the street outside the window for signs of Mom or one of her Jazzy Chicks, half afraid of what would come next. "Mrs. Hams?"

She turned to me with a handful of fiberfill and a look of disgust. Her coal-black eyes set deep beneath thick salt-and-pepper brows. "Is there somewhere we can speak privately?"

"Of course." I patted the bakery counter on my way past and looked at Paige. "If my mom stops by . . ."

Paige lifted her eyes as she sealed a full bakery box for the woman with the stroller. "I'll let her know you're with someone."

I led the severe faced, colorfully dressed woman to my cluttered desk in the stockroom and uncovered a chair for her to sit. She didn't.

"What can I do for you, Mrs. Hams?" I folded my hands protectively in my lap.

She clutched her purse against her chest and dug inside. "I'd like to hire you. I hear you're quite the seamstress, and word around town says your love of animals is akin to Noah's. I don't trust my llamas to just anyone. This is a compliment." Her snub nose wrinkled. Life under the harsh Louisiana sun had leathered her cheeks and spotted her arms. She smoothed a piece of paper against a bare spot on my desk. "I need twenty-four leg warmers for my girls. We're putting on an old-fashioned farmer's parade down Old River Road."

"A llama parade?"

"A livestock parade. My girls are just one component, but they're accustomed to being the stars. I'd like to keep the tradition."

"A livestock parade?" This was new. Was it some kind of trick? I scanned the room for hidden cameras.

She huffed. "There's plenty of young families and elderly folks who still farm my area and can't or won't come into the city for festivities. The Llama Mamas don't think they should miss out. Do you?"

"No, ma'am." My mind scrambled for a polite reason to decline her proposal. This was what southerners called a rock-and-a-hard-place situation. "My mother would kill me" was neither a professional nor grown-up reason to decline her offer, but obeying my mama was nonnegotiable. Going against her, which Mrs. Hams must have known she was asking, would put a smudge on my reputation as well as Mom's. In southern law, the "respect your mama" rule was followed closely by the "behave because you represent your family name" rule. Of course, if I named Mom as the reason for passing on the Llama

Mama offer, Mom would be furious with me for bringing her into it. Tension coiled in the pit of my stomach. I smiled sweetly and brought out my best manners. "I'm honored, Mrs. Hams, but I don't believe I'm the best choice for this job."

Though, I could use the money in case Detective Oliver didn't get his butt in gear. It had been two days since Miguel's murder. Were the police making any progress?

"Nonsense." She pointed to the paper placed on my desk. A stick figure animal with four legs and curly hair anchored the page. Each leg wore a design from ankle to knee. "We need them made of something airy. It's hot out there. Nothing too cumbersome, but make them flashy. Everyone loves flashy. Spare no expense. You can bill me at this address." She slid a business card across the desk with the drawing. "If you're opposed to leaving the city, I can have someone pick them up or you can have them delivered. The country's not for everyone."

"I enjoy the country," I said, bristling. "I couldn't do the job without meeting the girls. I've never worked with llamas before. I don't know their temperaments or how much material they're likely to put up with. I'd want to see their coats against the color choices and take measurements." Jeez. This wasn't amateur hour. Did she think I'd whip something up without meeting them and send it off with no details or research? Obviously I wasn't a livestock professional, but I had ethics. I had standards. There was a process involved. My thoughts wandered as I tried to imagine myself fitting llamas for leg warmers.

"Miss Crocker?" She scowled.

I bit my lip. "Hmm?" Clearly, I'd missed something.

"I asked how soon you can come for the measurements."

"Oh, no. I'm afraid I can't." I raced back through the conversation. "I have a packed schedule this week. I can't possibly prepare twenty-four leg warmers."

"I'm in no rush. Take two weeks. Come Friday afternoon for the measurements. I'll serve sweet tea and shortcakes. I'll have the girls groomed and ready for company." She pulled a stack of cash from her purse. "We'd like you on retainer. This should be enough to get started." She set the money on my desk. "Mr. Tater assures me you're a dedicated, talented young woman and you'll be an asset to the Mamas. Now don't be late." She disappeared through the stockroom door without a good-bye.

Mr. Tater had put her up to this? I warmed at the thought. He needed to distance his name from the murder, but he still wanted to help me. Hope lifted my chest. He believed in Furry Godmother, and so did I.

I grabbed the phone and left messages with two more banks about securing a small business loan. Just enough to get past this mess and back on track.

"Lacy?" Paige's voice drifted down the short hallway.

I imagined my mom's face on the cash before me. I snatched it off the desk and folded it around Ms. Hams's business card and drawing. I tucked both into my top desk drawer. "Coming!" I hastened into the studio.

Soft jazz filled the cozy space. Paige's phone rested in a speaker dock on the counter where she stood with a girl her age. "Hey." She waved me closer. "Lacy, this is Mack. She works at the Barrel Room."

"Ah." My memory kicked into gear. I smiled at the young lady who'd served Scarlet and me dinner. "Right. We met last night. What brings you by?"

Mack lifted and dropped one shoulder. "Paige said it's important you find out what happened to Miguel. I told her I'd help if I could, plus I need a gift for my mom's tabby."

I beamed at Paige. "That's fantastic."

Mack drifted toward the bakery display. "Got anything for finicky cats?"

"Always." I didn't tell her that "finicky cats" was redundant. Better to stay on her good side until I knew what she knew. "Most felines love my tuna tarts. Oh, or how about some purrlines. They look like pralines, but I make them for kitties. Everything is organic and safe. I color them with berry extract."

She cocked a narrow eyebrow. "I thought you made pet clothes."

"I do, but I also enjoy baking. How about a tiara?" I led her to a display of rhinestone headpieces. "If you think she might be interested in something specific, I can give her a call or invite her in for a consult."

Mack fingered the tiaras. "Maybe." She didn't look convinced.

I turned to Paige for a little help with her friend.

"Mack," Paige said, dropping three purrlines into a bakery box and tying it with a satin ribbon, "you said Miguel had a girlfriend at the restaurant?" She handed the box across the counter.

Mack helped herself to a tiara and stacked it on the box. "Her name's Sunshine, but if you ask me, she's more like a hurricane and not the good kind from Pat O'Brien's. I heard her say she's staying late tonight. If you want to talk to her about Miguel, stop by after ten. I'll let you in."

"Thank you."

"Can I get a bag?"

Paige whipped a logoed shopping bag into the air and set Mack's booty inside. "Thanks again. We really appreciate it."

Mack gave me a look and left.

Paige bounced on her toes. "What do you think?"

"I think Sunshine had better be there tonight. That information just cost me fifty bucks in merchandise."

"Aww." Paige pushed her bottom lip out and wrapped a long arm around my shoulders. "How about I buy you an ice cream before your three o'clock session?"

"I could probably eat some ice cream."

She tugged me against her side. "I'll pick it up and bring it back here. We can make a plan for Sunshine's interrogation and decide what to tell your mom about Ms. Hams's visit."

"Blah." I'd temporarily, conveniently, forgotten about that. "You'd better make mine a double scoop. Chocolate."

Chapter Seven

Furry Godmother's pro tip: Let sleeping dogs lie.

I drove along Mable Feller's street more slowly than necessary. She'd placed a custom order for her blue ribbon–winning Himalayan and elderly French bulldog more than a month ago—weeks before Mrs. Neidermeyer had asked me to make the tutus, which normally would have been Mable's assignment. Call it paranoia, but the idea she might've hired Miguel to destroy me had crossed my mind a time or two. The same part of me understood the theory was ridiculous. The shamelessly cynical part reminded me of all the heinous crimes committed by folks no one had ever suspected.

Before I opened Furry Godmother in April, all pet fashion orders went directly to Mable. She'd been sewing much longer than I'd been alive, but her designs were straight off of *Little House on the Prairie*, completely without flair. The district wanted pizazz, and zhushing up was my specialty.

I parked in the drive at Mable's Audubon Boulevard estate and gathered my things. The handsome brick Dutch Colonial was loaded with natural lighting thanks to an abundance of windows and Louisiana in July. Her lush garden was the envy of half my mother's social circle.

Humidity curled around my skin like a wet blanket as I slid from my car into the thick summer air. An instant bead of sweat formed along my temple. Most people hated the stifling subtropic temperatures of the Deep South, but I found them invigorating. Some of my best memories happened on days like these. I adjusted my bag over one shoulder and a slow smile spread over my face.

"You look like you're up to no good." Mable's knowing voice staunched my nostalgia. She stood on the opposite side of her garden gate, stroking her Himalayan, Miss Peabody.

"No, ma'am." My smile widened. Caught thinking of a midnight swim with my closest friends on graduation night.

"Well, fess up. What was that cat-that-ate-the-canary face about?"

"The heat." I headed her way. "Sometimes I'm slapped with a memory that makes me wonder how I ever forgot."

She looked me over from head to toe and freed a tiny garment bag from my fingertips.

"Would you like me to stay and check the fit?" I asked.

"Absolutely." Mable motioned me down an uneven cobblestone walk to a grand courtyard. The knotted roots of grand oak trees had long ago shoved the pavers into random peaks. "You know, we're all glad you didn't marry that doctor. You don't belong in Virginia. You belong here." She released the gate, and it snapped shut behind her. "With us."

The moment reeked of horror movie openings. I dragged my gaze from the gate to her decided expression. "I'm not sorry I went, but I'm certainly happy to be back. Life lessons and all that."

She nodded.

Happy or not, coming home had felt like defeat. It was practically a miracle Mr. Tater agreed to sign for my lease. He didn't know me, but he knew business, and he gave me a chance. Furry Godmother would still be a dream without him. All the more reason to clear my name and his simultaneously.

* * *

A raspy bark drew my attention.

"Oh dear." Mable shifted her cat into one arm. "There you are, Sir Peter." She opened the glass door to her sunroom and released the Kraken.

A squat, white bulldog with tall bat ears and a square head rumbled through the open doorway, circled Mable's feet a hundred times, and headed for me. He huffed in the heat, licking his flat nose and rolling on the bright-red pavers in a flurry of energy and clowning. "Woof!"

"You remember Sir Peter," Mable said. Sir Peter Piccadilly of Audubon was an elderly French Bulldog who thought he was a puppy.

I fell at his side, depositing my bags in a pile. "Yes, I do." I rubbed his belly as he writhed on his back. "He's a good boy. Yes, he is."

He sneezed and rolled onto his tummy, his little piggy tail flipping and whacking as he huffed and panted.

I rubbed behind his ears and squinted into the sun. "I think he's worn himself out."

"Good. Maybe he'll be still while I dress him. The costumes need to be perfect. I'm hosting the next Daughters of the Confederacy dinner and I'd like a portrait of these darlings on display."

Sir Peter rolled onto his side and closed his eyes. The tip of his pink tongue poked free.

Mable scooped him into her arms with a grunt.

Miss Peabody stretched away, growling in complaint. "I'll only be a moment." She retrieved the discarded garment bag and headed for the house.

"Okie dokie." I dusted myself off and went to explore the tiny waterfall in her garden where honeybees swept in and out of massive vibrant blooms climbing her trellis.

The glass door rattled open several minutes later, and Mable emerged. Miss Peabody was in one hand and Sir Peter was in the other. Mable's sleek, platinum bob was tussled, her silk tunic slightly askew. "Perfect," she trilled.

I met her halfway and gathered Miss Peabody into my hands, enjoying the feel of soft downy fur between my fingers. Her aqua belle gown and coordinating wide-brimmed hat were painfully adorable. "Well, aren't you the bee's knees, Miss Peabody." Pride welled in me as I arranged her gown over four tiny paws. I had spent hours hoping to impress Mable with the ensembles she had ordered. The verdict was still out on her, but I'd definitely impressed myself.

Mable settled Sir Peter on a bench beside her trellis. "There now." She smoothed his waistcoat and adjusted the snub brim on his matching hat. "Who's a handsome boy?"

Sir Peter panted. His tongue curled skyward and bounced in his open mouth.

I set Miss Peabody beside him. "They look lovely."

Mable hummed. "I can see why Neidermeyer asked you to do the tutus. You have a gift."

Guilt reared in my chest. "I'm sorry if it was poor form to accept the tutu job. In Arlington, it's every woman for herself, but I know that's not the case here, and I probably should have asked you how you felt about it before agreeing." The last thing I wanted was to step on any toes or start any gossip that might tarnish my name professionally. Furry Godmother would be doomed before it had a chance. Reputation was everything in a community as tight as ours, plus I valued good manners. "I should've come to you."

"It's fine. I've always wanted to take up needlepoint. Now I can. Besides," she said motioning to the tiny couple before us, "I couldn't have done anything like this. The workmanship is outstanding. The stitches are so tight and small, I barely see them. The details are magnificent. You're very good, Lacy. Very, very good."

I hoped the blazing heat hid my blush. "Thank you." The feeling she'd more likely hug me than hurt me settled in my chest.

"How are you holding up this week? It's terrible what you went through."

The words startled me. I hadn't had time to think of how the ordeal affected me beyond my business. I took an internal inventory. I was stressed, sleep deprived, and crazy enough to suspect a nice, old lady of putting a hit on me. "I haven't opened the back door since that night. I'd be better if the detective assigned to the case would investigate someone other than me."

"Darling," she cooed, "I'd give my prized hydrangea to be investigated by Jack Oliver, if you know what I mean."

* * *

I left with my fill of sweet tea and a basket of fresh berries from Mable's garden. I wouldn't need much in the way of dinner, which meant more time to get dressed for the after party at the Barrel Room. Detective Oliver's warning wouldn't keep me away two nights in a row.

When I found my favorite little black dress in an unopened drycleaner bag, I knew the day was blessed. I had a quick peanut butter and jelly sandwich dinner while leaning over the sink, so as not to dirty any dishes; brushed my teeth; and ironed my hair to flat perfection. A quick glance in the hall mirror confirmed it. I looked nearly as good as I felt. Those Barrel Room workers would never know what hit them.

I grabbed my purse and strode out the door like I belonged on a runway. Chin up, shoulders back.

My patent leather peep toes ground to a halt on my porch.

A stupidly handsome man in black wayfarers leaned against the door to my car. His messy black hair and two-day stubble dried my mouth.

"Miss Crocker." Detective Oliver whipped off the glasses and ended my stupor. "You look . . ." His lips moved, but nothing came out for a long beat. "Nice."

"Thanks." The disappointment in my voice irked me. "What are you dressed up for?"

He adjusted a Louisiana University ball cap over his still-damp hair. I shoved the image of him in the shower out of my head. It didn't help that humidity had applied the robin's-egg-blue T-shirt to his chiseled chest like a sticker or that his dark couture jeans fit well enough that I knew in which pocket he kept his keys. "I'm headed over to the Barrel Room to chat up the workers."

My jaw dropped. "What? Why?"

"I heard you're headed out there to talk to Miguel's girl-friend. I thought I'd come with."

"Come with? Why are you talking like that?"

"Like what?"

"Like you're a frat boy. Where's your urban cowboy gear?" I drifted closer. "Are those track shoes? Where are your boots?"

"I'm undercover. None of those kids are going to want to talk to a homicide detective. What about you? Where'd you put the responsible-business-owner clothes and good-girl ringlets?"

I ran both palms down the shimmering material of my slinky black dress. "I don't know what you mean."

"Care if I drive?"

"Yes," I squeaked. "Who's the snitch? The only ones who knew about my plans tonight were Paige and Mack." I doubted either girl would have narced on me to the cops. "Did you bug my store?"

"I'll drive." He tossed his keys into the air and caught them.

"Mack won't let you in after hours without an invitation."

He wiggled his badge between us.

I rolled my eyes. "You just said they won't talk to a cop. Mack knows you're a detective. You're stuck." I shooed him away from my car and beeped the door unlocked. "I'll let you know what I find out." The smug expression creeping over my face couldn't be helped, so I didn't bother stopping it. I gave him a little index-finger wave and tugged the door.

He whipped a hand out to stop it midswing. "Nuh-uh."

"Nuh-uh?"

"Nope. You go alone, and I'll charge you with obstruction."

"What?" I hopped back out, tugging the hem of my dress. "You would not." He totally would, and I knew it.

He tipped his head and waited.

"If I let you tag along, you'll let me ask the questions?"

A stiff dip of his chin in agreement.

Lies. "Fine."

He smiled, and his damn dimple sunk in.

Chapter Eight

Furry Godmother's fashion tip:
Better to be overdressed than underinformed.

I locked the door and stomped gracelessly behind him to his truck, parked parallel at the end of my drive, successfully blocking me in. "You trapped me in my driveway."

He opened the door and motioned me inside.

I climbed in and ignored him, choosing to concentrate on the beautiful evening drive instead. Outside my window, tourists meandered on sidewalks, smiling and pointing at things I'd long took for granted. Couples snapped selfies outside majestic neighborhood homes. Walking tours flowed in and out of Lafayette Cemetery No. 1, our district's own "City of the Dead," nicknamed for New Orleans's unique above-ground burial style. A family on bicycles pedaled past us as we stopped at a stop sign. I fidgeted with a line of bangle bracelets until I couldn't stand the silence any longer. "Who was the fink?"

He angled his truck into the parking lot and snuffed the engine. "Does it matter?"

"Yes."

He observed me with his usual smug expression. "I ran into Mackenzie when I went out for a jog."

"Mack?" That was unexpected. I recalled her comfort with him at the restaurant. I'd mistaken familiarity for flirtation. Sadly, it wasn't the first time. "You live in her neighborhood?"

"Yep."

I bit my tongue to stop myself from asking which neighborhood that might be.

"Ready?" He opened his door and climbed out.

I did the same and met him at the hood. "Would you really have arrested me?"

A glimmer of mischief danced in his eyes. "I'm glad we didn't have to find out."

"I bet you aren't," I mumbled. I turned on my toes and headed for the door. I'd get more answers from the people drinking than I'd ever get from him anyway. Why waste my time?

A guy in a dirty, white T-shirt, jeans, and work boots answered the door. A green apron hung loosely from his neck. His eyes lingered at my neckline before jumping to the hulk at my back. "Yo, we're closed."

I stepped closer and smiled big, trying not to stare at the silver ring in his eyebrow. "Mack invited me."

He sniffed and lifted his chin, careful to clutch the door in one hand and the frame in the other. "Who are you?" No one was getting past this bulldog without some effort.

I needed a strategy.

I softened my voice and tried looking sexy but probably missed by ten miles. "I'm Lacy."

I ignored the throaty cough behind me.

The doorman looked over my shoulder. "Yo, who's he?"

I looked over my shoulder and shrugged. "I don't know. He was in the parking lot when I got here."

The guy stepped aside to let me in. He didn't extend the same courtesy to Detective Oliver, ball cap or not. I didn't dare a look back. I had work to do.

I headed for the bar where a knot of early twentysomethings poured a line of glasses to the top with red wine. Every one of them wore cutoff shorts and tank tops. Most were barefoot. I was massively overdressed.

Mack frowned when she recognized me. "Did you come from a fancy party?" Confusion danced across her youthful face.

I nodded and slid onto the nearest empty stool, tucking my skirt securely beneath me. "Yep. How was work?"

"Sucked."

"Is Paige coming tonight?"

A girl with wild, sandy hair bounced behind the bar. "You know Paige?"

"Yes. Do you?"

Mack nudged my elbow. "Lacy, this is Trish." She nodded to the bouncy girl, then the others one by one. "Hayden, Kelly, and Sunshine." She put heavy emphasis on the final name. If she'd stopped to stage wink, it would have been less obvious.

"Hi." I lifted my fingers in a tiny wave. Something flashed in Hayden's eyes. She must've picked up on Mack's less-than-smooth introduction. Had Mack confided in her about what I was up to tonight?

Mack shoved a glass my way and wine sloshed over the rim. "We're chugging."

Well, there was a verb I hadn't heard since college. "Oh, no, I can't."

The girls stared, openmouthed. Their gazes drifted to Mack. I could almost see the wheels turning: *Who was this weird, overdressed woman who didn't chug?*

Mack smashed my toe with her foot.

I winced. "Sorry. I've already had a few drinks at the party I just came from."

"Drink, drink, drink, drink," they chanted, pounding their fists against the lacquered bar top and lifting their overfilled glasses with their free hands as I watched.

Mack finished first and raised her arms into a victory *V*. She winked again, and I got the impression she had planned this little game to loosen Sunshine's lips. I sipped from my glass.

The red Moscato was delicious and classified as a dessert wine for good reason. I savored the sweet burst of flavor on my tongue.

The other girls tipped their heads back in unison, completing the challenge. Crimson liquid clung to their glasses as it drifted into their open baby bird mouths.

Mack freed the phone from her pocket and smiled. "I'll be right back."

I watched as the other girls slapped high fives and laughed. There was a strange energy between them, but I couldn't put my finger on it. It felt like tension, but they all appeared happy. I scanned the scene for some less obvious source of drama.

Sunshine swept the glasses away and dropped them in the sink, looking peckish. The drops left in her glass were strangely dark and opaque. Had she helped herself to a better bottle than the rest of us had shared? "I'll be right back."

I lifted my now half-empty glass and sipped again. "What's her story?"

The girl with the wild hair leaned across the counter and lowered her voice in confidence. "Her boyfriend just died. He like *died* died. She's a mess. The boss told her to take some time off work, but she says she really needs the money. Can't afford to take a break, not even to grieve. The rule for paid leave is family only. No boyfriends."

"I'm sorry to hear that." My face tingled, either with anticipation of answers to come or in response to half the wine that seemed to have disappeared from my glass. "Is she going to be okay?"

"It's bad enough, but they got into a massive fight that day. The last thing she ever said to him had a bunch of expletives in it, and not the good ones."

I pondered the idea of good expletives. "That's awful. What'd they fight about?"

The taller girl, whose name I couldn't recall, looked up from the counter where she pushed a rag in circles, sopping up spilled wine. "He was seeing someone else. I told her to leave him, but oh, no. No one wants to listen to me. See where it gets them?"

"Dead?" I asked.

"No!" She balked. "Brokenhearted." She wadded up the towel and tossed it on the counter before stalking away.

"Ignore her," Bushy Hair said. "Hayden hated Sunshine dating Miguel."

I sipped my wine and worked the information over in my mind. "He was that bad, huh?" That didn't take a lot of imagination to believe. I tipped the glass to my lips and nothing

came out. I pulled it away for a quick examination. *Empty.*
Huh.

"Having fun, sweetie?" Detective Oliver glared from a closing distance. Mack hustled along beside him. "Funny story. I
had to call Mack to get inside."

I waved and smiled. "Bummer."

Mack rounded the bar and poured him a glass of wine. He
swirled and sniffed it with authority.

"Excuse me, do you know about wine?"

He tented his brows. "A little. For example, I know you've
had enough."

I harrumphed and slid off my stool. His fresh glass reminded
me of Sunshine's empty one and its weirdly colored contents.

His long fingers flashed out to clutch my wrist. "Where are
you going?"

"Bathroom. Apparently, I've had too much wine." I shot
him a warning look. I wasn't a big drinker, but I didn't appreciate the implication I'd had too much or that he knew me well
enough to judge. Honestly, I liked very little of what he'd said
since we met.

He released me. Wisely.

I wandered the restaurant, checking room by room for Sunshine. Ironically, I found her in the bathroom. She was crying.

She patted a wet paper towel under her eyes. "Sorry. I'm not
usually so emotional."

I fished a travel pack of tissues from my purse and handed
them to her. "It's okay. I heard about your boyfriend."

She sobbed into the tissues. "Thanks."

"That other girl out there was kind of mean. She said she
didn't like him for you."

Sunshine scoffed. Her round, freckled face bunched. "One hundred dollars says that was Hayden talking. She said she didn't like him? That wasn't the problem. The problem was that she *did* like him and he chose me. She hated not getting what she wanted for once."

That explained a lot. "She was jealous."

"Yeah, and he was guilty. He led her on, and they hooked up sometimes, but he never let me go. That's what I always told her. Yeah, fine. He's a man. Maybe he thinks with his pants once in a while, but who does he go home to? And what did she think she proved by getting in bed with him over and over?"

I had so many opinions. I held my breath so I wouldn't ruin my investigation with a lecture on the merits of fidelity, integrity, and basic feminism.

"Lacy?" Detective Oliver's voice boomed through the ladies' room door. He rapped on the thick mahogany.

Sunshine ducked around me and whipped the door open to make her escape.

Detective Oliver's expression said he knew I was ahead of him on information and he didn't like it. "Are you ready to go?"

"Yes." I brushed passed him and waved to the girls at the counter. "Thanks, guys. I had fun."

He caught up easily and paced his gait with mine. "How much did you have to drink?"

I stumbled, looking over my shoulder. "One glass, yeesh. What are you, the party police?"

"No." He pressed the door wide. "I'm the regular police."

A gust of humidity stole my breath and warmed my skin. Across the lot, I saw Sunshine and Hayden arguing. The words were hard to make out, but the tone and facial expressions said plenty. Hayden vanished into a tiny sports car and burned rubber out of the lot. Sunshine ran back inside, crying.

Detective Oliver sauntered to his truck and opened the passenger door.

I climbed inside, debating the benefits of calling a cab.

He started his engine and applied his seatbelt. "What do you suppose that was about?" He tipped his head toward the place where the sports car had revved out of sight.

I contemplated how much to share with him from my girl talk at the bar and in the restroom. Much as I wanted to squirrel away the newfound information, he was the police, and I needed him to close this case. "Both of those women were sleeping with Miguel."

"Both?"

"Yep."

"And they both knew?"

"Yep."

He slid his phone from his jacket pocket and scrolled through his contacts before exiting the parking lot.

"Who are you calling?"

"Mack. I need the addresses for those women so I can send black-and-whites to pick them up and haul them in for questioning." He made the calls.

I listened intently for any new information. Nothing.

He set the phone in his cup holder when he finished.

"You're bringing them in? Don't you want to know what they told me?"

"Nope." He flashed his brilliant white teeth my way. "I'll take it from here, but I will drive you home first."

"Oh, gee. How chivalrous, considering you invited yourself along and insisted on driving."

"This is a murder investigation." He enunciated and drew out the final two words, breaking them into their syllables. His gaze trailed over my face, returning to my eyes. "You know, Mack gave me an open invitation to drop by after hours. I didn't have to tag along with you tonight."

I tucked the ends of my skirt under both thighs and fiddled with a loose thread at the seam. "I didn't kill him. You have to know that."

He flicked his attention back my way as we rolled along St. Charles Avenue.

I turned my face to the window.

"Either way, you need to leave this alone. Civilian involvement is a bad idea. We don't know what we're dealing with, and Miguel Sanchez wasn't a good guy. Let NOPD handle this."

"Maybe." I watched homes flash past. Pets walking their people. Couples holding hands. Logically, I knew it was his job and not mine, but it felt like my entire world depended on clearing my name, and frankly, it didn't seem like a big priority to him. He didn't even want to know all the details of what I'd learned tonight.

"I mean it, Crocker."

In two days' time, I had gone from the sole suspect in Miguel's murder to a woman with two viable leads. "Me, too." Not bad for a fashion designer.

Chapter Nine

Furry Godmother's business tip:
Blowing up is messy. Buy a broom.

Electricity sizzled through me on the way to work. After receiving two new e-mail rejections on my small business loan applications during breakfast, I'd gone back to obsessing over Miguel. By my third cup of coffee, a new idea had also percolated. If I couldn't find any solid information on Miguel, maybe I could contact his accomplice, Levi Marks, in the big house. If anyone would be willing to dish the inside scoop on Miguel, it would probably be the former partner he'd flipped on. After a couple sketchy impersonations on my part and several terrible attitudes on the part of the correctional facility administration, I learned Levi had been released on parole five days ago.

Plenty of time to get to New Orleans and exact his revenge on Miguel three nights earlier.

I parked along the crowded street and thanked my stars I didn't work in Arlington anymore, where creepy multilevel parking garages were the norm. My cell phone had 9-1-1 on one-touch dialing thanks to those terrifying memories. I jumped

into the sunshine and dashed through a line of manicured flow-
erbeds and a mass of animated morning shoppers. Inside my
studio, I flipped every light switch and slouched in relief.

Three days. Three suspects. I wasn't sure if I should feel
proud or overwhelmed, but at this rate, I'd never know who
killed Miguel.

I set Roomba-Spot in his charger and fed the turtles, Brad
and Angelina. The place looked magnificent considering the
black cloud raining on it. I shook the tension off my shoulders
and turned the "Open" sign in my window.

The bell above the door jingled. A line of people moseyed
in, sucking lattes and munching beignets, dusting everything
they touched with powdered sugar and judgment.

I shifted into congeniality mode. The crowd wasn't my
enemy. It was my opportunity to hold onto Furry Godmother,
my lifelong dream come true. I wouldn't see it go belly-up
because some thief had dragged me into his mess. "Good
morning." I nodded and welcomed every patron. "I'm glad
you're here."

The doorbell rang all morning as people poured into the
tiny space. Most made their rounds, peeked at the murder suspect behind the counter, and left. Others came with actual
pertinent questions.

"Do you make house calls?"

"Do you cater?"

"Can I order three dozen . . . ?" Tuna tarts. Pawlines.
Purrlines. Pupcakes.

"Can you replicate . . . ?" Versace. Gucci. Kate Hudson's
Golden Globes gown.

I said yes to everything, buoyed by sheer Crocker determination.

A few hours later, Mom marched into the studio. Oversized white sunglasses covered half her face. A frown covered the rest. "Have you seen the paper?" She smacked the daily news against my counter.

I pushed it aside and finished taking a phone order for the local pet spa. "That's five dozen tuna tarts, five dozen pawlines, and ten dozen peanut butter pupcakes. Anything else?"

Mom rolled her eyes and slung her giant Kate Spade bag into the space beside mine under the counter. She left her glasses on the newspaper and went to assist the line at my bakery counter. "Where's Paige?"

"She's only part time. She doesn't work today."

Mom clucked her tongue and plastered on a smile. "I'll call Imogene. She can take over when Paige goes back to school. I suppose you'll have to make do with me for now."

By three thirty, my tummy was outraged I'd missed lunch, but the store traffic had somewhat settled. I opened my digital calendar and typed the information I'd taken by phone. The rest of my month was full. I couldn't take more requests for anything, and I'd have to live in work mode to meet the promises I'd already made.

"Well?" Mom shoved hair behind one ear and stared.

"What?"

"Have you read the paper or not?"

I gave her my best crazy face. "I haven't stopped moving since I got here." Based on my calendar, this trend would continue for three to four weeks.

She swiped her sunglasses off the paper and shook it. "You made the news. Again."

"I figured." I took the paper and skimmed the article beneath a grainy black-and-white photo of my store. *Local Pet Fashion Designer and Caterer Accused of Murder Gallivants With Victim's Friends.*

"I don't gallivant."

"For goodness' sakes, Lacy. You're thirty years old. Why were you hanging out with a bunch of kids? And after hours at your boss's restaurant." She shook her head in disapproval.

The article mentioned my appearance in the Barrel Room's parking lot around midnight. "I wasn't hanging out. I was investigating, and I don't have a boss."

Mom made a strange strangling sound. "You're a Crocker. A woman of position in this district. Not a gumshoe. Don't you hold our family legacy in any regard at all?"

My skin heated. "Maybe I'm making a new legacy. I'm following a dream and building a business that will be here long after I'm gone. My kids can take over, expand, grow, or do whatever else brings them joy."

"Your children, you said?"

Here we go. I went back to entering obligations into my calendar.

Mom mashed a stack of order slips for baked goods onto the counter beside me. "Unless you're planning to adopt or marry a twentysomething restaurant worker, I suggest you remember your place in this community and stop your feminist hijinks."

Oh. My. Sweet. Lord.

I bit my tongue so hard I flinched.

Silence fell over the buzzing room. Dozens of strangers stared openly.

Mom looped her bag over one shoulder and shoved her glasses back onto her face. "I've volunteered you for the Legacy Parade Committee. Civic duty is a Crocker responsibility. One not to be taken lightly. They're expecting you at the next meeting. I'll send you more details this afternoon. Right now, I need to go prune something."

I'd learned years ago why all the fancy ladies kept gardens. They could rip weeds out by the roots and pound gloved fists against the earth when they really wanted to scream and swear. The latter would have ruined their genteel reputations. The former earned their houses a spot on the Circuit of Homes.

I closed the shop at five to tidy the mess left by a busy day of onlookers and order placers. People continued to try the door until after eight.

Unfortunately, my business boom came with a catch. No money. Customer deposits on orders were slim, and the balances weren't due until the time of services rendered. The four-page list of supplies I needed to fill the orders would have to come from my sparsely lined bank account.

Dozens of new customers, and I was somehow poorer.

I stuffed the lists into my purse and headed for the door with a box of accent materials for Mrs. Neidermeyer's tutus. Whatever else I accomplished this month, those tutus needed to blow her mind. Her stamp of approval had the power to change everything.

I stepped into the night calculating the amount of work I could finish before dawn. What had gotten into everyone today? It was like the bad press had inspired them to hire me.

A thin evening crowd strolled the sidewalk outside my store, moving toward the restaurant-sated blocks where food and sultry jazz seasoned the air. A few straggling tourists and locals on evening power walks nodded as they passed. I balanced a box of design books and shiny appliqués on one hip and locked the door behind me.

An uneasy sensation crept over my skin, lifting the fine hairs on my arms and neck to attention. I scanned the scene again. Everything seemed normal, but something was wrong. I hurried to my car on instinct, wrestling my phone from one pocket and bringing up my speed dial for 9-1-1. I hovered my thumb over the green send button, ready to call the cavalry if Miguel's killer was thinking of eliminating me as well.

I jerked my gaze around the street and up the sidewalk in both directions before reaching the curb. My car sat at an awkward angle. "No. Nononono." Not a flat tire. I set the box on my hood and abandoned 9-1-1 in favor of Dad's cell phone number.

My muscles turned to stone when the damaged tire came into view. It wasn't just flat; it was murdered. A Furry Godmother flyer was pierced to the rubber with a railroad spike. The corners of the paper curled and waved in the breeze. I checked over both shoulders before sinking into a squat beside the tire. Dark, hasty scribble covered the paper: *Don't end up like Miguel, Lacy Crocker.*

* * *

Red-and-blue lights cut through the night as cruisers filled the street with cops and, by default, attention that I didn't want. Pedestrians and onlookers crowded previously empty patches of sidewalk, and a local reporter snapped pictures of my car. Detective Oliver moved from one person to the next, canvassing the area for witnesses of the tire impaling. No one had seen anything. Shocker.

I leaned against the detective's truck and tried to disappear in the shadows. More bad press. Mom would have an aneurysm when she saw tomorrow's paper. And if the negative publicity increased customers any further, I'd go bankrupt.

"Well, kitten," Detective Oliver said, striding to my side and toting the box of materials I'd left on my hood, "let's go. We're towing the car to the shop for a new tire, but you can pick it up tomorrow." He opened the passenger door and tossed my box onto the seat. "I'll drive you home."

I was fresh out of energy for arguing. "I need to go get groceries."

He raised a brow and almost smiled. "Okay, but I drive the buggy."

"As you should." I slid onto the passenger seat of his truck and gladly shut the night out.

I waited for the display of red-and-blue lights to disappear from view before gulping the oxygen I desperately needed.

"You okay?"

I bobbed my head, formulating a plan to harness my courage and use the adrenaline assaulting my veins for good and not emotional paralysis. "I'm going to throw myself into my work. I have a full schedule for the month, and that's what I'm going to think about."

"Fair enough." He took a front-row space at Whole Foods and quieted the engine. "I guess Mable Feller didn't hold your success against you."

"What do you mean?" How'd he know about that?

"I hear she made some calls, inspired her contacts to support a struggling local."

That onslaught of orders had been spawned by a woman I suspected of putting a hit on me? I pressed my complicated emotions of guilt and gratitude into something I could handle at the moment. "I have a long shopping list." I shook the papers in my fist. "Lists. There are four. You can wait in the truck if you'd like."

"Nah."

He drove the buggy as promised.

An hour later, I wrote a questionable check, and we headed uptown to my beloved home, where I planned to put on a pot of coffee and bake until dawn.

I opened my front door with trepidation and ran my palm over the switch plate before entering. "I'll take it from here." I extended a hand toward Detective Oliver, motioning him to hand over the bags he'd insisted on carrying up my walkway.

He brushed past me and continued down the hall to my kitchen. "Where do you want this stuff?"

"On the counter is fine." I twisted the dead bolt and turned on the porch light. "Where are you going?"

He disappeared around the corner toward my bedroom. "I'm sweeping the residence." He moved in and out of every room, peeking through windows and checking closets for boogeymen and/or note-writing creeps. "Due diligence."

"Gee, thanks for putting that thought into my head." I kneaded my hands and centered my attention. *Focus on the work.*

By the time he returned, I'd unloaded the bags, fired up the coffeemaker, and preheated my oven.

"All clear." He stopped in the doorway behind me.

I didn't look. No need. His presence was undeniable, disconcerting yet strangely comforting. "Coffee?"

"Maybe one."

I rubbed my palms against my apron. "Cream or sugar?"

"Black."

I measured my breaths, willing the panic at bay.

In accordance with my life, Pete's *Psycho* shower scene ringtone erupted.

Detective Oliver cocked an eyebrow.

I flipped my phone over on the counter and swiped my thumb against the screen. "Never mind that."

"Hello? Lacy?" Pete's voice drifted from beneath my hand.

I jumped as if it'd burned me. Fire coursed over my cheeks and dried my throat.

Detective Oliver stared.

I grabbed the phone and spun my back toward him. "Hello? This isn't a good time. I hadn't intended to answer. My apologies. Thank you for calling."

"Wait!" Pete screeched before I could hang up. "Lacy, wait. Give me two minutes. Please."

My stomach bottomed out. I couldn't tell him where to stick his pleas and excuses with Detective Oliver listening in.

"Lacy, I'm an idiot." Pete picked up on my hesitation and took full advantage. "I never meant to hurt you. I honestly don't know what I was thinking. I fell in love with two women, and I was too cowardly to do the right thing when I should have, but in the end, I chose you. The other woman meant nothing. I've let her go."

The man behind me scoffed audibly.

I pressed hot fingers against my temple. This was worse than the dream where I went to work naked. I fumbled to reduce the volume on my phone. I'd heard Pete's pathetic excuses a dozen times, both in person as I packed and on voicemail via messages when I'd rejected his calls. Detective Oliver didn't need to hear them ever. I cupped a palm around my mouth, uselessly attempting to shield my voice. "I can't do this with you right now. I have company." I raised my palm to cover my eyes. I hadn't meant to call Detective Oliver my company. Huge mistake. Company implied all sorts of things we weren't. He was probably reading into it already. I forced myself not to look.

"I swear it," Pete whispered. "On my mother's grave."

"Your mother's not dead!" I tapped the phone against my forehead.

"It's an expression," he growled. "Why are you always so impossible?"

I moved the phone against my lips. "It's not an expression. No one says their mother's dead if she's not dead. You're a horrible person. You know that, right?"

Detective Oliver moved into view. Concern creased his brow. Emotion burned my eyes. How humiliating. "I have to go."

"Don't! I'll do anything for your forgiveness," Pete pleaded. "Anything at all. You name it, and it's done."

"I want Penelope." The words were out before I'd had time to consider them. He'd taken Penelope somewhere on the morning

I was set to leave. He tried to use her as a means to manipulate me into staying, but my will to go was stronger than my will to take her with me, and I fled. I'd felt like gum stuck on a shoe sole every moment since. "I want Penelope back," I repeated. I knew he was good to her, but she was my baby. I hadn't had a chance to say good-bye. She didn't know where I was or why I'd gone. She didn't deserve to be left behind by the woman who'd saved her from icy Arlington rain as a kitten. I'd saved her just to abandon her all over again.

A white handkerchief appeared before my blurry eyes, pinched between Detective Oliver's fingers. "Thanks," I whispered, hiding my face as I wiped my features back into submission. I peeked at him. *Who carries a handkerchief anymore?*

"Fine," Pete huffed into the receiver. "Fine, but I'm coming down there to deliver her myself, and I want to see you in person."

"What?" Was he really agreeing?

"When can I come?"

I locked eyes with Detective Oliver, as if he could somehow help, or at the least hold Pete to his word.

Detective Oliver's expression was firm and unreadable. I returned his handkerchief.

"How soon can you get here?"

I held my breath during the long silence.

"Let me check my schedule and confer with the airlines."

"Okay."

"You'll have to answer my call next time so we can make plans."

I bit my tongue. Pete always wanted control.

"If I miss the call, just leave a voicemail. I'm certain you know how."

"Fair enough." His voice was low and soft. "Can I ask you something?"

I didn't answer. His questions were always loaded and never fair.

"You said you have company. Is it a man?"

Detective Oliver curled his lips into a cocky grin.

It occurred to me that he'd moved closer to hear my conversation better. As he said, *Nosy comes with the job.* The handkerchief was a stage prop. "Call me when you have a date set for arrival." I disconnected with Pete.

Detective Oliver shifted his stance. "Was he the reason you left Virginia?"

"Yes." I took a cleansing breath. *Pete might bring Penelope to me.*

He seemed to weigh my answer for a long moment before motioning to the organized chaos on my counter. "What are you baking?"

"First, six dozen canine carrot cakes for Happy Tails Day Spa. They're doing a fundraiser in conjunction with the Jazz Festival to promote adoption." I poured him a cup of coffee and slid it across the counter.

He sipped and watched. "You make dog food?"

I fumbled the sifter and gawked. "Seriously?"

"Canine carrot cakes? Those are for dogs, right? Unless they're made with dogs."

"Ugh. You're disgusting." I dusted my palms and braced them on my hips. "Get over here. You can run a hand grater, right? Before you ask, it's not for grating hands."

He set his coffee aside and moved to the sink. He washed his hands, then turned confidently to the counter. "I can probably figure it out."

I handed him a stack of fresh carrots from beside my sink. "You grate. I'll explain." I dumped eggs, peanut butter, oil, vanilla, and honey into the bowl of my favorite mixer. "The carrots go in here."

He went to work grating carrot slivers into the bowl while I sifted the powdered ingredients together.

I slid my eyes his way. Curiosity got the best of me. "You're awfully at home in the kitchen."

"I'm over thirty and single. A man's got to eat."

"Really? I thought single men only ate takeout and whatever they could grill."

"Funny."

"I have my moments."

We finished the tasks, and I set the mixer to blend.

He went back to his coffee. "Why do you make pet food?"

"Do you know the kind of gross things that come in store-bought food? Overprocessed, outdated meat, ground-up, unwanted animal parts like hooves and testicles. There's grain in there animals don't need and no actual nutrition. My treats are made from fresh, garden-grown, pesticide-free vegetables; brown eggs from free-range, local hens; and peanut butter from real, actual peanuts. Period."

He smiled. "You're passionate about pet food."

I wiped my forehead with the back of my hand. "A little."

"Where'd you learn to make it?"

"Mom." I sighed. "She raised me on food from her garden and fresh meats from the market. I never understood why we took so much care to prepare our own foods but fed our beloved pets from cans. As soon as I was old enough to use the kitchen, I experimented with recipes on our pets. I learned what they liked and hated. Quizzed Dad about proper nutrition. It was fun."

He scanned the floor, twisting at the waist. "Do you have a cat?"

"No." But I would soon, if Pete wasn't lying.

"Well, you don't have a dog or he would've been under our feet by now, plus I checked the rooms. Not a single bark. I didn't see a fish tank or hamster cage."

"No pets."

"None?" He turned his nosy face on.

"No. Not anymore. I left Penelope in Virginia with my ex-fiancé and the woman I caught him riding his office chair with. She's a Tabby. Penelope, not the woman."

"Yikes."

"Yeah, yikes." I stuffed a spoonful of peanut butter in my mouth. "I miss having a cat, but getting a new one would be like cheating on Penelope, so I just stay busy and don't think about her as often as possible."

"I'm sorry."

I lifted my weary gaze to his sincere face. "Thanks."

"And that was him on the phone? The one professing his regrets?"

"Yeah."

He rubbed the back of his neck. "He's coming here?"

"Allegedly. He says he'll bring Penelope. I'll believe it when I see it." I filled miniloaf pans with carrot cake batter and slid them into the oven, twisting the timer when I shut the door.

"Are you planning to stick around for two more rounds of carrot cake prep?"

He hesitated. Reluctance changed his features. "Nah. It's late. I'd better get going."

I walked him to the door. "Thanks for everything tonight. I'm sure it's not protocol to run errands for citizens without transportation. Wasted time. Taxpayers' dollars and things like that."

"I'm not on duty."

The shock I felt must have registered because he flipped the switches beside my door and changed the subject. "Your porch light is burnt out."

"I know."

He worked his jaw. "Do you have any idea who might have vandalized your car and threatened you tonight?"

I shook my head. "You've already asked me that." Several times.

He heaved a sigh. "You aren't always forthcoming."

Okay. That was true. "Did you know Miguel had a partner in a diamond heist?"

He bristled. "Yes. Levi Marks."

I stared past him, wondering how much he'd researched their situation. "Did you know Miguel turned on him, and Levi spent eight years in jail?"

His brows furrowed. "He was sentenced to twelve and paroled six days ago." Detective Oliver blanched. "You already knew?"

I rolled my aching shoulders and gripped the tender meat of my neck in one hand. I didn't know much of anything anymore. "I also know I didn't kill Miguel Sanchez."

"Me, too."

It took several beats to process his words. "You do?"

He narrowed his pale-blue eyes. "Yeah. I've been watching. You're too soft for murder. If you were guilty, I'd see it."

"Unless I'm a sociopath. They don't care enough to show signs of guilt."

"True. I wouldn't be doing my job if I didn't keep you on a short leash, in case you turn out to be a sociopath." He turned for his truck and sauntered away. He waved a hand over his head.

I shut the door before I could tell him where he could tie that leash.

Chapter Ten

Furry Godmother's tip for using leashes:
They require someone at both ends.

I met Detective Oliver on my porch the next morning with a box of canine carrot cakes and twelve dozen tuna tarts. The balmy wind clung to my skin and tousled my frizzy hair. "Detective," I said, nodding in salutation.

"You should probably call me Jack." He took my packages and traded me for a steaming go cup of café au lait. "This is what you drink, right?"

"Nice try," I told him, "but I haven't forgotten that line about keeping me on a leash."

He shook his head and turned for his truck. "I thought you'd like the pet reference. Obviously, I have no intentions of putting you on an actual leash. What sort of things did you get into up north?"

I followed him to the sidewalk and climbed onto the passenger seat. "I'm not dignifying that with a response." I buckled up and nestled my purse on my lap. "My dad would have taken me to get my car."

He gunned the engine to life and pulled into morning traffic. "Like I said, it's better to keep you close. I'm not getting a real think-ahead vibe from you."

"Joke's on you. All I do is think."

He slid his eyes my way briefly but kept his thoughts to himself.

I sipped my latte and relaxed against the warm seatback. "Thank you for the ride and the coffee." Summer sunlight drifted through the passenger-side window, warming my cheeks. I squinted at passersby and oak trees soaked in moss. "Did you really bring Miguel's girlfriends to the police station for questioning?"

"Yep."

"And?"

"We took their statements."

I huffed. "I wish you wouldn't play coy with me. This is important."

An ornery smile raised his cheeks.

"I'm sorry, was something I said funny? This is my life you're messing with."

The smile fell. "Don't even get me started, lady."

"I'm sensing hostility. Maybe you need to settle down."

"I suppose I need to remind you this is my job, and I'm pretty damn good at it. You'd know that if you weren't running around digging holes like a dog with a bone and giving me fits. I've got to keep you safe and chase my own leads while you're chasing your tail."

"You took the dog references too far that time."

"I probably could've closed this case by now if you'd listened to me and stayed out of it. Now my time and attention are divided between doing my job and saving your ass. How's that for clarity?"

My mouth fell open. "Did you just swear at me?"

"Oh, believe me, there's more where that came from if you don't knock it the hell off."

I snapped my lips shut and turned away from him. If I thought for a second I could have carried all my things the rest of the way to Furry Godmother without him, I would have. "If I'd left it up to you, I'd probably be in jail. I was your only suspect until I started asking questions."

He took the next right. "You were the obvious suspect, but that doesn't mean I wasn't exploring every option. The only person who expected me to keep you apprised of my work was you. It's not any of your business. You weren't arrested, were you?" He adjusted his grip on the wheel. "For the record, I brought the girlfriends in. They answered my questions. No, I'm not sharing my findings with you. There's no grounds for you to be upset by any of that."

I shook off the sting of his tone. "I'm curious. What did you ask them? What did they say? How do you know they told the truth?"

"I don't believe anyone until I have reason to trust them."

"So you assume everyone lies?"

He wheeled into the auto shop parking lot at the end of the next block and took the space beside my car. "Don't they?"

"I don't."

He snorted and rubbed heavy palms over his sullen face, paying particular attention to his puffy eyes and wrinkled forehead.

I shifted for a better look at him. "Are you okay?"

He leaned across my lap and opened the glove box. "It's just a headache." He shook a pair of pain relievers into his palm and closed the compartment.

"Are you sure?"

"Oh, I'm positive I have a headache." He tossed the pills into his mouth and chewed them like a madman.

I climbed down from the truck and headed to the office. The squat brick building was covered in graffiti and posters for bars in the Quarter, but it was the cheapest tire place around. I turned back, thankful and aggravated to have someone looking out for me.

Jack loaded his arms with my box and bags. "Something wrong?"

"The note stuck to my tire said I'd end up like Miguel. What do you make of that?"

"It means dead."

I pursed my lips. "I don't think the note was from his ex-partner, Levi. I don't think anyone who knew him before he came here would address him as Miguel. Levi and the other people from his past knew him as Anthony."

Jack seemed to consider this theory. "Maybe Levi didn't know you knew Miguel as anything else. Imagine you were like anyone else in your position. You wouldn't be researching the victim. You wouldn't know Miguel was an alias. If he used the name Anthony in his note, anyone else would have wondered who that was."

"I don't think a guy who spent eight years in prison for a busted jewelry heist thinks that much about anything. I think the note and tire stabbing were a heat-of-the-moment thing. Whoever wrote it knew him as Miguel, too." I swept inside, signed the bill, and collected my keys from the man at the desk.

Jack unloaded the contents of his arms onto my back seat.

"Thanks for the ride. I've got to go." I slid behind the wheel and pulled the door shut. "I'm volunteering involuntarily on a parade committee today."

He tapped my roof. "Good idea. You should stay busy doing your own job for a while."

I white-knuckled my steering wheel. The man made me want to weed a garden.

* * *

Paige texted at nine to let me know she'd opened the shop and all was well. I made a stop at the Himalayan Rescue to deliver the tuna tarts and sign a contract for two more jobs with them before dropping the carrot cakes at Happy Tails.

The temperature gauge on my dash climbed by the minute. I swept my unruly hair into a messy bun and jammed a charcoal pencil through it. It was officially hotter than blue blazes, and the traffic lights on Magazine Street were set to aggravate me. I stopped at every intersection against my will.

A parade of dog walkers in brightly colored tank tops and tightly cropped yoga pants turned on a lightbulb in my head. I needed a peacock-inspired line for Furry Godmother. Jade-and-royal-blue feathered pieces with golden curlicues and those exotic eye-shaped patterns in purple. I yanked the pencil from my hair at the next light and drafted a messy sketch in shades of gray on a sales receipt. The look was perfect for pet pageantry:

showy like Vegas and completely customizable. "This is my ticket into the big time."

A car honked behind me, and I jumped into action, trading focus on my pencil for some effort with the gas pedal.

Ten minutes later, I dashed along the sidewalk toward my store, tapping details into the notes app on my phone. Pet pageants were like beauty pageants. I couldn't make the same item for more than one contestant, but I could expand the concept for over-the-counter items to sell in the studio, like boas, hair clips, and one-size-fits-most wraparound skirts. My mind overflowed with things to work out as soon as I got to the studio. The big Animal Elegance gala would be the perfect venue to introduce a new line. I just needed some prototypes and a pet to model for me.

I must've been more consumed than I realized because I screamed when someone grabbed my shoulder.

"Whoa, hey, it's only me." Miguel's girlfriend, Sunshine, waved an extralarge smoothie cup between us. Condensation ran down the side and over her tanned fingers. "I met you the other night. Do you remember? You asked a lot of questions about my boyfriend, Miguel."

I pressed my phone to my chest and thanked my stars she wasn't a tire-popping lunatic. "Hi. Yes, of course I remember you."

Her eyes glossed with tears. "The cops picked me up after that."

Her voice cracked, and my heart stopped hammering. I went into caretaker mode. "Sit." I motioned to the bench outside my shop window. "Let's rest a minute."

She wavered. Heartbreak reddened her eyes.

"I'm glad you're here," I said. "I wanted to talk to you again. I planned to come back to the Barrel Room, but this is better." I sat and patted the space beside me. "Did you come to talk to me or is this a coincidence?"

"I came for you. You weren't in the shop, so I got a drink to cool off and waited. We get discounts at Frozen Banana, so I'm up this way a lot lately."

I cringed at the memory of the last smoothie to visit my storefront. "You get a discount?"

"Yeah. Mr. Tater gave cards to the Barrel Room employees. He has them for a bunch of places in town." She lowered her body onto the bench and batted teary eyes. "Sorry. My emotions are all over the place this week."

"I can't imagine." I gave her a thorough once-over. She wore threadbare flip-flops and a maxi dress that clung slightly to her middle. "How are you feeling besides emotional? You weren't well the other night."

She rested the drink in her lap and cupped protective fingers around her abdomen. "I'm fine."

"You're pregnant."

Her eyes widened. "Yeah. I wasn't really drinking the other night. That was grape juice. I would never hurt my baby."

I nodded, recalling the odd hue at the bottom of her glass. *Grape juice.* I smiled. "Why are you hiding your pregnancy?"

She gave me a one-shouldered shrug. "Miguel wanted me to keep it a secret until he had a chance to break things off with Hayden."

Wow. What a keeper. I cringed internally at judging him so harshly. He was gone, and creep or not, Sunshine now faced single parenthood. "Was Hayden the one you argued with in the parking lot that night?"

"Yeah." She rubbed her nose. "Miguel and I were leaving here and starting over. He said he had something to take care of, and then we were going to go out west to make a life for ourselves. Just the three of us."

"Do you know what he needed to do?"

"No. He didn't say, but I know what you're thinking. Mr. Tater was going on for weeks about all the local thefts and how important it was for us to stay vigilant at work. We were supposed to report any shady activity. But Miguel wasn't a part of that. He's out of the game."

"Have you seen anything shady?"

She wrinkled her face. "This is New Orleans. I don't even know what would classify here."

Touché. "I haven't heard of any new break-ins. Have you?" Not since her boyfriend had broken into my store.

Sunshine launched onto her feet. "Miguel wasn't a thief anymore. He was done with that life. He told me so, and he never lied to me."

"I believe you." Well, I believed that *she* believed her lying, cheating baby daddy. Personally, I thought his criminal record spoke for itself. That and the fact he had broken into my studio.

"When was the last time you talked to Miguel? Did he seem like anything was bothering him?"

"No. He was happy. We were happy." She swiped renegade tears from her cheeks.

"Did he have any enemies? Can you think of anyone who would want to hurt him?"

"No. Everyone loved him. Especially Hayden. She followed him around like a lost puppy, begging him to choose her. He said she showed up everywhere he went."

"Did she know about the baby?"

"No. I don't think so, but she was really jealous."

I chewed my lip. "Do you think she was mad enough to hurt him? Maybe if she couldn't have him, then you couldn't either?"

She paled. "I don't know. Oh my goodness, I hope not. Who would be that crazy?"

I didn't dare tell her. Lots of people used that exact excuse to clobber cheating spouses and significant others. Still, it seemed a long reach, and Jack had let her go after questioning. "Did Miguel ever mention a guy named Levi Marks?"

"No. Who's he?"

"Never mind. It's nothing." I lifted my hand in the air and dropped it, unsure what I could do to comfort Sunshine. "I'm really sorry about your loss." My gaze drifted to the gentle curve of her abdomen. She seemed far too young to carry so much loss and face so many challenges. "I'm sure your baby will be perfect and loved beyond reason."

"Thank you."

The street around me burst to life, infiltrating my single-minded focus. No matter what happened to me, I'd never be left alone to grieve or raise a child. I had an uptight, pretentious mother who meant well in her way and a father who, as far as I was concerned, hung the moon.

"Is there anything I can do to help you?" I asked. I didn't have much at the moment, but I could listen. I could cook.

I had a network she could access for prenatal care, housing, or anything she needed. Where did she live? Where was her family?

"Find out who did this. Give my baby justice."

"I will."

She squared her shoulders and tossed the cup into a trash bin. "See you around, Lacy."

Chapter Eleven

Furry Godmother's advice for dating: Don't.

I stopped at the French Market for junk food and squirt guns, then drove to the Garden District for lunch with Scarlet and her kids. I was in desperate need of decompression, and I always left the Hawthorne estate feeling lighter. The stress of the week had me leaking brain cells, and permanent lines were forming on my forehead.

"Only you would come here to unwind." Scarlet waved a loaded squirt gun at the minirebels moving too close. "This place is a circus without a ringmaster."

"You're the ringmaster," I told her.

"No. I'm more like a trained monkey. I do what they say, and I have very few thoughts of my own these days." Her fantastic red hair was swept into a bun and her red baby doll dress matched her lipstick. She'd thought to coordinate. That was something. My mom would love the monochromatic effect. She'd hate the baggy, bohemian number I'd chosen, especially paired with my messy ponytail.

"Well," I turned the knob on Scarlet's garden hose and hefted the green weapon in both hands, "I have enough thoughts for ten people, and I need some help sorting what's real and important from what's imagination and Froot Loops."

"Now you've done it."

"Froot Loops!" Her youngest son ran circles around my legs. "Froot Loops! Froot Loops! Froot Loops!"

I trained the nozzle at him and waved a bag of kid-sized graham cracker bits his way. "Here."

He nabbed the bag, and I shot him. Water sprayed off his little back as he squealed through the grass. He dove behind the slide for cover.

I lowered the hose.

Scarlet dropped her gun on the table and rubbed her eyes. "Nice diversion tactic." When the other pint-sized Hawthornes went after him to get their piece of the cracker action, she collapsed into a white wicker chair lined with floral print cushions. "You have about two minutes before they're back."

"I have to drive out to the Hamses' plantation and measure the llamas for leg warmers this afternoon. Mrs. Hams insisted. She didn't seem like a lady to trifle with. I can see why Mom chose her as a nemesis. Before you ask, no, I haven't mentioned the job to Mom."

"Uh-oh."

"Yeah. I'm only getting started. Someone stabbed a threatening note into my tire last night, and Detective Oliver had to drive me home."

"Oh my stars! Are you okay?"

"He helped me bake carrot cakes, and he drove me to get my car this morning."

She raised a perfectly sculpted brow.

"He said I should call him Jack."

A grin slid across her face. "And?"

"Miguel's girlfriend is pregnant. She came to see me outside the store today. She says they had planned on leaving together. They were going to be a real family, but now she's alone. I can't imagine how she approached the woman accused of killing her boyfriend."

Scarlet drained her glass of ice water. "That wasn't what I meant by *and*."

"I'm sorry. It's a lot to take in. Mr. Tater is distancing himself from me, but I've got appointments and orders coming out of my ears. Probably enough to make the lease payment, but I've got only two hands to work with and no money until the jobs are done. Mable Feller arranged the windfall of customers. Actually, I should contact Mr. Tater. Maybe everything that's going on is enough for him to keep investing. Jack isn't looking at me as a suspect anymore, and with Mable's approval, my name is clear around here again." I tugged my lip between my thumb and index finger. It would be tough—practically impossible—but maybe I could do it without Tater's help. "I've still got twelve days before my lease payment is due."

Scarlet straightened in her seat and nodded stiffly. "Okay. What can I do?"

I scanned the chaos tearing through her perfect green lawn and sighed. "You've got your hands full. I just needed to spill my thoughts so I could attempt to sort out the pieces."

"I could reach out to Miguel's girlfriend through the restaurant. Maybe she needs a friend who's been in her position about four times." She traced the bump of her upturned belly button.

"That would be amazing. I don't know if she'll be receptive, but it would be good to know we tried."

"She's the overly independent type? Those are the worst."

I nudged her foot with mine. "The very worst."

"What are you going to do about your mom and Margaret Hams?"

"I don't know." I imagined Mom's face as I explained my reason for helping her archenemy with llama leg warmers. "She'll see this as mutiny."

"Undoubtedly. I suggest telling her before she gets wind of it from someone else."

I stroked a tuft of windblown hair behind my ear. Scarlet was right, of course, but the whole thing was complicated and delicate. "That's going to get ugly."

"What isn't?" Her creepy grin returned. "So you baked with Jack last night? How was it? Please tell me *baked* is a euphemism."

"Stop," I chided. "He was oddly at home in my kitchen, and I appreciated it. Also not a euphemism."

Scarlet's smile fell. "That's too bad. Did you ask him about himself?"

"No." I made a point of watching the children instead of asking the plethora of questions I had on the topic.

"You want to know why he seemed at home in the kitchen?"

"Nope."

"I can't believe I didn't tell you this before," she hedged. "Obviously I wasn't thinking."

"The last time we talked about Jack, you also tried to set me up with Chase."

She wasn't listening. Whatever she had on her mind was consuming her. I'd seen the look a thousand times. "It was pretty interesting around here when his grandpa died. Women were throwing themselves at him."

Good grief. I swiveled to give her my complete attention. "What women?" Presumably, Garden District women, but they wouldn't look twice at a man making a detective's salary, or even have reason to know he existed.

"His grandpa left him the family trust and his entire estate. Jack cried at the funeral. It was a free-for-all after that. He moved back into the district, and ladies lined up at his new doorstep with casseroles and ripe ovaries."

"He cried?" He hadn't struck me as a guy with emotions. Jack was more like a modern version of RoboCop, wheeling around town, chasing the wrong suspects with his big truck and serious face.

"Believe it. I guess his grandpa raised him, but we never saw Jack around the district because his grandpa's interpretation of 'raise' was 'send to exclusive boarding schools abroad.'"

"Shut the front door. He's a Garden District kid? He went to boarding schools? What is happening? Why would he join the military? Kids here have every opportunity at their fingertips."

"You mean like Ivy League medical schools?" She beamed. "Interested now, aren't you?"

"Yes. Well, not like that, but yeah." How did I not know he existed before? I smacked the table. "Did you know he takes his cat to my dad for her care? I couldn't understand why he'd come all the way out here to see a vet. He lives here. That makes sense. Wait. Who was his grandpa? There aren't any Olivers here."

"That's because Grandpa was his maternal grandpa, and his mother's family name was Smacker."

"No." I dragged the word into several syllables. "Grandpa Smacker was Jack's actual grandpa?"

"Yep."

Jack inherited Grandpa Smacker's Homemade Preserves.

Scarlet folded her hands over her round belly. "Jack has a cat?"

"Jezebel," I deadpanned. "Oh!" I straightened in my seat. "Pete called again last night."

"While Jack was there?" She leaned forward, mouth gaping. "What did he say?"

"He says I can have Penelope back. He said he'd bring her to me if I agreed to see him when he came."

She blinked. Her mouth closed slowly. "I don't trust him." She reached out for me and laid a palm on my arm. "I won't let him hurt you again."

I gave her a little smile. "Are you my muscle now?"

"Always have been. Always will be."

The patio doors behind us swung open with a flourish. "There you are," a familiar voice boomed.

The children abandoned their inflatable pool and sandbox with a squeal and flew past us. I hadn't heard that voice in a decade. It was ridiculous that I identified it so easily all these years later.

Scarlet hoisted her body from the seat beside me. "Chase! What are you doing here?"

"I came to see my nieces and nephews." He kissed Scarlet's cheek and smiled. "How's my favorite sister-in-law?"

"Enormous. Thank you for asking." She motioned me out of my chair. "You remember Lacy Crocker."

I blew out a long breath before turning to face the district golden boy. "Hello."

He whistled long and slow. "Lacy Crocker. It's been a long time."

"Yep."

"What have you been up to the past ten years?" His deep-set green eyes sparkled in the sunlight. Black Ray-Bans sat atop his cropped chestnut hair. He looked every bit the part of professional volleyball player. A measure of commonality linked us together. His mom went nearly mental when he dropped law school in lieu of shirtless days on sandy beaches.

"Not much." I forced my attention back to his face.

"We were just about to have lunch." Scarlet pulled up a third chair. "Why don't you two catch up while I get something started in the kitchen?"

I shot her a dry expression.

She herded the kids inside. "Come on, y'all. Let's get cleaned up. Who wants sliced peaches?"

Chase lowered his body onto the seat beside mine and rubbed the arms of his chair with mammoth palms. They looked like the perfect size to grip a volleyball.

Heat crawled up my neck and into my cheeks as the mental volleyball I'd conjured slowly became a number of other things unrelated to his sport. I snapped my gaze to his face.

His smile widened. "Are you seeing anyone?"

"What?" I'd temporarily forgotten I didn't like Chase Hawthorne on principle. He was a shameless playboy. "No. I'm single and happy."

"Playing the field, huh?" He waggled his brows.

"No."

"Oh, come on, Lace. I'm just playing with you. You were always too uptight. Relax. Tell me all about Virginia."

The patio door flung open, and the trio of mini-Hawthornes spilled out again. They marched single file to a kid-sized picnic table, complete with striped umbrella, and sat with their hands in their laps.

Scarlet brought up the rear. A tray of crust-free triangles, stacked four tall, teetered on her palm. A bowl of sliced peaches balanced precariously in the crook of her arm. She had bags of pretzels, paper plates, and napkins jammed between her fingertips. She looked at us. "Can you grab the fruit punch?"

Chase and I knocked into one another getting to the door.

"Sorry." He steadied me with strong hands.

I blushed like an idiot and took a baby step back while he grabbed the punch. The zip of heat racing down my arm from his touch must obviously be thanks to a sunburn I hadn't realized I had.

Chase delivered the punch to the kids and disappeared back into Scarlet's kitchen. He reemerged with a similar feast for our table. "I think this is for us." Croissant sandwiches lined a milk glass tray with chunked cheese and grapes in the center. Peaches filled a crystal serving bowl. "Almost done." He made another quick trip and returned with a pitcher of sweet tea and three glasses. We split the duties setting the table while Scarlet served the kids.

"Nice." Scarlet nodded in approval when she returned. "Teamwork. I like it."

I shoved a grape between my lips and smiled. "This looks amazing. Thank you."

"Don't mention it." Scarlet gave Chase the gory details of my life drama while I made faces and groaned appropriately.

Chase looked unnaturally at ease. "Man, it's good to be home." His ultrawhite shirt and teeth emphasized the extent of his hard-earned beach tan and illuminated his eyes.

I tore the corner of my croissant. "That's what you got from all this? You're glad to be home?"

"Yeah. This place is real. I missed it. The world of professional volleyball is a hot mess. Literally."

"I guess I missed the District, too. I didn't know it until I was home, but I did. Things were going predictably well until last week. Now my life is in upheaval." I tossed the bit of buttery pastry into my mouth and checked the time on my phone. "Yikes. I've got to go." I collected my plate to drop in the sink on my way out. "I need to get those llamas measured before four and it's already after one."

Scarlet followed me into her kitchen. "What happens at four?"

"Mom volunteered me for the parade committee."

She laughed. "I can't say I miss those days. Small groups with power scare me. You know," she teased, "kids get you out of stuff like that. Husbands, too. Family always comes first. That's the rule."

I set my plate in the dishwasher and gasped as authentically as possible. "Are you suggesting I get married to avoid my civic duty? How dare you, ma'am."

She smiled. "What about your duty to continue the Crocker family bloodline? You have zero siblings. Lots of pressure."

Chase appeared in the doorway and leaned against the jamb. "I hear Hawthorne genes are impeccable. Above reproach, really." He motioned a thumb over one shoulder toward the lawn where Scarlet's kids were slinging cups of fruit punch at one another.

"Ugh." Scarlet took off across the yard at a clip, threatening naps and showers.

"How about dinner sometime?" Chase asked.

"Sorry. I'm off men."

He tented his brows. "I didn't see that coming."

"Not like that. I'm not dating. I'm busy building a business and investigating a murder."

"Not tonight then. Tomorrow at your place?"

I couldn't stop the smile that popped onto my traitorous lips. "You're insane. I have to go."

He followed me to the front door and leaned out. "See you tomorrow night."

I'm not going to lie—I ogled him a little as I drove away.

Chapter Twelve

Furry Godmother's secret to a shiny coat:
Avoid Llama Mama drama.

Measuring llamas for leg warmers turned out to be easier than I'd imagined. The animals were beautiful and mostly docile, except one who liked to spit and gave me the evil eye. The drive was lovely, and Mrs. Hams's plantation was nothing short of spectacular. She gave me a tour of the grounds and estate, then plied me with enough sweet tea to send me into one of my Civil War–era fantasies. My punishment came later, in the form of traffic.

According to the dashboard clock, I was late for my first committee meeting. Mom was guaranteed to hear about it. She'd want to know why I was late making a ten-minute trip through the District to Commander's Palace, and I'd have to tell her I'd been halfway to Baton Rouge visiting the Hamses' plantation. Then she'd kill me, and the llamas would never get their leg warmers.

I tapped my thumbs against the steering wheel and waited for the light to change. Cabbies and tourists crept, bumper to bumper, along streets most locals knew to avoid. I, meanwhile, had no other route options.

I left my car with the restaurant valet and hastened inside, ready to beg forgiveness for my tardiness and to promise free pawlines to anyone who appeared dissatisfied.

To my great relief, the committee hadn't yet come to order. They were lollygagging and gossiping around a large table in a private room, sipping mint juleps and munching nuts and fruit.

I slipped into an empty chair and helped myself to a glass of ice water on the table. I'd nearly forgotten how much fun the proper ladies were after a few afternoon cocktails. District committees weren't like the stringent events in Arlington, where everyone was in a hurry and the judgment never ceased. These gatherings were more social than business.

Seven women in pearls and fancy dresses chatted animatedly about their neighbors, family, and friends, utterly unconcerned with the time. In minutes, I learned someone was having a dinner party, someone else's daughter was running for local office, and someone had bought the home on Seventh Street. Not much had changed in the last decade.

I shook my glass and readjusted the ice. No one had noticed my tardiness. It was a good day.

"The Crocker girl was arrested for murder."

Hey! I snapped into the moment and cleared my throat. The table went still.

"Oh, dear." Fanny Hesson pressed a hand to her throat. Fanny owned a riverboat, a sugar farm, and half the orange groves in Florida. Her abundant resources and no-nonsense disposition made her a natural leader. Her quick wit and shrewd mind had made her rich. "I didn't believe your mother when she said you were coming."

A rush of soft giggles coursed around the table.

I cocked my head and smiled as authentically as possible. "I'm glad to be here. Thank you for inviting me. And I wasn't arrested," I pointed out. "I was questioned after I called to report an intruder. No one knows why that man was in my store after hours. I don't suppose you've heard anything?"

Fanny scanned the table. "Anyone?"

The committee stared wide-eyed. No one knew anything, but everyone wanted to get wind of any scoop.

Presley Masterson shifted in her seat, drawing the group's attention. She fiddled with her pearls and leaned in my direction. "What can you tell us? You know, about the murder?"

The others fell silent, their rapt attention locked on me.

"Well." This was my chance to make a public statement. A golden opportunity. Anything I said here would be texted and e-mailed across the District in minutes. "Not much. When I ran away, he was alive. When I came back, he was dead."

Fanny shook her head. "The whole thing is tragic. Pearl Neidermeyer said that man was a heel."

I hated to speak ill of the dead. "He wasn't pleasant."

Presley raised her drawn-on eyebrows for dramatic effect. "I heard he was a jewel thief."

Fanny adjusted the cuffs of her blouse, feigning nonchalance. "My granddaughter knew him, and she said he was trouble. Bad news from up north."

"Noooo," the ladies responded in near unison. A few faces turned my way. *I* had just come from up north.

I wiggled a finger at a passing waitress. "I'll have what they're having."

"Yes, ma'am." She spun and disappeared through the nearest archway.

"Is that true?" Fanny's voice ratcheted an octave.

"What?" I startled.

"The man attacked you? You hit him with a gun?"

"No. Of course not. He came at me, and I sprayed him with my glitter gun. I've never hit anyone." Outside of the self-defense courses I'd taken in Virginia.

She pursed her deeply creased lips. Fifty years of smoking had made an impact even plastic surgery couldn't wholly erase.

"Glitter!" Another round of quiet laughter swept over the table.

I turned in my seat, hoping the waitress would return soon with that drink.

A petite blonde in a baby-doll sundress and Chanel sunglasses breezed past me to say hello to Fanny, kissing her cheeks.

The waitress followed her as far as my chair. "Your mint julep."

"Thank you."

I kept an eye on the blonde. She was young to be at a meeting like this one. Every woman at the table had at least two decades on me, and I was thirty. The girl chitchatting with Fanny wasn't more than twenty-five and could probably pass for high school with less makeup. Could she be the granddaughter who knew Miguel?

Fanny brought the meeting to order and passed a stack of floral folders around the table clockwise. Matching pens clung to the covers.

I opened my folder and stole another look at the girl beside Fanny.

"We'll begin by introducing our newest committee member, Lacy Crocker." Fanny motioned for me to stand. "Lacy owns Furry Godmother. I'm certain you've all heard of it."

To my utter shock, the group nodded.

None of these women had ever stepped foot in my boutique.

A flicker of recognition illuminated the girl's bored expression. She dropped her gaze to the table and fidgeted with her nail polish.

I forced a congenial smile while my heart tap danced in my throat. She knew me. If she was Fanny's granddaughter who knew Miguel, then I needed to talk to her the moment the meeting ended. "Thank you. I'm glad to be here."

The girl suddenly raised her eyes to mine. She caught me staring. Her face turned a strange shade of pink, and to my horror, she excused herself.

She was getting away!

"You know, Lacy," a woman I recognized as Cecelia Waters began, "I could use a dozen star-spangled capelets for the kittens I plan to include on my float."

My brain screeched to a halt and put on the backup beeper. "You have twelve kittens?"

"No, but my float's drab Americana. It needs some action, and everyone loves kittens." She snapped her fingers. "I'll adopt them from a shelter and find them good homes after the parade.

This is fantastic. My float just became an awareness campaign. Do you know how many homeless cats are in New Orleans?"

I shrunk under her stare. "No."

She slapped the table and her mint julep sloshed. "Me either, but it's too many, and I'm going to do something about it."

"Right on." I lifted one fist in a weak power-to-the-people move.

I glanced at Fanny. "Excuse me. I need a quick break." I dashed down the narrow hall where the blonde had disappeared as fast as etiquette allowed and swung the restroom door open with a silent prayer. Fanny's blonde friend stood at the mirror applying lip gloss. She was younger than I'd originally guessed, probably still in college. She eyed me warily in the mirror's reflection as I scurried past, checking under stalls for feet.

The girl stuffed her lip gloss into a tiny clutch. "What are you doing?"

"Making sure we're alone. I want to ask you a question. Privately."

She spun slowly to face me.

"Are you Fanny's granddaughter?"

"Yes. I'm Emerson Hesson."

I shifted the words in my mind. Emerson Hesson. Another heiress in line to never run out of money. "How do you know about Miguel Sanchez?"

She blanched.

"Your grandmother gave us your very insightful input before you arrived. I can't figure out how you and Miguel managed to cross paths."

"I don't want to talk about this. It's not worth the drama. Nana hates how I spend my free time."

"With people like Miguel Sanchez?"

Emerson tapped the end of her nose with one finger.

"Gotcha." I knew firsthand what kind of community chaos choosing inappropriate friends caused. "Your family wouldn't have approved."

"That might be the understatement of the century." She rolled her eyes and leaned against the sink.

Adrenaline spiked in my system. Another lead. "What was the nature of your relationship with Miguel?"

"He taught me to play cards and took me dancing in the Quarter."

I blinked. "He taught you to play cards?" Confusion set in, along with the feeling I'd been away from the table too long.

"Yeah. You should've seen the looks on those uptight losers' faces when they called the boys' club for poker night and I showed up. You *really* should've seen their faces when I beat them."

An irrational wave of feminist pride hit me on the head. "You won? How much?"

"Twenty-five thousand and one kid's mom's Birkin, but I couldn't really take that."

Good grief. This was definitely Fanny's granddaughter. I checked the time. I didn't want to be gone so long that I'd need an explanation. "Can you tell me anything that might lead to the capture of his killer? I met his girlfriend. She's pregnant and needs closure."

"I heard Mr. Tater pulled your store's funding and you want to clear your name."

I slouched. "That, too. Does everyone know about Tater?"

"Pretty much."

Mable had apparently spread the ugly details about my shop needing support.

"Anything you can tell me will help."

She pressed her shiny lips together, visibly warring with herself. Helping me, a complete stranger, meant helping Miguel but also possibly starting drama with her Nana.

"I won't tell anyone," I promised.

"Miguel liked to gamble. He liked to play pool for money at Boondocks. He took a lot of cash from this guy named Adam. I was there last night and heard Adam say Miguel got what was coming to him."

"You think this Adam might have killed Miguel over bad billiards?"

"Miguel liked to hustle. Sometimes it went his way and sometimes it didn't. I don't know Adam well, and I don't know how much of his money Miguel took, but people say it was a lot, and Adam has a temper. If he hurt him . . ." Her eyes welled with unshed tears. "Please don't mention me if you talk to him."

"I won't."

She dotted her eyes with a tissue and waved me away. "We'd better go before they think you've got troubles." She gave my midsection a frown. "I'm going to text Nana and let her know I'm meeting friends. Your meeting is boring."

I opened the door, and Emerson sashayed past, turning toward the kitchen instead of the dining room.

I returned to the meeting with an abundance of fresh energy. "Sorry. I had to take a call." I took my seat at the table and did my best to look more interested in parade floats than pool sharks.

* * *

Furry Godmother was empty when I returned, except for Paige thumbing through a fashion magazine.

She straightened when I entered. "Hey, have you thought of doing a mock runway show and making pet versions of this year's top lines?" She turned the magazine around and wiggled it. A group of bored-looking models dressed in Stella McCartney stared back.

"Every day." I skulked past her and unloaded my purse. "I'm exhausted, under caffeinated, and in possession of a new order for twelve kitten capelets."

"Aww." She dropped her magazine on the counter and made doe eyes as she followed me into my office. "I love kittens."

"Me, too, but this order has to get in line. I've got a six o'clock delivery in Algiers." I hoisted my bag over my head and secured it cross body. "Did the security company come for the quote?"

"Yep. I put a copy on your desk. They said Mr. Tater signed a preapproval last week and they'll be back tomorrow afternoon to get the system installed."

"Excellent." It was a little crazy I hadn't gotten one sooner. If Tater refused to rejoin forces with me, I'd find a way to pay for the system on my own.

"Does it make you nervous to go on appointments alone after that ghastly note?"

"Yes, but life goes on, and the sooner I find out who's trying to scare me, the sooner he can go to jail and I can get a normal night's sleep." My life had become a game of cat and mouse. If I hunkered down like a sitting duck, I'd be the mouse. Mixed metaphor, but regardless, in this situation, I needed to be the cat. Cats had nine lives.

"Anyone home?" A familiar tenor travelled through the air. Paige perked.

I slunk back to the front and braced for anything. "Hello, Detective Oliver. It's nice to see you today." Calling him Jack in front of Paige seemed wrong, especially after the big deal I'd made about him being the enemy. She'd never let me forget it.

He clasped his hands behind his back and appraised me. "How's the car doing? All four tires still have air?"

I smirked. "Cute."

"Thanks. I'm actually here to deliver bad news." He relaxed his stance. "The victim's former partner didn't check in with his parole officer last night, which makes his whereabouts unknown. Care if I take a look around in the back?"

I peeled my suddenly dry mouth open. "Please." I watched him disappear into the room where I'd just been.

Why did he tell me this? Did he think Miguel's ex-partner might be hiding in my stock room?

My mind turned to the Occam's razor solution: Jack thought I was in danger.

The front door opened again, and my mother blew in like her pants were on fire. "My Chicks' pianos aren't ready. They were supposed to be assembled yesterday and delivered to you today, but they weren't. The vendor says it could be another *two days*." Her voice reeked of despair.

"Nice to see you, too. The meeting was lovely. Thanks for asking."

She huffed. "You said you'd decorate the pianos."

"I will. When are they coming?"

"That's what I'm trying to tell you." She rolled her eyes to look at the ceiling. "The vendor's behind, and I don't know what I'm going to do. We've set up a tour around the county, speaking to 4-H groups about raising chickens. I need the pianos and the tuxedos finished ASAP."

I lifted my to-do list onto the counter. "Two days from now is perfect. Don't worry. That gives me time to finish Mrs. Neidermeyer's tutus and a few catering orders." I jerked the notepad away, realizing my error too late.

Mom's mouth popped open. She narrowed her eyes to slits. "Let me see that list."

I shook my head and tucked the notepad behind my back like a toddler. "On second thought, I'll work on your tuxedos tonight." After I make a delivery in Algiers and then visit Boondocks.

Mom rounded the counter on quick feet and took a swipe at my arm, attempting to get her hands on the notepad.

"Hey!" I jumped back, startled by her speed. "You've gotten fast since I was in high school."

"I do Zumba."

"Well, don't do it here."

Her chest expanded and her face turned red. "Let me see that list."

"No." I shook my head.

"Lacy Marie Crocker. Are you working for those *Llamas*?" She seethed the final word, as if I'd done something as vulgar as joining the Manson family or the Democratic Party.

"Mrs. Hams came to me. What was I supposed to do?"

Mom's jaw tightened. "You were supposed to politely refuse and show that harebrained interloper to the door."

I dropped my hands to my sides. "I couldn't refuse the job without a reason. I thought about telling her the truth, that my mom would lose her mind—"

Mom's eyes bulged. "You can't say that. She'd assume I'm too insecure or overbearing to allow my daughter to work for her." Mom sucked in her cheeks.

"Do you see? I was stuck, plus she ambushed me. There was no time to set a plan for polite refusal."

The color in Mom's face drained from rage-red to something more along the lines of her usual peeved-pink. "Fine, but I don't like it."

"Noted."

She cast her gaze back to the ceiling. "Can you at least make her products ugly?"

"No."

She turned a tiny smirk on me. "Sprinkle them in itching powder?"

"Mom!"

She turned her face away. "I was joking."

Jack and Paige emerged from the back. Jack offered a hand to Mom in greeting. "Hello, Mrs. Crocker. Everything okay out here?"

Mom managed to look quite pleased with herself. "Everything is grand." Her gaze slid to me. "I'd like to see those Llama Mamas find a worthier pursuit than what we're doing, educating hundreds of children on the importance of our local agriculture while endearing them to my adorable livestock."

I faced Jack. Agriculture and livestock were a bit of a stretch for piano-playing chickens, and I wasn't clear on how Mom was qualified to teach either topic. At least she was content and her Jazzy Chicks would win the round of Who Can Do More Good. "How's my stockroom?"

"All clear. Why do you look like that?"

"Like what?"

He cocked a hip and leveled me with those icy blues. "Like you're hiding something."

"Have you heard of a place called Boondocks?"

That stretched Jack to his full height. "Yes. Why?"

Mom lifted one perfect brow and stepped closer to him, arms crossed, designer bag dangling from one wrist. "What are you up to, Lacy Marie Crocker?"

Great, she'd gone to his side. They'd unified against me. Exactly as I'd predicted.

Paige went back to flipping pages in her magazine. "It's an Irish bar in the Quarter. They have a bouncer at the door, but it's a little rough. Lots of locals. Still, I wouldn't go alone."

That sounded like the right place. "No. I wouldn't. I just wondered."

"Why?" Jack pressed. "What made you wonder about a place like Boondocks?"

"No reason. Curiosity." I looked to Paige for help.

She obliged by dropping the magazine like it had burnt her. "Lacy! Your delivery for Algiers!"

"Oh dear!" I did a stage gasp a la *Home Alone*. "I have to go. I'll get started on the tuxedos tonight. Everything will be spectacular. Let me know as soon as the pianos are built.

They're my new top priority." I flung myself through the door and kept moving.

My phone buzzed with a text from Paige before I jammed my key into the ignition.

You're welcome.

That girl deserved a raise . . . as soon as I wasn't broke.

Chapter Thirteen

Furry Godmother's life lesson: Keep a costume on hand.
You're probably going to need it.

I took the ferry to Algiers, enjoying the balmy wind and views of the city. I climbed the wide cement stairs slowly once we docked, taking in the deeply curved bank of the Mississippi and a tiny St. Louis Cathedral standing sentinel across the way. The Kimbers lived in a comfortable working-class neighborhood where children rode bikes and traffic was light.

Mrs. Kimber met me on the porch with open arms. "Thank you so much for making the trip. It's not easy to get into the city with four kids in tow, and it's even harder to leave."

I handed her the carefully packaged costume. "It's no problem. I had a lot of fun making this one."

She removed the lid and folded back the layers of green-and-pink tissue papers. "Oh!" She gasped. "Jean Lafitte will love this!" She turned the material over in her fingertips, examining the cut, cuffs, and collar of her kitty's new pirate costume. "It's fantastic. Like a piece of art. I almost hate to give it to him!" She pulled me into a quick hug.

The Kimbers had named their cat after a famous New Orleans pirate. Jean Lafitte the human had his own museum in the French Quarter. He became a local legend after helping Andrew Jackson win the Battle of New Orleans with his legions of ships and experience. People still claim to see his ghost wandering Pirates Alley at night, swilling pints and whistling a song from the sea.

"Kids," she called through the open door, "bring Jean Lafitte."

Her children barreled onto the porch for a look at the costume. They squealed and laughed and bounced around their mother.

Her husband leaned in the doorframe. "Well, we've thrilled the kids. I'm not so sure the cat will feel the same."

"The cat!" The children swarmed into the house.

Mr. Kimbers kissed his wife's head and laughed at the costume.

I made my way back to the ferry with a strangely heavy heart.

As the little vessel chugged me back across the river, I realized the pain I felt was grief for the loss of my Penelope. Hearing Pete promise to return her had reopened a barely scabbed wound. I hated coming home to an empty house. No wide, judgmental eyes at the end of a long workday wondering where I'd been and why her bowl was empty. I took a small detour to Friends with Fins, the nearest aquatic pet store, on my way home.

I slowed at the last light before my house and put my hand out to keep my Friends with Fins packages from sliding off the passenger seat. Water sloshed gently in the lidded cup braced between my knees. "We're almost home, Buttercup."

Buttercup was a bright-blue female Betta fish with stumpy fins and an understated tail. The fish version of myself, and definitely not an act of betrayal toward Penelope. The salesman had assured me.

I carried my things into the house with added care and kicked the door shut behind me. Buttercup needed a special place to call her own. I settled her cup on the kitchen island and went to lock my front door. I scanned the lawn and street as far as I could see in both directions before going back to Buttercup. Tonight, I wouldn't come home to an empty house.

"Okay." I scrubbed my palms together. "Let's get you set up. I think you'll be happiest in the kitchen. I spend most of my time here. Everything's white and cheery. The lighting's good. There's coffee and food. I'm not sure why I ever leave."

I unpacked the new Betta owner supplies and read every instruction as if the fate of the world depended on getting each step right. Half an hour later, Buttercup was peering at her oversized home from the safety of her travel cup. "I can't get you out of that little house until I'm sure the water in the big house is the same temperature as what you're swimming in." I raised my palms. "Take it up with the people who wrote the books. I promise to move you after my shower."

I did a finger wave at my new roommate and headed to the bedroom. Tension rolled off me. It was nice to have someone to talk to again.

I brought up the Boondocks website and Yelp reviews on my laptop. I didn't want to show up overdressed, like I had at the Barrel Room. It looked like a standard dive bar. Clothes wouldn't be a problem, but I needed a new look for the night. Someone had tagged my car with a note. They could be watching me. *If they know what I drive, chances are they know where I live.* I pushed that horror from my mind. The sooner I found Miguel's killer, the sooner life could get back to normal. I couldn't keep up a frantic pace without the quality of my work taking a serious hit. Once that happened, my sales would fall and I'd be broke and hopeless.

I jumped in the shower wondering if I should barricade the front door and stay put until dawn and got out thinking, "I can't live like this." If asking a few questions in the Quarter could push this investigation along, then I was the woman to do it. I dragged a box of old college clothes from my closet and ripped off the packing tape.

An hour later, I faced Buttercup for a second opinion. "What do you think?" My co-ed ensemble included black leather riding boots, skinny jeans, a silver tank top, and a can of aerosol hair spray. "Is the hair too big?"

She stared at her new home next door and made a bubble.

"I agree, but it's just for the night." I unlidded her cup and lowered her into her new bowl. "Enjoy your pink-and-white marble flooring and handcrafted sandcastle." I drew a heart on the bowl in purple dry-erase marker and blew her a kiss.

She took a spin around her new digs and lowered herself behind the castle.

"Oh, Buttercup. If only we all had a sandcastle."

I applied another round of mascara and called a cab.

The night was gorgeous. A perfect mix of live jazz, oppressive humidity, and nostalgia. I lowered the window to breathe it in. How many times had I taken a cab to the Quarter at night? Too many to count and too long since. I leaned against the backseat door and window for a better look at the beautiful Spanish scrollwork on second-floor galleries untouched by time. A man with bagpipes played a low lament near the Moonwalk as horse-drawn carriages clip-clopped down Canal Street, pretending this was another era and the city was new. I'd been around the world, but there was nowhere else like New Orleans.

* * *

Boondocks was on St. Peter Street. The chalkboard outside advertised, "Soup of the Day: Whisky." Inside, a traditional Irish bar complete with authentic copper top and stools lined one wall. The remaining walls were exposed brick and worn from age, like the rest of the place. The movie *Boondock Saints* played on a flat-screen. A bevy of locals filled the seats, complaining about work and kids. A trio of tourists stood near the door, complaining about the heat.

"What can I get you?" A tall blonde jogged to meet me on the opposite side of the bar.

"Coffee?" I fished a ten from my pocket and slid it her way.

"Coming up."

I wiped a line of sweat and melted hair spray off my temple and noted the distinct absence of pool tables.

"Enjoy." The bartender delivered a tall, frothy drink on a little napkin.

My mouth watered in anticipation. "What is this?"

"Coffee." She winked and wiped the bar in big, wet circles. "Plus a little crushed ice, Irish cream, and whisky."

I admired the glorious concoction. "Have you worked here long?"

She slowed her rag on the shiny surface. "A while. Why? Where are you from?"

"Not far."

"No?" She smiled. "A local? Why haven't I seen you here before?"

"I was away. College. Do you know a guy named Adam? Likes to play pool?"

She glanced toward a door in the back wall. "No."

"No?" I gave her a disbelieving look.

"He's not here tonight."

I gave the door she'd glanced at a pointed look and improvised. "You sure? He said he'd teach me how to play, and he told me to meet him here."

She looked me over, clearly deliberating.

I feigned casual, slid onto an empty barstool, and helped myself to the coffee. The icy sweetness hit my tongue with a high five of fantastic. "This is amazing." I swirled the drink and marveled. "You just added the cream and whisky to regular coffee?" I took a long satisfying drag. I could make these at home. "It's brilliant."

"Plus the ice, a shot of Kahlúa, and some coffee liquor, but not much. You're tasting the cream and whisky."

I was tasting deliciousness.

I turned on the stool and gave the small crowd another look. No one seemed like a jewel thief on parole hoping to hurt me. The whole scene was charming in a dive-bar way. I would've loved this place in college.

The door on the back wall swung open, and a lanky-looking guy sauntered over to the bar. He had a beanie on his unruly hair and a Louisiana State jersey over baggie jeans. He gave me a toothy grin. "Hey."

"You know her?" the bartender asked.

I pulled in a breath for bravery and took a chance. "Of course he does. We met on Bourbon Street, and he promised to teach me how to shoot."

She leaned on her elbow. "I thought you were looking for Adam."

I shrugged.

Confusion rode the guy's brow, but he gave my cleavage an appreciative stare and nodded slowly. "Sure. I remember you." He lifted two fingers in the bartender's direction. "Get me another and a refill for my friend."

"Oh, I don't need . . ." I lifted my empty cup. Huh. I set the cup on the bar.

Two fresh drinks appeared. The guy paid. "You ready?"

Not at all. I slid off the stool and prayed the bartender didn't make another protest. "Absolutely."

We cut down the length of the room and through the rear door. The stockroom on the other side was arranged to accommodate two regulation-sized pool tables. The shelves and boxes were pushed against the walls. A handful of men and women hung around, smiling and canoodling. Two men circled the table, cues in hand.

The guy who bought my drink pointed around the room, assigning names I'd never remember to people I'd never recognize again. "And over there is Adam."

A guy with a smooth-shaven head swore as he lined up his shot. "Man, Tim, can you not talk right now? I've got a lot of cash on this shot."

Tim buttoned his lips.

A guy in a black hoodie and jeans peeled himself off the wall. The chain hanging from his pocket swatted his baggy pant leg as he ghosted to my side. "Is this your girl, Tim?"

I tried not to make eye contact, which was simple because Pocket Chain's hood covered half his forehead and hid his eyes. The hood, however, did nothing to hide the line of shiny rings in his lip.

Tim barked a deep belly laugh. "Nah, we met on Bourbon. I don't even remember going there. Crazy, right?"

"Yeah." The creep moved into my personal space until his body heat warmed my arm. "What's your name, kitten?"

My jaw dropped open, and I craned my head back for a better look at Pocket Chain. "Um."

It was Jack, all right. Jack's eyes were near slits of frustration beneath the hood. He'd shaved his ever-present stubble and added several shiny rings to his face.

Fight or flight kicked in as adrenaline beat back the effects of the boozy coffee I'd finished at the bar. The full cup in my hand felt like an anvil. Would Jack blow my cover? Would he arrest me for obstruction like he'd threatened? My instincts screamed to flee. Curiosity and sheer hardheadedness said I had every right to play pool in a weird stockroom with a murder suspect if I wanted.

I gave Adam another look. He didn't seem to be very good at pool, but he also didn't look like a killer. He seemed more like the loud guy at a frat party, running his mouth and getting punched a lot. Though he could've paid someone to do his dirty work. It was impossible to tell if he had any money. His scrubby outfit said he was blue collar or wanted to appear that way. The toes of his work boots were scuffed. His belt was worn. The logo on his pocket was familiar.

Tim swung a heavy arm over my shoulder. "Watch it, dude. Kitten's with me."

I shook him off and glared. "My name is not kitten. It's . . . Jack-ie." I did a smug face at Jack.

"Well, Jackie," Jack retorted, completely unfazed, "do you have the five hundred to cover your game?"

Tim scoffed. "Man, I just told you she's here to learn, not play."

Jack leveled Tim with a look that chilled the room. "Well, she can't have my time at the table. You don't come here to hook up. You come to play." He turned his icy gaze on me. "Maybe you should go."

Clearly not a request.

Adam threw a chalk cube against the wall and it shattered into pieces. He marched into our little squabble, eyes blazing. "You just caused me to miss my shot!"

Violent curses ricocheted off the walls and my brain. The crowd complained about having to wait. Tim complained about being confronted.

Jack grabbed my wrist and yanked me aside. "You need to leave."

Fear rooted me in place. I had a very bad feeling about whatever came next.

"What were you thinking by coming here? Are you crazy?" His whispered rant gained speed like a downhill snowball. "And what are you wearing?"

His cocky tone snapped my mouth into motion. "Me?" I waved a palm in front of his pierced face. "What are you wearing?"

His chest expanded and his eye twitched. "I'm investigating a murder. You're obstructing that effort. Leave now and I won't call your mother."

I gasped. "You wouldn't!"

He leaned into my space. "You don't seem to fear my badge, but you sure as hell fear her. I'm not above getting childish if that's what it takes to save your life or keep you out of jail." He liberated his phone from one pocket and swiped the screen to life. "What'll it be? You staying for a lesson, or am I calling you a cab?"

Adam suddenly shoved Tim and Tim knocked into me.

I tripped over my feet, trying not to grab onto Jack for support. I flung both hands in search of balance and my drink went flying. My back hit the wall. "Oh, no."

Adam gasped. Iced coffee dripped from the tip of his nose and eyelashes.

I untangled my feet and adjusted my tank top to show a little more cleavage. "I am sincerely sorry about that."

He delivered his thoughts on my apology with more swearing. Loud swearing.

I pressed a palm to one ear and blinked rapidly. The logo on his shirt snapped something loose in my memory. "You work at All-American Construction?"

He swore some more.

I'd take that as a yes and talk to Jack later. He could probably take it from here. No need to involve my mother. I slipped behind Tim and made my way toward the door.

"Hey, babe. Don't go." Tim shot an arm out to block my escape.

Adam capitalized on Tim's distraction and lunged at us.

I jumped.

Adam and Tim struggled, banging into the wall and cursing. They deflected and spun through the crowd until they crashed onto the table, scattering balls and snarling threats. A few beefy bystanders piled on.

I wrenched the door open and waved a silent good-bye to Jack.

He tapped his phone screen. "Go!"

I slipped through the open door but peeked at the chaos I'd left behind. Would Jack be okay? Should I call the police? Would that ruin his investigation?

He put his phone away and grabbed two men by their shirts, hauling the latecomers off the top of the pile. "That's enough. Knock it off."

Both men spun blindly toward the hands that had grabbed them and punched outward.

Jack's head whipped back. "Son of a . . ." He shook his head and checked his mouth for blood. When his fingers came up red, he unzipped his hoodie to reveal his detective badge on a shiny, beaded chain. "Against the wall." He cuffed the offending duo with zip ties. He readied another set of ties and raised his badge into the air. "NOPD! Don't move."

The room stilled.

Adam sprang off the table and made a run for the door I was behind.

I jerked the barrier between us and slid the lock.

The door bounced hard under my trembling hand. "That was close," I whispered to myself.

"You do that?" The bartender appeared beside me, and not too happy. She nodded at the door.

I blew out a shaky breath. "Not intentionally. Did you know Miguel Sanchez?"

She watched me in wonder. "Who's asking?"

"Me. I'm trying to find out who would've wanted to hurt him."

"Someone hurt him?" Her voice hitched with genuine shock. "Is he okay?"

"No." Apparently news didn't travel in the Quarter as quickly as it did in my district. I did my best to steady my voice. "I'm sorry to tell you this, but Miguel's dead. He was murdered four days ago. There are no significant leads."

Sadness tugged at her eyes. "You a cop?"

"No. Just someone looking for answers."

The hasty bark of sirens cut through the air.

My time was running out. "Anything you can tell me . . ." I looked toward the open front door where a line of cops in street clothes flashed badges and marched our way with authority.

She turned her back to the room. "There was a guy in here looking for him about four nights ago. You said that's when he died?"

"Who was he?"

"I don't know. He said to tell Miguel he came by and that he owed Miguel one."

A man the size of a barge pushed past us and unlocked the rear door. "Lacy Crocker?"

I gave an appreciative nod to the bartender as she slipped away. "Yeah?"

"Don't go anywhere. Detective Oliver would like to talk to you." He pulled the door open and steamrolled inside.

"I'll be at the bar." Ordering another iced coffee.

Chapter Fourteen

*Furry Godmother's advice for ladies: Don't flaunt your superiority.
It's bad form, and men don't pick up on it anyway.*

An hour later, I was still at the bar nursing a bottle of water.
Everyone from the stock room had been questioned and
released, except Adam. I hadn't seen him or Jack since the cops
arrived. The crowd at Boondocks had grown generously, and
the ruckus on Bourbon Street had, too. Knots of tourists wandered inside with giant plastic souvenir cups and flashing party
buttons. A woman in a hooker dress and wedding veil let men
kiss her for a dollar, while her girl crew cheered them on. Frat
kids bought shots for someone's twenty-first birthday. Retired,
divorced, and middle-aged friends stood wide-eyed and awk-
wardly in the corners, reliving their heyday or maybe regretting
that they'd missed it thirty years ago.

This night had definitely not gone as planned. Jack would
never let me speak with Adam, and Adam was so mad at me
for dousing him in iced coffee, he probably wouldn't talk to
me anyway. Everyone else from the secret pool room was long
gone. I'd already forgotten their names and faces. I had no

leads, and it seemed unlikely Jack would share what he learned from Adam with me.

The juke box suddenly blasted a long guitar solo from an eighties hair band, and I turned for a look at who had thought that song was worth his or her money. A pair of plainclothes cops brushed past me with Adam sandwiched between them. He wasn't cuffed, but the escort didn't look optional.

Jack mounted the empty stool beside me and tussled his sweaty hair with one hand. "Well, that was fun. Not at all useful, but fun." He pulled the faux studs from his nose and eyebrow with ease but flinched when removing the rings from his swollen lip.

"Yeah. That was a blast. Who doesn't enjoy bleeding from their face once in a while?"

He rolled his shoulders and stretched his neck side to side. "I haven't been in a bar fight since I was fifteen."

"Fifteen!"

His snarky expression stopped me short. "It's a joke. Relax." He pushed the jewelry into his pocket and swiped my water bottle off the bar. He pressed the cool condensation to the corner of his mouth. "At least I didn't have to arrest you."

I grimaced. "I'm sure they can get you some ice. No need to bleed on my drink."

He took a look at the bottle, twisted the cap off, and drank it dry. "Two more." He lifted a peace sign into the air. "Guessing you didn't want that bottle back."

"Correct."

The bartender dropped two bottles in front of us. Jack paid.

"You didn't have to do that."

He levered himself off the stool and placed a tip on the bar. "Calm down. It's bottled water, not an engagement ring." He stripped out of his hoodie and bunched it into one fist.

"Adam works at All-American Construction."

"That's what you keep saying. Feel like telling me why?"

I followed him onto the sidewalk and soaked in the tangible buzz of energy. "That was the company that put my shop together for me. Tater hired them. They made the built-ins and handled lighting and my display case. That company is ever present on Magazine Street. The crews are really good. Store owners rarely call anyone else for renovations or improvements."

"Good to know."

"Did you arrest him?"

"No."

"Are you kidding? He had access to my shop!"

"We haven't let him go. He's headed to the station for more questioning. If we find grounds, we'll keep him. How does he have access to your shop?"

My short legs scrambled after his on the crowded sidewalk. "They had keys. They let themselves in and out all week while they worked there this spring. It wasn't that long ago. He could've kept the key." I snapped my fingers. "Or had a spare made! We should find out where people get keys made in town and show his picture around."

Jack laughed. "I'll get right on that."

"I don't believe you." I waved hello to a passing group of goths in variations of Vampire Lestat costumes.

They leered suggestively and bared their fake teeth.

Jack dug in his pockets for keys. "You look more comfortable here than with most of those Garden District women."

I laughed. "Oh, you'd be surprised."

"Yeah?" He moved along the street, and I kept pace. "Heard any compelling stories about me from your circle?"

My circle? I didn't have a circle. Unless I could talk Paige and Scarlet into running around me a few times. "No. I didn't know you existed until four days ago. I'm comfortable here because everyone came here as often as possible when they were younger. Except you. You were overseas somewhere playing cricket and drinking tea."

"And you said you hadn't heard anything about me."

I clenched my jaw. I'd given him the impression I'd asked about him when I hadn't. Protesting would make it worse. I dodged a woman speaking with large hand gestures. We needed to focus on the reason we were both in the Quarter tonight. "What did Adam say back there?"

Jack cut through a crowd on the corner and headed directly for an intimidating-looking motorcycle.

I clipped along at his heels like the little dog following the big one in cartoons. "You talked to him for almost an hour. What did he say? What did you say?"

"He copped to having a gambling problem, and I gave him the name of a local gamblers anonymous group. They meet in the Central Business District. It'll be good for him if he doesn't end up arrested for murder."

I grabbed his swinging arm and released him instantly. "You know what I meant."

He looked at his sleeve where I'd touched him. "Ever been on a bike like this?" He stopped beside the fierce, gas-blue motorcycle.

I crossed my arms and tried looking defensive instead of terrified. "No."

"Looks like tonight's your lucky night."

"This is your bike? I thought you were going to give it a ticket or something. Where's your truck?"

"I'm going to pretend you don't think I'm a meter maid and answer your question instead. My bike is easier to park down here." He handed me a helmet. "Put it on."

I rolled the bulbous object over in my hands and gave the motorcycle another look. No seatbelts. No roof or doors. There was no way a helmet could protect me if I flew off of that thing, and where was I supposed to hold on? My traitorous gaze slid to Jack's torso. The heat index, coupled with hours in a hoodie, had applied his heather-grey T-shirt to his skin. I cleared my throat. Twice. "Sunshine came to talk to me today. She said you brought her and Hayden in for questioning."

"Put my helmet on your head and get on the bike."

"She didn't do it."

He took the helmet from me, turned it over, and stuffed it on my head. "There. Now let's go." He grinned and shook his head.

"Excuse me, are you smiling?"

He straightened his face. "No. Get on."

"You aren't listening to me. We need to talk about Sunshine."

"I heard you. She's innocent. What about the other one?"

"Hayden? I don't know about her, but Sunshine's pregnant. She didn't want to hurt Miguel. She loved him. They were going to leave New Orleans together."

Jack motioned to the bike. "Hayden's a mess over his loss. She had a rough upbringing, and she's a little worse for it, if you know what I mean." He tapped his temple. "If you see her coming, I'd go the other way."

"Why?" I squeaked. "She blames me for his death, too?"

He made a sad face. "No, but she knows about Sunshine's pregnancy, and she's livid. That spiel he gave Sunshine about leaving town together?" He cocked his brows. "He told Hayden the same thing. I'd advise anyone to steer clear of her right now. She's a ticking time bomb of rage and unsubstantiated entitlement. Add her boyfriend's betrayal and recent death to her lifetime in poverty, and she's not in a pretty place. You're everything she hates in one package."

"What's that supposed to mean? I had nothing to do with her socioeconomic background or Miguel's awfulness."

"You're pretty, classy, educated. All the things she thinks she can't ever be. Are you okay wearing that helmet? You're not going to freak out on me once we're on the road, are you?"

He thought I was pretty and classy? "No. I think this is okay." I slid onto the seat and scooted as far back as possible. What wasn't okay was his description of Hayden's temper. If she'd been following Miguel around town with an employee discount card to Frozen Banana, I had a solid idea of who'd vandalized my window.

I adjusted the helmet and tried to look natural while straddling a motorcycle. I may as well have tried to look natural riding an ostrich. "If my dad sees me on this thing, you're going to have a whole new set of problems."

"Why would Dr. Crocker be in the Quarter at midnight? Besides, you're the one with explaining to do. If I were you, I'd use this time to get my story straight before I'm questioned by

New Orleans's best detective." He climbed in front and settled onto the seat.

I ignored the distracting effect on his jeans and tried not to touch more than necessary. "I suppose you're New Orleans best detective? Way to be humble."

He revved the engine to life and eased away from the curb. Pedestrians with big smiles and go cups hustled out of our way. Men stared at the motorcycle. Women stared at the driver.

I got my story straight.

* * *

I headed for the kitchen, flipping every light switch I passed.

Jack followed. "I hope you're making coffee. I have a feeling this is going to be a long night."

I peered into the new fishbowl on my counter. "Buttercup? I'm home. Please come out of your sandcastle so I know I didn't transfer you too soon and accidentally kill you."

Jack hefted the coffeepot into the sink and turned on my water. "Where do you keep your coffee?"

"On the lazy Susan." I tapped the bowl. "Buttercup?" Panic laced my voice.

Jack reached around me, dripping water from wet hands onto the counter. He shook a food flake onto the water. "That's how you get a fish to come when you call it. Make it associate you with mealtime. They love mealtime." He went back to making coffee. "What kind did you get? A goldfish?"

"A Crowntail Betta."

Buttercup stuck her nose through the castle door and made a bubble. She darted to the surface and snatched the flake.

"Oh, thank goodness." I deflated against the counter. "She ate it. She's alive." My heart warmed to Jack. "How'd you know to do that?"

"Common sense." He pressed the Brew button on my pot.

Warmth gone. "Can we please talk about Adam?"

"All right." He pressed his backside to my counter and crossed his legs at the ankles. "What did you plan to ask him tonight when you found him?"

"I had plenty of questions, like whether or not Miguel had ever mentioned my store or his former partner. I wondered if Adam knew if Miguel participated in the recent jewelry store heists. I wondered if he knew anyone who might have wanted Miguel dead. I had lots of questions."

He seemed to consider that. "Coffee?"

"Sure."

He upturned two mugs from my drying rack and snagged the pot off a still-brewing coffeemaker. "Cream or sugar?"

"Black."

"I'd have figured you for a both. I thought you were a café au lait girl."

I made a you-don't-know-everything face. "I learned to love black coffee for its ability to keep me awake all night in college." Besides, I'd had enough doctored coffee for one night.

"Was that medical school or fashion college?"

"I was premed, which is nothing like medical school, and stop making my design degree sound like Monopoly money." I gathered my overteased hair into a messy bun, which had to look better than it did after being hair sprayed to death, sweat drenched, and smooshed into a helmet. I jabbed a pair of takeout chopsticks into the mess and breathed easier. Cool air on the back of my neck lowered my blood pressure.

"I'll stop teasing you about your foofoo degree if you agree to stay out of this investigation."

I blew over the surface of my coffee. Delicious tendrils of bitter steam swam up my nose. "I guess that's it for the banter portion of our evening."

"I'm serious. This investigation is a hairy mess, and you need to keep your distance so I can follow through on my leads without any distractions."

"Do you mean like the information I gave you on Miguel's two girlfriends?" I tapped my bottom lip with one fingertip. "Who told you Adam worked for a company that had a key to my shop a few months ago? Oh, yeah, me again."

He nodded along, unamused. "That's right. You're bringing me tons of intel on this case. Like the big-ass railroad spike you found in your tire. Thanks for handing that over. It was a case cracker."

"That was not my fault."

"No, but it was a direct result of you putting your nose where it doesn't belong."

"I was accused of murder. He broke into my store."

Jack rolled his eyes up at me, peering over the rim of his mug. "I'm aware of that. It doesn't mean you have to get yourself killed."

I set my coffee aside. The cold fingers of fear slid into my gut. "I really need to know who did this before I go bankrupt or my store goes under. There's a lot riding on this. My business. My reputation. My sanity." I rubbed my tired eyes. "Sorry. You don't want to hear this."

"No. Keep going. It helps me understand why you seem hell-bent on undermining me."

"I'm really not trying to do that."

He bobbed his head. "But you still have to stop. I'm on top of this, and you need to distance yourself. If anyone asks you how the investigation is going, tell them you have no idea because I iced you out. Okay?"

Something like fear flashed in his eyes. I didn't think fear was an emotion Jack possessed.

"I'll try."

"Don't try. *Do.* How's it going with the new security system Tater had installed?"

"It's not in yet. The company will be out in the morning for the installation. They did a walkthrough with Paige while I was at Mrs. Feller's place. I got the work order and appointment confirmation this afternoon."

He poured more coffee into his half-empty mug. "Good. Make sure you never leave without setting it, and keep it on after hours, even when you're there."

"Of course." Going to my storeroom in the middle of the day had given me goose bumps since running into Miguel that night. It would be nice to know the alarm was working to protect me around the clock.

"Are you ready for a refill?" He wiggled the pot between us.

"I think I've had enough. I'm going to get some rest tonight." Right after I mock up a few tutus and kitty capelets. "Did Adam tell you anything useful about the murder?"

Jack laughed. "You promised to drop this five seconds ago."

"I'm not investigating. I'm just asking. As a friend."

"You need to get dumber friends. You're asking about the details in a murder. That's called investigating. So stop."

"Why can't I ask you? Asking you isn't the same as interfering."

"I'm not feeding your sickness." The glimmer in his crystal eyes slid to his mouth, turning his reddened lips up in a smile.

I didn't hate the fresh-shaven look on him or the evidence he'd kicked some bad guys' behinds. "Let me get you some ice for your lip."

He waved me off. "I'm fine. It doesn't hurt, and it'll look better in the morning."

"What if it scars?"

"Ladies dig scars."

I lingered my gaze over the tiny, white dashes on his cheeks. He had plenty of scars. I wasn't sure I liked them or hated whoever caused them. I wetted my lips and looked into his eyes. "The bartender told me a man came in the day Miguel died and asked about him. She said she didn't get a name, but he wanted to leave a message. He said he owed Miguel one."

"One what?"

"She didn't ask, but that was a blatant threat, probably from Levi Marks."

"That theory wouldn't hold up in court. It's speculation. Miguel might've helped that guy with a flat tire, and now the guy owes him a beer or a return favor."

"Oh, sure. Miguel was a real Samaritan."

"Speculation."

"Fine. You're welcome for another lead." I hid a smile behind my mug. "What's your theory? Who killed Miguel Sanchez?"

Jack gave me a pointed stare. A little chuckle rumbled his chest. "You said you weren't obstinate. I asked you the night we met and you lied."

"Didn't." I bit my lips to stop supporting his argument.

He lowered himself to my height and softened his voice. "Please drop this. I want you to change up your routine until we find out who stabbed your tire. Consider talking to the security company tomorrow about getting an alarm system for your home."

"Another monthly bill? Can I pay for it in blood or cellulite? Because I've already told you I'm out of cash."

"Then adopt a big dog or put some NRA stickers on the windows. Did you take any self-defense classes in Virginia?"

I wrapped my arms around my middle. "A few." The self-defense classes wouldn't have helped me on the night I was mugged, though. Not against a man with a gun. "I got my concealed carry license."

He set his cup in the sink and took mine, too. "I know. I made a few calls after we met." He didn't have to say more. He knew my secret. He knew I was a victim.

I swallowed the lump of fear that came with those memories. "I don't carry. I never did."

Jack watched me, giving me time to say more, but I couldn't, and he didn't push. "If you ever want to go to the range, I'll take you. It's a good release when you're tense, and it's a confidence builder. Criminals tend to be lazy. If you look vigilant, they'll find an easier hit."

"The average criminal, maybe, but what about someone who's already threatened me once?" I'd spent countless hours at the firing range in my lifetime, honing my concentration and steadying my nerves, but none of that would help me with my current problems. A burst of boldness squared my shoulders. "What are you really doing here? Driving me home. Coming in for coffee. Am I in danger right now? If so, you need to tell me."

"I'm being proactive. If I'm with you the next time the tire popper makes a move, you'll be safe and I'll be a hero. Win-win." He smeared a cocky grin across his face.

"Very chivalrous. Thank you. What if you're wrong, and I'm not in any danger?" I begged him silently to say this was a possibility.

He pulled his phone from his pocket and frowned at the screen. He pressed his lips into a tight line and groaned. "I've got to go."

"What? Why?"

"Lock up behind me."

"Where are you going? You just said you were staying here to protect me."

"There was another break-in on Magazine Street." His gravelly voice sent chills over my skin.

I scampered along behind. "What? I thought Miguel was the one breaking into jewelry stores. Wait. Which shop? There aren't any more jewelry stores on Magazine Street."

He stopped on the porch and turned his phone to face me.

1211 Magazine Street

"That's my store!"

Chapter Fifteen

Furry Godmother's fun fact: Cleanliness is next to godliness,
but it won't wash away bad juju.

Cruisers sat outside my store, half-cocked onto the sidewalk, announcing their importance. Where had they been thirty minutes ago? Their colored lights flashed across my front window, giving the tiny, winged drawings painted there an evil-fairy look. A uniformed officer spoke with pedestrians. I ran toward the broken door, praying the damage was minimal and nothing had a railroad tie through it.

Jack drove his motorcycle onto the sidewalk in front of me and shut it down. "Look out. There's glass."

"Thank you, Captain Obvious." I spun in a small circle, fighting tears. "If I'd known it was Park on the Sidewalk Night, I could've saved myself some time."

Jack approached me slowly, with his palms turned up.

"Can I go inside?" I bumped the broken door open without waiting for an answer. Glass covered the floor inside.

Jack snapped pictures with his phone. "Looks like someone punched in the window to reach the lock." He pressed the phone into his pocket and snapped surgical gloves over his hands.

"I can't see anything," I grouched. Misery crawled like spider babies over my skin.

He flipped the line of switches beside my door. Tiny chandeliers cast fluorescent light over the colossal disaster.

"Oh my goodness." I crunched a path into the store. Every display and shelving unit was overturned. The bakery treats were torn apart. "Was this a hate crime? Did the jewelry stores look like this?"

"No. Those were textbook smash and grabs." The flash of Jack's camera came again. "This is something else entirely."

"Yeah. Like the Incredible Hulk had enough of me."

A line of men in navy shirts crossed the floor to Jack. White stencils painted on their little plastic brief cases read, "Property of NOLA Crime Lab."

Jack shook their hands. "We just got here. That's Miss Crocker, the store owner. She's taking an inventory. Pull prints on the lock, door frame, and handle. Maybe some of the overturned pieces, register, usual drill. Let's get them matched up to the jewelry heists and stop this son of a gun."

I shuffled through the store, saving my precious work from the debris-covered floor and setting it in stacks on the counter beside my register. All my framed pictures lay wrecked on the floor like artistic carnage. "There's so much glass." I shook slivers off a pile of headscarves. "Who would do this?"

Jack tipped his chin toward the stockroom. "Better take a look in the back."

I followed at a distance.

The lights were on.

Jack reached for his sidearm. "Anyone check the stock-room?" he called over his shoulder.

"All clear," the outside cop answered back.

Thank heavens. "Why were the stockroom lights on and the storefront lights off?" I asked.

"Turning the front lights off makes it harder to see inside. Cuts down on witnesses."

Jack kept one hand on his gun as he moved methodically through the pummeled stock, looking utterly at ease as he checked corners, behind doors, and under large piles of dumped boxes.

My throat tightened. I struggled to swallow the knot forming there. It was a record-breaking week for awful things. My store had been violated twice. My car had been attacked. My store window defaced. My life had been threat-ened. I'd been accused of murder. I forced my breaths to slow. There was a proper time and place for a breakdown. It wasn't here or now.

Bulk containers of overturned glitter flooded the room. Spilled paint and glue mucked it up in patches.

I fell onto my desk chair and shoved a wad of tissues to my nose. "It'll take days to clean up the mess. I'll have to replace a ton of stock. The floor needs to be refinished." Even if my insurance replaced everything, I'd never have all the materials I needed to fill orders already waiting. Not if I wanted to make the next lease payment. So which would it be, buy supplies and fill the orders as promised but risk missing the lease payment and losing my shop? Flake on the orders I'd already committed to and lose customers but keep my space? Who would ever work with me if I got a bad reputation for not following through on my services? No one. Then I wouldn't need a space. Problem solved.

Something moved in the mix of overturned supplies. Jack raised a silent palm and kicked a wad of crinoline and rickrack. Roomba-Spot rolled out, bumped Jack's boot, and headed back into the pile.

A bright smile spread over Jack's face. "Your sweeper says 'Spot' on top."

"So?"

"He's got big googly eyes and felt ears."

"At least something survived this awful night." I set him on his charger and sighed. "I won't be able to open for a week. I'll have to work from home." I scooped a pen and pad from my purse. "I'll make a list of the supplies I need and see if I can salvage any of them from this mess. Tomorrow." Too much stress and a bar fight had turned my stomach. This catastrophe didn't help. "Can I take some things home?" I turned to find Jack rolling bolts of fabric.

He tossed the tidy bolt onto the floor and grabbed another. "I need you to take an inventory. We need to know if anything's missing. It's probably hard to tell right now." He set the second bolt with the first and lifted another. "You don't have to do this alone, but we need to know what was taken. With help, it won't take a week."

I burst into tears. The sincerity in his voice was too much. "You have no idea. Those fabric bolts are the biggest things back here. All these other boxes were filled with thousands of appliqués, pins, and buttons." I mimed the infinitesimal sizes with my thumb and first finger.

He waved me off. "Make your list. I'll lift and count, you mark."

"Why are you doing this?"

He rooted for a pair of scissors and cut off a tattered line of fabric. "It's what friends do. I might not have spent a ton of time here growing up, but I know how this district operates, and I guarantee I'm not the only help you'll see before the job's done."

I wiped my eyes on my arm and crammed the soggy tissue against my nose. "Thank you."

"Don't thank me. Get to work."

* * *

I dragged myself out of bed long after the sun had risen and drank coffee until I felt better than I looked. Shampoo and shower gel had met their match after the night I'd had. Even my megaduty concealer was useless against the zombie-grade circles under my eyes. I pulled on a pair of cutoff shorts and a blue cotton shirt with a cartoon dog in the center and "Pugs not Drugs" scripted over him. This would be the first of many cleanup days.

Thirty minutes later, I hauled bags of cleaning supplies through the busted door at Furry Godmother. Jack had used plywood to secure the store against further intruders until I could call the glass company. I left them a message before I fell asleep. The ball was in their court.

I locked the door behind me and unpacked my bags on the counter. I hadn't touched the storefront and had barely made a dent in the stockroom before going home to have a breakdown. Jack slept in his truck in front of my house. I didn't know when he'd left, but he was there when I fell asleep and gone when I went outside to bring him coffee in the morning. He refused my offer to sleep on the couch. I had mixed feelings on the refusal.

The work ahead was almost daunting enough to return me to bed, but if I didn't get started, I couldn't get finished. I grabbed a broom and pushed glass chunks into a pile. Unfortunately, the filthy floor was polka-dotted with fallen shelving and broken stock. I moved on to righting displays and rearranging the store. I stopped at the turtle tank and fished a bunny bonnet off the rocks. "You guys were lucky," I told the turtles. "I should have you outfitted with security cameras. You've got a perfect view of the whole place. If you can talk, this would be an excellent time to tell me." I dropped a handful of heirloom strawberries into Brad and Angelina's tank. "I'll clean your place after I finish with mine."

Someone rapped on my new plywood door cover. "Hello? Good morning? Lacy Crocker?" a sweet, little-old-lady voice called.

I peeked through my window. "Sorry. I'm closed."

The woman jumped when she noticed me at the glass. "Oh my!" She fanned her face. "I know. I brought you a snack. Homemade cinnamon rolls. They just came out of the oven. I'm Matilda Golden. I live on First near Coliseum Street." Her raspberry muumuu and orthopedic sneakers didn't scream danger, and I could almost smell the cinnamon rolls through the window.

I unlocked the door. "Thank you. I'd invite you in, but I've got a mess. I don't want you to get hurt."

"Nonsense." She beeped the doors of a nearby Jaguar unlocked. "Give me just a minute." She passed me the dish with rolls and waddled across the sidewalk.

I held the door with my bottom while she fished an espresso machine from her trunk. "Now we're in business." She carried the machine through Furry Godmother and set it up on my bakery display case.

"You really don't have to do that. I've got a ton of work to do, and honestly, I'm in an awful mood. Maybe another day would be better." I checked outside for suspicious-looking individuals and closed the door.

"I didn't come to visit. I came to help." She produced a speaker dock from the box with the espresso machine and set her phone inside. Soft jazz filtered through the air. "Leave the door open. Get the air circulating. Do you like cinnamon rolls? You're not one of those young people who are allergic to everything, are you? Whey, nuts, gluten, oxygen."

I shook my head.

"Fantastic." She dropped a pastry the size of my head onto a paper plate and jammed a fork into it. "Eat."

I pinched my wrist in case I was still at home in bed. "I'm sorry, did you say your name is Matilda Golden? The recluse?"

"I rarely find ample reason to leave home, but I'm not opposed to it. Ah!" She waved her hands overhead. "Here they are." She wobbled past me in a flurry of silk and heavy perfume.

A cluster of women my grandmother's age appeared at the doorway in floppy brimmed sunhats, toting bags in every size and pattern. They kissed Matilda's cheeks and gasped appropriately at the mess around me.

The smallest one with fuzzy, bluish hair took my sweaty hands in her small, soft ones. "Don't worry about a thing. We've all heard what went on here, and we've come to help."

I opened my mouth to speak but only managed, "Thank you."

My mother arrived next, wearing white capris and my high school Converse shoes. She said her hellos, then focused on me. "Why are you standing there?" She clapped her hands.

I jumped behind the counter and gawked. The sexagenarian posse before me scooped up trash and wiped down walls. The combined net worth of my cleaning crew was probably enough to buy the block, maybe the street. Mom sprayed and wiped the glass on my bakery display with gusto. I didn't even know my mother could work a household cleanser bottle.

Another round of neighbors rolled through the front door like this was completely normal. They got assignments from Matilda and went to work.

A lump formed in my throat. My eyes stung and blurred. I turned my back to the crowd and pulled the hem of my shirt to my face, dabbing away the renegade tears.

"Lacy?" Dad's voice echoed from the doorway.

I turned and gave him my brightest smile. Imogene stood at his side. Her hair was shocked with gray, but her eyes were as sparkly and mischievous as ever. I kissed Dad's cheek, then wrapped my arms around her. "Thank you for coming."

She patted my back. "Where else would I be when you need me?"

I pulled back and waved a hand at the carnage of my store.

Her frame went rigid, as if she'd finally noticed the disaster around us. "Whoa. Someone did a number in here. They left bad juju all over this place, and you didn't need any more of that." She shivered and rubbed her palms up and down her arms. "It feels like angry, fearful juju. That's a dangerous combination."

Dad slid one strong arm around my back and squeezed me to his side. "Don't listen to her. The worst of this is over, and we're all here to help lighten your burden." He pressed his lips to my head. "I'm so sorry this is happening to you, but you're going to be fine."

I shook free with a confident smile. One more fatherly assurance and I'd be a blubbering moron. I lifted my chin. "You're right." Jack would figure this out if I didn't. I just needed to stay alive until one of us did. "Where did you find all these people?"

He nodded to my mother.

Mom looked up on cue and heaved a stage sigh. "Now there are three of you just standing around. If I look up again, will there be six?"

I laughed through a bubble of emotion. "Thank you," I managed to croak.

Her eyes widened and a blush crossed her cheeks. "Well." She smoothed her palms over her pants and glanced at the busy folks around us. "You're welcome. I knew you wouldn't ask for help, so I took it upon myself. I thought you might get angry, but someone has to get things done properly around here."

"You didn't need to ask to help me clean up, but you could've asked before borrowing my shoes," I laughed.

She looked at her feet and smiled. "We bought these together before you went to college. Do you remember?"

"Yes." I was shocked that she did, but I hadn't forgotten. "It was a really good day."

She raised her eyes to mine. "Yes, it was."

A man in navy-blue dickeys poked his head into the open doorway, breaking our moment. "Crocker?"

"Yes?" Mom, Dad, and I answered in unison.

The man checked his clipboard. "Someone called about a window replacement."

"That was me." I waved. "I left a message last night with the measurements."

Dad shook the man's hand and signed for the bill.

Clipboard took more measurements and went back to his truck on the curb, where two men in matching uniforms commiserated over coffee from the shop next door.

I leaned into Dad's side. "You didn't have to do that. Insurance would have paid for it."

"Then they can pay me back. No sense in waiting when the Clean Team's here now."

"The Clean Team?" I snickered. "This crew has a name?"

"Sure. Names make everything friendlier. Like Vinnie. Without a name, this group, for example, might seem like just a bunch of pushy old broads."

Mom glared.

Matilda laughed.

"Come on." He took me by the elbow. "Let me introduce you to the crew."

* * *

By dinner, Furry Godmother was clean, tidy, and repaired, save one massive fallen bookcase. We'd worked around it until it seemed more like a strange part of the ambience than the huge obstacle it was. Mom had even wiped down the back and sides.

I'd taken complete inventory of everything on the sales floor. Nothing was missing. The last of the District Clean

Team had dissipated by late afternoon, and Imogene had left promptly after shaking a feathered rattle around every window. I didn't ask. I only hoped whatever she did to the windows was as effective as the sleeping magic she had worked on me as a child.

What a difference a day made. Yesterday I'd bought a fish to cure my loneliness, and today I'd been kissed and hugged half to death by a dozen neighbors and friends. Working with Mom had been nice, too. She wasn't nearly as intimidating without her haute couture.

I needed some fresh air. "Who wants a smoothie?"

No one responded. Mom made a face and pointed to all the refreshments lined up on the bakery counter.

"I'll be right back." I slipped into the sticky evening and exhaled. I needed to clear my head. A little red sports car zipped into traffic and revved its engine. I stopped moving. It was the car from the Barrel Room parking lot. Hayden's car.

I hustled up the block to the Frozen Banana and waited impatiently for my turn at the counter. "Hi. I'm Lacy Crocker. I work a few doors down. I own the pet boutique, Furry Godmother."

The guy behind the register didn't seem to care. "What can I get you?"

"I think a woman was just in here. She has really big, brown hair and tan skin." I struggled to remember something else about her besides her bad attitude, but I hadn't paid much attention to Hayden the only time I'd seen her. My focus had been on Sunshine. "I think she's taller than me." I lifted a hand over my head to indicate how tall I thought she might be. "Athletic looking."

The clerk patted out a drum solo on the register's sides. "Are you going to order?"

"Yes, but can you tell me if a girl who looks like the one I described was in here a few minutes ago?"

He stared. "No."

I dragged an agitated hand through my hair. "Are you sure? I think she was just here. She drives a red sports car with tinted windows."

He raised his brows and looked through the store window.

"You remember her now?" My heart leapt. I remembered something, too. "She has an employee discount card from the Barrel Room."

"Oh, yeah." He smiled, proudly. "I know that girl. She's hot. Are you going to order?"

"Yes. What else can you tell me about her?"

"I don't know. She's a regular. She used to buy two strawberry smoothies every night, but she missed a few nights and only ordered one today. Same thing last time." He peered over my head at the line forming behind me. "Dude, if you aren't going to order, I have to ask you to step aside."

I dug in my pocket for some cash. "No. I'm ordering a small piña colada smoothie. Was she here last night?" Was Hayden the one who trashed my store?

He took my money and turned for the stack of bright-yellow cups. "Nah. She hasn't been here in a few nights."

"How about five nights ago? Was she here then?"

He snapped a lid onto my cup and shoved it across the counter. "Yeah, maybe. Thanks for stopping at Frozen Banana. Have a fruity day. Next."

A couple in matching "I Heart New Orleans" shirts pushed their way around me to the counter.

I unwrapped a straw and pondered the new information all the way back to Furry Godmother. Hayden didn't stop at Frozen Banana last night, but she could've trashed my shop without buying a smoothie. Not buying a smoothie didn't mean she wasn't in the area.

It also didn't mean she was.

I pushed the door open to my shop and relaxed at the sight of my loved ones.

Dad gave the room a proud once-over. He toed the toppled bookcase. "Sorry I couldn't raise this for you. When you've only got one man under sixty, it's hard to do any heavy lifting. Bad backs. Bad hearts."

I gave him a fast squeeze. "You did enough. Forget that for tonight. I'll figure it out tomorrow."

"Don't forget to send thank-you cards for the help and the food," Mom instructed. "I have addresses if you need them."

I couldn't muster the urge to grumble about the thank-you cards. I hated writing them, but this time I wished I could do more than write a few words on cardstock. "I'll take care of it."

She dug in her purse and handed me a fancy black-and-white invitation. "I'm having a benefit dinner tomorrow. You always say no, so I don't invite you as often as I should." She pushed her shoulders back. "If I don't invite you, you can't reject me, but you also can't say yes. So think about it."

I nodded. Appreciation for all she'd done bubbled in my chest. However, making emotional decisions wasn't the best practice with all my tasks piling up. "I'll see if I have anything on my calendar."

Dad lowered reading glasses onto his nose and pushed buttons on my new security system. "They installed this in no time. How do we know it works?"

"They showed me. I've got an instruction booklet, an emergency number, and passcodes in my purse."

He traced his finger around the outline of the wall unit. "It doesn't look like much. We probably should've had our guys come out here. Our house has a bigger pad than this. More options."

Mom dusted her shirt. "Our home has more to lose."

I bit my tongue. If I pointed out that my stock was handmade, and therefore irreplaceable, she'd list family heirlooms and art, which was valid. Insensitive, but accurate.

The locked front door wiggled, and the silhouette of a man in dark clothing and a ball cap came into view.

I knew that silhouette.

Dad stepped in front of us. "We're closed for renovations."

I nudged him. "It's just Jack."

Dad's face lit up. "Why didn't you say so?" He flipped the dead bolt and welcomed Jack inside.

Jack pulled his hat off and stuffed it, brim first, into his back pocket. His cheeks were red from sun or exertion. His eyes were droopy from lack of sleep.

"What's this?" I reached for the baking dish in Jack's hands.

"Banana bread with cranberry jam. It's a family recipe."

"You made me a banana bread?"

He looked away. "Tabitha made it. I would've stopped by sooner, but I chased a dirty lead halfway to the Mason–Dixon line."

I set the dish aside and tried not to care who Tabitha was.

Mom huffed and floated past me on indignation. "Can I get you some coffee, Jack? Maybe you'd like a bite to eat?" She stood behind the casserole-laden bakery display and gave me the stink eye.

I shooed her away. "Fine. Let me play hostess. You've done enough. Go home and open a bottle of wine. Enjoy your night."

She sidestepped me and hooked her hand in the crook of Dad's arm. "What about the shelving unit? You can't open tomorrow with it like this."

"I can't open tomorrow at all. I still have to clean and organize the stockroom. We've made a dent, but there's plenty for me to do before I can go back to business as usual."

Jack cracked his knuckles and approached the fallen unit. "What was taken?"

"Nothing, as far as I can tell. A few dozen items were total losses due to damage, but nothing was taken, not even the cash register. There's no apparent reason for any of this."

Dad moved opposite Jack and crouched low. Together they grunted and huffed until the enormous bookshelf was back where it belonged. The front edge of each shelf was scratched and chipped, but the structure was no worse for wear.

I sighed in relief. Imogene was wrong to worry about bad juju. "It's perfect. A little elbow grease and a dab of paint and no one will know anything bad ever happened here."

Mom suddenly squeaked with fear.

Jack whipped out his phone. "I need the CSU back down here at 1211 Magazine Street."

"What?" I followed his gaze to thirteen choppy letters carved into my beautiful wooden flooring, revealed by the now-upright bookcase.

You were warned.

Well, that wasn't going to buff out.

Chapter Sixteen

Furry Godmother's advice for your waistline:
Eat your feelings, not a pound cake.

Scarlet arrived on my doorstep approximately twenty minutes after her husband got home from work that evening. She brought homemade sugar cookies and a carton of my favorite ice cream. She was the best friend ever. The A-line on her vintage yellow sundress was working that baby bump like it was the summer's hottest fashion accessory. My cotton yoga shorts and alumni shirt were feeling a lot like jammies.

I peeled the top off the ice cream carton and loaded two mugs to the tops. "How was your day?"

She drew the outline of a fish on Buttercup's bowl with a red dry-erase marker, then kissed the glass. "Oh, it was *great*." Her facetious tone dripped from each word. "Someone broke into my pet shop on Magazine Street and destroyed everything." The sarcastic expression would've made me laugh, if she wasn't aiming the jibe at me. "I would've called, but I didn't want to bother you."

I waved a spoon between us. "Listen. You're right. I have no excuse for not calling."

"You'd be a terrible defense witness."

"I'm sorry. I really didn't want to bother you. That's true, and my head's spinning with all the nuts and crazy this week."

She dragged her mug across the counter and jammed a cookie into the moose tracks like a makeshift spoon. "I'm pregnant, not an invalid. Let me help you."

"Can you still sew? I need a dozen capelets, among other things, but the capelets are simple semicircles with satin lining and ties."

"Maybe," she hedged. "First, tell me about the investigation."

I stuffed a heaping helping of ice cream between my lips. The cool sweetness slid over my tongue in delicious perfection.

"Come on," she insisted. "We used to be partners in crime. I'm really good at puzzles. I know this town as well as you do. I'm an excellent resource. Ask me anything."

"How many little people are counting on you?"

She glared.

"I know you want to help, but if you start receiving threats on your life—or worse—because of me, I'd never forgive myself. Please don't put me in that position. It's scary enough thinking a lunatic might be stalking me. I can't have them stalking you, too."

She tapped her nails against the bowl. "I saw Detective Hottie outside. Is he stalking you?"

"No, but I see you've been talking to Paige."

"Maybe, but I'm also a woman with a pulse."

Jack had insisted on staking out my house again. He refused to come inside, and it was starting to get on my nerves.

I smiled over another spoonful of utter delight. "And a healthy libido, apparently. How many kids is this for you? Eight? Ten?"

"Shut up. Talk."

I laughed at the ridiculous orders. She joined me eventually.

I stretched a hand over hers and squeezed once. "I missed you."

Humor drained from her face. Fear crept into her eyes, and she turned her hands to squeeze mine. "Are you okay? Really?"

"I will be. I've got Buttercup to keep me company and enough work to keep my mind off whatever's happening until the killer's caught."

"What did they take last night? Maybe that will give us a clue about where they'll hit next."

I wiggled my hand free and nibbled the end of a cookie. "That's the weird thing. As far as I can tell, they didn't take anything, not even my cash register. They left a hate note, though. So I assume this is about me. I just don't know why."

"What else?"

"I saw Miguel's second girlfriend nearby today, so I asked about her at Frozen Banana. Sunshine said all the Barrel Room employees have a discount card. The clerk said she was a regular, but she wasn't around last night or five nights ago."

Scarlet tapped her spoon against the mug's rim. "How reliable is the clerk?"

I shook my head. I had no idea. How reliable was anyone?

We finished our desserts in companionable silence, but I could see Scarlet sorting the facts she had to work with. She'd looked just like that while plotting senior pranks and revenge on cheating boyfriends.

"So," she shimmied off her stool at the island and headed for my sink. "I called Sunshine."

"Yeah?" I met her at the sink and took her mug. "How is she?"

"She's terrified of being a single mom, but what can be done about that? When I heard about the break-in at Furry Godmother, I worried she might've changed her mind about you and gone berserk."

"Did she?"

"No. She's young and pregnant and scared. That's all she's thinking about right now."

I finished rinsing our empty mugs and wedged them into the dishwasher. "Were you able to help?"

"I think. We had a long talk. She feels terrible that all this is happening to you and that Miguel was somehow a part of it. She wondered if it had anything to do with his travels."

"Travels?"

"Mm-hmm. It seems Miguel made regular trips out of town."

I reminded myself to breathe. This could be the lead I needed. "Where?"

Scarlet shrugged. "I don't want to get involved," she deadpanned. "I'm pregnant. Which way to the sewing machine?"

The doorbell rang before I could strangle her.

I pointed at her as I ran past. "Stay here. If this isn't a murderer, you're going to tell me the rest of that story when I come back."

I skidded to a stop on socked feet and peeked out the side window. Jack wasn't in his truck. I crossed my fingers and whispered to my ceiling. "Please let the person on my porch be Jack and not a killer." Slowly, I inched the curtain back and checked the porch. "Uh-oh."

Scarlet cursed. "I'm not as fast as I was, and I'm too big to hide. Should I call nine-one-one?"

"Maybe." I opened the door. "Hello, fellas."

Chase and Jack stared down at me from their lofty heights, all squared shoulders and raised chins. They looked like three hundred and fifty pounds of testosterone ready to explode. Chase had a bottle of vintage red wine and a wide, blinding-white smile. Jack's tanned fists were firmly on his hips.

Jack angled his chin in Chase's direction. "Who's this guy?"

Chase's smile grew impossibly wider. He shifted the wine into his left hand and extended the right to Jack. "I'm a dear childhood friend of Lacy's."

Jack eyeballed Chase over a long, slow hand squeeze. "You have a date?" Shock and distaste soured Jack's tone.

Chase wiggled the wine. "She's off men, but we have plans to find the bottom of this bottle and catch up on old times. Whatever happens then is anyone's guess. How about you, champ? What are you doing here?"

"I'm Detective Oliver. I'm here on business."

Chase freed his hand from Jack's grasp and clapped him on the shoulder. "Good. No need for fisticuffs then." He breezed past me, dropping a good-natured kiss on my raging-hot cheek. "Sorry I'm late, sugar. You didn't forget about our date, did you?"

"Actually, yes." My eyes slid shut on autopilot. I counted to ten before reopening them to Jack.

Chase was in the kitchen, asking Scarlet about his nieces and nephews.

My attention was on the six-foot Y chromosome still rooted to my porch. "What?"

He rubbed the back of his neck. "I knew Scarlet was here, so I didn't think you were expecting a date. I didn't mean to make a scene."

"You didn't, and I'm not having a date. That's Chase, Scarlet's brother-in-law. He's not dangerous. He's all dental caps and self-importance." I flashed a toothy grin. "He told me we were having a date tonight, so he thinks we have a date tonight. That's how Hawthornes work."

Jack dropped his hand back to his side. "Chase Hawthorne." He barked a humorless laugh. "I thought he looked familiar when he kissed you. I saw something similar while I was home for spring break senior year. Last time, it was my girlfriend he was kissing, and it wasn't her cheek."

"Yikes."

"Yeah. Good times." His attention fell to his phone, buzzing in his pocket. He read something on the screen and looked past me to Chase with a grimace. "Don't let him leave until you see my truck outside again."

"Why? Where are you going? What did that text say?"

He jogged off my porch and across the lawn to his truck. Ten seconds later, he was nothing but taillights.

Didn't he know it was rude to ignore people? Especially terrified young women with pregnant guests?

I locked the door and considered installing a chain and security system. I could probably sell my eggs or plasma to foot the bill.

In the kitchen, Chase leaned over the island, mimicking a volleyball move. "And bam! He went down like a house of cards. One big heap on the sand. He had a bandage on his nose for the rest of the tournament like Marcia Brady when Greg hit her with a football."

Scarlet roared with laughter. She wiped tears and motioned me into my kitchen. "We used to watch those old-timey reruns with Imogene. Do you remember?"

Chase uncorked the wine and hoisted two glasses off the rack. "Imogene's your old nanny, right? She has crazy eyes and talks to herself?"

I smiled. "I don't think she has crazy eyes, but she does like to talk to herself."

He tipped his head back and laughed. "I was always afraid of her. How is she?" His butter-yellow button-down looked fantastic with his tan, accenting his unnaturally white teeth and making his impossibly green eyes greener.

I touched my glass to Chase's. "She's good. She came into my store today and told me I had bad juju, then whispered something into all the corners and shook a feathery doodad from her purse around the windows and doors."

Scarlet stretched her back. "She's right about the juju. Did she give you something for protection?"

"Like a handgun?"

Chase laughed. "No. Like a creepy dried-up alligator head from the bayou or a ragdoll with push pins that wards off evil or protects you from harmdoers."

"*Harmdoers* is not even a word. Imogene is a nice old lady, not a witch doctor."

He shook his smiling face. "Wrong. I bought a spell from her once when I got stoned and hit a guy's Aston Martin with my Segway. Worked like, well, I was going to say a charm." He frowned. "Magic doesn't sound right either, though both are correct."

"Did you hit your head in the accident?" I swirled the wine in my glass and pictured his stupidity. "You got high and took your Segway on a joyride?"

He rubbed his face. "I was young and stupid. I didn't want a DUI, but I wanted to go down the street to a big party, and I knew I couldn't walk that far."

"A DUI?"

"Turns out you can't drive a Segway under the influence and pot's illegal, so double trouble. Plus, the guy was totally unreasonable. He tried to sue my family for astronomical amounts of money in damages." He held up his pinky in promise. "I swear to you, I went to her just for help to stay out of jail. I paid her two hundred bucks for an other-lawyer-be-stupid spell, and it worked. That guy was a total moron. I'm surprised the Aston Martin owner didn't have to pay *me* for wasting my time in court that day when I could've been riding my sweet Segway."

Scarlet rubbed her belly through another round of laughter. "Other-lawyer-be-stupid. Oh, geez. I need to use your bathroom."

With Scarlet out of the way, Chase narrowed his eyes on me. "How are you holding up?"

"I'm okay. I got a fish." I pointed to Buttercup.

"If you need any help at the store, I can swing by tomorrow. I heard it was a real wreck."

I took a step back. "No. The Clean Team took care of it. They're like geriatric ninjas or really rich carnies. They came in like locusts and devoured the disaster. My door is fixed. The new security system is in place. I just have to finish the stock room inventory and it's back to work as usual."

He looked relieved not to have to help. "Was anything missing?"

"Nope."

"So what'd they want?"

How many times had I asked myself that question? "I have no idea. I also don't know why Miguel was there that night or why someone killed him. I don't know why I'm caught in the middle of whatever is happening, and," I lifted a finger, "I don't know what is happening."

Scarlet returned with a sigh. "Someone broke in to trash her place and left a threat on her life carved into her floor," she told Chase. "She's trying to find out who killed Miguel so Mr. Tater will continue to be her investor. Meanwhile, she's pissed off this nut job and he's coming at her every day. Earlier this week he stabbed her car. I think she should stay with her folks until Jack catches this guy."

Chase gave me a strange look. "They stabbed your car?"

"My tire. She exaggerates."

"Which is why Detective Oliver is staking out her house right now."

Chase's face lit up, and he snapped his fingers. "Jack Oliver! I knew that guy looked familiar. Where is he?" He craned his neck down the hallway, as if just noticing Jack hadn't followed him inside.

"He got a text and left. He asked me to keep you here until he gets back. He plans to sit out front and catch whoever's after me."

Chase refilled our glasses. The bottle was looking emptier by the pour. "I'd go on a wine run, but I forgot my Segway."

Scarlet helped herself to a big glass of ice water. "I'd go for you, but I'm too jealous to watch you have any more."

I took her water away. "I haven't forgotten you have information I need."

She beamed. "I do? How is that possible?" She flipped her rosy curls. "Here's a hint: it's because I'm useful and really good at this."

I returned her water. "Fine. Spill."

She wiggled into a comfortable position on the stool and put on her best campfire face. "Sunshine says Miguel would disappear for a couple days at a time. Some weeks he was off the grid more than he was around, but he'd never give her details, and he forbade her from asking any questions. She assumed he was cheating, so she started checking his cell phone for hotel reservations, anything shady like that. She discovered he was out of town all those days. He'd visit different cities within a day's drive. Travel all day there and all day back."

I finished my wine and refilled the glass. This was getting good. "What was he doing?"

Scarlet lost steam. "She doesn't know."

I slapped the countertop. "Well, that was a horrible story."

"You're welcome."

Pete's ringtone burst from my phone. I lifted a finger to my guests and braced myself for whatever Pete wanted this time. "Hello?"

"Hey, beautiful, how's it going?" His tinny voice echoed through the phone at my ear.

Chase snorted. Scarlet frowned.

I stepped away. "Have you made your travel plans? When will you be here?"

"I'm looking into the details. To be honest, this is going to be a more expensive trip than I'd expected."

I ground my teeth. "Then don't come. I'll buy Penelope a ticket if you'll get her to the plane."

He huffed. "Our agreement was that I see you."

"You just said it was too expensive." Pressure built in my chest. He was backing out. *I knew he'd do this. I knew not to trust him. I knew it, I knew it, I knew it.* I slid my eyes shut to force back the crushing disappointment.

A broad hand landed on my shoulder. Chase pulled me against his chest. Scarlet gripped my free hand.

"You could come to Virginia," Pete said. Likely that was his plan all along. Get me alone and try to keep me, using Penelope as leverage.

"No." Scarlet and Chase spoke in unison.

"Who was that?" Pete barked. "Are you on another date or is that the same guy from before? You've been gone for four months and you can't spend one evening alone?" He breathed heavy into the phone. "You know what? Forget it. You're clearly too busy for Penelope." He disconnected.

Chase gave me a quick squeeze and stepped away, leaning one lean hip against the counter. His bright-green eyes were shining with wine and fascination. "Wow. That was your fiancé? You've got really bad taste in men."

"He's my *ex*-fiancé, and I hate him." I swiped tears. "He's a liar who screwed everything up and stole my cat. He knew I was leaving, and he took her somewhere on the morning I needed to leave for the airport."

Chase shrugged. "I'll get your cat back."

"What?" I froze, tissue pressed to my cheek. "How?"

"Don't worry about it. No one will find Pete when I'm done."

My heart stopped.

"I'm kidding!" He laughed loudly. "You should see your face right now. It's priceless." He pulled his phone from his pocket and pointed it at me.

I whacked it away. "Don't take my picture. That wasn't funny. Tell me about getting Penelope back."

His smile turned ornery and his eyes darkened. "I will trade a tersely worded letter from my prestigious New Orleans law firm for a kiss from you."

"Ooo," Scarlet cooed. "This is getting interesting."

"No." I shook a finger at her. "No, it's not." I turned to Chase. "You don't have a law firm. You dropped out of law school."

"No, I didn't." Chase smiled. "I finished law school. That was the deal I made with my old man. If I finished law school, I could do anything I wanted. I finished tenth in my class, and I didn't want to practice law, so I didn't. I wanted to make my college volleyball career a professional one."

"So you know what you're doing?" I couldn't stop the smile spreading over my face. "If Pete looks you up online, he'll find your family practice." I puckered up.

Chase pressed a finger to my lips. "Uh-uh. That doesn't count. You have to want to kiss me, and it can't be the kind of kiss you give your mother."

I pulled my face away from his hand and ignored the silly pinch of rejection. "You kiss your mother?"

He swigged the dregs of his wine and stared into the empty glass. "No, but when you're ready, I'm going to kiss you, and you're going to enjoy it."

Oh, boy! I turned to Scarlet, hoping the heat racing up my throat and through my chest wasn't visible.

She looked past me to her brother-in-law. "Do you write bogus legal letters often, or did this idea just pop into your head?"

He refilled his glass and added more wine to mine. "I had a lucrative practice in college. All anonymous, of course. I'd write the letter on official-looking letterhead and leave it at the drop. Swing by later and collect the cash."

"The drop?" I asked. An idea scratched the corners of my mind. "Do you mean a drop location? Like in spy movies?"

He straddled the stool beside me at the island. "Mm-hmm. It was all very James Bond. Are you impressed?"

I scooted closer, matching his body language. "What if my store was a drop location? I've gone over everything in the studio and at least half of the stockroom. Nothing was taken, but everything was overturned. What if the burglar was looking for something left behind by Miguel?"

"Clever." Chase tapped the end of my nose. "But what?"

* * *

Jack's truck was gone when I got out of the shower in the morning, so I drank both cups of coffee and hit the road, too eager to sit around waiting for daylight. I passed overeager joggers and pajama-clad dog walkers in droves. Chase had set my mind in motion with that whole drop location concept. What if there was something hidden in my overturned stock?

I arrived at Furry Godmother in time to enjoy the sunrise. I locked up behind myself and set the alarm, then scurried to the stockroom to finish what I'd started.

By eight, the excitement had worn off and I had sequins embedded beneath my fingernails. "Ugh." I pried my body off the floor and shook half a pound of sparkles and miniscule embellishments from my clothes and skin. I hefted the final box of miscellaneous onto my desk and cracked my back. Sitting on the floor was for toddlers and Miss Molly.

My toe caught on something that skittered across the floor. "What the heck?" I fetched the small tool with care, turning it in my hands, trying to remember what it was for. The smooth, wooden handle was stumpy but easy to grip. The short, pointy metal protruding from the handle was completely unfamiliar. "What are you used for?"

I checked my toolboxes of craft supplies. Nothing in my collections had a similar handle, so it wasn't part of a set. I dropped into my desk chair and went online to find out what it was and which box to store it inside.

After a few misses, I landed on an image of the exact thing I held in my hand. A jewelry burnisher. I jumped up and paced the room. Maybe this was the thing the burglar had been looking for? Or maybe he'd dropped it while he was destroying my stock. Maybe it was evidence from one of the heists. Gooseflesh rose up my arms to my neck.

I zoomed through the storeroom toward the front register and dialed the cell number on Jack's business card. I took a plastic bag from behind the counter to keep the burnisher safe.

No answer.

"Come on." I dialed the office number next.

An unfamiliar voice picked up Jack's desk phone at the station. "Detective Ansel."

"Hi. I'm calling for Detective Oliver." I grabbed my purse and keys, prepared to meet Jack anywhere he wanted.

"Detective Oliver comes in at ten. Can I help you?" The scratchy no-nonsense in his voice said everything. I was wasting his time.

"Did you say Jack's still at home?"

The detective huffed into the receiver. "I don't know, lady. Do you need actual police help or is this something personal?"

My gaze caught on the angry message carved into my floorboards. I gave the burnisher a hard look and disconnected with Detective Ansel. Then I moved slowly toward the threat on my floor and lowered the metal point of the burnisher into one of the perfect-fitting grooves.

Chapter Seventeen

Furry Godmother's advice on aging: Never mention it.

I motored over to the Grandpa Smacker estate on Sixth Street, keeping a close watch on my rearview mirror as I rolled through stop signs with reckless abandon. Someone had used the jewelry burnisher, currently riding shotgun, to carve into my floorboards. There could be prints, besides mine, that would lead us to whoever was threatening me. Maybe even Miguel's killer.

I swallowed and pushed the images of the deep scratches from my mind. If the burnisher could do that much damage to finished wood, what could it have done to me?

I slid my car against the curb outside the Smacker place and checked my surroundings. No one was on the street in either direction. An eerie calm blanketed the neighborhood. Ancient sprawling oaks formed a canopy overhead, dripping moss in tiny veils and filtering the morning sunlight into dancing patterns on the road and walkways.

I rubbed sweat-slicked palms over my thighs and steadied my breath. Mom's voice echoed in my head. *Never arrive unannounced.* I'd called and Jack hadn't answered. This had to qualify as a "desperate times" situation. *Never visit for the first time without a gift.* I grabbed the baggie off my passenger seat. A clue in Jack's open investigation seemed like a solid gift. I dialed his cell phone again on my way to the door.

He answered on the first ring. "Oliver."

"Good morning. This is Lacy." Hands full, I shoved my hip against the intricate, wrought iron gate protecting his property. It swung open with a groan. I checked the street once more before dashing up the walk to his front door.

"What's wrong?"

"How do you know something's wrong?"

I stopped short of knocking. Holy Chihuahua! His estate was enormous, far bigger than it looked from the street. I tipped my head to examine the massive columns supporting galleries overhead. My entire house could fit on his porch.

The door sucked open. Jack squinted at me. His hair was wet and pointing in every direction. His basketball shorts and bare feet made him look ten years younger. The sight of his bare chest made me *feel* ten years younger.

A gray-muzzled cat wound around his ankles, purring loudly.

I disconnected our call. "Good morning."

"Why are you here?" Jack stepped aside.

I crouched to rub the cat behind her ears. She was a beautiful Snowshoe Siamese, and the natural markings of her fur made her a dead ringer for the grouchy cat everyone loved online. Jezebel was actually kind of a hilarious name. "Mom told me she was a sweet cat. She was right." I loved Jezebel. She flopped onto one side and lifted her head. Her paw reached to me, pleading for more. "So you are a cat person," I mused.

"Come in."

I hurried inside, unimpressed by his lack of enthusiasm. "They say people start to look like their pets."

Jack leaned against the open door. "Why are you here?"

"I called before I came, but there was no answer."

"I was in the shower."

In the shower? Now there was an image. "I assumed you were at the range shooting something and couldn't hear your phone or you were ignoring me." I handed him the bag. "I couldn't wait, so I brought you something."

I waited for a thank-you.

He shut the door. "What is it?"

"It's a jewelry burnisher. It fits into the letters on my studio floor perfectly. I found it among the boxes in my stockroom."

Jack searched me with his gaze. "You want coffee?" He didn't wait for an answer.

He padded through his house, and I followed, gawking and ogling his magnificent home. No signs of Tabitha, the banana bread maker, or any woman for that matter. Jezebel passed us on silent feet. She stopped in the kitchen and shoved her face into a water bowl with a fountain feature and paw prints painted on the side.

I slowed a few feet shy of the grand center island to take it in.

The high-polished wood we'd traveled on abruptly gave way to miles of mosaic tile flooring. "This is your kitchen?" I raised my arms in reverence. "Are you kidding me?" I fought the urge to twirl like Julie Andrews in *The Sound of Music*. "Do you know how many pawlines I could crank out in this place?"

I pressed a palm to my heart. "You're a cat person who has a gourmet kitchen."

"Impressed?" His frown deepened.

"Your hospitality could use a little help, but I do like the cat and kitchen."

A delicate scrolling letter *S* was embossed in the endless copper backsplash. *S* for Smacker. "I keep forgetting Grandpa Smacker was your *actual* grandpa. No wonder he had an amazing kitchen like this."

Jack poured two cups of coffee. One chipped, ceramic NOLA PD mug and one go cup. "He loved to bake. I didn't realize you knew."

"Hard to keep secrets around here. Probably makes your job easier."

"You'd think."

I climbed into a luxurious, high-backed barstool at the massive island and sighed. "I'm sorry about your loss."

He gave one stiff nod. "He was a good man."

"How long have you been here? Is it lonely?"

"I've been home almost three years. Grandpa passed last fall, and I moved in here. Jezebel keeps me company."

Yeah, her and the horde of casserole ladies with their ovaries.

I pulled his open laptop toward me. "Do you mind?"

"I'm still trying to decide why I let you in." He lumbered around the island and leaned over my shoulder.

"You're a riot in the mornings. Ever try stand-up?" I feigned bravery as I searched the web for jewelry burnishers. "I brought you another clue for your case. See, this is a jeweler's tool. I bet it's evidence from one of the local heists."

Jack straightened. "You know how to leave messages, right?"

I spun the big stool in his direction, and he jumped clear. "What?"

"You didn't have to drive over and ring the bell. You could've left a message or gone to the station. I'm going to work in an hour."

I dropped my jaw. "You're not going in until ten. I talked to someone over there. Plus, it's not like you go there and stay for any amount of time."

He grinned. "Anything you don't know about me?"

"Yes." I dragged the word out several syllables. "I have more questions by the minute, like why aren't you more upset about this burnisher?"

Jack rubbed one eyebrow with his fingertips. "I have a level head."

"Also, no one threatened *you* with it. Can you get prints and arrest someone?"

He tipped his coffee mug toward the front of the house. "I'll see what I can do. Thank you for the evidence. I'm glad you're okay." He took a step in the direction from which we'd come. "Consider staying with your parents a few days while I wrap things up. Let me walk you to the door."

I scoffed. Humility burned my cheeks. "Wait! I know something else."

He lifted and dropped an arm at his side. "Go on."

"Miguel made a lot of overnight trips to cities within a day's drive."

Jack crossed his arms and managed to look irritated at *me*.

"You know, I keep delivering more intel and you keep looking like that."

"Where did he go?"

"I don't know."

He widened his stance. "What was he doing?"

"I don't know." I tapped my fingers on the keyboard. The proverbial light bulb flickered on in my cluttered head. "Is there a law enforcement database you can search for jewelry store heists within a day's drive of here? Maybe I can cross-reference with Sunshine and see if she remembers any specific dates or the cities where Miguel visited, and you can see if there were any break-ins there while he was in town."

"Move over." Jack squeezed between the next stool and me. He typed onto the keyboard, and a printer buzzed to life somewhere in the cavernous home.

"That was fast," I muttered. "Did you already have a list?"

He ignored me and headed down a wide arching hall beyond the kitchen.

Jezebel sniffed my legs and dripped water from her mouth onto my shoes, the floor, and herself.

"What'd you do? Stick your head in the fountain?"

I texted Scarlet.

"Who are you texting?" Jack's voice nearly sent me onto the ceiling. Sadly, he pulled a T-shirt over his head as he walked.

"Scarlet. She's the one who learned about Miguel's travels. I'm asking her to ask Sunshine if she can remember any specific dates or cities Miguel visited."

He groaned long and loud. "When did my murder investigation become a girlfriends' game of telephone? You know how that game ends, right? With a big load of mashed-up details that sound nothing like the original message."

I hopped off the stool. "You're right. I should go straight to the source."

"Stop." Before I could see myself out, his strong fingers snared my forearm. "I will talk to Sunshine. You will find a vault somewhere and lock yourself inside until I finish this."

"Can't I come with you?"

"No."

"Why?" I loathed the hint of whine and desperation in my voice. Sure, he was the cop, but wasn't I the one with all the information? "You wouldn't be talking to her again if I hadn't told you about Miguel traveling."

"Listen, kitten, you're finished here. Hit the road. Take a vacation. I don't care how you do it, but stay out of my way, or I'll make that phone call to your mother. I was joking before, but now I'm wondering if she can shake some sense into you."

I glared. "Do not call my mother."

"Hey, I don't want to be a drag on your good time playing cop, but someone has made multiple threats on your life. Go home and knock it off or I'm turning you over to your mama."

"Keep it up with that attitude and I won't share any new information with you."

A vein pulsed near his temple.

I scooped my go cup of coffee off the island and took the hint. "Tell Sunshine I said hello. I'm thinking of having lunch at the Barrel Room later, so I'll probably see her." I backtracked to the front door with Jezebel at my feet and Jack bringing up the rear. "Have a nice day at work."

"Go to your parents' house." He shut the door before I made it off his porch.

Men.

* * *

I spent the afternoon locked in my storeroom sewing tutus and leg warmers. Every time someone tugged on the front door (which was clearly marked "Closed"), it gave me enough adrenaline to run a marathon.

My nerves were strung tighter than ever, and there wasn't enough comfort food even in New Orleans to help me. When I'd gone into the front looking for a measuring tape, the mailman had dropped letters through the mail slot, and I nearly had a coronary. One of the letters was from Mr. Tater. Inside was the bill for my lease payment and paperwork to reroute the bill permanently to my store. I had nine days left to get answers or make the payment myself. Both options seemed fairly unrealistic.

I shook the daylights out of the mail before throwing it onto my desk in the stockroom and diving headlong into my work. I'd considered working from home after the mailman scare, but the scene of the crime felt safer. If lightning wouldn't strike twice, maybe criminals wouldn't either. It didn't hurt that my crime scene was newly equipped with an alarm system, and every restaurant on the street delivered.

I poured my raging emotions into the work. Every stitch was carefully made and tested for quality. Every custom-ordered dose of show-stopping shazam was performed with a smile and prayers for the animal who would wear it. All I thought about for hours was the work. Until I ran out.

A closed shop and a boatload of energy had wiped my overflowing to-do list clean. No new orders had come in since the original wave of Mable Feller's magic wand. All I had left to occupy my mind was a set of undecorated chicken pianos, delivered by my dad. Even the kitten capelets were down to minor touch-ups and a few errant rhinestone reattachments.

I folded leg warmers into sleeves of tissue paper and fought the return of endless questions I had no answers to. I packed the leg warmers carefully into a box for Mrs. Hams and hung Mrs. Neidermeyer's tutus from hangers on my pint-sized rolling rack.

I didn't want to call Mom about the pianos yet. *What else could I do before dinner?*

I extracted a pile of thank-you cards from my drawer and addressed them to each member of the Clean Team. There weren't strong enough words to express the appreciation I had for each of them and their unconscionable efforts. Emotion crept into my throat as the stress of the past few days rushed over me.

The desk phone rang, and I crossed my fingers for a megamoney work order that would cover my lease payment. "Furry Godmother, where every pet is royalty. Lacy speaking."

"Lacy Crocker? This is Damon Foster from Central Business Bank."

I perked and engaged my most entrepreneurial voice. "Yes. Thank you so much for returning my call, Mr. Foster. How are you?"

"I'm good. Thank you for asking."

I smashed my eyes closed and crossed my fingers. "Do you need any additional information about my small business loan? I have copies of everything here. Financials. Testimonials. References. I can e-mail them to you."

"No. Your business plan was thoughtful, well-researched, and professionally documented, Miss Crocker. We rarely see work of this caliber from our applicants. Unfortunately, we can't approve you at this time. Perhaps there's someone you could ask to cosign?"

I opened my eyes and pasted an inauthentic smile on my lips, even though he couldn't see it. "I'm sorry, but no. I don't have a cosigner, but thank you for the call."

I returned the receiver to its cradle and rested my forehead on the desk. *There's always another way.*

I sat up tall. Yes, there was another way, and I knew where to find it.

* * *

I arrived at the Barrel Room in time for the dinner rush and took a seat at the bar. Sunshine zipped around the bar, mixing drinks and wiping spills with agility and precision. If she'd tossed bottles in the air like Tom Cruise, I wouldn't have been surprised. She was lithe, cheerful, and impressive. No one would suspect the amount of weight on her poor grieving shoulders.

When she spotted me, her smile fell. "Hey."

"Hi. Can I order the grilled chicken salad, a bowl of fruit, and a glass of ice water for here?"

"Sure. Anything else?" She wrote the order on a little green-striped notepad. "I get bonuses for selling house wine." She tipped her mouth into an ornery smile. "I'm teasing."

"Lucky for you, my book club loves wine. I'll take a bottle of the Pinot Grigio to go."

She lowered her pen, looking a little bewildered. "I wasn't serious."

"And I don't have a book club, but I'll still take the wine if it helps you. I'm sure I can find someone to help me drink it." Chase and his promise came to mind.

She nodded silently and disappeared into the kitchen. She returned with a bottle of wine and a slip from her notepad. "Your dinner will be right out. This is for you."

I examined the paper. Names of cities and random numbers. "Dates and locations."

She piled dirty glasses onto trays. "Yep. Scarlet called."

The smile sliding across my lips stretched my face until it hurt. "I came to ask you about these. I forgot to text Scarlet back and tell her not to contact you. I wasn't sure you'd remember anything specific. This is amazing. You have no idea how much this helps or how much I needed it right now."

"Funny," she said. "That's exactly what I told Scarlet the first time she called me. Thank you. Both of you."

"You're welcome." I logged into the free Barrel Room Wi-Fi and searched for recent jewelry heists, then reduced the hits by adding a timeframe starting six months back.

Sunshine settled a plate and bowl beside my list. "Enjoy."

The salad looked like heaven. I speared a fresh slice of cucumber, then scrolled through the articles. I worked methodically through my salad and search results until the bottom of my bowl came into view.

"Lacy?" Mr. Tater smiled from a few feet away. "I thought that was you. I didn't want to interrupt." He gave my phone a meaningful glance.

"You're not interrupting. Why don't you join me?" I turned my phone over and wiped my mouth with a soft linen napkin.

"I can't. I only have a minute, but I wanted to say hello."

"Well, it's nice to see you. I'm swamped at the shop." I drew out the word *swamped*, hoping he'd hear money and come back to me.

"Did you get the letter about your lease? I sent it a few days ago. I've been meaning to call and ask."

"Yep."

"Good. How are things?"

"Everything's great. I'm very busy. The alarm was installed right on time. Nothing was taken during the break-in." Not that he'd bothered to ask. "I'm making strong progress on our agreement from earlier. You remember?"

"Of course." Distraction changed his features and he looked away. "It looks like Mr. Fraser from Harrah's has arrived. Time to seal the deal and bring the Barrel Room label into the casino. Take care of yourself, Lacy." He patted my shoulder and left to schmooze Mr. Fraser.

Way to make a girl feel second class. I turned back to my phone. Why had I ever worked with him? Oh, yeah. I was broke.

According to Sunshine's list, Miguel had been to five cities in the last three months: Gulf Port, Mississippi; Fairhope, Alabama; Pensacola Island, Florida; Galveston, Texas; and

Memphis, Tennessee. I sipped my ice water as I checked the local papers in each town for references to a jewelry store break-in. Gulfport papers made no mention of a jewel heist. I went back another six months just in case I'd made the parameters too small. Nothing. Fairhope results came back the same way. No jewel heists. Maybe he had to case the places first? Maybe some stores were too fortified to take the risk?

I thumbed through the next round of search results and clicked on one that looked promising. The Pensacola Island search came back with two jewelry store hits in one weekend. I sent the links to my e-mail and tried Galveston. Another heist on the day Sunshine reported Miguel as being in town. I searched through the Memphis papers. Bingo again! Maybe it was sheer coincidence, but it looked a lot like a pattern.

Miguel took a road trip, and the destination town lost some diamonds.

I grabbed my new bottle of wine and ordered chocolate cheesecake to go. This girl was on a roll.

Chapter Eighteen

Furry Godmother's business tip: Without proper marketing, zealous admiration is just stalking.

I headed to my parents' house on the way home. I needed to review ideas for the Jazzy Chicks' pianos with Mom and brag to Dad about the connection I'd made between Miguel and the other jewelry heist locations. He would know what to do with the information.

I slowed at the end of their block. I'd completely forgotten that tonight was Mom's benefit dinner. Twinkle lights lined the wrought iron fence around their property. Lanterns hung from the reaching limbs of the ancient oak. Spotlights illuminated the master craftsmanship of their home's nineteenth-century architect. Neighbors were walking the path to the front door wearing Armani and thousand-watt smiles.

As much as I wanted to find exasperation with the fact Mom was on her second dinner party this week while I was on my second death threat, I couldn't. A flutter of nostalgia wiggled in me. In high school, Scarlet and I would steal abandoned champagne flutes at these events and pour them into sports bottles until we'd accumulated enough to have a party of our own. We'd climb to the widow's walk and talk about boys and the future. Mostly boys.

I rolled closer, feeling the urge to peek inside.

A man in an emerald vest smiled and waved from his position behind a portable stand at the drive's end. He jogged into the street and waved through my closed passenger window.

I powered the barrier down and weighed the merits of jumping a side road home to watch Netflix with Buttercup.

"Are you attending the Crocker dinner?"

I gave the twinkling house a long look. *Nostalgia or microwave popcorn and seven seasons of* Gilmore Girls*?* "Yeah. I think so."

"Great! May I see your invitation? I'll get you a ticket and take your car."

"I don't have my invitation." I scanned the street, rehashing my options. This was my last chance to drive away. Acceptance pulled my shoulders away from my ears. I was already at the party. I might as well say hello. I shifted into park and freed the driver's license from my wallet. "I'm on the list. Probably at the top."

He looked at the identification and passed it back. "Of course, Miss Crocker."

He rounded my hood while I prepared mentally for whatever awaited me. My mind had a habit of jumping to the worst possible conclusions and absolute ugliest scenarios. *Everyone will stare and whisper.* They had to wonder by now how I was involved with a murder and a break-in. I'd been listed on more police reports this week than I'd thought was humanly possible.

I'd use the back door and ease into the party. It'd been a long time since I'd attended one of Mom's dinners. Party situations were tough enough when I lived here. Now that I was grown and involved in a murder, the experience would probably be worse.

Unless I was wrong and everyone would be thrilled to see me. After all, meeting a single thirty-year-old woman in high society was like finding a unicorn. I'd be the belle of the ball. Mothers would drag their newly divorced or obviously gay sons to my feet, listing their grand attributes and smoothing their hair for them.

Soft music drifted from the kitchen on the clang of glass and dishes. I opened the door and slid into the steamy room.

"Oh!" A woman in a gray pantsuit jumped to attention. "Guests enter through the front. This is the service door."

I dodged her attempt to capture me before I could move farther into the house. "I'm Lacy Crocker."

She gave me another look. "Lacy?"

"Yep." I lifted my palms hip-high.

She raised her arms, like security gates, and corralled me toward the rear staircase. "You need to change. Go this way so your mother doesn't see you, and make a proper entrance via the grand staircase in the foyer." She gave the French pronunciation: *foy-ay*.

I did a slow blink and took the first step.

Maybe coming inside was stupid. I'd already eaten. I couldn't talk to Mom about the pianos in the middle of a party, and upon second thought, Dad might not be as enthusiastic as I was about the jewelry heist link I'd found. He seemed to side with Jack on the topic of me leaving this alone.

"Go on," the lady shooed.

The narrow passage was lined in wainscoting and had made the perfect escape route for a rebellious teenage girl. I opened the door to my old bedroom. Everything was exactly as I'd left it ten years before. Every blue ribbon, book, and stitch of clothing was precisely where I'd left it, though someone had obviously kept up the dusting.

When I turned sixteen, Mom hired an interior designer, and I'd spent months with her designing and outfitting my room with the perfect color scheme and accessories for my life. We'd trimmed pale-blue walls in white woodwork, and I'd chosen accents in various shades of silver or gray. Glass jewels dripped from the chandelier and lampshades. I used to imagine they were diamonds and I was the queen of a kingdom. The down comforter on my bed was as puffy and inviting as any cloud in heaven. My exhausted body begged to sink into it and sleep forever.

Across the room, an overflowing pair of bookshelves spilled their treasures onto the floor and every flat surface a book could call home. A pile of paperback copies of *Wuthering Heights* anchored my closet. I still bought a new copy whenever I saw one with a cover I didn't already own.

Someone rapped on the wall inside my open door. "Lacy?"

I turned to greet the voice I heard in my sleep most nights. "Hi, Mom."

"What are you doing here?" Her simple black dress was perfection with Grandmother's striking white pearls. Her hair was pulled into an elegant chignon. Her shoes and nails were understated but noticeable. She was one hundred percent casual elegance. "Are you alone?"

"Yes."

"Is everything okay? Are you hurt?"

"No."

She wrinkled her nose and stepped back. "Are you ill? Are you contagious?" She turned in a helpless circle, proving I got my conclusion-jumping skills honestly. "I have fifty guests who will blame my cooking if they leave here sick."

"You have a caterer."

"And?"

I shook my head. "Never mind. I'm not sick or hurt. I just came to talk to you about the Chicks, but then I saw the party and thought you'd like me to stay."

She lifted her eyebrows into her bangs. "You're staying?"

"If my invitation's still good. I left it at home. I had to dodge security."

Her smile came and went in a heartbeat. "You need to change."

"Of course." When I'd left home this morning, I'd planned to spend the day sorting the Furry Godmother stockroom. My white tennis shoes and T-shirt weren't exactly party ready for this crowd.

"I have a rack of LBDs in my room. That's pop culture speak for little black dresses."

"Thanks, I know." I stifled an eye roll. "I'll take a look."

She wrung her hands together. "You can stay as long as you like, you know. If you want." She motioned to the bed. "I haven't touched a thing in here since you left. It's still your room. Always."

"Thanks."

"Jack thinks you'd be safer here than at your place."

I once again fought an eye roll. "I'm fine."

"Don't do that," she snapped. "Don't say you're fine as if I'm worrying about nonsense." Lines raced over her forehead and gathered between her brows. "You're my daughter. My only daughter and my whole world." She cleared her throat. "I won't have you dead." Her eyes were glossy, but her attitude was as firm as ever. "That's an order."

"Yes, ma'am."

"Now change. I'll make you a plate and find a way to keep the desperate men at bay."

"Thanks."

She nodded and turned away. "I can make no promises if I see a solid catch."

"Deal." I followed her into the hallway. "That was funny, Mom. When did you get to be funny?"

"Where do you think you get your sense of humor?" Her eyes twinkled. "Certainly not your father. I'm the personality on this cruise."

"If this week has been a cruise, it was the *Titanic*."

She turned for a trip down the grand staircase. "You see? We're comedy gold."

"I'll be down in a few minutes."

She adjusted her hair and dress. "Maybe this is my lucky night and your father will come in from the office where he's monitoring a patient." She used finger quotes around the last three words. "He doesn't think I know he drinks brandy in there and watches sports."

"Men, right?"

She took the first step and looked at me over one shoulder. "Like you would know. Zing!"

I turned the spotless glass knob on her bedroom door and inhaled thick scents of makeup and Chanel No. 5. The master bedroom was layered with cast-off dresses. The plush carpet was speckled with shoes that didn't make tonight's cut. I opened her closet and walked in. Motion sensor lights lit my path. The rack of black dresses was in the back, near her dressing table, where a collage of photographs had nearly overtaken the mirror. All shots of me, from pageants to proms, graduation to college.

I thumbed through the rack and chose the dress I thought she would've picked for me. It was an elegant, knee-length number covered in a layer of Chantilly lace that formed a modest scoop neckline. Little satin buttons hid the zipper in the back, and a wide, matching ribbon formed a belt around my center. The dress was a little loose in the hips, though not as much as I would have liked. I smoothed my hair into a low ponytail and borrowed some earrings. Simple. Classic. Not bad for a girl who spent the day sorting stock. One pair of black slingbacks later and I was on the grand staircase, pretending I'd been there all along.

Mom met me at the bottom with a warm smile and a plate of hors d'oeuvres. "I'm so glad Jack came. He always draws a crowd."

I accepted the plate from her.

He was easy to spot. Handsome, brooding, and several inches taller than the throng of women surrounding him. My heart did a dumb flutter. "He's stalking me."

"That would be difficult, since he arrived first. And from the looks of your previous outfit, you made a last-minute decision to come here, probably while driving by."

What was she? A psychic?

"I've arranged the cover story, as promised, to avoid any unwanted advances from male suitors tonight." A sly smile reached her eyes. "I'm spreading the word that you're dating."

"Oh?" I stole another look at Jack in his timeless black jacket and slacks.

This time he lifted his glass in response.

"Isn't that clever?" Mom said.

I didn't hate the idea, but he had been a little short with me this morning. He probably needed to apologize.

Mom's smile grew. "Here's your boyfriend now."

I turned to see who she was referring to. Jack hadn't taken a step away from his position across the room.

Chase materialized from a crowd of similarly dressed men in khaki pants, white dress shirts, and brown shoes.

Mom stage winked. "You two make such a lovely couple."

He squeezed her to his side. "What can I say? I'm a lucky fellow."

"You two have fun." She patted his cheek and slipped away.

My "boyfriend" wiggled his eyebrows.

I shook my head slowly. "All these men and Mom chose you as my love interest?"

He furrowed his brows. "I'm not sure how to take that."

I sampled a cheese chunk from my plate. "It's not you. It's her. I assumed she'd pick an overachieving, work-obsessed show-off with a high personal station and coffers of money."

"Maybe she picked the guy she thought you'd have the most fun with."

"I don't know. That doesn't sound like her."

Mom worked the room, looking for me every few minutes and smiling as if we shared the most delicious secret. I'd never been in on something with her. It was kind of fun.

Chase nudged me with an elbow and took my plate. He set it aside and wrapped my hand around his elbow. "Shall we?"

I stood taller. "Let's."

We made a slow but appropriately cordial circuit through the room, greeting guests and listening to fuddy-duddy rants on local politics. I found my people quickly. They were buzzing with enthusiasm for the upcoming Animal Elegance gala. They knew the keynote speaker and the menu. They recognized me right away and drew me in with questions on my time in Virginia, my fashion degree, and finding the right pet ensemble for any occasion.

Mrs. Neidermeyer arrived on the arm of a man half her age. She dismissed him with a kiss and drifted into our circle with dramatic flair. "Ladies." She looked me over, taking care to examine Chase as well. She took a seat on the Queen Anne chair across from me and crossed her legs to reveal the telltale red soles of her Christian Louboutins. "Has Lacy told you all about the fabulous ensembles she's creating for my girls?"

The little crowd lit up. Their eyes went wide at the possible scandal.

Nerves pricked the back of my neck. "I've spoken with Mrs. Feller. She's okay with the change, and she was really pleased with the work I did for her babies."

The women exchanged mildly disappointed smiles.

Mrs. Neidermeyer fluffed the layers of her chiffon gown around her calves. Her gaze fell to Chase's hand on mine. "When did this begin?"

The group fell silent. People on the fringe seemed to lean in closer.

"It's very recent," I stammered.

"For you," he said smoothly. "For me, this has been a lifetime in the making."

One woman covered her heart with both hands. A pair of eavesdropping college girls frowned and left the vicinity. The other women in our circle traded looks.

I nudged Chase. "Well, we should see if my mom needs anything."

"Anything you want," he agreed.

I led him away from the circle. "I can feel eyes burning holes in our backs," I whispered as we made our way through the crowded room.

Chase lifted my hand to his lips and murmured quietly. "Did we greet everyone?"

"I think so." The only person we'd missed was Jack, and I hadn't *missed* him as much as *outright avoided* him.

"Then our work here is done."

Voodoo darted through the room and up the steps on silent feet. She stopped several feet up and peered through a set of wide cherry balusters.

Chase stared. "Is that your cat?"

"Yeah."

"Voodoo, right?"

"Yep."

He rubbed his forehead. "I think I remember her from high school. Is that possible? She's got to be the oldest cat in the world."

I laughed.

"I'm serious," he said. "Your dad's either a really good vet or a magician."

"A little of both, I think." I tugged his hand. "Thanks for being my boyfriend for a night."

"The night's not over. How are you feeling?"

I smiled. "Good."

"Let's go somewhere quiet, eat sugar, and reward ourselves for not leaving sooner."

"I like how you think, Hawthorne."

He scooted into my personal space and dropped his lips to my ear. "Did you find any more pieces to that puzzle we talked about last night?"

"Actually, yes, thanks to you. Do you want to hear?"

"Absolutely." He looked over his shoulders. "Have you told Scarlet yet?"

"Yes, this morning."

He groaned. "I like to get things over on her, but she's got the red line to this town, I swear. The only person who manages to hear things before her is my brother, but being everyone's favorite attorney helps in that area. I don't know how she gets the scoop on anything while she's home with three kids." He hooked his arm with mine and swiped a plate of petit fours and lemon tassies off the buffet.

"She's got that face. It's all those freckles. People want to tell her things."

He added one more tassie to his pile. "It's all about the freckles."

I sniped an unopened bottle of champagne from an ice bucket. "Ever seen my widow's walk?"

He tapped his plate of sweets to my bottle. "Not personally, but I'm sure it's fantastic."

I led him to the stairs. "Oh, it's fabulous."

We climbed onto the railed rooftop platform and settled onto Mom's designer chaises. The space was narrow but cozy and lined with plants and solar lights. Warm winds tussled our hair. I set the bottle on a little stand and pulled my feet onto the cushion beside me.

"So," he prompted, "tell me about your investigation."

"Well, I've obsessively rehashed every detail of my awful week and come to one conclusion."

He tossed a pink petit four into his mouth. "What?"

"After looking at each situation—the break-in, the threats, the jewel heists—from every angle, I've found two consistent common denominators. Sadly, one of them is dead and the other is me."

"Maybe you should stay with your parents until it blows over. This place is Fort Knox." He pushed another petit four into his mouth.

I pulled a pillow onto my lap, barring against the wind. "Not really. It's all smoke and mirrors. I walked right through the back door earlier."

"Care if I open the champagne?" Chase stretched one long arm to reach it without getting up. "I think I have a sugar flower petal stuck in my throat."

"You aren't supposed to swallow mini desserts like aspirin." I kicked off my shoes and wiggled my toes. "Why didn't we hang out more when we were kids?"

He twisted the muselet off the cork and wedged his thumbs underneath. "I was your best friend's boyfriend's little brother. Not a big selling point in high school romance." He pointed the bottle toward the streetlight, the trees, the moon. "What should I shoot for?"

"Not my car." I relaxed into the chaise. "I've always loved it up here. I feel like I can see forever, like we're in a big snow globe where it's always sunny, or starry, I guess." Thousands of historic oaks and other Garden District trees muffled the city sounds, making the world beyond our home seem surreal. "Living here is a little like living in a very green storybook."

"Never thought about it." The cork burst free, flying into the night and swan diving through the amber glow of a gas street lamp below. Chase swung the erupting bottle away. "Glasses?"

"Oh. No. Oops. Do you want me to go get some?"

He slid onto the floor by my feet. "Nah." He sipped from the top and passed it to me. "I shouldn't drink tonight. I'm having breakfast with the folks and a seven AM tee time with Dad."

I sipped from the bottle and set it aside. "How's that going?"

He leaned his head against my chaise. "They forgave me for having a career in volleyball and offered me a position at Dad's law firm."

"Ah." I handed him a lemon tassie from the comfort tray.

He chewed and laughed. "If I get unlimited dessert for having disappointed parents, what do you get for living in fear of a psychopath?"

"So far? A headache." I admired the sky full of stars, light-years away from the mess in Storybook Land.

He tipped his head back and looked into my eyes. Curiosity played on his handsome face.

"What?" I hoped the light was too dim to see my blush.

He shifted, swiveling onto his knees and rising over me without needing to stand. "Have you given any more thought to our deal?"

"Trading a kiss for a false legal document?" I held his gaze, torn by desperation to flee, memories of a too-recent heartbreak, and a certain detective I couldn't quite shake from my mind.

"The caveat to our deal was that you have to want the kiss." His voice was a soothing purr as he inched closer. Soft scents of cologne, sugar, and champagne enticed me to curl my fingers into the fabric of his shirt and seal the deal. "Do you want me to kiss you, Lacy?"

Our breaths mingled in the unreasonably romantic moment. I lowered my eyelids to think.

"Lacy." His warm lips brushed mine as he spoke.

My eyes popped open. "I'm not ready."

"Fair enough." He returned to his spot on the floor with a look of immense satisfaction. "Another time, then."

I flopped against the backrest of my chaise and exhaled pure adrenaline. "Wow."

He popped another sweet into his mouth. "And I haven't even touched you yet."

Jeez.

When the sweets were gone and the wind had worn away my resolve to hide, Chase walked me to the valet and kissed my cheek. "Goodnight, Lacy Crocker. I fancied being your gentleman tonight."

I curtsied. "Thank you for a lovely evening, Mr. Hawthorne." Why couldn't actual dating be as pleasant?

"Keep me posted on that deal we're negotiating."

I slid behind the wheel and eased onto the dimly lit street. If a letter from an attorney could help me get Penelope back, I wasn't above hiring a real one the minute my stalker was caught.

A man in traditional livery waved me down at the corner. "Miss?" He had something that looked like a cell phone in his hands.

I checked my purse and pulled over. Jeez. I powered down my passenger window.

"You dropped your phone."

"Thank you so much. I can't believe I did that."

He jogged to the passenger door and pulled it open, pointing a handgun at me from beneath his jacket. "Scream and die." His dark eyes were hard and bloodshot. "We're going to go for a ride. You're going to take me to the diamonds. Those are mine. He owes me. He knew it. He doesn't need them anymore, so they're leaving town with me. Got it?"

"I don't know what you're talking about," I blathered, desperately scanning the scene for someone to notice my despair. From outside my car, I looked like someone casually speaking to a member of Mom's evening staff. Not like someone about to die a bloody death because I hadn't been able to read the mind of a dead man. "I swear. I don't know anything about Miguel's diamonds." My bottom lip quivered, and I sucked in a fresh breath.

"They're *my* diamonds," he growled. He raised the barrel of his gun inch by inch. "I know Miguel had them when he went into your store, and he didn't have them when the coroner hauled him out. The only other person in there was you. You're going to take me to them, now, or I'm going to shoot you." He emphasized the final words.

Whoever he was, he'd lost his blessed mind. Panic coursed through my veins like lightning. I'd been through this before. I wouldn't do it again. I said a prayer and crammed the gas pedal against the floorboard.

The phone toppled onto my floor. His gun clattered onto the road.

He vanished with a grunt and a swear.

I sped through stop signs, screaming and pounding my horn while burning rubber down my parents' street. My car door hung open in the wind. There was no one in the rearview. Did I imagine a carjacking? Was I losing my mind? Had fear finally taken my sanity, too? I fumbled for the phone with one hand and took the next left turn on two wheels. My door slammed shut and someone honked at me.

I hit speed dial and prayed Jack could find the guy before he shot anyone at Mom's party.

No answer. *Why did he even have a cell phone if he wasn't ever going to answer it?*

I dialed Dad's cell next and spewed the information while barreling through the district with nowhere to go. "You need to pull over and calm down," Dad insisted. "Don't drive like this."

"Hang on," I sobbed. "Jack's calling me back on the other line." My teeth chattered as I took the call. "Jack?"

"Come back," he answered. "I've got the guy, and I need your statement."

"You've got him? Already?" I pulled into a bookstore parking lot to hyperventilate and wipe my nose. I rested my forehead on the steering wheel since I couldn't get it between my knees. "Really?"

"I told you. I only needed to be at the right place at the right time."

I sucked in a painful breath and let it out slowly. My fingers were numb from my grip on the wheel. "You were at Mom's party because I was there?" I whipped my head up and the world spun. "I told her that and she didn't believe me. How'd you know I was going?"

"I saw your invitation at Furry Godmother the day she gave it to you. For the record, stalking is subjective. I was on the lookout for this guy. I knew he was on the lookout for you. Take a minute to get it together, then get back here. I need your statement before the ambulance arrives."

I reversed out of the lot and pointed my car back down Prytania Street. "I think he was Miguel's partner. He said those diamonds were his and Miguel owed him. What ambulance?"

"He's Levi Marks, and I had to call for medical. You ran over his foot."

Chapter Nineteen

Furry Godmother's advice for managing stress: Try a new lease on life. It's exhilarating and extremely affordable.

A crowd had formed outside my parents' home. Guests and staff made a human wall along the sidewalk three people deep. Neighbors had gathered behind fences in nearby yards, tying floppy robe belts around their middles and snapping pictures with cell phones. I pulled my car over at the corner, several yards away, and practiced breathing. Searing pain ripped through my throat and chest with every deep inhalation. Too many shallow breaths had blurred my world.

Dad ran toward my car with terror in his eyes. His black jacket fluttered in the wind behind him. "Lacy!"

Tears rolled over my scorching cheeks. I unlocked the door and waited for his help. My limbs were heavy and shaking. My teeth chattered violently, and my head ached from the fresh load of stress that had tipped my mental scale. I wasn't built for this kind of excitement. I liked puppies and kittens. Sunsets and books.

Dad wrenched the door open and dropped into a squat. His soft palms warmed my cheeks. "Are you hurt?"

I turned my chin left and right, unable to trust my tongue.

He released my face and checked my pulse, then ran a critical gaze over my torso and appendages. "I heard the honking and came to see what was happening. There was a bleeding man in the road, and Jack had a gun on him. Jack said the man tried to hurt you. Did he touch you?"

I shook my head again. Without his hands to stabilize me, I was a life-sized bobblehead doll. "He tried to get in." I slid my eyes toward the passenger seat.

"How'd you get away?" Dad's voice wobbled.

"I think I ran him over." I peered through the windshield. "Is he okay?"

"He's pretty banged up. Jack wouldn't let me treat him, but there's an ambulance on its way. They should check you over. You could've been killed. I think that man's on something."

"Drugs?" I sputtered. My attacker in Virginia was high when he hurt me. Drugs turned normal people into time bombs. They couldn't think. Couldn't rationalize.

"I don't know." Dad gave the man another look. "He reeks of alcohol, but he's clearly taken something else. His pupils are dilated. Alcohol would've constricted them. His eyes are bloodshot. He's got a tremor, and he's extremely agitated."

The man sat in a heap on the sidewalk, propped against a tree and handcuffed to a historic metal hitching post. The poles were topped with stallion heads and rings for securing horses in another era. I'd strung colored yarn through those loops as a child and hung signs for tea parties and playdates.

I'd never look at them again without seeing Levi Marks and his gun.

I swallowed. "Jack says that's the murder victim's old partner."

Dad's eyes widened. The skin on his forehead pulled tight. "Let's go inside."

"I have to give a statement."

"They can come inside to take it. You don't need to face that man right now."

Dad escorted me from the car and led me toward the house. The distant cry of emergency vehicles drew closer with each step. An uneasy hush rolled over the street as I pulled away from Dad and moved toward Levi. His pants were ripped and his cheek was raw and bruised. One of his shoes was missing. The bare foot was swollen, bloodied, and black.

Jack stepped between me and Levi. He nodded to Dad.

I leaned around Jack for a clear view of Levi. Anger burned away my fear like the silver coating on a sparkler. Surrounded by my people, bolstered by the presence of Jack and Dad, I felt primal, livid, and dangerous. "Why did you do that?" The words were feral. I wanted to frighten him the way he frightened me.

Jack reached for my shoulder.

I pulled back and jumped around him to look Levi in the eyes. "Why did you do that? Were you planning to kill me? For what?" Angry tears welled in my eyes. "Why are you doing this to me?" I screamed. A tremor rocked my limbs. My teeth chattered harder, knocking against one another until I feared they'd break. "I don't understand what I've done to you."

Levi narrowed his red, beady eyes and spat on the street at my feet. "What have you done?" he growled. "You've thrown me from a moving car and crushed my foot. You fled the scene of a crime."

"Your crime!"

A smirk played across his filthy, road-rashed face. "I hope you have a good lawyer."

My mouth snapped shut. I curled my fingers into fists at my side. Fire lit in my veins.

Jack lifted an arm between us. "That's enough."

Dad tapped the screen of his cell phone. Mom covered her mouth with a handkerchief.

I pulled oxygen into my stinging lungs and braced to spring. "How badly can I hurt him before the cops arrive?"

"*I'm* the cops." Jack gripped my shoulders and steered me away from Levi. "Do not engage him anymore. I need you to think about your statement." He lowered his voice. "Keep a level head. Don't let him win."

Levi spat at my feet again.

Jack pushed me onto the sidewalk with my parents, stepping on Levi's foot as he passed. "Whoops. Sorry about that."

Levi screamed and flailed, overselling his pain.

Hopefully the neighbors hadn't caught the accident on camera. Someone might think it looked intentional.

The ambulance wailed onto the street, blinding me with too-bright lights and too many reflectors. A pair of NOPD cars brought up the rear.

Chase blinked into view beneath a cone of streetlamp light. He raced over the mossy, uneven sidewalk. "What happened?

I was halfway home when I saw the emergency vehicles headed this way."

Mom stretched a finger in Levi's direction. "That man tried to kill her."

Chase pulled me to his chest and wrapped long arms around my back.

"What are you doing?" I mumbled into his shirt.

He kissed the top of my head and lay his cheek on my hair. "All these people think I'm your boyfriend," he whispered. "I'm selling it. Plus, you nearly scared the cookies out of me."

"That's enough." I pulled away to watch the events unfold behind me.

Jack's ghostly blue eyes were locked on us. His stance was rigid. His expression was blank.

"That's Levi Marks," I explained to Chase. "He tried to carjack me, and I drove away, but he hurt his foot. I think I ran it over."

Jack opened and closed his right fist, clenching and stretching his fingers.

I cringed. "Jack might've helped his face get like that."

Levi called out in pain with every touch of the EMT's hands. He grinned slyly as he watched me fume helplessly.

"I wish *I'd* helped his face get like that. He says he's going to sue me for escaping his attempt on my life."

Chase puffed air. "Typical. I know where you can get a good Other-Lawyer-Be-Stupid spell."

A short laugh lodged in my throat and hardened into a painful rock. My bottom lip began to tremble. "He wanted to kill me, and I don't even know why."

Jack snapped out of his stupor and approached me with a look of shocking remorse. "I'm sorry I didn't stop this."

I waved a trembling hand. "You tried. You were here. What else could you have done?"

"I could've driven you here." He ran a heavy hand through his hair and settled it on the back of his neck. "I could've kept a closer eye on the staff tonight. I should've had a second set of eyes on the premises, but I didn't. You should be proud. Keeping a level head in a situation like that isn't easy, and it probably saved your life."

"Thanks."

He dipped his chin. "Levi won't hurt you again. He's in violation of his parole and in possession of a firearm. He attempted an abduction and is clearly high. He's going back to jail for a long time."

"Yeah?"

"Yes, ma'am."

I savored the sweet drawl in those words. Relief washed over me like rain.

"Party's over," Jack called into the crowd. "If you believe you saw or heard anything tonight that could be useful to the police, or if you know anything about this man"—he pointed to Levi, who was being loaded onto a gurney—"please see me now. Otherwise, form a line, collect your cars from the valet, and go home. I'll get a guest list from Mrs. Conti-Crocker and contact you individually this week if I have any further questions."

I wrapped shaky arms around myself and leaned against Chase for support. "It's over."

He rubbed his palms up and down my chilled skin. "Got any coffee left, Mrs. C?"

"Of course." She extended her hand to me.

I accepted.

Mom swept me against her side. "I can make some herbal tea if you don't want the caffeine."

"I want the caffeine." I wouldn't be sleeping again until I knew Levi Marks was behind bars far away from New Orleans.

* * *

Slowly, the coffee spread through my icy veins, warming me from the inside out. Mom put me on the couch and covered me with Grandma's favorite afghan. She slid booties over my feet and patted my head. Imogene arrived minutes later and whispered frantically with Mom in the kitchen.

Chase left the minute the crowd had dispersed. The caterers had the house back to preparty status in twenty minutes. Dad made plans to go to the firing range and unload some frustration first thing in the morning.

I set my empty cup aside and rubbed my palms together. "Want some company when you go?" Shooting was something Dad and I had done together all my life. His dad bought me my first BB gun when I was eight. We shot old cans off fence posts at his farm until I couldn't miss. Dad took me skeet shooting at the club when I was older. He bought me my first handgun as a graduation gift, but I'd left it at home when I went to college. Dad had been a military sharpshooter. I wasn't half bad ten years ago, but I hadn't held a gun since I completed my concealed carry training. I'd wondered a thousand times about my mugger. What if I'd been carrying? Would I have taken his life to save my own? I couldn't answer that question, which meant it was a good thing I'd left my gun in a safe where it belonged.

Mom pushed a swath of hair behind my ear. "What are you thinking about?"

"Bad juju."

Imogene clucked her tongue. "Didn't I tell you?" She unwrapped a brilliant silk scarf from her hair and dropped onto the edge of the couch at my side. "Your mama told me everything."

I gave Mom the stink eye.

Mom gave it back. "I think you should stay here tonight."

Imogene pressed one of my hands in both of hers. "Listen to your mama. There's blood on the moon tonight. You shouldn't be alone."

I squeezed her hand and smiled. "I missed you at the party. Where were you?"

"I was babysitting my granddaughter, Miss Isla."

"How's Isla?"

She shook her head and dug into her purse. "Better than you. She's tucked in tight. Swaddled in love." She liberated a small hunk of clay from her bag and pressed it into my hand. "For good luck. Chanchito will keep you safe."

I opened my palm. A little three-legged pig figurine looked back at me. "Thanks." I closed my fingers around it and reevaluated my life. "How long can it take to talk to the guests?" I wanted to go home, away from another crime scene. I wanted to be tucked into my bed and swaddled with love. What did a lady have to do around here for that?

The muted glow of red-and-blue lights disappeared from outside the window. "I think they're all gone now," Dad said.

"Thank goodness." A few days ago, I'd worried about ruining my family's name when coverage of Miguel's murder hit the paper. Tonight I'd lured a jewel thief and killer to my parents' home and run him over with my car. "I'm really sorry about this."

Dad pulled the curtain back and scanned the street. "This isn't your fault. You can't blame yourself for the actions of a criminal." He released the curtain and headed for the kitchen. "Anyone need anything else?"

"No." We all answered.

The back door opened and closed.

Jack's voice cut through the air. "I'm sorry to do this now, but I'd like to get Lacy's statement while it's fresh in her mind."

As if I wouldn't replay it frame by frame for the next thirty years.

I tensed as his footfalls grew nearer and sighed in relief when he came into view.

Imogene made a long humming sound before going to stand with my mom.

"May I?" He motioned to the chair beside me.

"Of course. Do you want coffee? Tea?" I wiggled into a seated position on the couch.

"Whisky?" Dad offered.

Jack smiled. "I plan to have plenty of that later." He turned anguished eyes on me. "Are you sure you're not hurt?"

"Yeah."

"Do you think you can give an account of your night for the record? If you need more time, we can wait until morning, but I'd rather not push it longer than necessary. Images and recollections can become hazy or inflated as time goes by. We rehash, add, and eliminate things from memories as necessary for our mental health."

"Now's fine."

Dad extended a hand to Mom and Imogene. "Come on. I missed the party, and I'm starved. Let's see what's in the fridge."

Jack scooted forward in his chair until his knees bumped the couch. "Do you want to call them back for moral support? This can be a difficult process so soon after a trauma."

"I'm okay."

"Maybe you want your boyfriend with you."

"I don't . . . Chase Hawthorne is not my boyfriend. Mom cooked up that scheme so I'd stay at her party. When men flirt with me at these things, I never know what to say, and it makes me uncomfortable."

"It's hard to be young, wealthy, and attractive."

I scoffed. "Shut up."

"What?" He smiled. "I was talking about me."

A laugh bubbled up from my core. "Yeah, you looked miserable, surrounded by all those women."

"Like I said." He turned his cell phone over and rested it on the coffee table. "I'm going to record this. I'll take notes, but you can talk as quickly as you like and get it all out. I'll replay and review the statement later."

"Should I write anything down? Do you need a written statement?"

"When you're ready."

I wrung my hands. "You have a good bedside manner. Ever think of becoming a doctor?"

"Maybe when I get too old to chase crooks."

"You call them crooks? You might be older than you think, Bugsy."

He tapped the pen against his paper. "I'm sorry I was short with you yesterday."

"Do you mean when I stopped by, unannounced, and told you I was digging around in your murder investigation?" I smiled. "I was mad about that for a while, but I guess you had a point."

"I knew Levi was in town. I assumed he was following you, which is why I've been staking out your place. I didn't want you leading him to my house. The goal was for me to surprise him and not the other way around."

"Why didn't you tell me he was in town?"

"I wanted to protect you without worrying you."

"How'd you know for sure?" I'd speculated but hadn't found any proof.

He gave me the bored, it's-my-job face. "I went back to Boondocks and talked to the bartender. She gave a description of the man asking about Miguel. I showed her Levi's mug shot, and she confirmed it was him, so we put out a BOLO and pulled some footage from local business cameras. We spotted him catching a cab, got the number, and called the cab company to see where he went."

"Just like on television."

His cheek twitched, barely avoiding a smile. "Yeah. Just like."

"Where'd he go?"

"Magazine Street. No address, just asked for Magazine, so they dropped him off around lunchtime. We assume he waited for Miguel, followed him into Furry Godmother, and killed him."

"So I'm really safe." I loved the sound of those words.

"I think so," he said, working his tie loose and unbuttoning the top button on his shirt. "Yes."

I retold my story of the night's harrowing events in detail, then did my best to write it out. It was after midnight when I finished. "I guess I should head home. Maybe I'll open the shop tomorrow. Paige keeps texting me, wanting to come in."

Jack stretched to his feet. "Sounds like a plan. I'm going to say good-bye to your folks, then follow you home."

I tossed Grandma's afghan off my legs and toed off the booties. "You don't have to do that. I know the way."

"I don't mind. You may find it harder than you think to be alone the next few days or weeks. Knowing the bad guy's in custody is logic, but logic does little to quell fear. Believe me. I know. I think you do, too."

I couldn't imagine Jack fearing anything, but he was right. I still dreamed of the monster in that Virginia alley. "Fine. You can follow me home, but don't try to come inside or I'll tell my boyfriend."

He snorted. "Wouldn't want that."

* * *

The houses on my street were appropriately quiet. Humidity clung to the ground in a haze beneath my headlights as I bounced over the warped brick road. A colony of bats swooped past the moon, swallowed quickly by the inky darkness. I pulled into my drive and cut the radio. Jack was right. I didn't like the idea of going inside alone. Imogene's warning of bad juju and blood on the moon niggled in my mind. I didn't know what either meant, specifically, but they sounded bad. I unlatched my seatbelt and tried not to see my house as a place where someone could get me alone for nefarious reasons.

I hadn't been home since the morning. Buttercup was probably worried and hungry—two downsides to having a roommate. Even after a night like mine, someone had to serve the brine shrimp.

Jack parked behind me and climbed out. His gait was tight as he approached my car door.

I popped my door open and planted both feet on the ground. "I thought you weren't going to try to come inside."

He turned cold eyes my way and flicked a warning finger in my direction. He slid the opposite hand under the back of his high-end black jacket. A moment later he pointed a gun at my front door.

I slapped both palms over my mouth and tried not to vomit. I yanked my feet back inside the car and locked the door.

He moved onto the porch like a panther, touched my doorknob, and swung the front door open.

Chapter Twenty

Furry Godmother's recommended reading for single ladies:
How to Jiu Jitsu.

Jack returned to my car several minutes later and knocked on the window. "Someone's been inside. I called it in."

I powered the window down an inch and directed my voice toward the crack. "How'd you know something was wrong?" Was he a psychic? What if I'd come home alone? Why didn't I see what he saw?

"Your porch light was off."

I gave the house a disbelieving look. "You know it burnt out."

He looked away. "I came by this afternoon and changed the bulb."

"Oh." That was nice. A little creepy and presumptuous, but not an awful gesture. "Thank you."

"You should come in and take a look around."

A NOPD car pulled up behind Jack's truck. One of the officers who'd been at my parents' house climbed out. "Busy night." He shook Jack's hand.

Jack straightened. "Looks like Marks planned to wait here for her, but she hasn't been home since breakfast. When she didn't show, he rifled through her kitchen and found the dinner invitation."

I resisted the urge to smack my forehead. One more reason formal invitations were awful. They cost a fortune, killed trees, filled up my recycle bin, *and* led gun-wielding nutballs right to me.

The officer bent forward and looked in my car window. "How are you holding up?"

"I think I'm in shock."

He looked at Jack. "Is she up for this?"

"You'll have to ask her."

The officer looked guilty. "Hey, I don't mean to be a jerk. You've had one hell of a night." His troubled eyes were a strange comfort. Validation, maybe. Tonight was truly awful.

"I've got to ask you to look around. Make a statement."

I forced my stiff fingers off the steering wheel.

"Lacy?" Jack's smooth voice beckoned. "You'll have to turn the car off."

I made my fingers cooperate. I must have restarted my car while contemplating how far away I could get with the gas in my tank.

I followed the men up my walk. Fragments of a shattered bulb crunched under foot on the dark porch. Inside, nothing seemed different. I lingered in the doorway, buoyed at least by the fact my home wasn't in complete upheaval like my store had been.

Jack made a trip to the kitchen and returned with Mom's invitation in one freezer bag and my red dry-erase marker in another. "We'll get prints off these, the light switches, and doorknob, maybe her kitchen counter. Remember, Miguel's killer wore gloves. If gloves are Levi's thing, it's going to be difficult to attach him to your break-ins, but either way, he's going back to jail for the stunt he pulled earlier."

I considered the statements. "How long do fingerprints take? When will we hear about the break-in at Furry Godmother last night?"

"We should have the results tomorrow. I'll check on the prints from yesterday first thing in the morning."

I walked through my rooms slowly, hoping to find an obvious clue to who'd lurked in my home. Maybe Levi's photo ID or a note signed by him. Whatever it took to make sure he didn't come back.

Jack snapped a photo of Buttercup with his phone.

"Is my fish a suspect?" Poor Buttercup. Alone with a killer.

Jack took another picture. "No."

I crossed the space to his side.

The little red heart Scarlet had drawn was wiped away and replaced with a cartoon gun and four letters: *B-A-N-G*.

I grabbed a paper towel and scrubbed the glass. "I hate this guy." I dropped three fishy pellets into the water. "I'm so sorry you were adopted into my mess, Buttercup." How could I even think of bringing Penelope into this? I was a terrible mother.

The officer appeared with his little notebook. "Anything missing or damaged?"

"No."

"Are you certain?"

"I'll need more time to know if he stole chocolate from my sock drawer stash, but everything looks just like it did when

I left this morning." I turned to Jack for advice. "Should I go through every drawer before you leave?"

He stuffed his phone into his back pocket. "No. Take your time. You can add to your initial statement anytime."

A little shiver ran down my spine. "So this really wasn't a robbery?"

Jack lowered his head and lifted his brows. "Based on what I see here, I think this was attempt number one on your life, or at the least, on your abduction. I think he let himself in and waited in the living room for your car to pull up." He pointed to my front window. "The chair's been angled away from your television and positioned for a clear view outside. Your personal calendar is open on the kitchen counter and the dinner invitation is with it. This guy was looking for you."

"Now I've got to move," I groaned. "I can't sleep here."

Jack handed the evidence bags to the officer. "You don't need to move. We've got Levi in custody and nothing here is damaged. Maybe burn the chair and buy a new calendar. Get an alarm system."

"Maybe I should move to Peoria and raise bunnies."

He stretched his eyes wide and mouthed, "Wow."

I wiped a sneaky tear off my cheek.

"Did he say anything to you before you ran him over?" Mischief glinted in his eye.

"He wanted Miguel's diamonds. He was adamant I had them and they were his. He wanted me to take him to them, but I knew if he got into the car . . ." I choked on a knot of fear.

"Look," Jack whispered, containing our conversation. He turned his back to the officer. "I think you're sleep deprived, scared, and polka dancing toward delirious. Why don't you pack a few things and let me follow you back to your parents' house for tonight?"

I nodded woodenly. "I'll research Peoria tomorrow. I could surround myself in bunnies. Make that a thing. Move over, cat ladies. The cool crazies collect bunnies."

He pressed one hand to the small of my back and steered me toward the bedroom. "You aren't that crazy. Get your things. I'll call your Dad and tell him we're on our way."

"Okay. Don't forget my fish."

* * *

I opened Furry Godmother the next morning with trepidation. Logically, I knew the danger had ended, but Imogene's concern about bad juju plucked at my skin like a thousand tiny needles. Jack was right. Fear was irrational.

I slapped a borrowed throw rug over the warning carved in my floorboards and tacked it down with finishing nails. The rug was Mom's. The nails were Dad's. The unresolved emotional issues were all mine.

The little bell over my door jingled, and I jumped to my feet.

Paige waved. "Feeling edgy?"

"Yep." I checked the rug from every angle. The nails were invisible in the braided strands. "Thanks for coming in." I probably wouldn't have opened today if I had to work alone.

"No problem. I'm glad to be useful, and I could use the money."

I relaxed a fraction, thankful for normal conversation. "Party plans?"

She swept long bangs off her forehead. "No. I'm saving for fall semester. The bad thing about growing up in New Orleans is how fast it seems dull when you've seen it all before. I'm looking forward to school starting."

I lined colored pencils on the counter and unfolded plans for four Jazzy Chicks upright pianos. "What do you think of this?" I turned the sketch to her.

She wrinkled her nose. "It's a little punk rock for your mom's crew, isn't it?"

I tapped a gum eraser against the sleek black drawing. Gas-blue-and-green flames climbed the side and turned to silver confetti above the keys. "I was being ironic."

"Are they hipster chickens?"

The door opened once more, and Mrs. Neidermeyer swept inside. Her jangling bracelets echoed through the quiet studio, punctuated by the steady clip-clop of designer heels. "How are you?"

"Super."

She stopped to lean against the counter between us. "I can't believe you're here today after that mess last night. Jack Oliver looked ready to rip everyone's heads off. I gave my statement to the uniform cop who didn't have smoke billowing from his ears."

Paige crept close to Mrs. Neidermeyer. "Sounds like the detective was feeling a little overprotective, maybe even territorial."

Mrs. Neidermeyer's eyes widened. "You don't say."

I shook my head. "No. Jack and I are friends." Were we friends? I stopped midthought to ponder the question. We were. When had that happened?

"What about Chase Hawthorne? You two looked awfully cozy, and everyone noticed you disappearing upstairs for more than an hour."

Paige steepled her fingers and smiled brightly at the older woman. "Oh, really?"

I feigned rapt attention in my chipping nail polish. Memories of Chase's lips near mine lifted the soft hair on my arms to attention.

Mrs. Neidermeyer raised her eyebrows to her hairline. "You should've seen Jack. He didn't know whether to shoot or wind his watch."

"What?" Paige laughed. "What did he do?"

"He stood cross-armed at the bottom of the staircase and frowned. It wasn't until he heard them coming back that he made himself scarce. He blended in at the buffet until they passed, then followed them outside."

I pressed a palm to my tummy as an irrational bout of guilt and anxiety swept through me. Nothing had happened, but it looked completely scandalous. The whole district was probably talking. "Would you like to see the tutus, Mrs. Neidermeyer?"

"Of course."

"Great." I stepped around the counter to meet her. "Come on back. I've got them pressed and ready for inspection."

I led her to the storeroom and waved a hand at the rack of custom tutus. "I added little bodysuits to keep the skirts in place. What do you think?"

She fished glasses from her bag and pushed them over her snub nose. "Let's see what we've got here." She unclipped the first tutu from its hanger and inspected the hem. Stretchy black-and-white chevron bodysuits topped an abundance of bunched, hot-pink tulle. "Nice tight stitching." She turned the material over in her palms and rubbed it between her thumb and first finger. "Not too scratchy for their tummies. That's good. They'll fuss and chew if it's uncomfortable." She handed the skirt to me. "I like the rhinestones at the collars and cuffs. Very nice touches. Stage lighting will work wonders with those. When can you come by and fit my girls?"

I turned the costume belly-side up and demonstrated the closure. "The elastic and Velcro makes them the perfect size for any pet."

Her eyes narrowed. She snagged her glasses off her nose. "Do you mean to tell me you don't do fittings? I'm sorry. Are you a custom designer or the buyer for Kmart?"

I sucked air. "Kmart?" *Flies and honey, Lacy.* I gathered my pageant voice and forced a congenial smile. "You're absolutely right, Mrs. Neidermeyer. I'd be glad to measure your girls for these one-size-fits-all ensembles. When's the next time they'll be together?"

"Forty-five minutes. Bring the costumes and whatever you need to make adjustments. Don't dawdle."

She dismissed me with the flick of her hand and abandoned me in a cloud of frustration and high-end perfume.

I rolled the rack of tutus into the studio and set the box of leg warmers on the counter.

"Whatcha doing?" Paige asked.

"I've got to go to Mrs. Neidermeyer's dance studio and measure the Shih Tzus. I'll be back in time to close up, but I may take the rest of the day and run the llama leg warmers to Mrs. Hams's plantation."

I loaded the tutus into an extralarge garment box and set the box of Mrs. Hams's leg warmers on top.

"No problem. This place is dead. I'll text you if anything comes up."

"Great. Have lunch delivered and leave me the bill." I hefted the boxes under one arm, lugged my purse over the opposite shoulder, and headed into the sunlight.

Across the street, a lean man in dirty jeans crushed a cigarette beneath his shoe and glared at me. His grubby shirt matched the worn belt and boots. "All-American Construction" was written on his ball cap. *Adam.* The guy Miguel had beaten in a few rounds of high-dollar billiards at Boondocks. The guy I'd splashed my drink on and the cops had hauled in for questioning.

I swallowed hard and dropped into my car. *Adam's not lurking outside my store. All-American Construction is always on this street doing something at one of the shops. They'd released him after questioning because he wasn't the culprit. I am safe.* I brought my cell to life and considered calling Jack anyway. What if he hadn't looked into Adam thoroughly?

Before I finished dialing, a group of men in similar dress joined Adam on the curb. They opened paper bags from a local deli and passed the contents out.

Adam pointed his sandwich at me.

I hit the gas.

The drive to Fancy Paws was riddled with traffic. I hit every light and spent the time circling unanswerable questions. Was Adam watching my store for a reason, or was it a coincidence his crew had chosen that deli for lunch? And, further back, how could I have escaped Levi Marks and avoided a lawsuit? What if I'd gone home where he was waiting for me instead of having dinner at the Barrel Room or staying for Mom's party? The night could've ended unbelievably worse.

What had been his plan? Where was he taking me last night when he tried to get in the car?

I pulled into the parking lot at Fancy Paws and texted Mrs. Hams to let her know I'd deliver her order this afternoon.

First, I needed to impress Mrs. Neidermeyer. Her approval could change everything for Furry Godmother. The Fancy Paw dancers headlined every canine show from here to Atlanta.

I hauled the big box from my back seat and hip checked the door shut. I'd never measured an actual Shih Tzu, but according to my research, the elastic and Velcro I'd used would accommodate variations in their girth and hairstyles.

Seven ten-pound dust mops met me excitedly at the door.

Mrs. Neidermeyer brought up the rear. "Come in. Come in." She stuffed two fingers in her mouth and whistled. "Ladies!"

The mops froze and turned to face her.

Nine reflections of the two humans and seven dogs gazed back at us from mirror-covered walls. Spotlights shone down on the high-polished floors. Posters of dancing dogs and a pin board papered in flyers decorated the wall closest to the door. The studio schedule was four pages long and taped beside the pin board. Fancy Paws was the premiere location for every talented dog in the district. Bulldog Ballet had three time slots, all filled from the looks of the schedule.

"Line up, ladies." Mrs. Neidermeyer flicked her wrist, and the mops formed a row.

I applauded. "That's amazing."

"Oh, honey, you haven't seen anything yet. The wooden waves and boat props will be here soon. We're performing 'On the Good Ship Lollipop' at the Animal Elegance gala." Pride oozed from her words. "Let's get the girls dressed and watch them work."

"All righty." I wiggled the lid off my tutu box and examined the little dance troupe.

Mrs. Neidermeyer stepped out of one shoe and rubbed her foot. "Where's your assistant?"

"I don't have an assistant."

"What about the little girl at the register today?"

I tugged my hair into a ponytail. "Paige isn't a little girl. She's twenty-one."

"Honey," Mrs. Neidermeyer deadpanned, "I've got shoes older than that child. You need an assistant for things like this."

"Thanks. I'll take that under consideration." She was right, of course, but I could barely afford Paige, and she worked for minimum wage. "Are you okay?" I watched her rub her heel and circle her ankle.

"New shoes. I'm wearing them a bit day by day so I can wear them all day for Animal Elegance."

I recognized the Louboutins from the night before. I could buy a new wardrobe for what she'd paid for those shoes.

"Do you need my help?" she asked.

"Can you remove their collars and smooth their fur? I'll slip the tutus on and check them for fit."

She rubbed her chin. "Or I could hand you the outfits and make notations for alterations."

"Who's first?"

"Laney." Mrs. Neidermeyer bent a finger. "Come, darling."

A little brown-and-white mop with an *I Dream of Genie* ponytail pranced forward. She was clearly the belle of any ball and knew it.

"Hello, pumpkin," I cooed. "Let's show them how to look fabulous."

Seven dogs and eighty-five minutes later, Mrs. Neidermeyer insisted I stay to see them perform before I left. She also insisted I help her disrobe the little starlets and rehang the costumes. On the upside, she accepted the garments as they were and wrote me a chubby check I could cash in the morning.

By the time I dropped the leg warmers off with Mrs. Hams, the workday was done and so was Paige.

She had her keys in hand when I walked through the shop door.

"How did it go today?" I asked.

"I sold some pawlines and a couple headscarves. Nothing exciting. Now I have a date with a bartender from Bourbon Cowboy. He's going to let me ride the mechanical bull."

"Congratulations."

She spun her keys around one finger. "I'm meeting friends for coffee before my date. You want to come?"

"No, but thanks. I've got to talk to Mom about those pianos." I dropped my purse behind the counter and sifted through the messages. "These are all from Jack."

Paige pushed the door open with one hip and flipped the "Closed" sign for me. "I want to hear more about why you're calling him by his first name now, but I guess I could stay and see for myself."

A familiar black pickup pulled against the curb outside.

"No. You should go." I tried to look boring and serious, but my insides fizzed and swirled with anticipation of what had caused Jack to leave four messages. Instinct and experience said it couldn't be anything good.

Paige waved Jack inside. "Have fun." She strode into the evening sunlight like the debutante she knew she was.

I gripped the counter and prepared for bad news.

Jack turned the dead bolt. "Did you get my messages?"

"These?" I lifted the little pile of papers. "Yes. About two minutes ago. What's wrong?" The urge to panic tightened every fiber in my body. "Wait. Am I jumping to conclusions? This could be good news. You wanted to deliver it in person and see my happy face when you told me."

"What kind of good news?"

"Like you've connected Levi directly to Miguel's murder, and I can call Mr. Tater and get my business back on track."

"Afraid not."

"Then you matched fingerprints recovered after my home invasion to ones found here, and they all belong to Levi."

"Nope." He latched his hands behind his back. "Technically, you had a break-in, not a home invasion. However, we got the results back from both, and all the prints belonged to you."

I waved the messages at him. "You called four times to tell me you found nothing significant? A-plus detective work." I mentally collapsed. "Why didn't you call my cell phone?"

"Paige said you were on the road, and I didn't want you to take the call while driving."

"That's dumb."

"It's the law."

"I wasn't in my car the entire day."

He waved his hands between us and admitted, "I thought I should tell you in person. I called to see when you were here so I could stop by. You didn't call back so I took a shot stopping by at closing time."

"What's so important you wanted to tell me in person?"

He ambled to the counter. "Traces of cornstarch were found on the light switches at your home, in your stock room, and on the glitter sprayer."

I wrinkled my brows. "Cornstarch?" I glanced at the bakery display. "I don't use cornstarch."

"No, but cornstarch is often found in latex gloves. It makes them easier to put on."

I worked that information around in my head. "My gloves don't have that."

"I know. The lab tested one found here after Miguel was killed, and I confirmed your standing order online for monthly shipments of that same glove."

I bit the insides of my cheeks. Having my life picked through was unsettling and felt a little like betrayal. Then again, he didn't know me then, and I had been a sensible suspect, all things considered. "So we know the same person who destroyed my studio also killed Miguel and broke into my home, but you can't prove it was Levi."

"Correct."

"Levi's still headed back to jail for holding me at gunpoint and trying to abduct me. Even if he isn't charged with the break-ins, he's out of my life, right?"

"Yes. What's wrong?"

Sadness pinched my heart. "I wanted Sunshine and her baby to get justice. If we can't pin the murder to Levi, they won't have the peace of knowing someone paid for taking Miguel from them."

Jack erased the space between us in slow, steady strides. Concern pulled at the corners of his eyes and mouth. "This is why I wanted to talk to you in person. Sunshine and her baby might still get justice."

"What do you mean?" I backtracked through the facts he'd delivered. "If there weren't any prints, but you know the same gloves were used by Levi in the break-ins and the murder, isn't that enough to charge him?"

Jack leveled me with a powerful stare. "There were no traces of cornstarch on Levi's hands or the clothes he ditched in your parents' linen closet before dressing as part of the waitstaff."

"That doesn't make him innocent. It doesn't prove anything."

"We located the abandoned home where he's squatting in the Lower Ninth Ward. There weren't any latex gloves there either. No traces of cornstarch."

I backed up until my heels hit the wall. "He probably threw them away." I pressed my palms to the cool surface for support. "He's a career criminal. He's smart." The words rang false on my tongue. Nothing about Levi was remotely smart. He acted on impulse and used drugs. He didn't have the patience or self-discipline to sit and wait for anything. Whoever stabbed my tire, carved into my floor, and broke into my house liked the chase. The psycho enjoyed playing cat and mouse.

"I think there's another party at play."

My knees buckled, but I managed to stay upright with the help of the wall. "Adam was outside the studio today. His crew from All-American Construction was having lunch across the street, but when I first went out to my car, it was only him. Staring." I shook my hands out at the wrists, recalling the fear his presence had incited.

Jack's expression went flat. "Did he say anything to you?"

"No. He stared. He pointed his sandwich at me."

"And you . . . ?" he prompted.

"I drove away. I had things to do, and I wasn't about to confront him. I've had enough homicidal men this month to last me forever, thank you very much. Besides, the police already questioned him and let him go. That's supposed to mean something. And I thought Levi was the culprit. You have him in custody. How crazy would I have sounded if I'd called to say a guy I dumped a drink on was glaring at me? We already know I'm not his favorite person."

Jack rolled his head over both shoulders. "You can always call me. Give me your phone."

"Why? Have I lost my privileges, Dad?" Curiosity got the best of me. I handed it over.

He snapped a selfie, then tapped the screen for several seconds. "There. I'm in your contacts if you need me."

I accepted my phone back and checked the screen. His sour cop face was memorialized for all time. "Thanks."

"I'm going to recommend you close up shop for a few days. Stay with your folks. Order takeout. Understand?"

I rested my head against the wall. *No.* I couldn't fathom who else could be involved or why I was of interest to him.

Jack ducked his chin. "I'm not trying to scare you. I think something else is going on here, and I want you to be safe. Levi's not talking, other than to say he had an alibi for the night Miguel died, so sit tight. I'm close. I can feel it."

"Are you sure it's not Levi?" Hope lifted in my words.

"Yeah. I dug deeper into the day Miguel died and watched security footage from local businesses all day. After the taxi dropped him on Magazine Street, he played pool at St. Joe's bar until closing. He said Miguel was supposed to meet him but never showed."

"And the bar staff confirmed his story?"

Jack tilted his head. "Yes. I confirmed the alibi. I know what I'm doing."

"Then Levi was in town to see Miguel but not to kill him? Why were they meeting? Were they just going to catch up on old times or was this a business meeting? Miguel is the reason he spent those years in jail. He has to be mad."

"I agree, but Levi's not talking. All he'd give me was the alibi on the murder. He lawyered up, and that was it."

I twirled a loose thread from my blouse between two fingers. "Is he still suing me?"

Jack smiled. "Yes."

"Great."

He grabbed my purse from under the counter. "It's nearly six. How about I follow you to your parents' house to drop off your car, then take you to my place for dinner?"

"Isn't there a law or police code of ethics or something against us spending time together casually?"

"I'm allowed to have friends." He slid a droll expression my way. "Even cops on television have friends."

I took my purse from his hands. He wasn't thrilled the last time I went to his house. Why the offer this time? "You're using me as bait again, aren't you?"

He flattened a palm over his heart. "That hurts."

"Truth hurts."

"Yeah, a little." He motioned me ahead of him to the door. "I can't help it. I want this guy bad, and you're not safe on your own. You get robbed and carjacked. Levi proved I'd underestimated how easy it is to reach you at your parents' house. Maybe I was wrong before about you leading him to me. Let's do that."

"Technically, whoever keeps breaking in hasn't taken anything, so I haven't been robbed, according to you."

He circled his hand in a universal hurry-up motion. "Call it what you want." He stopped by the new security panel. "Set your alarm. I'm starving. Tabitha won't keep dinner warm after seven."

I pressed the little plastic buttons on the keypad. "Who's Tabitha? Is she your cook? I knew you couldn't cook."

He held the door.

I passed under his arm. "Your maid? If you have a maid, you lose ten points of manhood. Seriously, pick up your own stuff and learn to use a washing machine."

The system beeped, and I tugged the door to be sure it locked.

Jack slid dark aviators over his eyes. "Tabitha was grandpa's girlfriend."

"What?" I made a crazy face. "Why is your grandpa's girlfriend making you dinner?"

He beeped his truck doors open. "She likes to cook, and she's cooking for herself, not me. I just take advantage of the leftovers."

I processed the nonsense and gasped. "She lives with you? You live with your dead grandpa's girlfriend?" I let my mouth hang open.

"What was I supposed to do when I moved in? Kick her out? She'll go when it's time, but I've got something to take care of first. Meanwhile, are you coming over or not?"

"Duh. Free dinner. If you're convinced I'm in such danger, why not assign a cop to follow me around?"

He swung his door open and smiled. "What do you think I've been doing?"

I climbed into my car and checked my rearview mirror before pulling into traffic. Jack followed in his truck.

Closed up in my car, the silence was deafening. I was alone.

Worse, I was unsafe. And I had no idea why.

I rubbed the three-legged pig in my pocket. "Feel free to start working anytime, Chanchito."

Chapter Twenty-One

Furry Godmother believes in equality.
Diamonds are everyone's best friend.

Jack walked me to the door at my parents' house while typing on his phone. The cuffs of his black dress shirt were rolled to his elbows, and he'd removed his jacket and tie. All formal pretenses of a proper detective were cast aside. Beside me, he was a bull ready to charge.

The sky was unnaturally dark, a poetic reflection of his mood and my building anxiety. I missed the snarky, even-tempered guy who'd threatened to arrest me so many times. This guy was on edge, and it did nothing to soothe my frayed nerves.

Wind whipped dirt and flower petals into tiny hurricanes around our ankles. The rising humidity had twisted my hair into clown proportions and plastered my dress to my body.

We reached the door, and he didn't look up.

"Everything okay?" I asked, squinting against the growing gale. "Is that bad news you're texting about?"

The clench and release of his jaw answered my question. Yes. Something was very wrong. So wrong it had the undivided attention of a normally vigilant man. "Jack?" His refusal to answer bit into my unraveling composure. "What's wrong?" The words dove off my tongue, louder than anticipated. I unlocked the back door and waited.

His eyes flashed up from his phone to meet mine. The crystal blue I'd come to enjoy suddenly looked lethal. Dark emotion marred his handsome face. "I need a rain check on dinner. Something's come up." He handed me the bags he'd carried from my car. "I want you to stay inside and call me if you need anything."

"What came up?"

"A thread I started pulling after you found that burnisher is paying off."

"What does that mean?"

He tipped one side of his mouth into a menacing smile.

A burst of wind whipped hair into my eyes and pulled the bags in my hands. "I'm just supposed to sit and wait? You won't tell me what your hunch was?"

"Hang tight." He turned away.

"Hang tight?" I followed him to the driveway. "Am I safe here? Are my parents?" Maybe I should go back to my house. If someone came after me, it would be better if they only got me, right? The coward in me said no. There was strength in numbers and an excellent alarm system here. Plus guns.

He pointed to the door behind me. "Go inside. Set the alarm. I'll be back as soon as I can. Let your parents know what's going on." He turned and jogged into the brewing storm.

"Hey!" I called after him, waving my hands overhead. "I don't know what's going on!"

The first fat drops of rain broke on my head. I jerked my phone from my pocket and texted Jack.

Be Careful.

I stood dumbfounded until his taillights vanished in the distance.

A blast of thunder cracked the heavens, and I nearly dropped my phone.

Dad's office door popped open across the lawn. "Lacy? Did you just scream?"

"Maybe." I slunk to his side, blinking rain from my eyes. "Jack dropped me off and told me to go inside and set the alarm, but he didn't tell me why he had to leave or what it was that called him away."

Dad scanned the twilight. "Well, how about I make some tea?" He locked his office door and escorted me to the house. "Why don't you have an umbrella?"

I shrugged. "They're like tiny lightning rods."

He chuckled. "Fair enough. I'm going to give your mother a call and let her know what's going on."

"Good. I'd love to know." I dragged my packages inside and set the alarm. "Are you telling her to come home?"

He laughed. "That would be the surest way not to see her until Christmas."

I filled the teakettle with water and cranked up a blue flame on the stovetop. "She's probably better off staying wherever she is until the storm passes. It's gathering fast. Plus, I don't know if we're safe here. Jack couldn't have been more ambiguous if he'd tried." I set the kettle on the flame. "Do you think he's intentionally vague, or am I too high-strung?"

"I think you could use some tea. Try chamomile." He dialed his phone and left the room to speak privately.

I checked the dead bolts on all the doors and pulled the curtains on the first-floor windows. Angry winds howled at the glass. Thunder shook the earth. I checked my phone for a response from Jack.

Nothing. *Shocker.*

I unpacked my things on the dining room table while I waited for the kettle to whistle. Tea wasn't my thing, but Dad loved it, and I probably didn't need more caffeine. My brain had swam in enough adrenaline this week to make me half loony. I sorted my materials into piles and ordered them for a streamlined assembly.

With my shop closed twice, plus my complete inability to sleep, I'd caught up on my orders and decided to make my Vive La France line after all. Who wouldn't want to see poodles in berets and skirts? *Literal poodle skirts.* The concept was adorable. I had to have it. If life stayed this way long, I'd finish Vive La France by Christmas and have my peacock line ready in time for Mardi Gras.

"Where should I begin?" I gathered a pink felt semicircle to use as a skirt mock-up and chose my embellishments. How could anything be wrong in the world when I got paid to make clothing for fur babies?

Nothing made sense anymore.

Dad emerged from the kitchen with two mugs. "You never stop."

"Sorry. I didn't hear the whistle."

"I don't mind being useful, especially to my little girl. You've always gotten lost in your designs. I think the pieces you made for my clients when you were young are half the reason my practice became so popular." He set one mug on the table beside me. "People brought their pets in for shots and left with a new tie or hair bow for their kitten or puppy. Do you remember those?"

"They were awful."

"You were a kid. A big-hearted kid with a flair for the dramatic. You were my world."

I stopped to hug him. His soft cardigan warmed my cheek. "I wanted to be you when I grew up."

"Well, I'm glad that didn't work out. I'm an overworked, underpaid man in love with his profession but with no time for a life."

Look at that. I did grow up to be my father.

"Do you remember the skirt we bought you in Paris when you were eight? It was covered in script. Words from a book, I believe, and it had a ring of crinoline underneath. You twirled and twirled in that skirt."

"I still have it. It was the piece that made me want to design my own things and make other little girls glamorous. It's the inspiration for this new line." I'd made an entire catalogue of French-inspired doll clothes the month we came home.

"It's good you have an outlet. People get caught up, living in their heads all the time, and they're miserable."

"I don't know what I'd do if I didn't do this." My mind had always been too busy for my own good. I'd drive myself crazy without books or projects to occupy my thoughts, and that was before a killer hunted me. Without an outlet at the moment, I'd go berserk.

"I hope you like chamomile. We could both use a little Zen, I think."

I sipped the warm comfort, and my shoulders slipped a little lower. "What about Mom? Will she be home soon?"

"Your mother could use a gallon of Zen, but she's with the Animal Elegance committee finalizing event details. They're probably on their second case of Pinot Grigio."

I inhaled another breath of the sweet steam and set my cup aside. "The parade committee put away a few dozen mint juleps the other day. How do these women get anything done when they're all snockered?"

"It's a gift." Dad headed for his den. "High tolerance. Let me know if you need anything. I'm going to sit and put my feet on the ottoman while there's no one here to boss me around."

I arranged fabric swatches and appliqués on the dining room table, imagining the ways I could make them sing. A line of crinoline would be cute on the skirt, but pets rarely tolerated scratchy fabrics. Maybe a soft tulle or lace instead? I set the felt over various materials as a visual aid.

The mention of Animal Elegance sent my thoughts in a new direction. Was I ready? Mrs. Neidermeyer had her tutus. I'd make her pupcakes that morning and take them fresh from the oven. My weighted crystal bowls and bottled water were set aside in the storeroom. The tuna tarts and turkey tots could be made in advance and frozen. I had a striking dress selected and my most comfortable heels.

The rest of my to-do list was done, except for decorating the Chicks' pianos. My finished kitten capelets were riding shot-gun until the next parade committee meeting, when I planned to deliver them to Cecelia Waters, and hopefully impress the other members as well. With any luck, Cecelia would pay in cash, and others would be inspired to place an order.

I lined straight pins in my teeth and mocked up a skirt and two blouses for small- to medium-sized pets.

If Jack's hunch was a dud and the whole case fell apart, I needed a plan B for Furry Godmother. Thanks to the cash from Mrs. Hams putting me on retainer and the fat check from Mrs. Neidermeyer, I had the lease covered this month, but what about next? Maybe a website with online ordering options would be enough to keep me going. There would be virtually no overhead. I could work from home if I lost my lease space. I didn't need an expensive lease on Magazine Street to succeed. I could chase my dream from home. Make my own hours. Use my spare bedroom as a workspace.

Thunder rattled the windowpanes, and I dropped a needle onto the carpet. I plucked it up and placed it on the table. I'd loved storms until Katrina. That summer changed everything.

The ghastly memories of hopelessness and fear drove my thoughts back to the subject of who wanted to hurt me and why.

I fed a needle with fuchsia thread and lined black-and-white beads on the table. I needed something that looked more Audrey Hepburn and less Katy Perry. I dragged my little bead box into reach with my fingertips and dug knuckle deep in the glass beads and rhinestones. "There you are." I lifted a package of Swarovski crystals and turned them over for inspection.

A tiny ember of an idea blazed to life in my mind. "Crystals."

Five days of hell crashed through my brain in fast-forward. There was no evidence of a break-in the night Miguel died because he came in with a key. I flipped my phone over and activated speed dial number five.

"Oliver," he barked. Wind blew into the receiver.

"Jack!"

"Lacy? Is everything okay?"

I shook the bag of crystals. "I'm fine, but I think I know what happened to Miguel. He stole the key to my store from Mr. Tater the day he was killed."

"What?" A car door slammed on Jack's side of the call. The storm quieted.

"Mr. Tater came in that afternoon and told me the Gallery was robbed. His *jewelry* store."

An engine revved to life on Jack's end. "What else did he say?"

"Not much, but that's why I'm calling you. I have a theory. My store might have been the location for a drop in a two-person operation. If Miguel came to make the drop, a second person could have ransacked my store when he came to look for whatever was dropped by Miguel. Mr. Tater had a key to Furry Godmother. He kept one when we signed the lease agreement, but he'd never used it. He said he was robbed. I think Miguel took the key."

"You think it was a drop?"

"What if Miguel hid the stolen goods in my store and someone else was coming to get them? Or what if Miguel planned to play both roles? Maybe he came into my store that afternoon looking for an unlikely, easily penetrable place to stash the jewels he stole. He needed a place he could get in and out of. Someplace with no alarm or security system. I think he planned to come twice. Once for the drop and again to recover the stolen goods when he'd covered his tracks. He was used to working with a partner, so this might've been something he and Levi had done together. He'd keep doing what worked. People are creatures of habit."

"You think he made a drop for himself."

"Yes. I think looking over his shoulder was probably second nature for Miguel. He must've known he was being followed, or at least had the instinct to bury the bone for later. He was a thief in a new city, with stolen jewels in his possession and someone on his tail. He needed somewhere safe to stash the goods until the heat died down. Preferably a place that another thief wouldn't link to him."

"Like your store."

"Exactly."

"Got any theories on who killed him?"

I wetted my lips and sipped my tea. This was where my imagination had probably gotten off track. "It's rough, but yeah. I think someone might have followed him into my store that night and killed him for the goods."

"You think a second criminal stalked the first one to steal the stolen jewels."

I couldn't tell if his exasperated tone was meant for me or himself.

"Why not?" I said. "If I wanted stolen diamonds, I wouldn't want to break into a jewelry store. They have tons of security. I'd find out who was stealing jewels and then rob him. It's not like the thief could go to the cops. If Miguel had already hidden the jewels, then the killer might've come back the other night to look for the jewels. I didn't know to look for hidden jewels in my stockroom, or else I might've found them."

A long pause stretched between us.

"Or," he finally added, "maybe whatever Miguel stole is still there."

I dropped my head back. Recognition dawned. "Oh my goodness. I know where the jewels could be." There was one place I hadn't looked. I'd been too busy. "Can you find out what Mr. Tater reported stolen?"

"Depends. Can you tell me where to look?"

I pushed the crystals aside and went to look out the window. "How's the storm?"

"Getting better. Why?"

"I want you to meet me at Furry Godmother in twenty minutes."

Jack groaned. "Why don't I stop by and get the key from you, and you can tell me where to look."

"No. I want to look."

"You're safer where you are," he grouched. "Why are you determined to get hurt on my watch?"

"This isn't about you. I want to see for myself. If I'm wrong, I'll feel stupid. If I'm right, I want to celebrate."

"Someone still wants to hurt you. Stay put and I'll video chat you from the store. You'll be able to see everything I see from the safety of your parents' fortress."

"No."

Silence. "Lacy."

"Jack." I imagined him rubbing the skin off his forehead.

"Fine, but I have conditions."

"Bring it."

"First, I've got another stop to make before I can meet you. I need you to wait an hour before you leave your parents' house, or you have to let me pick you up."

"No. I'll meet you in an hour." A coil of anticipation turned in my tummy.

"I shouldn't have expected you to take the better option. Fine, but if you drive yourself, you have to agree not to get out of your car until you see me. In fact, don't shut down your engine until you see me. Drive away if anyone approaches you. Understand?"

"Yes." I stomped my feet in silent victory. If I were right, he'd see I was valuable to this case and smart. I'd redeem my family name when a positive article printed in the paper. Assuming they didn't accuse me of planting the jewels so I could pretend to find them.

"I mean it," Jack rattled on. "Don't leave your parents' house for an hour, and don't get out of your car at the studio without me present."

I nodded at the empty room. "Fine. I agree."

"Lacy?" There was a new strain in his voice.

"Yeah?" I barely endured the pause. My muscles tensed and itched with anxiety.

"We know who killed Miguel."

"What? Who?"

"Hayden. We ran down all our leads after talking with her, but nothing panned out. Every alibi fell apart. We searched her apartment and found a stack of photos of Miguel. She's been following him for weeks. There were intimate pictures of him and Sunshine. It was ugly. She had a truckload of motive, and we pulled a string of escalating e-mails between her and Miguel from her computer. She'd threatened Sunshine and the baby more than once in an effort to control him."

Panic crushed my chest. "Is anyone with Sunshine right now?"

"Yeah. We've got her at the station until we bring Hayden in."

I released a shaky breath. "Hayden could've followed Miguel into the alley and confronted him or just followed him to hurt him somewhere there weren't any witnesses." Hayden had followed her cheating boyfriend into my store after hours. "The clerk at Frozen Banana said she was a regular, and someone assaulted my store window the day after Miguel was killed." That had definitely been her smoothie on my window. "Maybe there's security video footage of her from Frozen Banana or another camera on the block."

"We're already pulling footage from that night, and we're canvassing the city for her now. Wherever she is, you don't want to run into her. She's not stable."

"I'll meet you in an hour." I disconnected and busied myself clearing the adorable assembly line on my parents' table. Cleaning was something I'd always found soothing but had fallen short on a few tasks this week. Clean dishes were still not unloaded from the dishwasher. Laundry overflowed my hamper. I also hadn't made time to clean the turtle tank, and that beautiful lagoon of glass marbles could easily hide a plastic pouch of diamonds. I *knew* Brad and Angelina could have cracked the case if they could talk.

My phone buzzed on the table. Mrs. Neidermeyer's number appeared on the screen.

Your tutus are falling apart.
Get over here right now and fix this!

I responded with slight indignation. What did she do? Put them back on the dogs after I left? I'd rehung them, personally.

Me: I have somewhere to be in an hour.
Can I stop by in the morning?
Mrs. Neidermeyer: Absolutely not. We have an eight AM dress rehearsal. You will come now.

Jeez. I slung my purse on one shoulder and checked the time. I was in the middle of my own crisis at the moment.

On my way.

The tutus could wait, but Animal Elegance was the biggest performance of the year for Mrs. Neidermeyer. It was a huge deal to her, so I needed to make time to care. If I picked the tutus up on my way to meet Jack, I could bring them back with me tonight and make the adjustments. I'd deliver them early in the morning with coffee and a smile.

Dad blocked the kitchen doorway, arms crossed. A deep scowl wrinkled his usually pleasant face. "Where do you think you are going?"

"Out. I won't be long. I'm meeting Jack at Furry Godmother."

He raised his eyebrows. "Why?"

"I'm following a hunch."

"Why isn't he picking you up? The weather's awful."

"I insisted."

Thankfully, he relented his position as jailer and stepped away. "Don't go inside the shop without him."

I frowned. "You, too?"

"Always. Be careful. Let me know how it goes. Call when you get there so I know you're safe."

"Deal." I slid around him. I could've told him about Hayden, but I didn't have time. Mrs. Neidermeyer was already sure to hold me up.

He crooked an arm around my neck and kissed my forehead. "I mean it. Call or I'll worry."

"Yes, sir." I kissed his cheek and hurried into the storm.

Chapter Twenty-Two

Furry Godmother's words of warning:
The Good Ship Lollipop *is a misnomer. And an earworm.*

I parked beside Mrs. Neidermeyer's convertible in the lot at Fancy Paws. My wipers flopped back and forth at warp speed, unable to make a dent in the river coursing over my windshield. The storm had eased for a few minutes when I'd left the house only to rush back to life with fervor before I hit Prytania. Luckily, I was one of the few people crazy enough to be on the road. Storms in Louisiana came on fast and rough, though they normally subsided as quickly as they erupted. This one was hanging on like a bad omen.

The Fancy Paws lot was desolate. Mrs. Neidermeyer's white Beamer sat near the rear entrance. Every light in the building was on. I admired her dedication. It made me glad to be a part of her brand. When the Fancy Paws dancers pranced onto the stage in my tutus, spectators would associate me with her and vice versa. A partnership like that was priceless no matter how much she made me work for it.

I sent a quick text to Jack.

At Fancy Paws to pick up tutus.
Headed to Furry Godmother next.

It had taken longer than I'd planned to make the trip to Fancy Paws, and I wasn't convinced she'd let me grab the costumes and run. It was more likely that she'd insist I make the changes before leaving. Hopefully the adjustments would be nothing significant. The supplies I'd used for her pieces were at the studio. Maybe I wouldn't be late getting to Furry Godmother after all. As long as she didn't blame me for whatever had her so upset, I would be okay. The problem had to be something she'd caused. The costumes were perfect when I'd left earlier.

My phone screeched the *Psycho* shower scene theme. I debated not answering, but with Penelope on the line, I had little choice. "Hello, Pete."

"I can't believe you, Lacy!" he seethed. "You can collect your damn cat from the airport in the morning. I'm glad to be rid of her."

Emotions went up like fireworks in my mind. She was coming to me! In the morning! "Which airline?"

"Delta. I put her on the first flight out. I hope the plane's four hours late."

"Fine." I'd cheerfully wait forever. "Thank you."

"Whatever. Thank your hard-nosed attorney. He made the arrangements and sent her airplane ticket along with a letter threatening to expose me if she wasn't on the plane. How dare you tell him about my lab? I could lose my job over that!"

I pressed a palm to my mouth. He meant the time I'd caught him and his other woman enthusiastically christening the entire room. I'd never intended to tell anyone about that humiliating nightmare, but it slipped out to Scarlet in a deluge of tears and desperation.

"Good riddance," he yelled.

"Hey! It was supposed to be a clean lab, Pete. People expect their results to be accurate, not tainted by your body fluids and skin cells." I opened my car door and stepped into the blustery night. "I'll be at the airport tomorrow morning. Penelope had better be on that plane and in the same perfect condition as when I left her." I disconnected and jammed the phone into my pocket. The elation of victory overcame me. If Penelope was on that plane tomorrow, Chase was getting the kiss of his lifetime.

I texted him and Scarlet quick praises as I hustled toward the building. Loose flyers and debris skimmed across the wet parking lot, catching on telephone poles, trees, and shrubs along the building. I splashed through tiny rivers twisting across the asphalt. My shoes, socks, and feet were soaked before I reached the door.

The wind was frightening. I thrust the entrance to Fancy Paws open and dragged it shut behind me. I stomped sopping shoes against the welcome mat. "Knock knock." I shook my arms and hands, flinging raindrops over the floor. "Oops." If I were lucky, she wouldn't make me mop it up before leaving. "Hello?"

"On the Good Ship Lollipop" played on hidden speakers, giving the bright studio a lively feel. The Shih Tzus had looked fantastic prancing on their hind paws and spinning in little lines earlier. I should have stayed longer to see what happened after a couple rounds in the new ensembles.

Plenty had changed in the few hours I was gone. A dozen wooden stage props cluttered the floor. Stumpy waves on wheeled carriages stood among pinwheels of jumping fish and random nautical props: A boat. Oars. Life preservers. The little boat had a broad deck, pink ramp, and plenty of giant, foam gumdrops. A sign strung between two four-foot candy canes showcased the words *Good Ship Lollipop* in bright, chunky letters.

The tutus hung in a neat row near the window, swinging gently from their pint-sized rolling rack. Right where I'd left them.

I shifted my weight and squished a small puddle from my shoes. "Mrs. Neidermeyer? I don't want to ruin your floor." I leaned in the direction of her open office door and projected my voice. "Mrs. Neidermeyer?"

The bathroom door was open. It seemed to be the only room in the building that didn't have a light on.

Maybe she couldn't hear me over the music?

I stepped carefully onto the high-polished floor, accepting my fate. I wasn't going anywhere until I dried the gallon of water pouring from my hair and shoes. "Mrs. Neidermeyer?" I hustled to the stereo and turned the peppy tune down to a soft drone. "Are you here?"

She wouldn't have left the studio with all the lights on.

She wasn't in the bathroom. Her car was in the lot.

I turned in a small circle, surveying the possibilities. Maybe she was in the office. I tiptoe ran across the floor feeling awful. She was probably on the phone and unable to answer me. Meanwhile, I was in the studio yelling like a child.

I slid to a stop several feet before the office door, lingering in my self-made puddle.

The red soles of Christian Louboutins came into view. "Oh no." I stepped closer, hoping her shoes were cast off and not attached to the rest of her.

A gasp flew from my lips. Mrs. Neidermeyer was face down on the faux sandpaper beach behind the Good Ship. Her face was bloody, as if she'd fallen flat on her nose. Her legs were splayed in a less-than-ladylike manner.

"Oh my goodness." I yanked the phone from my purse and swiped it to life. I ran to her side and visually evaluated her condition. Her chest rose and fell in steady breaths. No gashes, extensive bruising, or obvious injuries. "Mrs. Neidermeyer? Did you fall? Can you hear me?" I tapped her cheeks and checked her pulse. She was knocked out. Probably fine, but better safe than sorry.

I twisted for a look at the situation around her. *Did she have low blood sugar? Trip on a prop? Fall off the Good Ship?* I brought the keypad up on my phone and hovered a thumb over the nine-one-one speed dial. "I'm calling an ambulance. We'll let the paramedics come to us. I don't want to move you, and the roads are a mess."

Thunder cracked and white lightning flashed outside, illuminating the dark world beyond her studio windows. Then splintering pain coursed through my skull and my world went black.

I woke to the dreaded refrain of Shirley Temple. I hated the Good Ship and everyone on it. I hated *everything* because everything I had hurt. My head felt like someone had mistaken it for a piñata. My eyes pulsed with pain. I pressed them shut and fought for comprehension. *What happened? Did I fall?*

My arms and shoulders were immobile. My wrists burned. My legs were heavy and nonresponsive.

I blinked the hazy world into focus with sheer force of will and took a personal inventory. I was seated on the floor and slumped uncomfortably forward. My wrists ached because they were bound behind me with heavy rope from the beach display. No wonder my arms wouldn't move.

I needed medical attention. My left shoulder was likely out of its socket, and I probably had a concussion. I peered through blurry eyes at my feet, tied at the ankles like an ugly mermaid tail. An unconscious Mrs. Neidermeyer lay inches away, breathing on my shoes. We were surrounded by ocean props and relentless speakers blaring that heinous song.

Thunder rocked the building, and nausea rolled in my gut. I definitely had a concussion.

I pointed and flexed my feet, wiggling the rope loose like Dad had shown me on endless camping trips. I tapped Mrs. Neidermeyer's head softly with the soles of my wet shoes. "Hey." My throat was dry and gravelly. "Wake up."

I raised my eyes and searched for clues. Was I dreaming? Was this real?

The cuffs on a pair of dress slacks came into view. Shiny, black shoes anchored the pants. "Good. You aren't dead." Mr. Tater's voice intruded on my nightmare. He squatted, and his face swam into view.

Thank goodness!

"Mr. Tater." I pried my sticky tongue off the roof of my mouth. "Help. Help us. My phone is . . ." Where was my phone? It was in my hand a minute ago. Wasn't it? I forced a bottleneck of thoughts into order. "I dialed nine-one-one.

There's help on the way. Did you see who did this? Was there another car in the lot when you arrived?" I wiggled against the ropes on my wrists. "Untie me, please!"

He shook his head in sad rejection.

A spear of pain sliced through my forehead. "Wait a minute. Why are you here?" What would bring him to Fancy Paws in a storm?

He wiggled my phone in one hand. The keypad was still on the screen. "You didn't make your call for help. No one's on the way. The storm is loud. The music's loud. You are alone. With me."

"What?" I squinted to see him in the blinding studio light. Two versions of Mr. Tater swam before me. "Help us." The words were a strangled mix of pain, fear, and confusion.

"Absolutely." He stood with a grunt. "First, give me my diamonds."

"Your what?"

Mrs. Neidermeyer released a low, anguished groan at my feet.

I ached to help her, but my hands were literally tied. My rattled brain strained to make sense of the situation. I squinted up at Mr. Tater. "Did you do this to us?" The truth fell slowly into position. "You sent those texts from Mrs. Neidermeyer's phone. She didn't demand I come here. You did."

Mr. Tater slid a grinchy smile across his spray-tanned face. He produced her bedazzled flip phone from his pants pocket. "Now you're catching up."

"You could've killed her! How long has she been like that?" I wiggled my wrists against the pain. "I knew my tutus wouldn't fall apart." I made my most fierce face. "Let me go. She needs help."

Mr. Tater swung his chin left and right with an expression doubly as frightening as anything I could manage. "First, the diamonds."

"I don't have your diamonds. I don't know what you're talking about."

He clomped his shoe against the floorboards. "You know exactly what I'm talking about. Miguel left the jewels with you, and I want them back."

"Miguel's dead." I scooted against the prop behind me, forcing my body into a proper seated position and levering my hands off the floor. "He didn't give me anything. The police thought I killed him."

"Stop lying!"

I longed to grip my head against his booming voice. Every move I made sent knives through my shoulder. "I don't have your diamonds. If I had them, I would've returned them to you. Why would I keep something that doesn't belong to me?" I bent my legs, prying as much of myself as possible off the floor.

"Oh, right," He hacked another laugh that made my ears ring. "Why would anyone keep diamonds that didn't belong to them?" He dropped back into a squat before me and pressed one corner of my phone to his temple. "Why? Why? Why?" he growled.

"I don't have your diamonds." I winced as the decibel of my voice sent shrapnel through my head. The move jerked my tender shoulder, and I cursed.

His face knotted in anger. "I saw Miguel in your store that afternoon. I know you spoke to him. I know you were in on it. What was your cut?"

"I don't know what you're talking about." Tears formed in my eyes and raced down both cheeks.

He scratched his head and huffed a small, humorless sound. "At first, I thought it was an unfortunate coincidence. I believed your gung-ho, solve-the-crime, save-my-store act. I worried you might dig too far in my direction, so I left you a note to knock it off before you forced my hand. Do you know how difficult that was for me? I don't want to have to do this."

"Then don't," I sniffled. "Don't do this."

He lifted and dropped his hands at his sides. "I combed your store, Lacy. Every box, every shelf. No jewels. At first, I was so confused. How could they be gone? Where could they go? Where could they be?"

"I don't know."

Mr. Tater groaned and rapped the phone against my pounding head. "You've had them all along. He gave them to you, and you hid them for him. I know what that pet shop of yours makes every month. It can't possibly keep you at the standard of living you're accustomed too. It was only a matter of time before you looked elsewhere for cash."

I rolled the back of my head against the stout, wooden prop. "Answer me!"

"No. It's not true. I never had them. I don't even know what he stole." I closed one eye to bring Mr. Tater into focus. "You wanted to distance yourself from me so I wouldn't tarnish your name. Do you know how crazy I've been this week, scrambling to make enough money to cover my costs and a lease payment?

You didn't want to be associated with *me*. And now you'd kill two women over some stolen jewels? What's wrong with you? You have insurance. Call them. File a report. They'll replace your lost inventory. You know that. You're a businessman."

He crossed his arms and furrowed his brow. "You still don't get it. Where do you think my jewels come from? The diamond store? You think I buy all my merchandise legitimately and still make a killing in a town like this? Don't be daft; it doesn't suit you."

I tried opening my other eye and failed. He was off his rocker, and I needed a plan. I worked my feet back and forth, wiggling and scrubbing the rope against itself, loosening the ties.

"Tell me where those jewels are, and I'll let you live."

"I have no idea where jewels come from." I pressed my back to the prop behind me, hoping it was less sturdy than it looked. "None of them. Not yours. Not Tiffany's. I make pet costumes."

He looked at the ceiling. "Have you heard the expression 'Pride cometh before a fall'? Miguel had too much pride. We had a deal, and he got greedy. He supplemented my collection with gems from his heists, and I paid generously. I reset the stones into my original pieces and no one was any the wiser until he came down here asking for more money. He robbed every jeweler in the district, including me."

Robbed by his personal burglar. Maybe karma was real. "You sell stolen jewels? What was Miguel? A freelance thief?"

"Close enough. Now I have to find another one, all because he wanted to cash in and run off with that girl."

If Hayden had threatened to hurt Sunshine and their baby, like Jack said, Miguel must've felt trapped. Hayden was stalking him. He had to get out. My heart broke all over again, for the three of them this time. Sunshine, Miguel, and their baby. I squinted sore eyes at Mr. Tater. "Everyone thinks you're a great businessman. You're a fraud. You're no better than Miguel. And now this?" I motioned to Mrs. Neidermeyer. "What were you thinking?"

"I'm thinking I'm tired of being jerked around. I sell a few stolen jewels. So what? They aren't enough to draw attention. I use the extra money to bankroll new investments. Like yours. I give back to the economy. That's called business savvy."

I nodded in faux agreement. "Shame on you."

My phone dinged with a new text. He turned it to face me before dropping it beside my leg and smashing his heel into it. Jack's selfie shattered. "Enough. I'm tired, and the storm won't last forever." He pulled a revolver from beneath his suit jacket. "I need to finish this while the storm's going, so talk."

Well, that wasn't going to happen. "How'd you know Miguel kept the jewels so he could leave with Sunshine?"

"I followed him all day after I spotted him in your store. When he went inside that night, I started after him, but a woman beat me through the door. I entered next and heard them out back." He switched to a high-pitched voice and made a whiny face. "'You never loved me. You can't leave me. You lied to me. Why are you doing this?'" He waved the gun in circles, as if the whole thing was ridiculous. "Eventually, it got quiet, and I opened the back door. Miguel was dead, and the woman was gone. Imagine my surprise when the cops showed up a few minutes later with you." His expression turned grim. "Last chance. Where did you put my diamonds?"

Tater shoved the gun closer to me.

A new idea sparked in my broken head. "Fine. You got me. I'll show you where I hid the jewels. Untie me, and I'll take you to them." Hopefully I was right about the turtle tank. Even if I wasn't, a car ride would buy me thinking time.

He tipped his head over one shoulder. "Where?"

"They're at my store." Where he would also find a very annoyed detective. "I'll show you." The knot behind my feet finally gave way, and I stilled.

"Liar!" Mr. Tater screamed, spittle flying into the air.

Panic pried at my brain. He was going to shoot me. What if I died tonight? *What a stupid way to die.* "Let me show you," I pleaded.

"I've already searched your store. The jewels aren't there and you know it!" He pulled the revolver's hammer back with his thumb. "Tell me the truth or she gets the first bullet." He swung the gun's barrel toward Mrs. Neidermeyer's head and inched closer, dropping into a crouch at her side. "Come on," he taunted. "Be a hero. I know you want to." He pressed the gun to her temple and looked at me. "Where. Are. My. Jewels?" Each word was a sentence. Each pause was a countdown.

I tensed my muscles and braced myself against the prop. "I. Don't. Know." In one excruciating move, I kicked my feet into the air and brought them down on his neck.

He cried out, tipping forward and grabbing his head with one hand.

I pulled my knees to my chest and pushed both feet into his face. They connected with a thud.

His neck snapped back, and he bounced against the floorboards. The gun skittered and thumped against the wall.

"Yes!" I scrambled to my feet, head pounding, eyes crossing, and stomach churning. The prop attached to my ropes slid down my back and fell away, drawn by gravity and aided by slightly loosened ropes. I bit my lip to squelch a scream and hurried to Mrs. Neidermeyer's side. I shoved her with my foot. Hard. "Wake up! Get up! Wake up!"

Mr. Tater moaned and rolled onto his back.

The gun was on the other side of him, and my hands were still tied behind my back. I couldn't hide. I couldn't use a doorknob or phone. He'd smashed my phone!

Mr. Tater rolled onto his side and grabbed his nose. Blood rushed over his lips and colored his teeth. "I'm going to kill you!"

I kicked his gun away and scrambled through the open office door, shoving it shut behind me. I pressed my back to the door and turned the lock on the knob with my fumbling fingertips.

The scent of burnt coffee and old paper overtook me. There was no other way out. No windows. I was trapped. I scanned the area for a weapon. I needed an envelope opener or another way to free my hands.

An enormous, tan rectangle in the corner caught my attention. The little black squares and spiral phone cord called to me like the savior that it was.

I jumped backward onto the desk and screamed as my left arm jostled and bounced against my side.

I leaned forward, craning my bound hands to reach the receiver. If I could unhook the phone, I could dial 9-1-1.

Outside the door, Mrs. Neidermeyer screamed.

"Come on," I cried. I swatted through the pain, aiming but missing the phone behind me.

"I warned you!" Mr. Tater's voice cut through the hollow office door.

"Please let her be okay," I whispered.

A gunshot exploded before I finished the prayer.

My ears rang, and I heaved onto the floor. My teeth chattered painfully.

An ugly sob shook my body. My fingers connected with the receiver behind me, and it rattled off the cradle and onto the desk.

"Thank you thank you thank you thank you." *One, two, three.* I counted the rows of buttons with my fingertips and pushed. "Nine." *Back up. One. Two.* "One. One." Tears fell over my face in hot, wet sheets.

"Nine-one-one. What's your emergency?" a tinny voice lifted from the receiver.

"Help!" I screamed, suddenly overcome with desperation. "We're at Fancy Paws dance studio. There's a man with a gun."

The office door burst open, and Mr. Tater walked in. The fingers of one hand were knotted deep in Mrs. Neidermeyer's hair.

Mascara blackened her cheeks. Lipstick smeared her chin and jawbone. Blood clung to her nose and upper lip. Awful sounds gurgled from her twisted mouth. "Please don't do this. Please."

He pressed the gun to her ribs with his free hand. "Shut. Up."

The storm drummed to a crescendo on the roof, flickering the lights and stopping my heart.

Mr. Tater stepped forward, leaving a trembling Mrs. Neidermeyer behind him. He lifted the gun toward me. "Last chance."

I dug deep for any semblance of composure and channeled my mother. "No, Mr. Tater," I corrected. "It's your last chance to run before you're arrested. I've dialed nine-one-one." I tipped my head slightly, indicating the phone receiver at my hip. "They're on their way, and they're recording every word. If you leave now, you can avoid a murder charge and maybe get out of town before they find you."

His crazed eyes flicked to the phone. "You're bluffing."

I tented my eyebrows. "I'm not, but it's your call. Waste some more time. Kill me before you go and never see freedom again, or make a run for it and maybe disappear before the police get here."

Beads of sweat lined his brow and upper lip. Rage and fear colored his face.

I thought of my parents. I'd promised Dad I'd call so he'd know I was safe. I'd never lied to my dad before. The weight of all I'd put my mother through crashed over me. I owed her more than I could repay. I'd never been as happy as I had been since moving home. I closed my eyes and sent loving thoughts to my folks.

I opened them again to see Jack step into view outside the office door, inches behind Mrs. Neidermeyer.

Tater's hand and gun shook. "If I'm going down, I'm taking the witnesses with me."

I worked up a cocky smirk. "Too late."

Jack set a hand on Mrs. Neidermeyer's shoulder, presumably to usher her away. She released a bloodcurdling scream and collapsed.

Tater spun in her direction.

"It's over," Jack said. "Put the gun down."

Gun shots erupted. Two in quick succession.

I released a wild, regretful cry. My ears rang and my vision blurred.

Mr. Tater staggered backward into the tiny office and sprawled onto the floor at my feet.

Jack appeared before me. His strong hands wrapped my cheeks, and his wide, calloused thumbs stroked the hollows beneath my eyes. His voice caressed my frantic heart. "It's going to be okay."

I cried louder. The chatter in my teeth spread to my limbs, and I vibrated with shock and excess adrenaline. "Mr. Tater bought stolen jewels from Miguel. He broke into my store. He left the note on my tire. He saw Hayden at Furry Godmother that night."

Jack paid no attention to my rambling. He prodded my skin with gentle fingers. "Is your arm broken?"

I shook my head. "My shoulder's dislocated."

He untied my wrists and rubbed them gently. He lifted the receiver on the desk. "Hello? This is Detective Jack Oliver."

I forced my attention to the dark-crimson stain spreading toward us over the office floor.

Jack put the old receiver on the cradle and took my hand in his. "This is going to hurt like hell." He braced himself and pulled my arm until the furious pain in my shoulder released with a snap.

"Ah!" I screamed. He pulled me against his chest. "You're supposed to count me down or wait for the paramedics," I sobbed against his shoulder. "Are you trying to kill me or save me?"

Jack leaned away and curved my arm against my tummy to stabilize the shoulder. "I'm saving you."

He bumped the body at his feet with the toe of his boot. "He'll live. I only gave him a flesh wound. I want him to stand trial."

"What about Mrs. Neidermeyer?"

"She fainted. I tapped her shoulder, and she went down like a bag of bricks."

I laughed. "Ow." I squinted. "I'm concussed."

Jack moved confident fingers through my hair and over my scalp, evaluating the report. "You know I told you to stay home, right?"

I flinched when he found a tender spot. "Really? You're blaming this on me?"

"If the tutu fits."

Outside, the distant whir of sirens cut through the wind and rain.

I tried to still my rattling teeth. "Thank you for saving me."

"No problem. Besides, you saved yourself. I was on my way here to yell at you after I got your text about making a pit stop. I called first, but you didn't answer, and I assumed the worst. Then I heard the nine-one-one dispatcher sending units to this address."

"Tater had my phone. He smashed it. What about Hayden? Did you find her?"

"We've got Hayden in custody. She admitted to the murder almost immediately. It was an accident. A crime of passion."

I held back a body-shaking sob and sought something good to think about while EMTs loaded Mr. Tater onto a gurney. "Pete's giving my cat back. I'm picking her up at the airport tomorrow morning."

Jack frowned. "I don't think you should be driving for a few days."

"I'll call a cab." Or Dad, or Scarlet, or Imogene, or Chase.

"I'll drive you."

Or Jack. I pulled in a deep breath. I had people. "Oh." I set my palm against Jack's stubbled cheek. "I didn't ask about you. Tater tried to shoot you." I did my best to look strong. "Are you okay?"

He made a sour face. "Haven't you heard? I'm indestructible."

I laughed. "Ow." I removed my hand from his cheek and used it to hold my head together.

He placed his hand over mine. "I didn't expect to shoot anyone tonight. I haven't done that in ages."

"Yeah? Well, stick with me," I muttered.

Chapter Twenty-Three

Furry Godmother's fashion tip: Cover your assets.

Three weeks later, the Animal Elegance gala was packed with the district's crème de la crème. It was a swanky red-carpet event with paparazzi and caterers galore. Local news crews had arrived hours ahead of time, along with reporters from pet advocacy groups, the Humane Society, and a few naked protesters who thought animals in costumes qualified as abuse. I'd been on my feet for twelve hours and in heels for eight. I needed a shower, jammies, and a soft bed. I'd been awake for more than a day, and my fantasies all boiled down to sleep. Too bad that when given the opportunity to sleep, my mind chose to replay the events of the night Mr. Tater tried to kill me. Even all this time later, it still hurt to brush my hair. Luckily, I had Penelope to talk to when I couldn't sleep. True to his word, Pete had put her on a plane, and Jack took me to pick her up. Life was infinitely better with her at my side. She was exactly what I needed to heal.

I swept my long curls over one shoulder and dropped fresh ice cubes in a line of crystal water dishes for any remaining party pets. Mrs. Neidermeyer's Shih Tzus were a hit, but they'd all gone home immediately after their performance. I caught a look at poor Mrs. Neidermeyer as they danced. She apparently felt the same way I did about the Good Ship Lollipop now. When the song finally ended, I'd exhaled ten pounds of tension and went for a glass of water. She wasn't far behind.

The tutus held up well and got plenty of nods. So many, in fact, that I was out of business cards by dinner.

A round of applause drifted through the walls. The keynote speaker must have finished. He represented the American Kennel Club, and I'd wanted to hear his ideas on pet health and nutrition, but being a one-woman company wasn't easy. Thank goodness for family and free labor. I had plenty of both by the names of Dr. and Mrs. Crocker and our dear friend Imogene.

The trio ducked into the private room single file.

"There you are." Mom had an empty silver tray. "We need more of everything and some business cards."

I topped the bowls off with fresh water and tossed the empty bottles into my recycle tote. "I'm out." I showed her my palms, then dropped them to my sides. The gesture was one I used with pets to assure them there were no more treats.

Mom gave me a narrowed stare. Her floor-length Elie Saab gown hung in layers of chiffon and silk over vintage Gucci pumps. "How am I supposed to make a proper impression without the right tools?"

I touched my forehead. "How was the speaker?"

"He looked like Mable Feller's bulldog. He's too squat for a pale-gray suit and Harry Potter glasses."

"I'd hoped to talk to him about my pawlines." A twinge of disappointment curled in my chest.

Mom huffed. "That's funny because everyone wants to talk to *you* about those."

I toed red velvet pet beds into a circle and dropped a peanut butter cookie on each. "Thank you for all your help today, but you should go mingle. There's no reason to spend the whole gala serving pet treats. Plus, we're all out, so . . ." I made a shooing motion. "Go. Have fun."

Imogene delivered air kisses and headed for the door. "You don't have to tell me twice. If you need anything else, you can find me on the dance floor."

"Thanks." I smiled and waved.

She stopped in the doorway. "I'm ready to take over for Paige at your shop when she goes back to Brown. Let me know when I start."

"Okay. That's . . ." I hesitated. I'd decided I didn't need an investor to keep the store open. I'd make it a success the same way other new business owners did: with a stress cocktail of debt, hard work, and sleep deprivation. Work would definitely be interesting with Imogene at my side. "It's great news." I hoped. "Thank you."

"You still got your little piggy?" She asked.

"Yep."

"Good girl." She patted the doorjamb and disappeared into the gala.

Mom handed me her empty tray. "If you don't want our help, we might as well go dancing too."

"Look at this." I waved my arms, indicating the room around us. The green room for performers and their trainers had been a simple conference room until Mom and I turned it into an Egyptian suite fit for any pharaoh. "You were here all day setting up, and now you're not enjoying yourself. You're working. You think my job is silly, and it kind of is, but I've got this under control. I want you to go enjoy what's left of your night."

Her jaw dropped in overly dramatic Crocker style. "I don't think what you do is silly."

I made a be-serious face.

"I think *you're* silly. I mean, you are your father's daughter." She wiggled her hands from me to Dad. What could she do? We were weird.

Dad tapped his empty serving tray against his palm. "What your mother means is that she's proud of you. *We're* proud of you, and we're glad to help however you'll allow us."

I eyeballed Mom. "You aren't ashamed that your only child dropped out of medical school in favor of a degree in fashion and now the only fashions she makes are worn by pets?"

She shook her head. "We love fashion and pets."

"Mom." I gave the face again.

"What? You said yourself it's a silly job, but that doesn't make it shameful. I've never been ashamed of you. I couldn't be. Your career choice, strange as it is, seems to fit you, and it makes you happy, so I'm happy."

"Really?" She didn't look happy, but she rarely did, so I couldn't judge based on that.

"Of course. My battle's half won. Now that you're back in the district, it will be much easier for me to find an established man willing to support your odd endeavors. Whimsy has its charms. I'll find someone."

I dropped my head forward and stretched an arm around her waist. "Thank you for your help tonight." I rested my head on her shoulder.

"You're welcome. Silly or not, the noblest thing anyone can do is support family."

The words were welcome but clearly at odds with her disposition. "You seem a little miffed for someone doing noble work."

She tensed. "That's because Hams is here with those Llama Mamas and their llamas."

"Really?" I tried to imagine how a herd of llamas could attend the posh event. "Where?" Not on stage, surely.

She pointed to the window on the far wall. "She brought them in a trailer lined in little twinkle lights and fenced off an area in the parking lot with signs on the benefits of llama love."

I must've made a face because Dad laughed and Mom sighed dramatically.

She fussed with her vintage sapphire necklace. "Now she's got the attention of two superintendents from prominent districts. If she gets those beasts into schools, what am I supposed to do?"

I went to the window for a look at the llamas and their little trailer. "Too cute." The llamas were adorable in scarlet-and-gold jackets bearing the Llama Mama insignia. I squinted. "They're behaving oddly." They were fussing and rubbing their sides against one another. "She should've let me design new jackets for them." What was the point of having me on retainer if she didn't call?

Mom peeked out the window over my shoulder. "They've worn those coats for two seasons now. She bought them online. They aren't even custom."

Dad looked at his watch. "Well, we can plan your pitch to the school systems tomorrow, dear. I think we should enjoy tonight while it lasts. Why don't the three of us take a break and enjoy the evening together?"

Mom was unusually quick to drop her llama lament and agree.

I hated to leave the green room but couldn't think of a reason to stay. The treats were gone. Waters were full. Things were tidy. It was probably the perfect time to shake hands and make contacts.

I slid my hand under Dad's arm and let him lead me to the crowded room of glitz and glam.

The grand ballroom overflowed with opulence. Well-appointed tables and high-backed dining chairs stuffed every inch of central floor space. Crystal bowls and glasses sat among a sea of crimson-and-gold linens. Lavish floral displays anchored the stage and adorned each table. A string quartet sat front and center, charming guests onto the dance floor.

The room was a showcase of New Orleans's finest. The mayor was there. There were several bigwigs from Harrah's casino and all the socialites from our district. I recognized most of the faces from a lifetime in these circles. Others I'd only seen on the news.

I released Dad when intuition kicked in. "When did you guys visit the llamas?"

He frowned. "Not long ago. Why?"

"Were they acting strangely when you saw them?"

He rubbed his chin. "No. I didn't think so. Do you think something's wrong?"

I turned my gaze on Mom. When she'd first learned of my involvement with the llamas, she suggested I sprinkle their products with itching powder. "Could someone have tampered with their costumes?"

Dad crossed his arms. "Violet?"

Mom clucked her tongue. "What do the two of you think of me? I would never harm an animal. You know that." She squared her shoulders in defiance. "That woman dressed her livestock in ugly jackets and penned them in a parking lot. They're probably plotting against her."

Dad turned toward the exit. "It could be too much attention or the traffic. I'm going to see if I can help."

"Maybe you should tell her they have fleas," Mom suggested sweetly.

I gave her a disapproving look. "Really?"

She matched my look and raised a self-important eyebrow. "I didn't bother her precious llamas. She, however, has covered every one of my 4-H posters with ones for her dumb parade. One day you'll have an archenemy, and then you'll understand."

"Great. Something to look forward to, then."

Dad left. Mom went in the opposite direction.

I found a quiet spot to people watch. Chase was easy to spot, even at the farthest corner from me. He wore a white James Bond tuxedo and was surrounded by women whose dates and husbands looked on. It wasn't often his kind of family money came with a contagious personality and a set of killer abs.

I made my way into his entourage.

He excused himself promptly. "Hello, Miss Crocker." He bowed formally and gave a sly wink.

"Have I thanked you for saving Penelope from a life with slime?"

"You have."

Though not in the way we'd agreed. "You never told me about the letter."

Chase fell in beside me to watch the crowd. "Scarlet had all the ammo I needed. The rest is basic law. You weren't married or living together long, so she wasn't property to be divided. You found her, brought her home, and are listed as her emergency contact on all veterinary forms. You paid for all her care with a personal credit card. You were Penelope's main caregiver. His only decent shot was an argument of abandonment, but I squelched that with the bit about his lab. Petty of me, but I'm not a real lawyer."

I nudged Chase with my elbow. "Thank you."

"Do you see that?" He motioned to his brother and Scarlet, his co-conspirator. "How do they do that?"

Scarlet and Carter stood nose to nose on the dance floor, leaning into one another over her bump and swaying infinitesimally. He smiled at her like they shared the world's best secret. Maybe they did. Scarlet was my first visitor at the hospital after that awful night at Fancy Paws. Jack had called her from the ambulance, and she almost beat us there. The effort was silly because I was fine, but it was nice seeing her fly into the room, eight months pregnant and ready to flatten Tater. Luckily, that job had already been done.

"Probably because they're both pretty amazing. Did you know she started a charity mission for single moms in New Orleans? She said Sunshine inspired her. Your family's law firm is drawing up all the paperwork and making the inaugural donation of a cool twenty-five thousand. Scarlet's tapping into established organizations for input and resources. She wants to provide parenting classes, support groups, and eventually an annual scholarship fund."

Pride welled in his eyes. "They aren't a bad bunch."

A man in vintage Armani and diamond cufflinks slid into the space beside me. "You look nice tonight."

"Hello, Jack," Chase said. He shook Jack's hand, then turned mischievous eyes on me. "I'll catch up with you later and see if I can sway you on that deal of ours." He kissed my cheek and strutted away. I did my best not to fan my face.

Jack slid a curious gaze over my figure, lingering on my exposed collarbone before continuing to the floor and back. "I'd like to redact my previous comment. You don't look nice at all. You look absolutely scandalous in that gown."

Suddenly the backless, sleeveless, high low number I'd chosen felt indecent. I glanced at the plunging satin neckline and resisted the urge to pull the sides together. "I'd hoped to make an impression."

"Mission accomplished." His sweet southern drawl sent shivers through places I tried not to think about. Heat swam across my cheeks, hot enough to melt my makeup and release my freckles. I cleared my throat and tried to look less exposed than I felt. "I didn't expect to see you here." I hadn't seen him since he drove Penelope and me home from the airport. Three weeks was a long time to wonder where he went and why he never called. "Are you here for work?"

"Something like that."

I gave the crowd another look. *Who was he watching?* "How is Mr. Tater?"

"He's recovering nicely. He'll be able to stand trial and be held accountable for his crimes."

I dashed my toe against the floor. "Thank you for not killing him. I'd had an awful night. Witnessing a murder would've been the worst."

"Well, I aim to serve."

I smiled. "Thanks. Did you get him to tell you everything he told me, or is he pleading the fifth like Levi did?"

Jack relaxed his stance by a fraction. "Tater cracked like an egg. Levi's a product of the system. He's hard and cold. He doesn't care about what happens to him, but Tater's a middle-aged white-collar criminal gone off the deep end. Once he realized how much trouble he was in, he told us everything. Even copped to plundering your store. We confirmed the cornstarch was from gloves he buys for the Barrel Room cleaning staff. He had no problem identifying Hayden as the woman he saw enter your store that night."

"How is she?"

"Not good. She was enraged when she saw Miguel at your shop after hours. She thought it was some secret rendezvous."

"I screamed and painted his face. What kind of rendezvous was she thinking?"

"She wasn't thinking. She was reacting. His death was a terrible accident. A blow to the head normally just leaves a person loopy. Take you for example."

"Ha." I touched my temple on instinct. The ghost of pain was still there with the memories. "Can you believe I didn't have a concussion?"

"Yes. You were the only one who thought you did."

"Apparently stress altered my ability to properly self-diagnose."

"You're obsessed with minutiae."

"What else did Tater say? Did he tell you Miguel worked for him?"

"Yeah. He subsidized his jewelry store with stolen gems. He sold a lot of fakes, too."

I guffawed. "Why hasn't anyone reported him?"

"I don't know. Maybe the price was so right, buyers didn't think it was worth admitting their stupidity. Two-carat diamonds for five hundred dollars online should be a giveaway. People are gullible."

"Not all of them."

He watched me. Whatever he thought of that, he didn't say.

I fidgeted under his gaze. "So the renowned businessman was a crook. I swear this town is all smoke and mirrors."

"Speaking of illusions, every missing diamond from Magazine Street turned up in your turtle tank. They've been logged and confirmed. Miguel dropped a half million dollars' worth of ice onto the layer of glass stones and no one had a clue."

"I guess Tater and Levi were right. I did have the jewels."

He slid his blue eyes my way. "Have you heard from Levi's lawyer?"

I shot him a dirty look. "No. He can't be serious about that."

Chase's laugh rose above the music as he high-fived his brother for something I'd missed.

I smiled. "If he does try to sue, I have an excellent attorney in mind."

Jack tracked my gaze to Chase and Carter. "Did I interrupt anything earlier? You two seem to have gotten pretty close."

"He saved my cat."

Jack looked me over. He knew that story and how much it meant to me. "I saved your life."

"I thought you said *I* saved my life by dialing nine-one-one."

He turned smiling eyes back to the crowd. "I was trying to make you feel better."

"You're changing your story, Oliver."

"Well, I have to. The credit's all mine."

I followed his lead and watched silently as couples floated arm in arm around the dance floor.

He glanced quickly my way. "I'm not used to seeing you smile. Too many cocktails?"

"No. I was thinking I'm glad to be home. I don't always understand the people here, but . . ."

"They're your people."

I turned to face him. "Yeah."

He nodded, eyes busily scanning the crowd. "I know."

I fiddled with the royal-blue satin of my gown and thought of Chase. His family adored him, despite the fact they had little in common outside of genetics. My family was the same. He and I had both left in search of ourselves, and we'd both wound up right back where we'd started. Maybe *this* was who we were. Prodigal children of the district.

A woman in thousand-dollar heels drifted by on the arm of a man whose watch cost more than my car. "Hi, Lacy." She waved as they passed.

A broad smile rose on my lips. No, I wasn't like my mother or most of the people I'd once left behind, but I was definitely one of them, and that was okay with me.

"I like to think of you as the hippie child of the neighborhood."

I laughed. "What?"

"It's nice. You make life quirky and interesting in a place that's too staunch." He turned on his shiny shoes and caught me with his gaze. "I remember watching you paint your store window before you opened. All those little animals with wings." He chuckled. "I thought you were a nut. I thought your shop would be bankrupt before it opened."

"You saw that?" I'd had paint everywhere. The glitter had stuck in my hair for a week.

"You wore a short pink dress and tennis shoes. Your hair was all twisted into a knot on top of your head. I stood across the street waiting for you to finish. I had to see what you'd do."

I grimaced. "What did I do?"

"You put the brush between your teeth like a rose and stepped back to admire your work."

"Well, that sounds conceited."

"No. There was pride in your eyes." His Adam's apple bobbed, and his brows inched closer together. His lips parted slightly, and my pulse quickened.

Mom swept into view with a silent clap of her hands. "Jack, it's so nice to see you." She gripped his hands and air kissed his cheeks. "I'm so glad you could come. I was just telling Lacy these are the sorts of events where great unions are formed. She should attend more often. Don't you think? Perhaps a fellow pet lover will find her and they can make a lucrative love match."

"Mom." I shook my head infinitesimally.

Jack laughed. "I don't believe I've heard the words lucrative and love match together before."

"Welcome to my world," I muttered.

Mom straightened her posture overtly, a reminder I was slouching.

I rolled my shoulders back. "I'm not looking for a match." Lucrative or otherwise.

She rolled her eyes. "Don't be silly. Everyone wants to find their one true love, darling. It's the American dream."

"That's really not the American dream."

Jack's smile widened, enjoying my mother's nonsense. "I'm confused." He crossed his arms and made a painfully serious face. "Are you saying you're against love, Lacy?"

I pointed a shiny, red nail at him. "I didn't say that. I only said I'm not looking for a wealthy man with societal status to validate me. I'm happy the way I am, poor or not, and I'd be happy with a regular guy who liked me for me."

Mom cocked a hoity eyebrow and turned back to the crowd. She hummed herself out of sight, enjoying my discomfort far too much.

"I like her," Jack said.

"That's only because she adores you."

"Not true. I like you, and you're a real pain in the ass." He trailed someone over my shoulder with his gaze.

"Is that so?"

A woman wearing gold, strapless couture appeared on my left. "Are you ready, Jackson?" she asked. She was gorgeous and clearly older than me, but it was unclear how much. Five years? Ten? Her figure was lethal, and her poise was long polished. Her gaze slid over Jack's neck and shoulders like they were dinner and she hadn't eaten in days.

I didn't like her.

"Yep." He turned to me and let his lids fall shut for a long beat. When he reopened them, he formed a tight line with his mouth. "Lacy, this is Tabitha." He glanced her way. "Tabitha, this is Lacy."

My mouth dropped. "This is Tabitha?" *The roommate? Dead Grandpa Smacker's girlfriend?* Holy gold diggers! Money bought at least one old guy happiness. She was even wearing gold. I snapped my mouth shut. "Nice to meet you."

She scrutinized me. "This is the girlfriend?"

Um, what? I looked behind me for another woman.

Jack took my hand in his. "Yep." He lifted our hands to his lips and kissed my knuckles. "Well, honey, I'm going to take Tabitha home. I'll be back to pick you up when you call."

He gently kissed my cheek, lingering his mouth near my ear. "Sorry. I didn't see her coming. Please go along with this and let's never talk about it again."

He bowed away and zipped through the crowd with the life-sized, female Oscar statue.

My phone buzzed a moment later. A text from Jack.

That never happened.

I dropped the cell phone back into my clutch. *Um, yes, that definitely did happen, and I'm going to find out why.*

Furry Godmother's Peanut Butter and Banana Pupcakes

Makes 6 full-sized cupcakes.

Pets love to party with their people, and these yummy treats are a safe way to include the furriest family members in every celebration.

Pupcake Ingredients

1½ cups whole wheat flour

⅓ cup rolled oats

2 ripe bananas

½ cup natural, unsweetened applesauce

½ cup natural peanut butter

2 eggs

1 tsp. vanilla

1 tsp. baking powder

1 tsp. baking soda

Creamy Peanut Butter Icing

6 oz. of cream cheese

4 oz. of smooth peanut butter

1 tbsp. of extra-virgin olive oil

Directions

1. Preheat oven to 350°F.

2. Line a muffin pan with paper cups or prep your tin.

3. Mash up bananas. Add eggs, vanilla, applesauce, and peanut butter.

4. Combine flour, oats, baking powder, and baking soda.

5. Add flour to banana mixture and stir.

6. Scoop batter into muffin tins or paper liners.

7. Ask your dogs to clean the bowl. They'll be great helpers!

8. Bake pupcakes for 18 minutes.

9. Remove the muffins from the oven and move to a wire rack until completely cool before icing.

10. Blend cream cheese, peanut butter, and oil in medium bowl until smooth.

11. Spread creamy peanut butter icing on cooled pupcakes and resist taking a big bite! These are for the dogs, silly.

Furry Godmother's New Orleans Pawlines

Makes approximately 2 dozen pawlines.

No candy is more iconic to New Orleans than the praline. Much like Lacy's family, pralines made their way to the city from France and grew into something uniquely New Orleans. Here's an animal-friendly version of the praline that's safe to enjoy with your pet.

Pawlines Ingredients

3–4 slices of bacon
1½ cups whole wheat flour
½ cup wheat germ
½ cup melted bacon fat
1 large egg
½ cup water
2 tbsp. all-natural maple syrup (optional)

Directions

1. Preheat oven to 350°F.

2. Fry bacon until crispy. Remove from pan and crumble. Set aside a small amount as topping.

3. Allow bacon grease to cool.

4. Add egg, water, and optional syrup to the bacon fat.

5. Mix in flour, wheat germ, and crumbled bacon.

6. Roll to ½ inch on a floured surface and cut into circles or use your puppy's favorite-shaped cookie cutter and move to lightly greased cookie sheet.

7. Top with remaining bacon crumbles for crunch and sass.

8. Bake 20 minutes or until lightly browned.

Furry Godmother's
Tiny Tuna Tarts

Makes 3 dozen tarts.

Show your cat you care with these homemade treats. Made from scratch and baked with love, Miss Mittens will never doubt your dedication again, unless you try to feed her more of that store-bought stuff.

Ingredients

1 can tuna in oil, drained
1 egg
1¼ cups of flour
½ cup water
1 tsp. of parsley, finely chopped

Directions:

1. Preheat oven to 350°F.

2. Mix tuna, egg, flour, water, and parsley into a sturdy dough.

3. Roll dough to ½ inch on a floured surface, adding flour as needed to handle dough.

4. Cut into 1-inch rectangle and move to a prepared cookie sheet.

5. Bake for 20 minutes. Tarts will rise as they bake.

Read an excerpt from

CAT GOT YOUR CASH

the next

KITTY COUTURE MYSTERY

by Julie Chase

available soon in hardcover from
Crooked Lane Books

CROOKED
LANE

NEW YORK

Chapter One

Furry Godmother's advice for the budding designer:
Never meet your hero.

I hefted an armload of miniature couture onto the counter at Furry Godmother, my pet boutique and organic treat bakery nestled in the famed New Orleans Garden District. A rainbow of crinoline and sequins splayed over the freshly cleaned space near a box of matching accessories. My heart fluttered. "I have thirty-eight minutes before I meet with Annie Lane. That gives me thirty minutes to make the final selections, pack up, and get to her house. And then eight minutes to freak out."

Imogene, my old nanny and new shopkeep, watched silently as I turned in a small circle, looking for a place to put the keepers. Every clean, flat space in sight was already covered in adorable creations.

I turned back to the counter and flipped through a flood of tiny formal wear. I hung my favorites over one arm with new-found discernment. "You know what? I'm starting to sweat. I should use the extra eight minutes to freshen up. I'll freak out on the drive over instead."

Imogene clucked her tongue. "Annie Lane is going to love you and your designs. Whatever you decide to take will be perfect."

I gave her an incredulous look.

Imogene had been with my family for decades. First as my grandmother's caregiver, then as my mother's estate keeper, and eventually as my nanny. She was heavily biased in my favor. At the moment, she was also wrong.

Annie Lane was a world-famous fashion designer. I was a budding pet couture creator. The pieces I chose to take with me to represent my brand mattered. A lot. This appointment could change everything. My career. My entire future. Together, Annie and I could be an unstoppable force in fashion. I just needed to convince her of that. When I'd heard she was returning to New Orleans for Faux Real, the annual arts festival, I pitched a meeting to her people, suggesting a companion line for Annie's Mardi Gras designs. I sent snapshots of my feline and canine king capes and nearly fainted when she wanted to see more.

Being crowned king or queen during Mardi Gras was one of the highest civic honors in New Orleans, so the pair dressed to impress. The royal garb was so significant that some of the most epic gear from over the years was enshrined in a French Quarter Mardi Gras museum. I'd loved going there as a child, imagining the designers' workspaces piled high with sequins and gold lamé. Royal apparel could weigh as much as forty to sixty pounds, not including the headpiece. In fact, one of the queen's gowns had had more than one hundred fifty yards of tulle over satin. Wheels had to be sewn along the hem to help her get around. Those costumes made the most elaborate

Vegas show girl ensemble look like amateur hour. With a little luck, one of my designs could be tucked safely behind museum glass one day too, if I made good choices. A partnership with Annie Lane was a very good choice.

Imogene eyeballed me from a closing distance. The tails of her red silk headscarf fluttered behind her, secured tightly around a puff of salt-and-pepper hair. "You're flushed. You should sit down before you fall over. Have a glass of water. I'll cleanse the air in here and try to clean up the bad juju."

My arm drooped under the weight of too many favorites. The logoed garment box I'd intended to pack my items into wouldn't hold half of what I wanted to show Annie. "I'm going to need a bigger box."

"I thought this was a Mardi Gras proposal? Why are you packing an Easter Bunny costume?" She handed me an ugly brown box from behind the counter.

"I want to show range." I offloaded the garments from my arm with a sigh of relief. It passed quickly as her words slipped through the clutter in my mind. "Did you say bad juju?"

Imogene was known to dabble in things I didn't understand, and she claimed she'd come from a long line of shamans and other mystics. I didn't believe in any of it, but the last time she'd said anything about my juju, my life had gone completely bananas.

"I can help." She fixed me with a pointed stare.

A bead of sweat formed on my upper lip. "I think I just need a moment to channel my inner debutante." I'd hated the years of grace and etiquette training forced upon me as a youth, but lately, I was thankful for the takeaways. For example, if I stood straight enough, strangers seemed to assume I knew what I was doing—and also that I wasn't having an internal meltdown.

"If you say so." She stuffed a roll of bundled sage back into her apron pocket and scanned the ceiling. She said burning sage cleansed the air, but as far as I could tell, it only made smoke and caused me to sneeze.

I thumbed a pile of headbands, hoping to accessorize the selected outfits. "Did you know Annie is half the reason I went to design school?" The other half had been to peeve off my mother. "A companion line to Annie's Mardi Gras pieces would put me on the map as a legit designer." Pet couture doesn't get the respect it deserves, but she could change that. Furry Godmother could be a pioneer brand in my field. A maverick.

Imogene delivered a bottle of water to the counter.

I dropped two headbands into the box, then sorted a stack of rhinestone-studded collars and optional charms. "Annie was born and raised in New Orleans like me." Unlike me, she'd chased her dreams around the globe, found stardom, and graced magazine covers. I'd made it as far as Arlington before a chance mugging and a cheating ex-fiancé had sent me packing back to the Garden District where my mother and her friends ran the world.

Determined to succeed in spite of my perceived failure, I opened Furry Godmother and put my fashion degree to work making designs for fur babies. As fate would have it, this was an opportunity I'd never have gotten in Virginia. I pulled my shoulders back and lifted my chin. Honey-blonde curls dropped over my shoulders. "I think I'm ready."

Imogene chuckled. "Be careful, Lacy Marie Crocker. You look like your mother when you get in that disposition."

I shot her a droll face. The similarities between my mother and I ended at the molecular level. I looked like my mother, right down to our narrow frames, blue eyes, and ski-slope noses, but I didn't care about keeping up appearances or embracing a legacy of social power like she did. I wasn't interested in marrying into the right family or accepting my family's bottomless coffers of cash. I wanted to make my own path in this life, and honestly, I could've also done without the pointy nose, but I had no control in that matter. "If only I could turn on Mom's Conti-Crocker charm and insist Annie love me."

"Why not? Works on everyone else. Annie Lane is no different. She's just people."

I could think of a certain homicide detective who'd disagree about my charm. Detective Jack Oliver had sauntered into my life four months ago, accused me of murder, pushed all my buttons, saved my life, then walked away. Was he also "just people"? Because so far, my Crocker charm hadn't done much for him. It seemed as if every time I thought our friendship was solidifying, he'd disappear for a few days and return emotionally distant. I squeezed my eyes shut and counted to three before reopening them. Part of me was determined to find out what was going on with him. The rest of me refused to spend another minute down that rabbit hole.

Imogene smiled. "Him, too."

I turned my face away and folded a sequined flapper dress onto the top of my pile. "What?"

"You forget I've known you a long time, Miss Lacy." She passed me a matching headpiece with scarlet plumes. "These look nice with the flapper dresses."

Imogene dropped a handful of business cards and store literature into the box.

"Oh!" I snapped upright. "I should take a few treats for Annie's kittens. They're nearly as famous as she is."

"I'll get those." Imogene hustled to the bakery display and slipped a pair of plastic gloves over plump, wrinkled hands. "I'll make them a sampler box."

"Thanks. That's perfect." My pet treats were one hundred percent organic and baked fresh daily. Baking added balance to my life. Some days it was the only thing that soothed my busy mind. As an added bonus, I could cater a pet's big party *and* dress him or her for the occasion. My life was kind of fantastic.

A line of bagpipers marched past the shop window. I pulled in a cleansing breath and smiled. "I love this town."

Banners for the Faux Real Festival hung from streetlamps up and down Magazine Street. The sidewalks teemed with locals and thespians in all manner of stage attire, enjoying the annual art fest. Tourists snapped photos with men painted silver and posed as statues with the Magazine Street sign. A cluster of mimes begged passersby to free them from invisible boxes.

My tabby, Penelope, leapt onto the counter and rolled in a shaft of sunlight. Happy vibrations rumbled through her lean body.

"Hello, gorgeous." I scooped her into my arms and nuzzled my cheek to her head. Penelope had been held captive, briefly, by my cheating ex-fiancé, but cheaters never win.

Imogene tied a ribbon around the little bakery box and set it inside my open purse. "Two tuna tarts, two kitty cakes, and two pawlines." Pawlines were pet-friendly versions of New Orleans's famous pralines and by far my best-selling treat.

"Thanks. I don't know how long I'll be with Annie. If I run late, don't wait for me. Go ahead and close up."

"Should I set Spot loose before I go?"

Spot was my vacuuming robot. I'd added large googly eyes, felt ears, and some yarn hair to help him fit in at Furry Godmother, but he mostly worked nights. "Yes, please. Do you have any plans after work? Visiting your granddaughter?"

Her smile faltered. "Not tonight."

"No? Is everything okay?"

Imogene clutched the pendant hanging from her necklace. "A friend in the Quarter needs help. She's got a ghost problem, but I'm sure things will be fine in the morning."

I blinked, lost for a response. "Should I tell you to have fun or be careful?"

She pulled Penelope from my arms. Her wide brown eyes twinkled. "Don't worry about me. You'd better get going before you're late. Those dopey mimes are slowing down traffic."

Right. I grabbed my leather hobo and big box of kitty couture. "You can leave Penelope here when you lock up. I'll be back for her as soon as I finish."

"What about Spot?"

"Spot's fine. She likes to ride him."

Imogene gave Penelope a funny look and set her on the counter.

I hustled to my car, dropped my bag on the floorboards, and buckled the box onto my passenger seat. I slid behind the wheel and attempted to settle my racing pulse. Air conditioning blasted my face as I gunned the little VW engine to life.

November in New Orleans was beautiful, but it wasn't always cool. I plucked white angora away from my chest and directed the vents at my neck, uninterested in accessorizing my favorite short-sleeved sweater with perspiration or three layers of deodorant.

The drive from my shop was short once I'd escaped the beautiful chaos of Magazine Street. Six miles of artsy shops, good food, and good times. Magazine was to the Garden District what Bourbon Street was to the French Quarter. A tourist magnet. A melting pot. But unlike the French Quarter, the Garden District was home to the elite, the megawealthy, and several eccentric aristocrats.

Annie owned a home on First Street, where sprawling mansions protruded from the ground in every form imaginable. Century-old Victorians with scrolling gingerbread designs stood beside mock chalets and austere Gothic architecture. Garden District homes were historic and sold more often by word of mouth than realtor involvement, moving from one socially acceptable owner to the next. Residents were choosy about their neighbors. After all, without proper vetting, who knew what sort of riffraff might buy the multimillion-dollar mansion next door?

According to my mother, I misinterpreted the intents of local customs.

I puttered along side streets toward First. Sunlight streamed through the canopy of reaching oak limbs above, filtered significantly by their mossy beards. I powered down my windows to enjoy the beautiful day. Hard to believe that only a few months ago, a dead body had turned up outside my shop and I'd found myself at the center of a murder investigation.

Eventually, the killer had come for me too, but things didn't work out for him. I was recovering slowly from the trauma, but at least I'd met Jack and reunited with Chase Hawthorne in the process. Chase was a childhood acquaintance who'd helped me rescue Penelope from my scheming ex-fiancé. Chase was great. Twenty-eight, a professional volleyball player, and a refugee from the Garden District, much as I'd been a short while ago. Unfortunately, he'd returned to his life-in-progress, probably on a sunny beach somewhere far from New Orleans. I missed Chase, but I had a complicated friendship going with Jack, and I'd grown closer to my mother, so there was that.

I stretched one palm against the rushing air outside my window. Knots of tourists jaunted after tour guides, snapping pictures of the historic homes and learning the most commercial facts about our area.

My phone buzzed to life inside my purse as I slid my car against the curb outside Annie's home and settled the engine. I found my phone and frowned at the little screen. "Hi, Mom."

"Lacy, it's your mother."

I pressed a palm to my forehead in exasperation. "Hi, Mom," I repeated more slowly. *At least it isn't Annie calling to cancel on me.*

"I'm having a gathering tonight to welcome a new neighbor. Cocktails and hors d'oeuvres. Nothing fancy. The caterers will set up around seven. My hairdresser and stylist will be here at six. I gave the stylist your dress size in case you're interested."

I rolled my eyes. "So nothing fancy then?"

"That's what I said. Nothing fancy."

"You know, in some parts of the country, delivering the new neighbor a plate of cookies works, too."

"Don't be so pedestrian."

I bit my tongue. If I wasted any more time, I'd be late for my meeting. "Mom I'm meeting with Annie Lane in a few minutes. I need to get off the phone. I don't know how long I'll be, but I'll keep your party in mind."

"It's just cocktails."

"And hors d'oeuvres," I said.

"Exactly. Invite Annie along. She'd love it."

"Okay. I've got to go. Have fun tonight if I don't see you. Welcome the new neighbor for me." I disconnected without waiting for her good-bye.

Mom's parties were out of control. She was a party addict. It was in her genes. The Contis had been throwing elaborate soirees in the city for the better part of a century. Contis were "old money," a group endlessly concerned with appearances and local influence. Mom was the last of her family line, so she hyphenated. Conti-Crocker. Dad's family was what the Contis called "nouveau riche," a.k.a. the *wrong* kind of rich. While Conti money had been handed down through the generations, Crockers had established personal wealth through a tedious combination of labor and penny-pinching. Both families thought the other was doing it wrong, and I'd been trapped in the Conti-Crocker cold war for thirty years.

Regardless of my feelings on the matter, I was Mom's only offspring, and I had a duty to support her. Unfortunately I'd already skipped two events last week. Tonight made three rejections in ten days. There was no getting out of whatever she came up with next.

I checked my face in the visor mirror and reminded myself to breathe. "Here we go," I whispered. I hung my purse over one shoulder and hustled to the passenger side. I hefted the giant box into my arms and hip checked the door shut. This was it. I was thirty feet away from meeting my hero. I marched forward, head high, and slipped through the front gate, moving confidently up the brick walkway as if I wasn't sweating bullets beneath my angora.

Annie's home was a stately Gothic number with black plantation shutters and galleries lined in stout iron railing. A famous author had once owned the home, and like everything in town, the place was believed to be haunted.

I'd toured the property with my parents years ago, but it had changed hands many times since then. I couldn't help but wonder what it might look like inside these days. The interior was beautiful in my memories. More than seven thousand square feet of ambience and history. Six bedrooms, six baths, stained glass dating back to the 1800s. The structure was such an astounding piece of architecture. I wanted to weep or pet it. Neither reaction was remotely acceptable or sane, so I rang the bell with my elbow.

A row of gas lanterns dangled above me. Gold-and-blue flames flickered behind ancient glass panels. I crossed the broad wooden porch for a look at Annie's rose garden in the side yard. The rear gate rattled. I leaned over the railing for a better look. Her gate bounced and banged against the supporting wrought-iron fence. Was I supposed to meet her outside? "Hello? Ms. Lane?"

I went back to the front door and tried the bell again. Nothing.

I checked my watch. Maybe she was in the bathroom. If so, where was her assistant? If no one answered the door soon,

Annie could think I was late. Not to mention my box was getting heavier by the second.

I peered through the leaded glass transoms around her door. Had she forgotten our appointment? I rapped the door with my elbow three times. The giant wooden barrier swung open under the assault. "Oh, my goodness. I'm sorry." I leaned in to continue the apology, but no one was there to listen.

My stomach knotted. Silent homes with unlocked doors screamed horror movie. "Hello?" Was it trespassing if I let myself inside? Even if I had an appointment? "Ms. Lane?" I took a timid step over the threshold and wedged the box between my hip and the wall. I liberated my phone and dialed the number Annie had given me.

"Wow." I absorbed the incredible beauty of intricately carved mahogany woodwork, baseboards, and crown molding. A massive cantilevered staircase stretched up one wall, lined in ebony-stained wainscoting. Thick wooden spindles carried a curved handrail into a loft overhead. An enormous chandelier scattered light fragments over the polished wood floor. I imagined nineteenth-century couples striding arm in arm through the space, dressed in their best and preparing to dance or flirt coyly in the parlor.

The muffled sounds of a ringing cell phone sprang to life somewhere in the house.

"Ms. Lane?" The call went to voice mail on my end.

One of Annie's Siamese sauntered into sight, rubbing its ribs on an interior doorframe.

"Oh, hello." I shoved the phone into my pocket and regained control of the box. "Is your mama home?" I gazed expectantly into the room behind the kitty.

"Meow." She inched closer, tail erect, and stopped several feet away.

I'd read a detailed article about Annie and her kittens, Cotton and Cashmere, in *Feline Frenzy* magazine last spring. She'd rescued them several years ago, and they meant everything to her. I related deeply. "Are you Cotton or Cashmere?"

She turned away with a flick of her tail and trotted back in the direction from which she'd come. A series of dark paw prints remained in her wake.

A bout of panic seized my chest. "Ms. Lane?" I checked behind me before following the crimson paw prints into the next room.

I followed the kitten through a stately doorway, careful not to trip over the jamb, drop my box, or ram it into anything. A series of stunning granite countertops lined the backsplash between a massive refrigerator and a stove that cost more than my house. One kitten perched on the center island, licking its paws and mewling.

A second Siamese stood in a puddle of scarlet goo.

I stubbed my toe on something and toppled my box of couture. "Oh!" I dropped on instinct, stuffing items blindly into the box until a handful of cloth came up heavy. I unraveled the gowns, now smeared at the hems with what looked too much like blood for my liking. Beneath the stack of my fallen designs was a Crystal Saxophone award. The base was covered in blood.

I held my breath and scrambled back against the counter. I dropped the award and grabbed my cell phone, dialed 9-1-1, and hovered my thumb over the green call button. For the sake of due diligence, I forced myself to peek around the kitchen island before sending the call. I prayed Annie had simply cut herself chopping vegetables and run to a nearby bathroom to bandage her hand. Anything other than what I knew in my terrified heart had happened here.

I sobbed on an intake of ragged breath. Inches from where I sat, on the other side of the gorgeous gourmet island, Annie lay in a growing circle of blood. Arms splayed, legs askew. Her skin was pale. Her chest no longer rose or fell. Unseeing eyes pointed at my shoes. Shoes now sticky with her blood. "Oh, no." The crystal award lying beside me, the one I'd handled, accidentally covered, and lifted with layers of my designs, was her murder weapon.

The glass-shattering scream filling her kitchen was definitely mine.